THE UNHOLY

This Large Print Book carries the
Seal of Approval of N.A.V.H.

THE UNHOLY

HEATHER GRAHAM

THORNDIKE PRESS
A part of Gale, Cengage Learning

GALE
CENGAGE Learning·

Detroit • New York • San Francisco • New Haven, Conn • Waterville, Maine • London

Copyright © 2012 by Heather Graham Pozzessere.
Thorndike Press, a part of Gale, Cengage Learning.

Thorndike Press® Large Print Core.
The text of this Large Print edition is unabridged.
Other aspects of the book may vary from the original edition.
Set in 16 pt. Plantin.

LIBRARY OF CONGRESS CATALOGING-IN-PUBLICATION DATA

Graham, Heather.
    The unholy / by Heather Graham. — Large print ed.
    p. cm. — (Thorndike Press large print core)
    ISBN 978-1-4104-4915-3 (hardcover) — ISBN 1-4104-4915-7 (hardcover)
    1. Paranormal fiction. 2. Large type books. I. Title.
PS3557.R198U56 2012
813'.54—dc23   2012016044

Published in 2012 by arrangement with Harlequin Books S.A.

Printed in the United States of America
1 2 3 4 5 6 7 16 15 14 13 12

Very especially and with
love for and thanks to
Michelle DeVille, a gifted
artist and fabricator!

For Doug and Laurie Jones,
talented beyond all measure,
sweet and all-around incredible.

And for the Wexler family,
Cindy, Bob, Dallas and Reese,
for their great kindness and
generosity to my family.

PROLOGUE

"So, you think you know the truth?" Dianna Breen, femme fatale, demanded. She leaned on the desk in the P.I.'s dingy office, skirt tight against her curvaceous form, eyes sultry as she stared at the hero, Sam Stone. The film was dark and shadowy, and sexual tension between the players was palpable.

Sam Stone made no pretense of looking away from Dianna Breen's chest, modestly covered in frilly white cotton beneath the linen jacket of her suit. "I do know the truth. I know you're a hussy and a thief, and I don't believe you'd think twice before resorting to murder."

"You know *nothing!*" Dianna Breen leaned down to bring her face close to Sam Stone's. She reached past him, drew a cigarette from a pack on the desk and continued to stare at him as he fumbled for his lighter, then lit the cigarette.

"I know that you'd do anything to own

the Egyptian Museum, Dianna. Anything," he added softly.

She moved away from him at last, striding toward the window, her walk a study in slow sensuality. There, however, in what remained of the winter light, her face told the story; she was being wronged. She was not a murderess. She turned to him, hurt and passion in her eyes. "You don't understand! You don't understand about . . . the museum," she said. She gazed back out on the Los Angeles street; beyond the window, day was dying. The city's shadows suited the ambience of the black-and-white film perfectly. "It was never mine — *you must understand.* It was never mine. It was Frederick's, and *it* killed him, not I."

The sound of the old reels flipping through the projector suddenly seemed loud as Sam Stone watched Dianna Breen incredulously.

Sam's thoughts were heard then. He was narrating as he stood and walked over to the gorgeous and seductive widow. "I couldn't believe it. A museum didn't kill. But the way she was looking at me, those enormous blue eyes of hers brilliant with tears, a trembling in her lips —"

"Hey!"

Alistair Archer nearly jumped out of his

seat; he barely managed to cut off the startled scream that threatened to escape him. Jenny Henderson had come running in, slipping her arms around him from behind, and nearly giving him a heart attack.

He was in lust — if not love — with Jenny. There was something about her, an aura of film noir seductress. She had Lana Turner dark brown hair that swept over her forehead, and she wore rich dark shades of lipstick. Today, she was in tight-fitting jeans and a cotton tailored shirt that reminded him of Marilyn Monroe.

"Hey!" he said, standing and allowing her to slide into his arms. His voice was a little tremulous, his muscles a little unsteady. "How did you get in here?" he asked, glancing back toward the door. Black Box Cinema was closed on Sundays; every other night of the week, a film noir movie played at 8:00 p.m. precisely. Or there might be more recent a movie influenced by the director's vision of film noir. The cinema was owned by Alistair's father, special effects whiz Eddie Archer, and stood just off Sunset Boulevard in the Los Feliz area. Eddie also owned the adjacent studio, and both buildings were situated on two acres surrounded by a very old cemetery.

Eddie Archer had bought the property twenty years ago when he started his special-effects business. For the previous five decades, the now-defunct Claymore Illusions had operated from the massive warehouse-style building in back. The company had been founded by the first Lucas Claymore and continued by his son, who'd eventually sold the place. All Eddie had needed to do was update it to create Archer's Wizardry and Effects. While his artists and artisans sometimes found the cinema next door a bit annoying, with tourists parking here and there and everywhere, Eddie was adamant that it would stay. He loved film noir, and having his own cinema meant he could watch his favorite old movies on the big screen to his heart's content. He made them available to the public as a way of sharing his passion, infecting others with his personal enthusiasm.

An underground tunnel — now a museum featuring posed mannequins in famous scenes from film noir and selected classic movies from the '40s and '50s — connected the cinema and the studio. But the main doors to the studio, which were next door and about fifty feet behind the parking lot, remained locked and guarded. During production, the studio often went into lockdown, as it was now.

Lockdown was for secrecy as well as security. No one wanted a big-budget movie's effects and surprises out on the internet before the movie reached the screen. Archer's Wizardry and Effects was busy creating the costumes and creatures for *The Unholy,* the next remake to come to the silver screen.

The Unholy was actually an updated version of *Sam Stone and the Curious Case of the Egyptian Museum.* Unlike remakes that simply *remade* an old film, like *Psycho, The Unholy* used the same characters and situations, but cast them in a contemporary light.

Sam Stone now had a cell phone and a computer.

Alistair was happy that the studio had the momentous task of bringing the film up-to-date, and he knew the effects would be splendid, but he still wasn't sure about a remake. In his opinion, some things were better off left alone. Film noir didn't really fit with computers and cell phones.

"What are you doing here?" Alistair asked as the film wound on and the projector *clicked, clicked, clicked.* "How did you get in?" Alistair had keys to the studio, to the doors that separated the underground tunnel from the studio, and to the Black Box

Cinema. His father trusted him completely.

He hated to betray that trust in any way. Even for Jenny. But he'd brought Jenny in with him before. It wasn't unusual that she'd come; it was unusual that she'd been able to just slip in.

She touched his cheek and smiled seductively. At twenty-two, his senior by a year, she already had the moves — as well as the appearance — of a femme fatale down pat. She eased away, flicking back the strands of hair that had hidden her eyes. "You left the front door open, silly," she told him. "I started to knock, but . . . it was open." She grinned, and looked more like any other young Hollywood hopeful. "The rest of the place is tight as a drum, but my dear, darling, *responsible* Alistair, believe it or not, you left the front door open." She paused to give him a charming pout. "I've been trying to call you. You didn't answer your cell."

He had to wonder what it was about one person that could turn the senses of another upside down. The senses and the sanity. Yes, Jenny was beautiful and perfect, but . . . it was Hollywood. The stunning, the perfect and the beautiful all walked about, ever hopeful, some willing to do whatever it took to get where they wanted to go, others starry-eyed and naive. He was the son of one of the most respected men in the movie business, and he suspected Jenny hung on to him because of what she thought he could do for her.

"Sorry," he said, and the tone of his voice was annoyingly husky. She knew she sent his libido off the charts, and he hated the pathetic puppy-dog tail-wagging demeanor he must put forth when she was around. "I was watching the movie. It's my favorite. *Sam Stone and the Curious Case of the Egyptian Museum.* I really love the film, and the special effects for it were actually done here, when the place was still Claymore Illusions." That fact added to the pride his father took in securing the special-effects contract for *The Unholy.*

Jenny shook her head. "Silly boy, living in the past! Except, of course . . ."

The production company was trying to keep the information about the *Sam Stone* remake quiet, but of course the rumor mill was already on the case. The company had neither rejected nor affirmed the claim. Rumors and anticipation could give a film a tremendous box-office advantage.

"So, um, why are you here?" Alistair asked.

Despite her imitation of classic Hollywood vamps, Jenny was not a fan of film noir, or

13

any other "old" movies. She loved silly modern-day romances and adventure flicks, the kind with überbuff heroes who lived exciting adventures and saved the world.

She threw her head back and touched her hair again, one of her moves calculated to be uncalculatedly sexy.

"I heard the studio's locked down!" she said breathlessly.

He nodded.

"But not to the son of Eddie Archer!"

He groaned aloud. "Jenny, you know it's not just my dad. It's the movie studio, the producers, the directors — they don't want information on pictures or anything on costumes and effects getting out."

She gave him her pout again. She did it very well, making a little moue of hurt. "Alistair, you *know* I'd never tell a soul what I've seen. I'd never tell a soul I was even in there. But they're still casting for extras — extras who *might* wind up with speaking roles. If I had a feel for what was going on, it would help me immensely. Please?"

He hesitated. Jenny always did pay up. If he took her through the studio, he'd be rewarded that night.

He was pretty sure she'd learned her love-making from the movies — dirty ones, at that. She was vocal; she liked to crawl on top and twist around like a voodoo queen dancing around a pole.

"You have a key to the studio," she said.

He groaned again. "If I tried to go in with a guest, old Colin Bailey, who's on guard at the reception desk, would push his alarm button and every cop in the area would appear," he said. Colin Bailey had worked for his father for the full twenty years he'd owned the studio — which was most of Alistair's life. He was like a fixture, dedicated to the studio. And during lockdown, he was fierce.

She moved closer to him. "I realize we can't go in by the front but we can sneak in because you have a key and the pass code to get there through the tunnel door. And Colin Bailey would never see us, because you know right where the cameras are so we can avoid them."

Almost involuntarily he felt his left pocket. He did have the keys. But he'd told her the truth. Colin Bailey would report Alistair to his father without blinking an eye.

She shimmied up against him, her body pressed to his in just the right way to elicit an immediate response. Her perfect breasts — albeit made that way with some saline enhancement — were firm against his chest and her groin pushed against his.

He forgot his father completely. He also forgot the danger — and the fact that he was being used.

"All right," he said. Now his voice was flat-out hoarse. "We'll go by the tunnel."

She smiled. She rose up on her toes and brought her lips to his and did things with her tongue that nearly made him climax on the spot. Then she stepped back. "That was a little promise of things to come!"

He nodded. He couldn't speak.

He turned around. On the screen, Dianna Breen was screaming. She was being chased by the Egyptian robe-clad murderer, who was forcing her deeper and deeper into the museum.

Alistair stumbled through the audience chairs to the back. He entered the old lobby, where wine and beer were sold, along with various forms of high-end movie snack food. To the far left of the lobby were a few offices and conference rooms, and at the back of his father's favorite little meeting room was a door, nominally hidden by a movie poster.

"Oooh, this is like a high-tech spy adventure!" she said.

"There's nothing high-tech about it," he said as guilt clashed with the near-desperate desire she elicited. "It's a movie poster covering a door."

She was pressed to his back. Desire won out over guilt.

Alistair swept the canvas poster to the side, dug in his pocket and twisted the key in the lock, fumbling for a moment as he did so.

There were auxiliary lights set into the steps that led down to the tunnel; on the days that the small museum was open, before and after movies were screened, the stairway and the landing would be ablaze with light. But tonight, no one was expected.

"Be careful," he warned Jenny.

"Of course!" she said.

Alistair walked slowly down the steps, ever aware of her sweet-smelling presence behind him. He reached the landing. He'd never been here before when there was no illumination except the emergency lighting. It changed the entire appearance of the place.

The museum's first scene was from *The Maltese Falcon*. Humphrey Bogart sat at his desk while femme fatale Mary Astor leaned toward him and a creepy Peter Lorre hovered off to the side. They were all caught in shadow, and even Bogie looked dangerous, ready to strangle Mary Astor. Across from that tableau, Orson Welles as the title character in *Citizen Kane* stood by the breakfast table, angry after ignoring Ruth Warrick, who played his first wife. The old mannequins, created in the mid-50s by the previous owner's special-effects studio, had been works of love, and in the dim red light and shadows, Alistair could almost believe that Orson Welles was about to speak angrily, his patience finally snapping him from the ennui of his marriage. Alan Ladd and Veronica Lake were together next, in a scene from *The Glass Key,* and then there were Dana Andrews, Vincent Price and Gene Tierney in *Laura.* The hall was long, and the exhibits were plentiful. A slim wooden barrier separated the walkway from the exhibits, and visitors could push buttons, which would let them hear the audio from the scene they were witnessing, along with information about the actors, producers, writers and directors. That night, to Alistair, all the characters looked as if they could speak without benefit of electronics.

Bogie made another appearance, with Ingrid Bergman in *Casablanca;* he was saying goodbye in front of the plane that would take her away. Bogie gripped Ingrid by the shoulders, and the emotion between them — and the greater good of the war effort, the sacrifice required — seemed palpable.

Toward the end of the hallway, Alistair stopped.

The scene was taken from the movie he had been watching that night, *Sam Stone and the Curious Case of the Egyptian Museum.*

There was hard-boiled Sam Stone, played by the ill-fated Jon de la Torre, arriving just a little too late in the fictional museum's "Hall of the Pharaohs." And there was the empty sarcophagus, and nearby, the man clad in the robes, his hands around the throat of femme fatale Dianna Breen, played by the equally ill-fated Audrey Grant. Snakes — Egyptian cobras — abounded on the floor, and Sam would have to make his way through them if he was to have any chance of saving Dianna.

Alistair stared at the scene and blinked; he could have sworn he saw one of the snakes move.

"Hey," Jenny said, pushing against his back.

"What?" Alistair asked, distracted. He kept staring at the tableau.

"The door is open. The door to the studio is open!" she told him, speaking softly.

He turned to look down to the end of the hallway. The door into the basement of the special-effects studio stood ajar. He frowned; it should have been locked. His father and upper-level management were adamant about the rules when it came to lockdown.

He glanced at Jenny. For a moment she seemed to look like every femme fatale who had ever graced a movie screen. There was something wrong here. He was being played, he thought, really played. Perhaps *punked*. There could be cameras somewhere that he didn't know about and other people ready to break into laughter. *Yes, he was a fool, ready to do anything for a woman's touch. And, as in so many film noir scenarios, the woman was luring him to his doom.* At least that was how it felt in his fearful and overheated imagination.

But there was something else about the night, the way the tableau seemed alive. Something that sent a chill raking his bones.

He warned Jenny with a glance that he was wise to the situation.

But when he started through the door to the studio he heard Jenny scream.

When he turned around, he was so stunned that at first his jaw just dropped.

The robed killer — the evil priest, Amun Mopat — had come down from the *Sam Stone* tableau. The *thing* seemed to have no face. There was only blackness where a face should have been. He, it, stood behind Jenny, and seemed to be staring at him, but it had no eyes. . . .

"Hey!" He wanted to scream. The sound came out like a croak.

An act. It had to be part of an act.

A hand appeared, brandishing a long knife.

It was a special-effects studio, for God's sake! Someone was playing a game, he told himself, maybe even at his father's request. Maybe his dad had suspected him of doing something like this, hoping for a hot night with his girlfriend. . . .

The knife looked very real.

"Hey, enough! Let her go!" Alistair said, willing his feet to move toward Jenny and her costumed attacker.

Jenny was no movie femme fatale. She implored him, her blue eyes wide and filled with terror. "Alistair!" His name was a shriek of panic.

"Enough!" he roared again.

Then he stood dead still. The thing attacked and, with a hard, quick motion, drew the blade across Jenny's throat. Blood didn't merely leak from the wound; it spurted. Her scream died in choking sounds that accompanied the blood, and it was cut off within seconds.

There was a scent in the air. Hot and tinny and fetid.

Because it wasn't stage blood being spewed.

The costumed form dropped Jenny and moved toward Alistair.

He'd spent his life among the creepy and the macabre, the greatest movie heroes and most terrifying villains. Monsters, vampires, ghosts, alien slime . . .

But something within him — logic, reason — turned off, his terror was so great.

And he fell toward the floor as blackness seemed to overwhelm his vision.

He fell into a pool of blood. And he knew, from its smell, that no, it wasn't part of any special effect.

It was Jenny's death, all bloody. Bloody, and *real.*

Vengeance.

In Hollywood, every character needed a name.

Vengeance was a good name.

And so Vengeance stood hidden, watching, feeling such a sense of glee, it was almost frightening. The scent of blood remained; the first few minutes after the scene were all but imprinted on the moving reels of memory.

Most people would consider the act, and Vengeance, crazy. Stone-cold crazy. But that wasn't the case. *Crazy* could not have worked out all the technicalities and the precise timing that had been necessary.

Crazy could not have figured out everything that was needed to pull off the stunt.

Crazy could never act it all out, as it must now be acted out. . . .

But it had gone better than could possibly be imagined. The girl . . . the blood.

And Alistair Archer, slipping, falling, knocking himself out.

Then waking, screaming . . . racing to the guard station.

And now . . . the blare of sirens in the street.

Cops would soon be crawling all over the place. But the cops would never suspect. Because the cops didn't know the studio, and the cops didn't know the past, and the cops would never recognize the brilliance that was bringing it all to fruition.

Ah, tomorrow!

Tomorrow . . .

Tomorrow, Vengeance would become normal, ordinary, once again. Vengeance would throw off the assumption of super-personality, sympathize, go about day-to-day business. . . .

And no one would ever, ever know.

Not in this lifetime.

Vengeance smiled, and Vengeance actually laughed aloud in the night; no matter, because Vengeance couldn't be heard.

It was all too good to be true. . . .

Time to move, but Vengeance needed to savor the moment. Alone in the dark, watching . . .

Vengeance was good, and vengeance was sweet.

And Vengeance had just begun.

1

Madison Darvil wasn't really awake when the phone rang. She was in that delightful stage of half sleep, when the alarm had gone off . . . but the snooze button was on and she had a few minutes to lie lazily in the comfort of her bed before rising. Her phone was loud and strident. She rolled over groping for it, swearing softly as it dropped to the floor and she had to lean down to get it, banging her head on the bedside table.

"Shit!" she muttered, and was further humiliated when she realized she'd hit Answer as she'd picked up the phone — and the caller had heard her.

"Hello?" she said frowning. Seven thirty-three. Who was calling this early?

She could hear a soft chuckle, and then someone clearing his throat. "Madison?"

Inwardly, she groaned.

"Yes, Alfie?" Alfie Longdale was her assistant at the studio. She loved the fact that she had an assistant and she loved Alfie. One day, he was going to rule the world, his eye for detail was so exceptional.

"You don't have to come in this morning. In fact, you *can't* come in."

Her heart seemed to sink to her knees. Had someone suddenly decided she was really a fake? That, despite her training, degree and experience, she was just a kid who played at working on the movies?

"What . . . what — ?"

Alfie's voice became hushed. "There was a murder last night! In the tunnel. Lord, Madison, Alistair Archer was arrested for murder! Some little starlet he had the hots for — they say her throat was slit from ear to ear. She's dead, Madison. And Eddie Archer's kid is saying that an Egyptian mummy — you know, the priest in the original *Sam Stone* movie, a *monster* — came down from one of the tableaux to commit the bloody carnage!"

Alfie was being dramatic. He *was* dramatic. But right now, what he'd said wasn't registering.

A mummy? A monster? Alfie had to be making it up. Monsters were what they did, what they created, quite frequently. Well, superheroes, giant rats for commercials, cute little pigs and other such creatures. But

26

horror was big; horror movies could be reasonable in cost and make massive amounts of money.

"Alfie, is this —"

"No! It is not some kind of joke. It is not a movie script. Madison, it's real. A woman was killed in *our* tunnel. Anyway, the crime scene units are there today, and Eddie Archer's closed the entire place. *No one* goes in until the police have finished with the tunnel, the security tapes, the studio — you name it. Anyway, I was up last night when it all hit the news. And Eddie Archer looked white — I mean, white as a ghost! — when they showed him on film. He said he wants the police to have complete access to *every-thing* because he's going to find out what really happened — his son is not a mur-derer!"

Alfie was telling the truth. As shocking as it was, she knew he was telling the truth.

Madison felt her heart break for Eddie Archer. He was such a good man.

Alistair was a good kid, too. Could he have snapped and killed someone?

No.

She couldn't accept that. He was too nice and decent, even shy.

"A monster," she repeated. "You mean — the Egyptian priest, the killer from *Sam*

Stone and the Curious Case of the Egyptian Museum?"

"Exactly! Is that movie stuff or what? Everyone suspects *The Unholy* is a remake of that movie, but most people don't know for sure. And now, right in front of that tableau . . . a real murder! Anyway, I thought I'd call because if you show up at work, you'll be sent home. This way, you might be able to get some more sleep."

Madison wrinkled her face at the phone, as if she could convey her expression to Alfie. What? Go back to sleep *now?*

"Thanks, Alfie. Thanks for letting me know. I'm sure I'll get tons of extra sleep."

"Keep me posted if you hear more," Alfie said. He seemed not to notice her sarcasm.

"Ditto," she said, and ended the call.

She crawled out of bed, drawing an indignant meow from Ichabod, curled up at the foot of the bed. "Sorry, my friend," she told the cat, hurrying out to the parlor of her old rented bungalow and switching on the TV, going from channel to channel until she found a news station covering the murder.

The information Alfie had given her was true. The news showed the crime tape blocking off the cinema and the studio, then cut to an earlier interview with Eddie

28

Archer in front of the courthouse. He denied his son's culpability, and swore that he'd learn the truth behind the shocking murder.

Mike Greenwood, creative head of the studio and Madison's supervisor, stood beside him. When Eddie finished speaking, Mike stepped up to the microphone. He reasserted what Eddie had said, that the truth would be discovered and, while Alistair had been arraigned for the murder, the D.A.'s office had acted only on what *appeared* to be the case — not what was. They would work toward his release, and by the middle or end of the week, when the police had gone over every inch of the place, Archer's Wizardry and Effects would be back in business. They would move forward with their various projects while the investigation continued. Mike spoke so earnestly, he silenced the spate of questions that should have arisen. He seemed concerned, but in control.

Mike was a steady man, excellent in stressful situations. Whenever they were on a tight deadline, Mike was the one who calmed down everyone at the studio, assuring them that, step by step, they'd get it all done.

Eddie had acted with his usual composure, but Madison felt so sorry for him.

Eddie, nearing fifty, was still fit, but his face bore the tension of sorrow. As Alfie had said, he looked white as a sheet. He'd run his fingers through his graying hair repeatedly as he spoke, his words calm but determined.

She was still staring at the TV in disbelief when her phone rang again. She'd left it in the bedroom, and raced to retrieve it, thinking it would be Mike Greenwood giving her the message that Alfie had already conveyed.

Her "Hello?" was breathless.

"Madison?"

The caller wasn't Mike Greenwood. It was Eddie Archer himself.

"Eddie!" she said. "Oh, Eddie, I'm so sorry."

"Then you've heard."

"Yes."

"Alistair didn't do it."

"I believe that, Eddie. With my whole heart."

"Thank you."

He was quiet.

"I heard not to come in, Eddie," Madison said. "Alfie called me."

"Actually, Madison, I do want you to come in. I have a friend arriving — a film effects artist I worked with years ago. He's a member of the FBI now, and he's going to handle a special investigation for me. I'd like you to meet with him, show him around the studio."

"I — I thought it was closed down, other than for the police?" FBI? How had he gotten the FBI involved? She wasn't savvy about law enforcement, but she'd always assumed the FBI only came in for serial killers or kidnapping or crimes that spanned several states.

And how the hell did a special-effects artist wind up in the FBI?

And, oh, God, why had Eddie chosen her?

She knew exactly why Eddie had chosen her. He'd never challenged her, he'd never forced her into a corner over this. But he believed — had reason to believe — that she talked to the dead.

"The police closed the Black Box Cinema. But *I* closed the studio. And Sean — Sean Cameron — won't be here until this afternoon. I just talked to him in the wee hours of the morning and he's coming from Virginia. I'm picking him up myself, so I'll swing by for you after I've collected him from LAX. If that's all right with you."

Madison exhaled on a long breath. The man she had hero-worshipped for his artistry throughout her formative years was asking for her help. The same man who'd

31

hired her and opened up a world that she'd only dreamed of knowing.

"Eddie, I would do anything for you," she assured him humbly. "And for Alistair."

"Thank you. I think you're the right person to work with Sean. And I deeply appreciate your friendship — for Alistair and me. You can expect me around five."

"Of course," she murmured lamely.

Eddie wasn't ready to hang up. "Alistair didn't do it — he really didn't." He was quiet for a minute. "He told me that the Egyptian priest, Amun Mopat, came down from the *Sam Stone* tableau, and killed her. Alistair tried to reach Jenny, but slipped in the blood, conked himself out . . . and then came to and saw it was real — he was lying in a pool of blood. I guess it's normal for the police to think that either he's crazy or his story is and that he's going to try for an insanity plea. But I know my son. I know he didn't do it. And only someone who's familiar with the studio can prove he didn't."

"We're in Hollywood — a place filled with actors and effects," Madison said.

"Yeah," Eddie agreed, sounding bitter. "But, oddly enough, I believe we're the only ones who see the possibility that Alistair didn't do it. Anyway, Madison, I'll be by for you. If you're sure you don't mind."

"I'm happy to show your guy around the museum, Eddie."

Eddie Archer ended the call. Madison sank down into her art deco–style sofa, setting her phone on the coffee table in front of it.

"Hey."

Madison nearly leaped a mile into the air at the sound of the voice. Her hand fluttered to her throat; her heart thudded.

She turned and saw the man who'd spoken, standing just behind her.

The voice was soft. The man was slight, with dark graying hair and a wonderful face filled with character.

She let out a breath. Her sometime-resident "invisible" friend — whether extension of her imagination or real ghost — was seated on the arm of the sofa, looking at her sorrowfully.

"You all right, kid?"

She let out a breath, realizing that the very concept of someone being murdered where she worked was terrifying.

"Yeah. It would help if you didn't startle me like that."

"I spoke quietly. And I'm not exactly a surprise now, Madison, am I?"

No, not anymore.

She could see him plain as day, as if he were flesh and blood, a good friend who'd stopped by in a time of need. He had a fascinating, ruggedly masculine face — including his slightly scarred lip — and a lean, slight form. When he stood, he was on the short side at only five feet eight inches.

"Um, I'm fine. I'm just stunned," Madison said. Then she rushed into words, well aware of how ridiculous she'd look if anyone else was there — because she saw Humphrey Bogart as he sat in her living room. "I don't know how much you hear or fathom from phone conversations, but there was a murder at the studio last night. A starlet who was with Alistair Archer. I can't believe he killed her. I *won't* believe it — not Alistair. Eddie must be beside himself, desperate to help him. He's such a loving father."

"Watching a child suffer is a hard thing," Bogie said, his voice low and slightly nasal.

Bogie.

Madison stared at him. *Was* he an imaginary friend? She would never be sure. She'd had strange experiences as a child. She'd tried chalking them up to growing pains, teenage angst and, as her parents had suggested, an overactive imagination — the kind that had led her right into a career.

She'd also had experiences that had broken her heart — and might be part of the reason she embraced her work, day in and day out.

Bogie hadn't come with the bungalow, though he'd lived there briefly in the 1920s. He'd told her once that he had loved it and loved living there. She'd first met him at the wax museum when she was a college student; she'd assumed he was a look-alike actor hired to play the part. They'd spoken and laughed together. . . .

And he'd followed her home.

Bogie showed up whenever he wanted to. Apparently he had other places to haunt, as well. Madison simply accepted him as a friend — imaginary though he might be. Sometimes she thought she was crazy; sometimes she thought she was incredibly lucky that such a man had chosen *her* to haunt. Although she believed that now, she hadn't always. He'd scared her to death at first, and had occasionally made her life hell.

He'd just startled her today; the first night she'd seen him sitting on her sofa, however, he'd practically given her a heart attack. She'd fumbled to call the police, and they'd come and almost arrested her, assuming she was another college kid trying to make trouble. Bogie had been apologetic and courteous — so sorry for causing her distress. He was what he was, and he'd tried to explain, but she hadn't believed him.

Maybe he *was* imaginary, but she didn't know what part of her mind triggered his appearances.

And if he was, what about the other dead people who'd spoken to her?

But imaginary or not, he was there for her now.

"Have some coffee, kid. That'll make you feel better."

"I'm not sure it will help me feel better. But at least it'll wake me up."

"What are you waking up for? You could go back to sleep."

"Why is it that everyone thinks I can sleep *now?*" she muttered.

Bogie ignored that, standing and stretching as he gazed out the windows. He turned to look at her. "The murder took place in the studio?" he asked.

She shook her head. "The underground tunnel between the Black Box Cinema and the studio — where Archer has his film noir museum."

"Interesting," Bogie mused. "By which display?"

Madison frowned. "The news didn't say, but Alfie told me it was by the tableau for *Sam Stone and the Curious Case of the*

36

Egyptian Museum. Sounds crazy, doesn't it? I mean, especially since the studio is now in lockdown because of *The Unholy* — the *Sam Stone* remake."

"A lot has been crazy in Hollywood through the years. You've heard about the case of the Black Dahlia? Poor girl, tortured and then displayed, chopped right in two," Bogie said, shaking his head. "There's always been murder out here — and out here, it becomes sensational, with more emphasis on the drama than the tragedy. You had Fatty Arbuckle and the murder of Virginia Rappe back in 1921, and later, you had the Manson murders and then the Simpson murders, and anytime anyone's killed here, the press is out looking for every sordid detail." He shrugged. "I watch the news, you know," he told her seriously, "as well as old comedy reruns. And, kid, this is a big place full of illusion. Murder isn't confined to Tinseltown, but there's no way it's *not* going to occur here, too."

Madison nodded absently. She glanced over at Bogie and wondered sometimes why he didn't haunt some of the other places he'd loved. And some of the people . . . He'd told her once, though, "They can't see me. I can't reach them. So it just hurts, kid. It just hurts." And he'd grinned at her.

"You reply when I speak to you and I like that. It's why I keep coming back, kid."

And now, most of the time, she was glad. Very glad.

"Sam Stone and the Curious Case of the Egyptian Museum," Bogie said. "I could've been in that movie. I think I was busy at the time. Something else going on. Might have been *Casablanca.* Yeah, probably. That was 1942. Anyway, I always thanked God I wasn't on that set, because there was a death back then — and it might have been a murder, too."

Madison tried to see if she could remember her Hollywood lore and legend well enough to recall a murder that had happened during the making of *Sam Stone.*

"I don't recall ever seeing anything about it — in any of the lurid books about true Hollywood murders or on any of the history or entertainment channels," she said.

Bogie joined her on the couch again. Watching him, she hid a smile. He seemed to sit differently from other people she knew. He was relaxed, and still, somehow appeared proper.

"It was 1942. The war effort was in full swing. Movies were being made to encourage heroism — or to try and divert the public from the war. *Casablanca,*" he said, and grew thoughtful. "Ah, that was a good one for me. There was some great writing on that movie. I wish some of those lines *had* been my own. That and *The African Queen* . . . some of those were my ad-libs. And both of them gave me a persona to live up to." He paused and looked at her with his famous lopsided grin. "Anyway, I digress, kid. And I'm talking out of line. The death of Pete Krakowski was never officially called a murder. No real inquiries were made, no one was investigated and no one was arrested. There were just rumors on the set, rumors that traveled around. Gotta remember, back then, the studios were king, and they were powerful. Krakowski's death was seen as a tragic accident, and that's the way it went. It was long ago and in the middle of a world war, and it wasn't particularly noted at the time — he was a bit player, not a big star."

"How did Krakowski die?" Madison asked, puzzled.

"There was some kind of fault with the wiring. He was electrocuted. From what I understood, he was fooling around on set before the filming was to start, and then he was dead. Fried," Bogie said, shaking his head sadly.

"We're doing a remake of that movie —

and I never even heard about it. Why do you say it might've been a murder?" Madison asked.

"You didn't hear about it because there *were* accidents on sets from time to time. Krakowski wasn't the only film person who died that you've probably never heard of — no internet back then. You just heard about these things if they happened to a major star or if someone was killed by a lover or a spouse." He cocked his head toward her. "Bit player, and what was deemed an accident. Nothing sensational about it, and Krakowski was hardly a household name. Like I said, no way for every little piece of news to be known across the country back then. No Twitter, no Facebook and no Google." He was quiet for a minute. "I woulda liked a Facebook page," he said.

"Actually, there are several devoted to you," she said. "But why would someone suspect it was murder? It sounds like an accident."

"I knew the key grip *and* the lead electrician on that film. They were the best in the business. If they were working the rigging and electric, both were safe." Bogie waved a hand. "Anyway, Krakowski's death is a far cry from a starlet being sliced up in the tunnel. A far cry, indeed." He leaned back, nostalgic. "I remember that old cinema from way back. Played silent films, even before my time. It's a shame, a damned shame. That Eddie Archer has a real appreciation for the past — this shouldn't have happened on his property. Shouldn't have happened to the poor girl, either."

Madison realized that she'd been feeling sorry for and worried about Eddie Archer and his son, Alistair. She'd almost forgotten the victim.

Was that how it had been when the death had occurred during the original filming?

"Lord," she whispered. "You're right. The poor girl."

"That's Hollywood for you," Bogie said. "It'll steal your soul, if not your life. There've been so many who came here with such dreams and wound up dead. Christa Helm, Dorothy Stratton, Dominique Dunne, Elizabeth Short or the Black Dahlia, Sharon Tate. Peg Entwhistle, the only one to really jump from the Hollywood sign. I remember that," Bogie said. "She found her fame in death. And we may never find out what really happened to Marilyn Monroe." He paused. "Did you know the young woman who was killed?"

Madison nodded, then shook her head. "I can't say I *knew* her. I met her a few times when she was with Alistair and once at an office party."

"You work too much, kid. You've gotta remember, none of it's worth anything if you don't have a life."

Madison arched a brow and refrained from reminding him that the last time she'd brought a date home, she'd acted like an idiot because Bogie had been watching something on her television and had said, "Don't mind me, kid." He loved TV. He couldn't do a lot on the physical plane, but he could manage such simple tasks as pushing buttons on the remote control. He adored old sitcoms and liked to keep up with the television news.

"There has to be some information on Krakowski's death," she said, returning to their previous topic.

"There was — one newspaper article. No follow-up. He died. It was sad. He was buried. And that was that. I'm sure many of us thought about it back then. But time goes by."

"This is so horrible. For the poor girl, yes, of course. And for everyone who will be touched by it." She sighed. "Alistair really loves his dad. He didn't usually bring people to the studio. I mean, I don't know what went on before — I've been there for about three years now. But as far as I can tell, Alistair respects the studio. And he loves film. He wants to get into directing rather than special effects, but . . . although I didn't really know Jenny Henderson, I saw the way Alistair followed her around like a puppy dog. He had a huge crush on her. I can't believe he would've killed anyone. And I *especially* can't believe he would've hurt Jenny. He was crazy about her."

Bogie shook his head sadly. "Sometimes I think it might have been better back in the bad old days when we were contract players for the major studios. Now, the young and the beautiful come out here willing to do anything for stardom. Anything. Can't help wondering what Jenny Henderson did — or was willing to do. Or maybe her dreams had nothing to do with her death. Maybe she was simply in the wrong place at the wrong time."

The wrong place at the wrong time. How could that be possible? The studio was in lockdown. There should have been no one with access to the museum — other than Alistair, Eddie and some of the department heads.

She winced inwardly.

It didn't look good for Eddie Archer. And it sure didn't look good for Alistair.

43

"*Sam Stone and the Curious Case of the Egyptian Museum,*" Bogie said. "You know, the costuming and effects for that movie were done where you work. The place was Claymore Illusions back then."

"I know," Madison told him. "That's why it seemed so perfect that the studio was hired for the remake. I think the fact that the place was used for creating props, costumes, illusions and whatever was needed for film noir is half the reason Eddie Archer loves it so much."

"Eddie appears to be a talented man with a real appreciation for the past," Bogie said, not for the first time.

Madison let out a little cry, startled as something pounced onto the sofa beside her. She laughed at herself.

As if he knew she was upset and needed some warmth, Ichabod meowed and settled his furry body next to hers.

"Hey!" Bogie said softly. "It's going to be all right. Don't go getting all jumpy on me now."

Madison forced a smile despite feeling a sense of dread.

It wasn't going to be all right.

Sean Cameron arrived in L.A. in the afternoon, when the sun seemed to spray down

44

light like a fountain, and the bustle of the city was as frantic as ever. This might be Tinseltown, and massive movie deals might be taking place in any coffee shop, but it was also where he'd learned that it was often the B-lister who had to put on pretensions, and where the working moguls could be as down-to-earth as their gardeners.

Such was the case with Eddie Archer.

Sean had spent five formative years working under Archer. The man was a genius when it came to creating creatures and special effects. To this day, Eddie loathed straight CGI or computer-generated imagery. Of course, effects were effects, but in Eddie's view, to create what *looked* real, you had to start with something real. Thanks to Archer, Sean had learned a great deal about physical illusion as well as computer-generated magic. He'd worked with Eddie in many capacities, learning to create costumes and attachments, build creatures, as well as work with computers.

Archer certainly enjoyed his income and the fact that he was customarily sought out by the most important and influential names in the business. But above all, he still loved his *art,* and he loved sharing that excitement and enthusiasm with promising young artists, wide-eyed and in awe of the chance to work for him.

Sean had gotten a frantic call from Archer an hour before he'd gotten the call from Logan Raintree, head of their Krewe of Hunters unit, telling him he'd received an official request that they be brought in. He assumed that Eddie Archer had used his influence with someone above the local police and even the state police, because just when he'd been about to tell Logan Raintree that he had to go to L.A. one way or another, Raintree had asked him to head out on the first flight and look into the situation.

"Remember, if something's impossible — then it's impossible," Logan had said. "I know this man is an old friend of yours, a mentor. And I know you don't want his son to be guilty of murder. But our job isn't to hide things, fix things or help with creative defense mechanisms. Our job is to discover the truth."

"I'm aware of that, Logan," Sean had been quick to reply. He hadn't taken offense. Whenever a team member had any personal involvement in a case, it was important to note what priorities had to be maintained. He'd gone on to say, "But I knew Alistair when he was a kid. Nice boy. He's trying to figure out how to be his father's son and his own man. And no, murder wouldn't be how he'd plan to make his name. From what I understand from Eddie so far, the kid loved this girl. She used him, but he was crazy about her. And he's a basket case now. He was immediately arraigned, and he's out on bail — Archer money and pull, I imagine — but he's basically locked up, anyway. He's wearing an ankle monitor and he's at a mental hospital that deals with dangerous and suicidal clients. A posh place, I understand. Apparently it's where the A-listers go when there's some kind of serious question about rehab, sanity . . . or possibility of a criminal offense."

"I'm sure this place is the best money can buy," Logan had said.

"Yeah. Archer loves his kid," Sean had told him.

And Eddie Archer did love his one and only son. Married three times, Eddie Archie had just the one child. Alistair was the son of his first marriage, to Annie Smith, with whom he'd grown up in Valencia, California. Annie had been a fledgling actress, but her first love had been her family. She'd died when a vicious flu strain had swept through the world, shocking everyone with the deaths it had caused. Eddie had been absolutely bereft.

And then lonely. And Alistair had been left without the mother who'd adored him. Eddie made up for that the best he could; he was always there for his son.

But although Annie had been as sweet and dedicated to a man as a woman could be, Eddie hadn't had much luck with women since her death five and a half years ago. When he'd married Benita Lowe two years after Annie's death, Sean had come to the wedding. He could have said right then that it wouldn't last. Benita had practically snatched the bill from the caterer's hand and had a few things to say about the cost of the reception. Turned out she wanted Eddie to save his money — for her. That marriage had ended in a matter of months. A year ago, Eddie had given marriage another try, again with an actress, Helena LaRoux. Sean knew Helena; she'd attended Eddie's second wedding with her third husband. Sean hadn't gone to that wedding. He'd sent his best wishes to Eddie, hoping he was wrong in his judgment of Helena. They'd had a few minutes to talk at Eddie's wedding to Benita, and he'd discovered that Helena apparently thought Benita's then-husband was superior to her own, as far as contacts and possibilities went.

Sean heard a horn beep and when he saw

Eddie's car across the divider realized he'd been waiting in the wrong place, pretty sad considering the fact that he'd lived in L.A. for five years and visited frequently ever since. He threw his garment bag over his shoulder and hurried over to slide into the passenger seat of Eddie's sporty little Ford hybrid.

"Hey, old friend," Eddie greeted him. "I'd give you a big man-hug, but they don't let you sit here long these days!"

"Just drive, my friend, drive," Sean said.

Eddie nodded and focused his gaze on the road ahead and the insanity of LAX. "Thank you for coming," he said.

"Ah, Eddie, you knew I'd come if you called me."

Sean glanced at Eddie, who looked drawn and haggard, a lot older than his years. That was natural under the circumstances.

"You're sure you're okay, Eddie? Okay to be driving around?"

Eddie nodded gravely. "I wouldn't risk your life — or my own. Alistair needs me. I'm strong. I know my son is innocent, and it has to be proven."

Eddie did seem rational and in control, driving like an expert as he maneuvered the complicated airport exit and the California highway system.

"From special effects to the FBI?" Eddie asked. He tried to smile. "I still marvel at that. I was in shock when you told me. Guess it must be your ability to create giant man-eating rats against a green background."

"Hey, now," Sean said, trying to speak lightly. "They didn't just pluck me out of the studio, you know. All right, well, they did at first, but you remember I'd done some work with Texas law enforcement groups. And now we've gone through the training system at Quantico. My team and I, that is," he added. "None of us was FBI when we formed. But you must know something about my team, Eddie — besides the little we've exchanged in phone conversations. Because I got the call from our team leader not long after I talked to you."

Eddie nodded. "Ever since I was informed that my son was in a jail cell, covered in blood, I've done nothing except rack my brains to figure out how we can prove that Alistair didn't do this — that he couldn't have done it. I thought about you instantly, and the fact that you've become part of an elite unit."

"I'm not so sure they call us elite," Sean murmured.

"Sean, the cops have gone through the

security tapes. There was no one in or out of the cinema or the studio, other than Alistair and Jenny Henderson. There were no cameras running in the museum. It was closed. The whole thing is impossible. I *know* Alistair didn't do it. My attorney is suggesting we consider an insanity plea . . . but Alistair isn't crazy. He didn't do it."

Sean studied Eddie as he drove. The man was a father, desperate to save his son. Sean groaned inwardly; he hoped Eddie hadn't wanted the Krewe involved because he believed he had an old protégé working with a group that was part of the federal government. Did he figure Sean might help with an insanity plea? It seemed to him that a good defense attorney could get a person off on insanity in a dozen different ways. *The television made me do it. The voices in my head made me do it. A video game made me do it, a book made me do it. The ghosts living in the old Black Box Cinema did it, not me.* And if you *imagined* that a ghost did it — or made you do it — was that as good as actual insanity?

"Eddie, a ghost — or a creature — didn't kill the girl. I mean, if you're hoping we can come up with the spirit of a dead noir actor, it's not going to fly."

Eddie looked at him, frowning. "Sean,

I . . . I know that. I don't believe a ghost killed anyone, either. *Can* ghosts kill someone? Or if a ghost ever did kill anyone, wouldn't it be that guilt or fear or terror simply overwhelmed that person? Sean, trust me, I don't think a ghost killed Jenny Henderson. But someone did," he said grimly. "Someone who knows the studio. Whether it's someone working there now or not, I have no idea. The police checked out the security footage and said, Hey, cut and dried, no one in there that night except for the security guard — who never moved. The guy didn't even take a piss until Alistair came running in to get him. Someone else was in that studio, Sean, and you know as well as anyone that what we see isn't always real, and that what looks real can be illusion."

"Of course, Eddie," Sean said, feeling a little foolish. Was he a bit testy about being part of a unit that many questioned? *The Ghostbusters of the FBI?* They were still a new unit, and they'd met all the members of the original Krewe, so they knew what they were up against. He'd been involved in the case that had put this second group together, and it had been unusual, to say the least. But like most evil, it had come down to human greed and the horrible twists and turns the mind could take.

But . . .

He'd also learned that there were others like himself and his cousin Kelsey. Those who could hear voices and see visions of people who'd departed the physical realm.

He'd also gone through rigorous training. He was an excellent shot, should the need occur, even if he'd always planned on living his life creating fantasy for entertainment purposes.

On both fronts, he'd learned that perception was everything. They were dealing with a locked-room mystery, he thought. A classic puzzle, and every puzzle had a solution.

And Eddie had seen this, the key to vindicating his son.

"I haven't been in the studio in years, Eddie," Sean reminded him.

"Yeah, I figured that, and some things have changed. Some storage has been moved around, but most of the structure is the same. Climate control or cold room, sewing section, construction — those areas are all the same. Anyway, I've asked one of my top young protégées to be your guide. She'll take you through the studio, answer any of your questions. She's the perfect assistant for you right now."

"Oh? Why is she so perfect?"

53

Eddie glanced his way before looking back at the road, somber and thoughtful.

"Because she's a lot like you. She's quiet, doesn't say much about anything that affects her, but . . . well, she's either certifiable, crazy as a loon, or just like you. She talks to the dead."

2

Los Angeles County was known for its smog, but this afternoon was worse than usual. When Madison stepped outside to wait for Eddie Archer, she felt as though the day itself was in mourning for Jenny Henderson and the Archer family.

It was just the beginning of summer, and in the past few days the sky had been powder-blue with wonderful puffs of snow-white clouds; today, a fog had rolled in from somewhere and joined with the pollution of the massively populated area. She almost expected to hear crows caw in warning while bats took flight across a darkening sky. Like something of a '50s horror movie . . .

Eddie Archer's little hybrid car pulling up in front of her place brought her back to reality.

Eddie pulled to the curb. A man slid out of the passenger seat watching her as she approached. He seemed to fit right in to the

California scene. He was tall, wearing dark glasses, and appeared to be fit and athletic, with a lean muscled frame. She slipped her own sunglasses on; sunglasses camouflaged a multitude of sins, or so they said — and allowed one to hide one's emotions.

As she reached the car, he extended a hand. "Sean Cameron, Ms. Darvil. Please, take the front. I'll get in behind you." He had a low, smooth, throaty voice that suited his physique. Bogie, she thought, would label him "a man's man." There was a quality about him that conveyed an inner easy confidence. She sensed his compelling masculinity and realized that meeting him, just feeling his handshake, made her want to know him. She lowered her head for a swift moment, willing herself not to flush.

Why on earth was she instantly attracted to a man she'd barely met?

She steeled herself mentally, disturbed and annoyed with her own thoughts. Eddie was troubled. Alistair was in a grave situation. A beautiful young woman had been murdered. She was here to escort this man around the studio today, and that was it.

"After you," he said.

She wasn't short, but neither was she exceptionally tall, at five-eight.

"No, no — you take the front." She managed a casual grimace. "Since I'm staring up at you, it's obvious you have much longer legs." He had to be six-three or six-four, she estimated. She felt she should tell him it was a pleasure to meet him, except that seemed kind of ridiculous at the moment. "I'm glad you're here for Eddie," she said instead.

He gave her a tight-lipped smile and a nod. "I'll say the same," he told her huskily. "Please, take the seat next to Eddie. There's plenty of legroom in the back. Humor me — it's a Texas thing."

Madison decided she wasn't going to wage a war over a car seat and got in.

When she was seated, Eddie turned to her. "Thanks, Maddie," he said quietly. "Thank you, sincerely."

"You're welcome, Eddie."

"So, the police still have the museum area — the tunnel — cordoned off. Naturally, Sean has jurisdiction anywhere, but I'd like you to show him the studio. You can answer any questions he might have." Eddie's voice grew emotional as he added, "I'm going to abandon you two and get back to the hospital to see Alistair. I don't like leaving him alone. I don't mean alone — I mean, without seeing me as much as possible."

"I understand, Eddie," Madison said

quietly. Alistair — assuming he was innocent — definitely needed family support at a time like this.

But he had a stepmother, too, although it was true that Alistair had never called his father's wives "Mother." But he seemed to have a friendly relationship with Helena LaRoux, and as far as she could tell, Helena liked Alistair. Alistair was happy if his father was happy, and he found it amusing that Helena had made no bones about the fact that she'd loved Eddie and wanted to be Mrs. Eddie Archer. She claimed to love Eddie and maybe she did. It was a nice bonus that he was as powerful as he was — and Helena never pretended that she wasn't eager to be rich and famous on her own. It seemed, however, that she was happy to share her journey with Eddie's son.

Appearances, Madison thought. Hollywood was all smoke and mirrors.

"He's got family there now," Eddie told her. "Helena is with him. But we've only been married a year, and although she and Alistair get along fine, she's not his real mom, and certainly not his dad, you know?" he ended hoarsely.

"No one else is you, Eddie."

She noticed that Sean Cameron reached over from the backseat, placed a hand on

58

Eddie's shoulder and squeezed.

She'd heard about Cameron before; she knew his name, and that he'd worked at the studio. Now that she was with him, she realized she'd even seen pictures of him with past creatures created at the studio and at industry parties. Once she'd actually wondered about him and joked with Carla, a seamstress, about him. *Why didn't he still work there, huh?* she'd asked. She often worked a double shift, seventy to eighty hours, with a group that was seventy to eighty percent male. All those hours and all those men, and they were like fathers, uncles, little brothers or obnoxious cousins. Or uninterested in the opposite sex.

Carla had reminded her that she dressed some of the hottest actors in the business, and she'd been asked out often enough.

It wasn't as if she was totally averse to a whirlwind romance — here today, gone tomorrow — it was just that the right opportunity hadn't come along. She preferred to remain friends with men she might work with again, and she *didn't* want the girlfriends, wives and lovers of actors or colleagues not wanting her to be part of future projects. So she kept her distance. Sometimes the actors she worked with could be cold and full of themselves, but luckily, that was seldom the case. And when she kept her distance, she earned their respect. Maybe men always admired and longed for what they couldn't have. Maybe women, too.

And maybe she was just damaged. Maybe a friend like Bogie was a reward for the strange and painful things that had happened to her.

Right now, she needed to concentrate and focus on the moment — and not on Sean Cameron. She didn't know the man. Not at all. She'd seen him standing outside a car. She'd heard his voice and shaken his hand. Watched how he'd silently laid his hand on Eddie's shoulder, a true sign of friendship and support. There was something about his voice, though. It seemed to enclose her and make her feel his words were sincere, that he was some kind of secure bastion against the world. Eddie had called on him in a time of need.

As they pulled up in front of the cinema and studio, Madison saw that there were four police cars guarding the entrance. She looked past the cars and the crime scene tape to the beautiful Art Deco–style Black Box Cinema with its terra-cotta sunburst facade, and the elegantly crafted sign. The building itself was a handsome and historic structure; it appeared sad, though, wrapped in crime scene tape as it was.

When she looked to the side she saw the parking lot, empty now of cars. During lockdown it was usually crowded even at night — all hands on deck.

She noted a vintage Cadillac that was out of place among the clearly marked patrol cars. It was parked at the far end; there was a man standing outside the car, staring at the buildings, as if he was carefully watching the police and every move they made.

He turned as they drove up. Before they could exit, he walked over to the car, and Eddie rolled down the driver's-seat window. From the passenger seat, Madison leaned over and saw that it was Andy Simons, Eddie's partner.

"Hey, you doing okay?" Simons asked Eddie.

Madison didn't know him half as well as she knew Eddie; Simons was money, Eddie was art. But the two were longtime friends and Simons — like everyone else associated with the studio — would stand by Eddie to the very end. Eddie and Andy were complete opposites in more ways than one. Eddie was slim and athletic, an attractive middle-aged man, casual and easy in his manner and dress. Andy was muscular and his clothing — even his jogging attire, as she'd seen once — was pure designer quality. He had a head of light blond hair that he kept artfully colored and his nails were manicured. He'd always been nice when Madison encountered him, he just didn't have Eddie's natural ease with the artisans and employees of the studio. However, that didn't matter much, since he was seldom around.

"Thanks, Andy," Eddie said huskily. "I'm doing all right."

"And Alistair?"

"The best he can be — under the circumstances." Eddie gestured at Sean. "Andy, you remember Sean Cameron —"

"Of course I do," Andy said, looking into the backseat and smiling. "Nice to see you, Sean. We missed you — and your talent — when you left. Odd timing, though," he added.

"He's not here for his old job," Eddie said. "Sean is with the FBI. His unit is going to take the lead on the investigation. I told you I was going to call in some favors to see that Alistair got a fair shake, that I wanted to bring in an FBI unit."

"Yeah, I know. But, Sean — you're FBI?" Simons asked.

"Career change," Sean said with a shrug.

"Life takes us to some strange places."

"That's a major change." Simons looked at Eddie, frowning. "I knew you wanted the FBI involved, but I wasn't sure you could pull it off. But then, you've always been able to create magic."

"Never hurts to have two law enforcement agencies working together — we can bring different specialties to the table," Sean explained.

"But from fabricator . . . to FBI?" Simons said, grinning.

"You never know," Sean Cameron said.

There was an air of expectancy in the silence that followed, but Cameron didn't say anything else and Eddie spoke up.

"Madison is going to show him around the studio. It's been a while."

Simons nodded. "Great." He smiled at Eddie and tried to sound cheerful. "No one works harder than Madison, and I'd say she's definitely a good choice for bringing Sean up-to-date. And we can't ask for anything better than the FBI," he said. He bent lower and grinned at her. "You're the best, too, Madison. We all appreciate what you're doing, but I have to ask — you okay with this? You don't have to be here, you know. We can only ask so much of you."

"I'm just fine. I'll do anything to help

Alistair," she said.

"Anything," Simons repeated. His comment seemed odd to Madison, or maybe not. To the outside world, there was no way that Alistair *hadn't* committed the murder. Maybe he was really asking if she'd be willing to lie, if necessary. Was *he?* she wondered. Andy Simons's fortune was tied to Eddie's, and while he might have had the seed money, it was Eddie's talent that had kept them both going.

The one aspect of the business Andy didn't have anything to do with was the Black Box Cinema. That was strictly Eddie's.

"Agent Cameron, welcome, and thank you," Simons was saying. He straightened a bit. "Glad you're with us. I've been standing in the parking lot for hours — don't know why, except that I want the police to realize that all of us at the studio believe in Alistair, and we'll be watching them."

"I know why you're here. You're my friend," Eddie said. "And I'm grateful for the support."

"Sure. With Sean on the case now, I'll head home. But, Eddie, if you need me — *for anything, anything at all* — just call."

"Thanks, Andy," Eddie said.

"Thank you. And I will be calling on you."

Sean Cameron reached through an open window to shake the man's hand.

"I'll talk to you later, then." Simons gave them all a grave nod and walked to his car.

"Thank God I do have friends on board, and we're not just throwing Alistair to the wolves," Eddie said.

"Character can mean everything, Eddie. And a vicious murder isn't in Alistair's character." Sean Cameron opened his door to exit the car and Madison did the same.

"Keep the faith, Eddie," Sean said, ducking his head down to the window.

"I will." Eddie nodded, and eased the car toward the road.

One of the police officers on guard duty approached Madison and Sean. Madison felt awkward about this; Sean Cameron did not. He smoothly produced his credentials and they were ushered through the massive gates. They were stopped once again, at the entrance to the cinema.

"Even though you're FBI, are you sure they're going to let us in here?" Madison asked.

"Yes, they're required to. The agencies will be working in tandem. I want to see the studio today. The crime scene experts are probably still in there — looking for anything and everything. But it's important that

I meet the LAPD detective in charge," he told her. "How do you feel about Andy Simons?" he asked, looking at her closely.

"Andy? Honestly, I don't see him that often. Neither Eddie nor Andy comes to the studio daily, although Eddie's in far more often and is usually with us when we go on location," Madison said. "When Andy does come in — maybe once every couple of weeks — he's cordial, interested and decent to everyone."

"How do you *feel* about him?" Sean persisted.

She smiled suddenly. "Well, I guess Eddie's a man of the people. Andy is more like royalty condescending from on high. But like I said, he's always been decent, and, odd couple though they are, he and Eddie have been friends for years. You don't think Andy —"

"I don't think anything yet. We've got a long way to go, Madison."

He'd paused to look at her and she was startled by the little tremor that rippled down her spine. She'd just met him, and she was alarmed by her strange and instant admiration for him. She liked the steady gravity in his eyes as he spoke, and still felt touched by the sound of his voice and the honesty and sincerity with which he seemed to speak. He wasn't muscle-bound like a prize-fighter, but she had the feeling he was all lean strength.

"Yes, of course," she said quickly, stepping back. She was making far too much of a simple moment they were sharing in the pursuit of justice.

They were approached by another officer and stood at the door, waiting, while he went into the building.

"We *will* get in there," Sean muttered.

The officer returned, leading a tall, bald-headed man of about forty. The newcomer eyed Sean suspiciously, but had apparently expected him. He was Detective Benny Knox, and he was polite enough, although he glanced at Madison as if he wasn't impressed and was, in fact, indifferent to her presence. She wasn't sure how he'd figured out that she didn't know a thing about crime scenes. Sean, however, introduced her as "Eddie Archer's most trusted studio artist," and the detective assessed her again and nodded grimly.

"I heard you worked here once, Cameron," Knox said.

"I did."

"I assumed they brought you in because you know the place yourself."

Sean gave a slight shrug. "But things

change over time. Madison has the position I had years ago, so she'll know what I'm talking about when I ask a question."

"And she's Eddie's girl," Knox said.

Madison frowned. "I'm not anyone's 'girl,' Detective. I'm here to make sure Agent Cameron has knowledgeable updates on any changes in the studio."

Knox raised his eyebrows, then nodded.

It was fine for them to be in the studio, Knox assured them. Fingerprints had been taken from the door that connected the tunnel to the studio, and the rooms had been searched. Knox actually managed something of a smile when he told her that some of his most seasoned people had been startled more than once, running into the creatures in production and in storage. She forced a weak smile in return.

The police were finishing up in the cinema and the tunnel, he went on to say, and, as law enforcement, Sean would understand that they didn't want tainted evidence. But before the biohazard teams were called in to clean up, Sean would have access to everything.

"Notes from the first officer on the scene?"

"Yes — and my own. Officer Braden was pretty thorough, and he knew the drill. He didn't touch anything until I was called. Of course, there's no such thing as a pristine crime scene in a situation like this — Alistair Archer had been slipping around in the blood, the guard rushed in and he had blood on him. But after that, the scene was contained. Let me know what you want when, and I'll see that you get it."

Once Knox had finished speaking, he studied Sean carefully. "What I hear — and this comes straight from the governor's office — is that you're lead investigator on this, along with your team. It's your ball game," he said.

"Not all — we need and appreciate you and your men, Knox. I'd like you to keep the lead until we're completely established. I want to get the lay of the land again, so to speak. Raintree is due tonight or tomorrow morning with the rest of the team. I'm not sure what plans they've made as yet. Now . . . we'll go through the parking lot to the studio, staying out of the way of the forensic experts."

Knox seemed mollified. He kept nodding.

Madison and Sean started across to the main studio entrance.

As they walked, Madison asked, "Is it always like that? I mean, it felt like he was throwing massive webs of power and testosterone there. Aren't you both working toward the same goal, as in the truth of what happened?"

Sean Cameron grinned at her; he was strikingly good-looking, she realized again, and could have been in the movies instead of the magic behind them.

Step back, think sanely. You're just here as a guide, she reminded herself.

She still wasn't quite sure how one went from being a visual fabricator and creator to an FBI agent, but she was glad to see his grin. She had to admit she hadn't relished this assignment and wished they could rewind time — go back twenty-four hours, make sure Alistair Archer was nowhere near the Black Box Cinema last night and that the entire place had been locked down tight. Then she'd be at work, consulting with her colleagues, studying sketches, and then computer simulations, discussing materials. . . .

"Sometimes the L.A. cops have taken a beating when they haven't been the ones to mess things up. And if you're asking whether law enforcement agencies can be territorial — you bet. I actually belong to a unit of people who are ready to stand down, suck up when necessary and just get our part done. But yes, we *are* all working toward the same goal, and a team like mine doesn't have the manpower to do it alone. If you have good cops on your side, you're ahead of the game."

"You worked for Eddie for several years, right?" Madison asked him.

"Yes. Then I returned to Texas — had a close friend with cancer, and I wanted to be around to help with what was needed."

"How did you find your way into law enforcement?"

"I didn't. It found me," he said.

They were in front of the studio door now. He indicated that she should get out her key, and she knew that their conversation on his history was over.

Madison fumbled in her purse and produced the key, then opened the door and stepped inside. As she'd expected, once they'd entered the vestibule, she saw Colin Bailey on duty behind the little glassed-in reception area.

During the day, when work was in progress, two people handled the reception desk. The hallways that led down to the studios, work areas and offices weren't locked, but a security officer usually sat in front with the receptionist. Today, no receptionist was on duty, but Colin Bailey was there, formidable despite his age. Colin had been a boxer in his day. Like the cop she'd just met, he was bald, but his bare pate was a present from nature, and not the work of careful shaving. He had bright blue eyes and jowls that would have done a bulldog proud. His nose had been broken a dozen times and looked it.

He could be gentle as a lamb, but when it came to defending Eddie Archer or his property and reputation, Colin turned into a cobra.

"There's no entrance! Absolutely no — Oh! Madison, it's you. And the FBI man, I assume?" Bailey rose from his swivel chair, opened the door dividing the entry from the reception area and came out to greet them. He inspected Sean, and then smiled. "Why, it's you, kid!" he said with enthusiasm. "I thought I got the name wrong or something!" He took Sean's hand and shook it with enthusiasm. "Wow, it's true! So you're a G-man, huh? For real?"

"For real, Colin, my friend, for real," Sean told him. "So, you're doing well?"

"Great!" Bailey said. "Well, until last night," he added, his smile fading.

"You were on duty?"

"I was. And I take that seriously, as you know, especially during lockdown."

"You had your eye on the video screens?" Sean asked.

Bailey grimaced. "For all the good it did. And the cops have the video now."

"The cameras still cover the same areas?"

Bailey nodded. He motioned to them to join him in the reception area. As they walked in, Madison realized she'd never been there herself; she'd never thought about the security cameras.

There was a bank with six screens. One showed the entry. Another focused on the main work area, encompassing the shop, the main construction area and, somewhat obscured, the rest of the floor. Another screen covered the parking lot, and yet another, the upstairs hallway. One showed the cemetery and parking lot to the right if one were facing the studio entrance, and another showed the side of the Black Box Cinema.

"You can't see the entrance to the Black Box," Madison noted.

"The Black Box Cinema has its own security camera that focuses on anyone coming through the main entrance," Bailey told her. "But as you can see, these screens will tell you if anyone is entering the studio by the main entrance, and if anyone tried to get through the fire exits, an alarm would have gone off."

"There's no security footage for the tunnel — the museum — itself?" Sean asked.

"Yes, but it's seldom used," Colin said. "There never seemed to be a reason. No one's allowed down there except by appointment or on movie nights, and there's always a guide with anyone who does go down. Film noir buffs always want to see it, but it's not like it's the biggest tourist attraction in Hollywood or anything. The cinema's Eddie's baby — has been from the start. He grew up loving film noir, and I guess he feels it's just a little collection he shows friends, even if the friends are people he doesn't know. You can ask for a tour if you've come to see a movie. You don't even have to pay the nominal five bucks, just bring your ticket stub during opening hours. Like I said, there never seemed to be much need for security down there."

Sean Cameron didn't respond to that. Maintaining a pleasant expression, he said, "Thanks, Colin. Madison's going to catch me up on any of the changes that have happened around here since I left. We'll check back in before we leave. Obviously, we have to leave this way, don't we?"

Bailey nodded. "Unless you open a fire door and, if you do, alarms will go off like firecrackers." He grinned at his own mild joke.

Sean looked at Madison. "If we go to the right, that'll still lead us to the main work areas?"

"Yes, the hallway to the left has two meeting rooms, plus the stairs up to the offices and meeting rooms on the second floor."

He moved quickly, heading to the right. She followed him at the same pace.

The studio seemed strange. Empty. She came in early sometimes, but a lot of workers did, and Madison couldn't remember a single time when she'd come in and one of the seamstresses or construction engineers hadn't already been at work. The sounds of sewing machines, electric saws, hammers and other work-related noises were constant, although someone usually had a stereo system playing pop music or rock classics. Today, there was no stereo on. Materials were piled up on the tables that stood by the sewing machines, and the shop area itself felt eerie. It was almost like walking into a home whose owners had mysteriously disappeared.

The walls were pinned with fabric and materials and drawings. Creatures they'd made for movies, shows or advertisements were lined up on the floor and arranged on shelves — some might be used again, and some were kept because they'd required a great deal of work and had turned out exceptionally well. They also kept some of the projects that *hadn't* worked quite as well, a reminder of the thought and care that needed to go into any creation.

A giant rat stood next to an equally large penguin. The rat had been used in a public service announcement and the penguin had been animated to advertise a new adventure park in Oregon. Robotic creatures from the last sci-fi movie they'd worked on were lined up together, and above them was an old bicycle being ridden by a very evil-looking big, bad wolf. Zombies created for *Apocalypse from Beneath the Sea* were against the far rear wall, and the bloodied victims from a Victorian-era murder mystery were on the high shelving ten feet above the floor — above the zombies. Madison noted that Sean was staring at the victims, Miss Mary, Parson Bridge and Myra Sue. He was thoughtful, and she suspected he was imagining that the appearance of Jenny Henderson's body must have been disturbingly similar to these props. The studio was known for the realism of what they created.

"Life imitates art and art imitates life. In this case, the question is which came first," Sean murmured.

Madison glanced down, troubled by the

creatures that were just rubber, plastic, fabric and paint. She'd drawn the designs for some of them; she'd dressed Myra Sue. Suddenly, Myra Sue and the other "victims" didn't seem like props designed for a movie. They *looked* like flesh and blood.

A lot of blood.

Madison found herself turning away from Myra Sue's one sightless eye.

"Fire door is still in the back, right?" Sean asked her.

She nodded. "Between these guys and the *Planet Mondo* air creatures over there," she said, pointing to the door. There was a large sign that said Fire Door, but it was partially obstructed by the wings of one of the *Planet Mondo* air creatures.

"Hasn't changed much," Sean said. He nodded to one of the giant robots across the workstations, beside the climate control room. "I worked on *Hugoman.* He's been here awhile."

"Really? He's fantastic. And I love the movie!" Madison said. She did love the creature in the movie *Hugoman.* He was the invention of a mad scientist who'd given him his son's personality through partial cloning; the massive machinelike creature was kind and fought only to save lives. Of course, he'd been misunderstood, and when

77

he'd saved the community from an attack by mutant creatures, he had died — a moral about judging people, or creatures, on appearances. *Hugoman* had actually been low-budget and promoted as an action/monster flick, but it had been extremely well written and had become a cult classic.

She flushed; they were here because of a murder, and because someone they both cared about had been accused of that murder. And yet, she wasn't sure why they were just touring the studio. The murder hadn't taken place *in* the studio; it had happened in the museum tunnel.

He wasn't appalled by her sudden enthusiasm; he smiled at her. "Thanks. I loved working here. I needed to go back to Texas for a bit, and then . . . then you get swept up in life, so I wound up staying and working there. But I did love the time I spent here, working for Eddie Archer. I was proud that we helped create a cult classic on a budget." His tone became businesslike. "So, as far as I know, that's our fire door on this side of the building downstairs, and we have another over by the offices?"

It took her a second to follow his quick change of subject, but she managed not to blink.

"To the best of my knowledge, yes," she

told him. "And there are corresponding exits upstairs, with ladders in case of fire. Eddie's always been very careful, dealing with some of the flammable materials as we do."

Sean nodded. "Okay, what's going on in the shop. What are you working on right now?"

"Don't you know?" she asked.

"No, I don't."

"It's kind of ironic. We're working on a remake of *Sam Stone and the Curious Case of the Egyptian Museum.* It's updated, and it's been retitled *The Unholy.* The script is really good — and different enough to make this a different movie. From what I've seen so far, I'd compare it to *Disturbing Behavior,* which was, in essence, a remake of Hitchcock's *Rear Window.*"

Sean frowned. "A remake of the movie — *and Jenny was killed in front of the tableau?*"

"Yes."

"That's not just ironic," he told her. "That sounds intentional. And it changes everything."

"The original movie was filmed well over half a century ago. What could this have to do with the movie we're making now?"

"Everything," he said curtly. "It could be a motive for murder. And lockdown —

that's incredibly important, too. Lockdown should eliminate anyone who isn't close to the studio."

Madison spoke through clenched jaws. She wasn't in the FBI or the police; she wasn't required to understand motive and investigation. "Even when we're not in lockdown, the curious can't just wander in. *I* have to have permission to bring in a guest on a regular day, and I wouldn't have been given permission at all now."

"Well, there's permission, and there's giving yourself permission by dodging the rules. On a regular day, someone could try to slip someone else in."

"What about the security cameras, Sean? People here don't want to risk their jobs."

"Of course not. Still . . ."

He walked toward the climate-controlled room, but looked through the windows for a moment, and never tried the door. He seemed uninterested.

"Where's your workstation?" he asked her.

Her work area was a few feet from the climate-controlled area. She pointed it out to him, and he went over to it.

It seemed bizarre that everything was just where she'd left it on Friday night. There were pieces of the leather coat she'd chosen for the costume of actor Oliver Marshall, playing antihero Sam Stone in the new movie.

"I saw the movie as a kid. But refresh me," Sean said.

What did this have to do with the murder?

"In a nutshell? There are a series of murders — people ripped to shreds by something in the night. Then an incredibly wealthy philanthropist with a gorgeous young wife is found murdered in a similar manner in his Egyptian Museum. The cops want to arrest the wife, so she goes to Sam Stone. Various clues suggest she's the murderer, but she denies it. The movie is great because it leaves the audience wondering — was something supernatural happening, or could it all be explained? The Egyptian mummy supposedly sent from the Department of Antiquities turns out to be a priest heading an ancient cult and in the end, needless to say, he proves to be the murderer. Sam Stone falls in love with the wife — Dianna Breen — but she dies at the hand of the priest before she's proven innocent."

"Who's playing Sam Stone?" Sean asked.

"Oliver Marshall."

"Hmm. How is he to work with?"

"He's fine. He's always in the tabloids for being a party boy, but he's polite and courteous, shows up for his fittings and works well with everyone behind the scenes. He's very pleasant and makes everyone at the studio think he's just one of the gang. I like him."

"Good to hear. When's the last time he was in?"

"Friday. I was working on his costume." She gestured at the fabric on the table. "He was in for fittings. Sam Stone carries concealed weapons, so everything about the costume has to fit perfectly."

"Those . . . creatures evoked by the Egyptian priest — what's his name?" Sean pointed to some of their newest creations, including giant fanged jackals, birds and bizarre giant snakes.

"The priest is Amun Mopat, and yes, they're for the movie."

"What will the priest be wearing? Same type of costume as in the film noir?" Sean asked. "And who's playing him?"

"That role hasn't been cast yet," Madison told him. "There's a mannequin over by the wall with a mockup of the robe he'll be wearing. It's an homage to the original film. Almost exactly the same."

"Where? Show me."

Madison walked over to the mannequin that stood behind one of the jackal-like monsters created for the movie.

There was nothing but a plain brown monk's robe on it.

She looked at Sean as shivers of fear streaked down her spine.

"The robe — it was just a mock-up. But it's gone," she said. "I suppose someone might have taken it. . . . Mike Greenwood could have shown it to someone. I'll ask Mike and Eddie where it is."

Sean shook his head. "They won't know — and the robe isn't coming back. It's been used," he said grimly, "by the killer." He turned to look at her. "Find that robe, and we'll be on our way to finding a killer."

3

"Hey!" Sean touched her cheek. "This is a good thing. Seeing that the robe is gone actually helps. I'm almost astounded that everyone assumes it was Alistair, to tell you the truth. The girl was killed in front of the *Sam Stone* tableau, the studio is doing a remake, the robe is gone. To me, all of that points to someone with an agenda against the studio or the movie."

Madison nodded. But she didn't agree that the robe's disappearance was a good thing! *A killer had been here, where she worked. A killer had used the robe she'd made to sneak onto a tableau or into the tunnel and slice open a young woman's throat.*

Sean turned her to face the construction area. "What are they working on here?" he asked.

"An old Western scaffold."

"For *The Unholy?*"

"No, that's the tail end of our last project

— *Ways of the West.*" She gave herself a mental shake and turned toward the sewing machines and a rack of clothing. "Projects overlap, but you know that. Or sometimes we work on several at the same time. Right now, though, as soon as the scaffolding's out of here, we'll be doing nothing but *The Unholy.* Or . . . I assume we'll still be working on it."

"The world goes on, despite murder," Sean said. He motioned to the far wall of the construction area. "And there's the door that leads from the tunnel."

It wasn't really a question. She said, "Yes," anyway.

He walked over but didn't touch it. Madison followed him and saw powder all over the whitewashed floor nearby. Black powder.

"The police dusted here," he said.

Madison felt a moment's discomfort. *Her* prints were on that door.

"They'll get a lot of prints," she said. "Including mine."

He looked at her, the curl of his lips gentle, slightly amused. "Elimination," he told her. "They'll take everyone's prints for the purposes of comparison."

"Elimination? But . . . you believe the killer works here, or is close to someone here? That means we've all known him or her. . . . Actually, any of us might have been killed."

"No, I don't think *any* of you could have been killed. The killer didn't want the police running around looking for a murderer. The killer wanted them to arrest Alistair. His habits were known — he was being watched way ahead of time."

"Are we going through there?" she asked, nodding at the door.

"No, we'll let the police find everything they can with their forensic units. I'll go into the tunnel soon. You don't have to come with me."

An uncomfortable sensation crept over her. A horrible murder had just taken place there, in the tunnel. She'd only seen crime scenes on television or at the movies. She didn't want to see the real thing.

But she was here to help. Help save Alistair. He couldn't be guilty — and Eddie had called her to assist this man who was somehow going to prove it.

She had to go to the site. If what she'd experienced during her life, the ordeals that had made it so painful, were worth anything at all, the one benefit might be that she could reach the dead girl. Did Jenny's spirit somehow remain, although her mortal life had been stolen? If so, wasn't she obliged to try to speak to the girl, to connect with her?

She shook her head, responding to Sean's comment. "No . . . if I'm going to help you, I should go all the way."

He didn't reply. He was staring at the area around the door. Close to it on the left was another rack of costuming, while a supply of wood had been stacked up on the right. She began to wonder if anyone could have hidden behind the racks of clothing or the wood, staying out of sight of the video cameras. But if someone had been there, waiting, how had that person gotten into the building? Some of the construction crew had been working Saturday; she'd been off herself, as had most of the shop. Sunday, as far as she knew, no one had planned on coming in. So that would've meant the person had hidden behind the rack of clothing overnight, with the intent of killing someone who might or might not have been in the tunnel on a night when *no one* should have been there?

Or did she know the killer? Was it someone who walked among them, someone she saw on a day-to-day basis, worked with, laughed with?

"Let's take a walk through the rest of the place," he said.

Madison turned and headed back to the

hallway, then passed by the reception area and went on to the offices. There were two on the ground floor, both conference rooms more than offices but supplied with computers, printers, screens and other work equipment. The walls were lined with movie posters; the hallway had two circular areas decorated with mannequins, all from different movies. There was an adolescent werewolf, a beautiful evil witch, a torn-up robotic trooper, a vampire complete with cape and golden eyes that seemed to follow you and a zombie, a poor girl from one of those "park by the lake and make out even though a dozen couples have already been killed there" movies. This girl had not done so well; she was missing most of her face, and the one blue eye that stared out at them was pretty gruesome.

Actually, with the exception of Myra Sue, their "creatures" rarely bothered Madison. She was accustomed to them. But there were a few mannequins in the offices that were far more upsetting. They were incredibly realistic. In the first office, there was one on an autopsy table, the sheet drawn up, eyes glazed and open, blond hair streaming around a beautiful face. She was the first victim in a murder mystery. In the second office, there was a mannequin of a beautiful, terrorized woman peeking out from the leaves of a bush. Neither victim had been played by a living actress; the work was so good, it just looked like they'd been real.

Entering the second office, Sean commented, "So Matilda is still here."

"Matilda?"

He flashed a smile. "We dubbed her Matilda. She didn't have a name, even in the script. She was just 'devoured victim number one.' But we all liked her when my crew was around, and we called her Matilda. She used to really creep out a lot of people. A guy named Harry Smith was working on digital back then, and he used to swear that he hated being in the office alone. He felt like Matilda was watching him."

"You *can* feel like our characters are watching you," Madison said. "The studio's always done great work. And when it's great, it looks real."

"I agree."

Sean left the office, and for the first time, Madison felt that "Matilda" was watching her and she, too, hurried out.

In the second hallway circle — complete with vampire, witch and slasher-movie victim — Sean paused for a moment, then headed to the hall with the elevator and the emergency exit that led to the fire escape outside. He didn't touch the door; he saw that the police had dusted here, too. Instead, he returned to the elevator, then saw that the police had dusted there, as well. "We'll take it." He pushed the button and they waited for a moment, listening to the whir of motors.

When they were inside the elevator, he said, "Did you know there's a key to get to the basement — or the end of the tunnel?"

"What?" Madison asked, surprised. As far as she was aware, the elevator only went down to the main level. There were two buttons to push in, for the first and second floors.

Sean pointed to a little metal piece where a key could be inserted. "The elevator can go to the first and second floors *and* to the basement . . . or to the tunnel entrance. As far as I'm aware, no one's used it — except for Eddie Archer, maybe — since Eddie's owned the place. I think there's only one key and he has it. But I saw the plans once, and this elevator will go to the basement. I wonder if Eddie thought to mention that to the police."

"I don't know if he did," Madison said. "I have my keys with me, of course. And I have keys to almost everything, but not the elevator."

"I don't want to try getting down to the basement yet. I'm going to ask if anyone's checked it out. For now, we'll stay clear until the crime scene units have gotten what they need."

Upstairs, the basic floor design was the same. They passed by a circle of prop creatures and came to Eddie's office — home to several charming little gnome-like beings from a children's fantasy movie — and then moved on to the large office occupied by Mike Greenwood, managing artist of the studio. Mike liked aliens, and his office was filled with sci-fi and space creatures and miniatures of a spaceship that appeared several stories tall on film.

A window in the back of his office looked over the rear of the property; it was high enough that the cemetery in back with its historic family vaults and funerary art could easily be seen. Sean paused there, gazing out.

"Peace Cemetery," he murmured, glancing at her. "Did it ever disturb you to work in the midst of a cemetery?"

"No," she said curtly, perhaps too curtly.

"That's an old, old place."

"And still accepting burials," Madison said. "I think Eddie loves that it's there. He says it's a place where history and contemporary life meet." She hesitated a moment. Eddie knew she had a sixth sense, as he called it, because of the cemetery, because of the times they'd walked there together — and the day he'd caught her talking to a ghost. "There are dozens of stories about the cemetery, secret burials and, of course, ghosts. Naturally, it's got a reputation for being haunted."

"Most cemeteries do," Sean said. "Eddie told me once that if he ever had time between the projects that paid the bills, he'd love to do a documentary on the cemetery." She had the uneasy feeling that he was looking inside her soul. Good Lord, Eddie hadn't told him she was some kind of a freak who talked to ghosts, had he?

"Does it mean anything to you?" she asked. "The cemetery being there?"

He shrugged. "Right now? I see it as a place where a killer could escape — that's what I see. Let's keep going, shall we?"

They returned to the first floor and stopped at Bailey's station. Sean thanked him and asked, "You're not working around the clock now, are you?"

"No, but I've always taken on the Sunday evening shift. You know how Eddie Archer loves his cinema. And it's not even like we have break-ins or anything of the kind, but I take over for Winston Nash at five in the afternoon on Sundays and work until morning. Today I'm in because I was already here, and because I'd do whatever I could for Eddie Archer."

"And Nash didn't report anything?"

"No, Nash said it was quiet as a tomb all day. I saw Alistair when he went into the Black Box."

"Did you see when Ms. Henderson showed up?" Sean asked.

Bailey flushed. He shook his head. "But she knew I was here. Even if I weren't, there'd still be a guard watching over the place. I think she parked on the other side of the cemetery — well, that's where they found her car — and came around through the graveyard. The front of the cemetery is only on the one side, but the graves stretch around to the back. I assume she slipped around the building. We must've caught her entry on the security cameras, but I admit I wasn't watching that screen when she got in. From what I understand, Alistair told his father that Jenny Henderson said he'd forgotten to lock the front door."

"And *had* he forgotten?" Sean asked.

"I haven't talked to Alistair since I raced over to the Black Box when he came for me. He was . . . he was crazy, hysterical, when I saw him. He was screaming that a monster killed Jenny. I went back to the tunnel with him . . ." He shook his head. "It was a pure zoo here last night! When Alistair ran up to this door it was as if he was being pursued by demons. I saw the blood on him and hit the call button for the police, and they were here within minutes. I tried to calm Alistair down enough to talk, but he just kept screaming about the priest and the mummies."

"Did you go down to the tunnel?"

"Yes. I walked in, saw Jenny Henderson and the blood and walked out again. But I had to check it out because he was so hysterical. It's my job."

Sean was thoughtful. Silent.

Bailey continued. "It was a slip-and-slide of blood down there. A slip and slide. When I saw the way the girl was lying there. . . . Well, I knew she was dead. I backed out, not wanting to mess anything up for the police."

"That was the right thing to do, Colin."

"I never had anything that resembled a coherent talk with Alistair. He was in shock. And then the police got here — and Eddie. Eddie seemed to be in shock, too, and they arrested Alistair. Eddie told me not to leave my post, and it's been a long time now, but

I haven't left," Bailey said, nodding with determined loyalty. "I haven't left," he repeated doggedly.

"Thank you, sir," Sean said. He handed Colin Bailey a card. "If you think of anything — even something that might seem unimportant, will you call me?"

"You bet, Sean. You know the police interviewed me for more than an hour. I think I said everything. But, Sean, yeah, you bet. I'll call you."

They walked out into the dying sunlight. Sean paused. Some of the police cars were gone; they could see that Benny Knox was still standing outside the entrance to the Black Box Cinema, like a sentinel.

"I'm going in," Sean said. "They should have finished up with the crime scene evidence by now." He turned to her. "There's no reason for you to come."

Yes, there is. The reason Eddie picked me to be with you.

She studied him, wondering how to explain that she somehow knew it was important that she go in without sounding like a fool. She didn't want to say she might get some kind of *feeling* from the place. He'd probably look at her as if she should be committed if she said, "There's a slim possibility that there's a ghost in there now, and that she might talk to me."

What would happen? This man wouldn't really react. He'd hold his thoughts, be polite — and *then* see that she was committed.

"I really love Eddie Archer," she began. "He gave me my life. I want to go in, I don't know if it'll help, but maybe . . ."

"I think it's a mistake," he said. He might be a legend, but she sensed that to him she was just the guide. No real help, just the guide.

"Eddie asked me to be here. I feel I should go in," she said stubbornly.

He knew she resented him at that moment and maybe he resented her back. He was the man in charge, so she understood.

"All right," he said. "I just wanted to know what we were doing before I challenged the buzzard."

"The buzzard?"

"Detective Knox," he said, rolling his eyes toward the entrance — and the man in question.

He didn't say any more as he headed toward the Black Box. Benny Knox had already been standing in a ramrod-stiff position, but his whole body seemed to straighten further as they approached.

"You going in now?" Knox asked.

"Yes," Sean said.

"You wait here, miss," Knox ordered.

"She's working with me, Detective," Sean said. "She'll be with my people on this." He kept speaking even though Knox's frown made it apparent that he planned to argue. "This case is looking more and more like an in-house situation, Detective. Madison knows all the players on the stage now, and I may not. She probably knows the killer, and I would say fairly well."

"In-house," Knox muttered. "The Archer kid was the only one here, Agent Cameron. Yeah, I guess you'd call that in-house."

"Come on, Knox," Sean said. "You're a good detective or you wouldn't be on this. And you know as well as I do that what's most obvious isn't always the truth."

"In this case? I don't know. I really don't." Knox wasn't being a wiseass, Madison thought; he was serious. The subdued way he spoke scared her for Eddie more than anything else.

Sean said, "We're not going with obvious. We're investigating. Madison is familiar with the working of this studio and the cinema, inside and out. She's with me." The last was quiet and firm.

Madison watched Knox's inner struggle. His longing to argue was clearly there, but he didn't persist. She wondered what kind of power Sean and his people had — exactly who they were, she wasn't sure.

Knox nodded. "Hands gloved, feet bagged," he said.

"Of course," Sean agreed.

At the entry there was a box of supplies. Madison followed suit as Sean put plastic covers over his shoes and pulled latex gloves on his hands. She fumbled awkwardly as she tried to get the gloves on, perhaps because Knox was behind them, watching her every move.

The three of them went inside.

A tech in a jumpsuit was leaving, a plastic box filled with vials in his arms. He nodded. As they headed through the theater, she saw that Sean looked at everything, from the Art Deco popcorn stand to the rugs, the cinema itself — and the office. As they reached the tunnel, she heard two of the techs talking.

"Hazmat will have fun with this one," someone said.

"This is nothing! You should've seen that murder site up on the hill. The killer wrote in blood everywhere. Wonder if that place will ever sell," another voice responded.

"This is Hollywood — you can sell anything," the first man said. "Let's finish up here. I'm ready for a drink."

The techs nodded as they passed Knox, Sean and Madison.

"Your team's covered everything?" Knox asked.

"Sir, if we covered any more, we'd have to take the walls," the man said.

"Good."

As they made their way down, Madison felt as if the place was closing in on them. It was actually a broad throughway, maybe fifty feet in width and a hundred and fifty in length.

When they reached the tunnel, she felt dizzy. The smell of blood was overwhelming.

The museum in the tunnel had always been fascinating. It was an homage to a bygone era of film, one that played an important role in the evolution of movies. Although Madison preferred romantic comedy, fantasy, adventure and horror, she loved the *feel* of the little museum. She'd learned new respect for film noir because of it, and she was impressed by the accuracy and detail of the old tableaux.

Today, it was different. The artistry seemed to be gone; it was merely a tunnel with props and policemen. There were little plastic clips with numbers, a photographer was still snapping photos and tape outlined the place where the body had fallen. The last tableau at the rear, the *Sam Stone* movie scene, was out of kilter. It had been photographed, fingerprinted and invaded.

Madison focused on that tableau, not wanting to see the blood on the floor.

It wasn't prop blood. It wasn't chocolate, as Hitchcock had used for the black-and-white murder scene in *Psycho.* It was real blood, and the person who'd shed that blood was now dead.

Thankfully, the body had been taken to the morgue. Despite what Madison had said, and despite all the time she spent creating creatures that were sometimes heroic and most often terrible, she felt somewhat squeamish about being down here. She wondered if she'd ever be able to come to the museum again without thinking about what had happened last night.

She'd come for a reason! she reminded herself. She *had* to be here.

She stood several feet from the tape that marked the position of the body and tried not to see the remaining techs or pay attention to Sean Cameron as he moved about the room. Eventually he came to the marked-out tape line.

She realized that he was standing as still

100

as she was, as if he felt the air and was waiting for some kind of message that would speak to him in silence from the tunnel.

The photographer packed up his equipment and told Knox he was done. Soon the other techs left, too, and then there were just the three of them. For a moment, the silence around them seemed . . . unnatural.

"Sam Stone and the Curious Case of the Egyptian Museum." Sean was looking at the tableau. "And Alistair Archer swears that someone — *something* — came out of that tableau and attacked Jenny Henderson."

"The priest — Amun Mopat, I understand," Madison said.

"Indeed, the priest. And he's still wearing *his* robe."

"There's something missing — something off in the scene," Madison said as she studied the tableau.

"I have that feeling, too. But what?" Sean asked. He stared at it, frowning.

Madison continued to study it, as well. Mannequins, snakes and the items in the "Egyptian Museum" had been moved by the police and put back, but they weren't experts on how the display had been set up. There was something wrong, but she couldn't pin it down.

Sam Stone was entering, ready to wrest

the priest, Amun Mopat, away from Dianna Breen. The sarcophagus, the mummy fallen to the floor, the stand with the canopic jars — all still there. So was the statue of the ancient Egyptian warrior, tilted to the wrong side, and the jackal and the sphinx.

"I wish I knew this place as well as Alistair does," Sean said.

Madison watched in silence as Sean noted where the body had been and he walked to the tableau, not touching the velvet cord that separated the scene from the hall passage. He stepped over the cord. There wasn't much he could do to mess up what had been a perfect recreation, since the police and the techs had already been through the entire place. She found it oddly disturbing, as if the characters were now out of focus, and far more haunting than the ferocious and bloody scenes in the studio.

Madison tried to shut herself off, tried to focus on the victim.

Jenny?

But she didn't feel the presence of anyone near her. She stood there alone in her little world, frozen. She could envision Alistair and Jenny coming here, Alistair walking ahead, Jenny sensing someone at her back, crying out desperately for help. . . .

And then feeling a knife cut through her throat.

Madison gave herself a furious mental shake. She was in the tunnel; the murder had happened only a few feet from where she was standing.

But there was nothing here that wasn't solid and real.

Jenny Henderson's body was at the morgue. If she was hanging around the place she'd been murdered, hoping to communicate, Madison could feel no impression of her.

She walked a step closer to the blood, hoping that didn't make her ghoulish. She closed her eyes and tried to imagine the scene. Jenny must have coerced Alistair into bringing her to the studio. Jenny was an actress, a budding actress who needed every possible opportunity. No casting was done at the studio, but she probably believed she could learn something that might give her an edge when they were casting bit parts.

Had Jenny and Alistair paused to look at the tableaux? Or had Jenny's mind been on her agenda — and Alistair's mind on Jenny?

She took note of where the body had lain. There was a distance of perhaps twenty feet to the door. Alistair had walked ahead. . . .

"All right," Sean said, startling her.

"Here's how I heard the story from Eddie — how it was told to him by Alistair. Jenny convinced him to bring her over — she wanted to get into the studio, see the costumes and the Egyptian creatures. Or the mythical creatures the Egyptian priest, Amun Mopat, brought to life. And according to Alistair —" Sean paused, approaching the door that separated the tunnel from the studio "— he came this way, and turned."

"And saw a monster — or the priest," Madison said.

"Which means —" Sean paused again, walking to the display "— that the killer was in the tableau. As soon as Alistair passed by, the killer came down." Sean moved up to the display, then got down, his movements silent. "The robed figure left his position and crawled over the velvet cord and attacked Jenny Henderson. He'd left Sam Stone and his femme fatale where they belonged as he stepped down to seize Jenny, and cut her throat."

Sean was suddenly standing behind Madison.

For a moment, she could feel the fear, feel as if the killer's breath touched her. . . .

She felt his hands on her shoulders, and the other girl's fear seemed to fill her. She could practically see — feel, touch! — what had happened.

Her throat closed; she could barely scream.

Alistair!

The sound didn't leave her lips. She managed to step forward before she began trembling noticeably.

She almost slipped on the blood.

Deep in his own thoughts, Sean hardly noticed her.

"This place, the movie — they have everything to do with the murder," he said, repeating what he'd told her before. *"Everything."*

4

Madison stared at Sean Cameron, feeling frozen at first, and completely lost. There was nothing she could do here. She'd hoped there would be, but she felt nothing except cold and fear and dread. She could picture what had happened but she couldn't see a face. She imagined the mannequin of the priest moving, saw him walking swiftly. . . .

Saw him kill.

"Poor girl, poor Jenny Henderson — and poor Alistair," he murmured.

"Alistair didn't do it," Madison said. Her voice was low, but her words were passionate. "It happened just the way you reenacted it. He was ahead of her and then he got to the door. Someone was already in here, waiting. Someone who knew that Alistair came to see the noir movies on Sundays, and someone who also knew about Jenny. Yes, it was taking a chance that Jenny would show up and that Alistair would fall in with her plans, but it wasn't really that big a chance."

"Someone — or the kid. The kid does tell it your way. But there's nothing to exonerate him."

Madison was startled by the voice of Benny Knox. He'd come in behind them. She'd been concentrating so hard, she'd forgotten he was with them.

"Yep, according to the kid, he walked to the door — and the *thing* came out of the tableau. I don't know what the kid was on, but temporary insanity or whatever is probably going to be his best defense," Knox went on.

"If he says that's what happened, it's what happened. Alistair isn't on drugs, and he doesn't drink. He's a good kid — which is pretty amazing when you realize the money he has access to and how everyone tries to suck up to him because of what his father might be able to do for them!" Madison said angrily.

"Whoa." Knox lifted a hand and took a step back in mock-horror. "Well, when they need character witnesses, they can call you to the stand."

Madison tried to check her temper, but he continued quickly, "Look, I'm sorry. We are going to investigate. If the L.A. police weren't determined on that, you can guarantee the FBI would be. But you've got to understand — you're looking at a locked-room mystery here, and the thing is, if a room is *really* locked, the people in that room are the suspects. Nine times out of ten what you see is what you get."

"What you see is a kid in shock and a brutally murdered young woman," Sean Cameron said. "And I wouldn't go counting on there being no other answer. For one thing, a costume is missing from the studio."

"Missing?" Knox asked sharply.

"It's not on the mannequin," Madison said, "where it should be — where it was before I left the studio on Friday."

"So it may just be somewhere else?"

"It's the robe the priest wears," Sean said. "That's definitely worth investigating."

Knox didn't dismiss his words, but he didn't seem too impressed, either. "That studio is filled with shelves and desks and nooks and crannies and . . . stuff. The robe may turn up easily. Yes, we'll investigate — I'm sure you will, too, Agent Cameron," he said to Sean. "I intend to go through all the steps on my end. I'm just telling you it isn't looking good for young Archer. When you show me another way in and out of this locked room, I'll be happy to reexamine the evidence." He pointed to the tableau. "As you can see, those mannequins just stand there — they don't move around. They don't speak, argue or step down to commit murder. But you're right. We have all kinds of hairs and fibers and plenty of blood. In fact, we've got forensics up the wazoo. We've checked the locks, we've gone over the security footage . . . and nada. So when you find something, let me know."

As he finished speaking, they were all shocked by a noise from the tableau. Some piece of the little scenario had shifted. The three of them immediately looked over at the characters. There was Sam Stone, ready to race across the room to save his femme fatale. And there was the man in the robe, his fingers twined around the terrified woman's neck. There was the sarcophagus and the snakes — cobras posed moving across the floor and in strike mode.

The scene had shifted, of course, because the crime scene techs had been up there, photographing, fingerprinting, moving things around. That obviously explained the odd, off-kilter look of the tableau. And yet . . .

Madison swallowed uncomfortably. Dianna Breen seemed to be gazing not at the mysterious man in the robes about to strangle her — but at Madison. Huge blue glass eyes seemed to stare across time and space.

For a moment — just for a moment! — she thought there'd been another presence in the tunnel.

Sean Cameron walked back toward and through the tableau. "Gravity, I guess. Something shifted from being handled by the crime scene techs."

"Of course," Knox said. His voice was harsh, and Madison looked over at him. Maybe the hard-boiled just-the-facts detective was a little on edge himself.

Madison tried to define exactly how the tableau had changed. The police and technicians apparently hadn't uncovered anything they considered evidence; they'd left the scene almost as they'd found it. But it *had* changed. And Dianna Breen still seemed to be staring at her with horrified eyes.

Last night, those realistic glass eyes had witnessed a murder.

"No sign of the weapon yet, right?" Sean asked.

"No. Before you arrived today, two dozen of our guys — the best at their jobs — went through the studio. We needed that many, which won't surprise you. The place is a hotbed of fake weapons and fake blood and fake — well, you name it." He shook his head. "But no, we don't have the weapon yet."

"So, how are you figuring that Alistair murdered the girl, fell in the blood, passed out, came to and got emergency help *and* somehow hid the weapon?" Sean asked him.

"Here's the thing, Agent Cameron. The kid was here alone. We have experts still going through all the surveillance. He *claims* he raced toward Ms. Henderson and the 'thing' killing her and that he fell in the blood, went down and passed out. According to him, he regained consciousness, called the security guard and came back with him when the guard rushed in, followed by the cops. He *claims* he passed out. God knows what he was really doing or what really happened. And if someone else was here, why kill the girl and not him?"

"How can you have a scapegoat if you kill everyone?" Sean asked reasonably.

"That's right," Madison said. "If Alistair had been killed as well, he couldn't have been blamed for the murders."

Knox was quiet a moment. "I'm not discounting any possibilities. I'm just not emotionally involved. Are you done here for the day? We're closing up until tomorrow and —"

"What about Colin Bailey?" Sean broke in. "Did you confirm that he was in the studio, in the security station, watching the cameras the whole time?"

"Bailey was the only other person on the property at all," Knox said. "Everything pans out — and, of course, we verified his background. His record is clean as a whistle, he's worked here twenty years and his story checks out. We're not stupid local dicks, Agent Cameron. So, are you done here?"

"Yes, thanks, Detective Knox. Can one of your guys give us a ride to Archer's place?"

"Sure. Go on out. There's a fellow named Duffy in his car."

"Madison?"

She nodded, said thank you to Knox, then followed Sean out. She noticed that Knox was behind them and had to wonder if he — hard-boiled L.A. detective — didn't want to be in the tunnel alone.

"You're going to Archer's house?" Madison asked Sean. Her part was finished for today, wasn't it? She felt as if she were in limbo. She had no idea what was happening with the studio the next day. Were they all on hold?

"I'll go with you," she said.

He looked down at her. "Why?"

She found herself bristling again. "Because

Eddie asked me to be in on this. Because the studio is my life. Because I may be able to help."

He stared back at her. She had the uncomfortable feeling that she was being assessed — and found wanting. He was going to tell her no, that she'd done her duty. To her surprise, he didn't.

"Fine. We'll both go," he said.

She looked away, wondering how she could feel so attracted to a man and so hostile to him at the same time. He was physically impressive, she decided. That must be it. He was also a stranger, even though he'd become a legend at the studio, and it was too easy to admire what she'd heard about him. She had to remember: he was law enforcement here, and she was not.

Maybe she was crazy. Maybe she should go home and get out of this now, while she had the chance.

But she knew she couldn't. She did have . . . an extra sense. And it was possible that she could help Eddie. She just hoped it wouldn't mean sucking up too much to Agent Cameron!

"Is Eddie there?" she asked. "I thought he was going to go and stay with Alistair."

"He'll come home," Sean assured her. "I need to get more of a feel for the lay of the land," he added.

"You suspect someone close," she said. "First, Bailey, who's been the most loyal watchdog in the world. Bailey! And now, someone in Eddie's household?"

"I suspect everyone," he said simply. "And this isn't your fight, not really."

"Oh? Think again. I live here and I work here, Agent Cameron. The studio — and Eddie — are everything to me."

He smiled suddenly and she had no idea what he was thinking. "Do you have plans for the day?"

"Yes, I'd planned to work. Now, I'm not working, so I plan to do everything I can for Eddie and Alistair. No, I'm not FBI or a cop, but Eddie asked me to help you."

She didn't want to tell him she wouldn't have had any plans. Not social plans, anyway. Life had made her too much of a loner.

Except, of course, for her unearthly friends.

She straightened, trying to appear calm, confident — and determined.

"Officer Duffy is waiting," Cameron said. "He'll take us to Eddie's. If you're sure you want to plunge in."

"I'm sure." She glared at him icily. He seemed amused. That was even more irritating.

■ ■ ■ ■

Officer Duffy was quiet as he drove. Sean didn't try to engage him in conversation.

Instead, he glanced over at his escort, Madison Darvil.

She's either certifiable, crazy as a loon or just like you. She talks to the dead, Eddie had told him.

She wasn't crazy; she was talented. But if she talked to the dead, she might wonder if there was something inside her that wasn't exactly normal. Most people learned early on not to admit that they could communicate with the souls of the departed. Madison was probably unaware that there were actually many people with her talent scattered around the world.

She was silent during the drive. Sean thought that Eddie had picked the perfect person to help him — even if he hadn't meant to draw her in this far. She did know the studio and everyone working there now; she was in on meetings and certainly trusted if she dealt with major names in the business. And aside from all that, she was slim and well-proportioned, with large, dark-lashed eyes that were exceptionally expressive and beautiful.

He suddenly wished he'd met her at a party or a bar or anywhere that would allow him to ask her out. He liked her passion when she defended Eddie and even her hostility when he suggested she was no longer necessary. Something within her — integrity, honesty — ran very deep, and it was compelling and seductive.

He turned away, surprised. He hadn't felt like this about anyone in a very long time. Work had been his escape for years now. It wasn't that he'd eschewed people, women in particular, but he'd never had this sense of *knowing* them as he already felt he knew her. He'd functioned well enough when he and Melissa had split, even though he'd really loved her, and she'd loved him, too. He hadn't hesitated to go back when she needed him, and it hadn't seemed like any kind of chore or sacrifice to be with her.

Her death had changed him.

He shook off the unhappy memory. Another friend needed him.

Eddie's place wasn't far from the studio. He lived in an elegant home in a cul-de-sac where the houses started at the seven-figure mark. There was a high wall around the property and gates protected it, but when they were dropped off and Sean pushed the call button, they were answered immediately.

Sean thought that Pierce Enderly, Eddie's "house manager," would be the one to greet them. He was wrong.

Mrs. Eddie Archer, Helena LaRoux, came clip-clopping to the door on high-heeled sandals as they arrived. She swiftly ushered them in, looking past them to the gates. "Were you followed?" she asked.

Sean shook his head.

"The paparazzi were out there for hours!" she said. The little lapdog she carried — some kind of designer Peke-teacup-poodle combo — let out a yap.

"Shh, little darling," Helena said. "It's Sean — and . . . Madison, right?"

Madison nodded. Helena gave her a puzzled look.

"Madison is taking me through the studio, Helena. It's been a while since I worked there," Sean told her.

"Of course." Helena smiled at Madison as if she was trying to be warm and genuine, except something in her tone made it clear that she was still confused as to why the "help" would now be at her door. "I knew Eddie had called you in, just didn't know there'd be anyone with you."

"Eddie asked her to hang around with

me," Sean continued.

He realized that although Madison was quiet, she meant to hold her own. "I would do anything for Eddie and *Alistair,* Helena. That's why I'm here."

Sean lowered his head to hide the smile that teased his lips. Oh, yes, Madison could hold her own.

"Eddie's still with Alistair," Helena said. "I've spent time with the boy, but . . . well, I'm not his mother. He really does need his father now. I'm so distraught! Forgive me if I've forgotten my manners. Come in, come in!"

She started clip-clopping across the marble floor again. Helena might claim she hated the paparazzi, but her platinum-blond swath of hair was sleekly brushed, her makeup was perfect and she wore skintight pedal pushers with her high-heeled sandals and a low-cut T-shirt that nicely displayed her expensive cleavage.

She led them through the grand entry to a family room connected to a huge kitchen. He didn't know if Helena liked to cook, but Eddie was a fan of culinary shows; he loved to watch and cook along with them. He must have put his foot down at some point because the family room was just that, despite Helena's high-end presence. There was a large-screen TV on the far wall and a pricey stereo system with speakers all around the room. The sofa was old leather, worn and comfortable, and there were a number of magazines spread out on the coffee table. Helena gestured at the sofa and sat in the massive armchair next to it.

"I'm so glad you're here, Sean. I mean, thank you for coming. You're so important to Eddie. I was heartbroken when you couldn't make *our* wedding," she said.

"I was on a project, Helena. I'm sorry."

Helena patted the little dog. "It was a beautiful affair! Oh, you were there, Madison!"

"Yes, it was quite an affair," Madison said dryly.

Helena frowned. "This is awful, so awful," she moaned. "I'm afraid it's just broken Eddie. Everyone in the media . . . they already have Alistair convicted, and Eddie loves that boy so much!"

"It's natural for a father to love his son," Madison said.

"Helena, the media craves sensationalism, and this is definitely a sensational case. But don't worry, the media might try someone, but there's still an investigation ahead, and I'm confident we'll prove Alistair innocent," Sean told her.

Helena's perfectly plucked brows shot up. "You think Alistair may be innocent?"

Sean felt Madison shift beside him and he almost grinned again. Apparently, she liked the newest Mrs. Archer about as much as he did.

"Of course I believe he's innocent. Now I have to prove it."

"Oh, yes! I've tried to be there for him. . . . Eddie asked me to visit Alistair. They both say he didn't do it. How wonderful that you think you can prove it," Helena said. Her voice seemed thick with an air of insincerity.

"Helena, you know Alistair. You can't possibly believe he could have done such a thing, can you?" Madison asked.

Sean couldn't help giving her a little nudge with his elbow. He heard the grunt she tried to swallow. Luckily, Helena didn't.

"I don't *want* to believe it. But . . . I've worried so often about poor Alistair. I mean, Eddie is a genius, and most people in the business can tell the difference between reality and imagination — but I've warned Eddie! Sometimes, being around all that gore and all that make-believe blood . . . it has to have an influence."

"You were with him earlier today, Helena. How is he doing?" Sean asked.

"Well, he's in bad shape."

"You didn't let him know you don't have complete faith in him, did you?" Sean half smiled to take the sting from his question.

"Oh, no! I *do* have faith in him," Helena said.

"Mrs. Archer?"

Sean turned to see that Pierce had arrived at last. He was glad; Pierce was one person who truly loved Eddie. He made a good wage for what he did, and he was another factor in Eddie's life on which he couldn't be dissuaded. Pierce had handled the household since the very first Mrs. Archer, Alistair's mother, had found him poring over classified ads at a coffee shop. She'd brought him home and they'd discovered that he could shop, clean and manage a school list without blinking an eye. He was indispensable. Pierce was gay and had been in a relationship with his high school love all of his adult life; his partner had died of bone cancer soon after Eddie's first wife, and since that time, Pierce had given his total love and loyalty to Eddie and Alistair. In other words, Pierce was family.

But not, apparently, to Helena.

"What is it, Pierce?" she asked irritably.

"I was wondering if you would like to offer *Mr. Archer's* guests some refreshment."

Sean rose, walking over to Pierce and giving him a hug. "Pierce! Great to see you. How are you holding up?"

"Getting through, Mr. Cameron, getting through," Pierce said. "Staying strong, because that's what Eddie and Alistair need now."

"It's *Agent* Cameron, Pierce," Helena drawled.

"Agent Cameron," Pierce repeated.

"It's Sean. You've known me forever, Pierce. I'm still Sean."

Pierce wasn't exactly the epitome of an old-fashioned butler. Or maybe he was the California equivalent. He was dressed in khakis and a short-sleeved cotton tailored shirt, and he wore sandals. He looked like an aging pool boy, still handsome with his blond hair turning silver and his year-round tan.

Sean imagined that it must be interesting to watch the dynamics between him and the newest Mrs. Archer — especially when no one else was around.

"Sean, what will you have?" Helena asked abruptly. "Madigan?"

"It's Madison, Mrs. Archer," Madison said politely. She had risen, too. Ignoring Helena, she walked over to Pierce and took his hand. "Eddie is in a bad way, and

Alistair's worse. I'm glad you're here for them."

"We all are!" Helena rose, as well, and walked over, handing Pierce the dog. "Will you take Perla for a walk?" she asked.

Sean wondered if she wanted him out of the way while they spoke or if she was just trying to prove that he was only the hired help.

"I'll tend to drinks for our friends," she went on. "Sean, a Jameson? That's your poison of choice, if I remember."

"To be honest, I'd go for some coffee right now," Sean said. "Madison?"

"Coffee would be great," Madison agreed.

Helena snatched the dog back. Clearly she wasn't interested in the effort of actually brewing coffee. "Fine," she sniffed. "Coffee, then, Pierce. Perla can run in the yard." She hurried toward the French doors that led to the pool and patio area. "Now, no doo-doo by the water, Perla! Take it out to the back, that's a good girl!"

"Coffee, coming right up," Pierce said. He walked over to the kitchen and began preparing it. Helena caught hold of Sean's arm, leading him back to the sofa and whispering, "Honestly . . . this house is impossible. These men — my husband, Pierce — they're so lost. Oh, it's dreadful.

Everything is at a standstill. Did you know I was about to read for the part of Lady Macbeth in a new Shakespeare project? It's going to be wonderful, filmed along the lines of *Game of Thrones* with lots of swords and sorcery. Even Eddie said that hot new director thought I'd be perfect for the role!" She pouted. "Of course now, God knows . . ."

The house phone rang and Pierce picked it up. "Yes, Eddie. They're here now. Yes, I'll tell them."

He hung up a moment later and turned. "Mr. Archer is on his way," he announced. He'd barely finished speaking when the phone rang again, and again Pierce answered it. As Helena looked at him expectantly, he covered the mouthpiece and said, "It's Benita, Mrs. Archer. She's calling to lend her support. Will you speak with her?"

Helena started to rise. "Benita?"

"Yes, the ex–Mrs. Archer," Pierce said politely.

Helena paused, eyeing him with venom. Sean wasn't sure if her dislike was now aimed at Pierce or Benita. She suddenly seemed to puff up. "No! You may tell her that I'm busy with the *FBI.* You may tell her that I'm far too distraught!"

Pierce dutifully did as bidden, assuring the second Mrs. Archer that he'd convey her feelings and support to her ex-husband. Sean suspected that Pierce used the word *ex–Mrs. Archer* on purpose, either to remind Helena that there were others who had loved Eddie and whom Eddie had loved, or that she, too, could be replaced.

"Oh, that woman! Calling now!" Helena said, shaking her head.

"I thought you two were friends." Madison smiled sweetly. "I always felt it was so wonderful that you could have remained such good friends."

"Yes, Helena. In fact, we met at Eddie's marriage to Benita," Sean said.

Helena waved a hand in the air. "Well, yes, we're friends! But this is an intimate time. *I'm* here to support my husband."

"I'm assuming you and Eddie were together when you got the call from Alistair last night?" Sean asked, keeping his tone sympathetic.

"Yes, yes. I was sound asleep," Helena said. "And then the phone rang, and . . . My Eddie! My poor Eddie!" She hid her face in her hands.

"You'd both been here all evening?"

"Earlier, Eddie was out at some meeting, but I was here all day. Pierce can tell you that." She turned, gesturing at him. He carried in a tray, then set it on the coffee table.

He was quick and efficient; the silver serving tray had three filled cups and saucers, milk, cream, sugar and artificial sweetener — anything they might have wanted — as well as plates of cookies and scones.

"I mean, if you're accusing me of anything!" she said, as if she'd just grasped the question, horrified at what it could imply. "Seriously? Sean! How could you even *imagine* that I . . . or Eddie! Oh, Sean! I thought you came here to be Eddie's friend."

"I'm not accusing you of anything, Helena." Sean kept his voice calm. "I'm trying to get a complete picture of what happened last night. Eddie had a meeting, but you were here. And then Eddie came home. What about Alistair?"

"I don't know. You'd have to ask Pierce. I was out in the afternoon." She paused, realizing that she'd just said she'd been home. "I was only out for an hour or so. Shopping. I was on Sunset. I can give you a list of the stores," she said coldly.

"Helena —"

"How would you like your coffee, Sean? Do you still take it black?" Pierce asked.

"Yes, thanks," he said.

"Alistair didn't leave until seven-thirty last evening. He was up doing homework until then," Pierce informed.

126

"So you weren't home until after seven-thirty?" Sean said to Helena.

"Was it that late?" Helena asked Pierce. "I'm sure I was home by late afternoon."

"No, Mrs. Archer. Alistair had gone about an hour before you returned."

"Well, then, there you have it. Our living calendar and timepiece here — Pierce — can tell you exactly where I was!" Helena said. "And when," she added.

Pierce ignored her, apparently accustomed to anything she had to say. "I saw her come home," he told Sean. "She retired to her room after that and I didn't see her again until the phone call came." He smiled.

"I hear a car!" Madison set down her coffee and rose. "I think Eddie's here."

Pierce strode to the door and opened it quickly, waiting while Eddie Archer parked his car in the drive. Eddie trudged toward the house, looking haggard and sad. He seemed to perk up as he entered and saw that both Sean and Madison were there.

"Sean, welcome, and Madison, my dear, thank you for hanging in with this. In this town, the people who love you can turn against you in the blink of an eye, so it's good to have friends," Eddie said. "Real friends."

"I just made coffee," Pierce said.

"Yes, darling." Helena walked over to Eddie, slipping an arm around him. "I was so enjoying conversation with your friends."

Eddie didn't seem to hear the edge in her voice. He was distracted, squeezing her in return and pecking her cheek, his eyes never leaving Sean's.

"Well, can you help me?" he asked anxiously. "Can you at least stop them from crucifying Alistair without even looking into other possibilities?"

"Eddie, there's definitely room for a great deal of investigation," Sean said. "Don't lose heart. I want to see the security videos myself and search the studio some more, plus the surrounding area, and check out everyone and everything in the immediate vicinity. The D.A.'s office will prepare their case against Alistair, but you and your attorneys have him at the best possible place for now. The kid has to be hurting, and they can help him there. Not only that, he's out of harm's way. Yes, you'll hear terrible things — and you'll have to expect that."

Eddie nodded, and Sean prayed he could prove that Alistair was innocent. In the meantime, he wanted Eddie to remain positive, but it was going to be a long haul. He could imagine what the court case was going to be like.

"Thank you, my friend. Thank you. Where do we go from here?" Eddie asked.

"Tomorrow night, the rest of my team arrives. We've already been invited in, so we can set up at the police station. I met Detective Benny Knox. We'll be working in conjunction with him."

Eddie made a face, and Sean tried to reassure him. "Eddie, I'm with you all the way on this, but you have to see how it looks to others. As far as anyone's been able to tell thus far, Alistair was alone at the Black Box Cinema, Colin Bailey was on guard at the studio and Jenny Henderson managed to slip in. We have to prove otherwise, and that means delving into *everything*. Alistair's life, your life, friends, enemies —"

"And me," Helena put in. "Eddie, Sean wanted to know where *I* was last night!"

Eddie remained distracted. He didn't respond to her complaint, if he even heard it. "Anything — anything. Whatever you need. I'm here, and I'll give you anything you want, and everyone around me will be as helpful as possible, too. Right?" He looked at Helena, and it was evident that he'd hardly been aware of her.

"Of course, sweetheart, of course," Helena said.

Eddie stepped away to face Madison, taking her hands. "Thank you, thank you, Madison. I know this isn't what you do . . . but I need you. This is Alistair's life," he said passionately.

Madison gazed back at him, and Sean saw himself, years before, when he'd first met Eddie. The guy was an absolute icon, an idol to anyone who loved special effects. And he was so down to earth, so generous . . . Sean could see that she was controlling her emotions as she listened to him and then spoke. "Eddie, Alistair is a great kid, a great person, and I'm happy to be there for him — and for you — in any way possible."

"Thank you, thank you," Eddie said again. "Sean, what do you need from me now?"

"Your schedule yesterday."

Eddie nodded. "Woke up, ate bran flakes here and ran by the studio, just to see that everything was okay for lockdown. After that, I left and met with Myron Silver and Harvey Anderson, producer and director on the Shakespeare movie that's gearing up. I went back to Harvey's home studio to look at his storyboards. I talked to Alistair on the phone about seven to see if he was up for dinner, but he'd already eaten at home with Pierce, so I went to a fast-food drive-through, grabbed a veggie burger and came home. I watched a few of my cooking shows

130

and went to bed. And then I got the phone call. I rushed to the Black Box, and then to the police station, where I called my lawyer. And soon after that, I called you and . . ." He shrugged. "Then I called the governor. I campaigned for him, and I said I needed help and that I thought I knew the people who could provide it."

"When was the last time you saw Alistair?" Sean asked.

"At breakfast."

Pierce cleared his throat. "Alistair was here all afternoon. He was on the computer for a while, and he took a swim."

"If you think the kid's innocent, why are you asking questions about him?" Helena demanded.

"Because it proves where he was before the murder, and that he wasn't at the studio or the museum stashing the knife," Sean said.

"But if he killed the girl in a jealous rage —" Helena began to say, then obviously remembered that Eddie was there, and that while Alistair might not be her biological son he meant the world to her husband. She flushed. "I'm just afraid that's how the police will probably see it," she mumbled.

"And that's why we have to find out who might've been at the studio. Who knows it well enough to hide there and escape and to do it without tracking blood anywhere," Sean said evenly.

"Someone could have planned this?" Eddie asked in horror.

"Someone would *have* to have planned it. Someone who knew the studio, like I said, but also your son's schedule, the movie and special-effects business, and either knew about evidence or studied police and forensics procedure," Sean told him. "The answer isn't going to jump out at us. We're going to have to dig until we find it."

"We'll dig. We'll dig into anything and everything. Everything." Eddie repeated the last word fervently.

"I'll need to visit Alistair tomorrow," Sean said. "For now, I'm sure Madison wants to get home, and I need to check in to my hotel."

"You can just stay here, you know," Eddie offered.

"Eddie, you made wonderful hotel arrangements for us. Actually, I wouldn't mind some time alone, until my team shows up. Space to think."

"Then, by all means, get checked in. I put your luggage in the little Prius outside. I figure you can use that while you're here."

"Great. Thanks, Eddie."

Eddie groped in his pockets and came out with a handful of keys. He dropped several; they all bent down to retrieve them at the same time. Madison banged into Sean and he caught himself once again studying the young woman with the wide eyes who was supposed to help him.

The girl who spoke to ghosts, or so Eddie said.

He paused for a moment. She was stunning, and in a way a woman like Helena would never understand. Those eyes of hers! Blue as the sky and framed by rich dark lashes. Her face was a classic oval that no amount of money could buy. Her dark hair was long and naturally wavy. He couldn't avoid noticing that her body was shapely, lean, athletic — with curves in all the right places. Curves that weren't exposed by a low-cut neckline or contained in sausage-skin pants.

Startled by his assessment — and trying to tell himself that it was so positive because he really disliked Helena — he stood again, glancing at her apologetically.

"I'm sorry, Madison. I'm fumbling all over the place."

"No, *I'm* sorry. I dropped the keys," Eddie muttered.

"It's understandable, Eddie," Madison

said. "And I'm just fine."

"I was driving competently all day, I swear it," Eddie insisted, half-humorously.

Sean grinned. "We know. We drove with you."

"All right. I'll talk to you tomorrow," Eddie said.

"As I said, I'll see Alistair," Sean told him. "Can you tell them I'll be there, midmorning?"

"Definitely, and he'll be glad to see you — and Madison, too. Will you come and assure him he has friends?" Eddie asked her.

"Yes," Madison said. "Of course I will."

Eddie nodded, his expression grateful. "They're giving Alistair a sedative tonight. Doctor says he'll sleep for hours." He looked at Sean again. "If the cops could just understand what this has done to him, how he's feeling . . . they'd know he couldn't have done it."

Helena put a hand on his shoulder. "Are they keeping the studio closed, Eddie? What about the work you have going on?"

"We're still down tomorrow. We'll be back up in a day," Eddie said, frowning.

"You have so many people depending on you for their livelihood, dear," Helena said softly. "Like Madison."

"I'm okay with whatever you choose to

do," Madison told Eddie. "As I'm sure everyone at the studio is."

Eddie almost smiled. "The police want to go through the studio once more. And then, apparently, it's all right for business to go on as usual, even if your son had been accused of murder and a girl died horribly on your property. Oh, Sean, I'm assuming your team will want to search the place, too?"

Sean nodded. He was fairly certain that Eddie believed their relationship meant there was someone who *cared* actively seeking the truth. He also realized that Eddie Archer had read up on the Krewe of Hunters. And he might have called them in simply because he had a greater belief in the FBI — or because he'd learned something about the Krewe and hoped that one of them could just speak to a ghost and come up with the answer he wanted.

It was never that easy. But tonight wasn't the time to tell Eddie that the Krewe worked like any other law enforcement agency, searching out clues, forensics and facts.

"Eddie, you need rest," Sean said. "I know it's hard, but try to get some sleep."

"Yes. Yes, thank you," Eddie murmured. "Oh, hey! It's late. How about dinner? Would you like me to cook something?"

Normally, Sean would've said yes. Cooking would have taken Eddie's mind off his situation. But he still had things to do, things he wanted done that night.

"We can stop at an In-N-Out Burger, if that works for you, Madison?"

"Nothing like a burger," she said.

They moved to the door.

"Thank you so much for coming." Helena nodded her head regally.

"Thank you for your hospitality," Sean said.

Madison waved to Pierce, who was hovering behind the group. He solemnly raised a hand in farewell.

As they went out to the front, Eddie followed them, pointing to a new Prius in the driveway. "I'll hit the key guard on the gate," he said.

"And get in, get in!" Helena called. "Eddie, that car over there — it's paparazzi."

"So let them take a picture of a grieving father," Eddie said. "I don't give a damn."

Eddie really didn't give a damn.

Sean observed rather cynically that Helena joined him, and that she posed, her face arranged in a mask of deep concern, her hips jutting out and her breasts high, hands draped with loving tenderness over the arm of her famous husband.

5

They walked to the car, with Sean pausing to open the passenger-side door for Madison. She slid in silently. He came around to join her, and waved as Eddie opened the gate. Then he eased the car out into the cul-de-sac.

"I'm sorry you have to drop me," Madison said. "Do you need some directions? Oh — there *is* an In-N-Out Burger on the way."

"I was with Eddie today when we picked you up, remember?" He laughed. "And I know I can find a burger place."

"Yes, of course, but you don't live here anymore. I wasn't sure you'd remember how to get around."

"I lived here long enough," he told her. "Although it's a little much to get used to again, after living in San Antonio. But I *do* still know my way around. I'm about to prove it — In-N-Out Burger ahead on the left. Shall we get something to go, or eat in?"

"I'm starving, so eat in, if you don't mind," she said.

They ordered and brought their food to a table. For a moment, they ate in silence; he was hungry, too. He found himself liking the fact that his companion ate with enthusiasm. She didn't play with her food or pretend she didn't intend to down her entire burger and fries, but she was fastidiously neat as she did so. It seemed they'd tacitly agreed not to speak about the case during dinner. Instead, they casually discussed California weather and the differences between Texas and California. *She* thought that Texas created a breed all its own; *he* thought that was equally true of California, whether people were born there or became Californians by choice.

Twenty minutes later, they were done and back in the car.

"I'm not sure I'm much help to you," she said as they entered freeway traffic. "I felt you knew the studio as well as I did."

"Not really. So much depends on the latest project. And that's especially important with this case."

"How so?"

"Whoever killed that girl knows the studio,

138

beyond a doubt. Knows everything about it — as it is right now."

She shook her head. "There are dozens of people who work there — probably forty full-time staff, and another twenty brought in on special projects, some of whom end up staying. And there are the different actors and actresses, set designers, directors, cinematographers, prop masters and so on who come in."

"No, the killer is not going to be a producer who stopped by to check on props or the costumer who drops in once. Whoever did this *knows* the studio. Backward and forward." He frowned. "This particular movie may well be a factor, too. Unless the connection — between *The Unholy* and the *Sam Stone* film — was intended to throw us off track."

"So, why didn't you start with the studio workers?" she asked.

"Everyone who's worked at the studio in any capacity is being questioned, and alibis will be examined. I'm sure that Knox already has a list, and if there were any red flags, he would've told me. When my team gets here, we can divide and conquer. But I have a feeling it's not going to be a regular employee or film person, unless it's someone really close to Eddie. Whoever did this not only knows the studio, as I said — they know Eddie Archer. And Alistair . . ."

"Someone like a stepmother? Because that little visit was . . . interesting," Madison said. "I'm sorry, I guess *interesting* is the wrong description. Were we making a courtesy call, or were we trying to make sure she's supporting Eddie?"

He flashed a smile. "*Interesting* was exactly the right word. And we were doing both of those things. In this kind of situation, you do try to draw out everyone who's close to the victims — and I'm considering Eddie and Alistair victims, too."

She looked down at her phone and then at him as he continued. "I haven't been here in a while," he said, "and it's been several years since I worked for Eddie. I've met Helena before, but I can't say I really know her. Still, they haven't been married that long."

She looked away from him then, and Sean thought she'd pursed her lips, trying to keep certain opinions to herself.

Then, apparently, she couldn't. "But it doesn't sound as if they're sharing a room."

"What makes you say that?"

She grinned, lifting her phone. "Just got a text from Pierce. I quote, 'Not trying to cause trouble, but FYI Helena and Eddie in different rooms. Eddie wouldn't know if she was there or not.' "

"Good old Pierce! Now, that doesn't necessarily mean the marriage is rotten — some people snore, or toss and turn, and if you're rich enough and have enough rooms, you can afford to sleep separately if you choose. But most people married a little more than a year are still enamored of being married and happy to sleep together regardless of the snoring, tossing, morning breath — whatever."

"I get the feeling that Helena likes her personal world to be ruled by her own desires," Madison said.

"Yes, and I'll bet she has Eddie believing that they're happiest having their own private domains. I think Eddie's still committed to his marriage. And who am I to judge? Maybe they do love each other."

"She won't treat us the way she'd like to in front of him, that's for sure. Well, me especially. I'm definitely *servant* status. But she's smart enough not to let Eddie know that," Madison said.

"Exactly." Sean chuckled. "Ah, come on, spit it out. You don't like her."

"And you do?"

"I didn't say that."

"I never had much to do with her," Madison explained. "I was at the wedding, and all she did was sweep by the tables as a beautiful bride on Eddie's arm. They filmed the wedding and reception, so she was all smiles. She comes through the studio now and then, and never acknowledges any of us. I didn't think anything of it — I was always working. Today is probably the most I've ever spoken with her," Madison said. She was quiet for a minute. "No, I can't say I like Helena."

"Good instincts," he said.

"Eddie loves her. He must love her, right? He married her."

"I imagine."

"She doesn't love Alistair. It's funny, I always thought she at least liked him and cared about him, but today I realized that her affection for Alistair is really just a show for Eddie."

"I agree, because I think Helena loves Helena too much to be interested in someone else's child. But to be fair, she's hearing what everyone's heard so far — that Alistair was the only person with a young woman when she was brutally murdered," Sean said.

Sean turned down her street, noting that Madison remained pensive. When he pulled into her driveway, she took a deep breath.

"Mrs. Archer is superficial, she's a caricature and she gives dozens of really great actresses a bad name. She's indifferent to Alistair at best, and I'm not convinced she loves Eddie for anything other than what she figures he can do for her. But I don't believe she murdered anyone."

"Oh?"

"As far as I can tell, she's not bright enough to have done it, and no person with the ability to pull off that kind of stunt would have her as a conspirator."

He had to grin at that.

"And," Madison continued, "*why* would she kill a budding actress who'd never be up for the same roles, not to mention the fact that Jenny was just breaking in, trying for bit parts?"

"I don't think it mattered that it was Jenny. I think the killer knew Alistair liked to go and watch movies alone on Sunday nights. *And* that Jenny planned to slip in and try to get Alistair to take her into the studio to learn what she could about *The Unholy.* That's what I'm saying. It's someone close to Eddie, someone who wants to hurt him."

"Alistair's the one being accused."

"Alistair being accused is important. But Eddie's had more time to make enemies."

143

"Everyone loves Eddie."

"Obviously, someone does not," he said. He saw her lips tighten and discovered that he liked her more and more. She was a loyal friend — and, of course, he shared her admiration for and love of Eddie Archer.

She stepped out of the car and peered at him through the window. "Thanks for the ride, Agent." She gave him a smile. "And the burger."

"Thank you for the escort," he told her.

He watched her as she walked up the pathway to her house and he found himself noting the way that she moved — the lift of her head and the sway of dark hair down her back. She turned and waved. He raised a hand in return. He liked her, he recognized again.

She was the real deal.

Sometimes that was hard to find in Hollywood — or anywhere.

She paused at the door, saw that he was still there and returned to the car, coming around to the driver's side. He lowered the window.

"Just curious — but are you this honest with everyone? I mean, should I be quiet about what you've told me?" she asked him worriedly.

"In my book, practically everyone is a

suspect, Madison," he said. "But Eddie trusts you, and wants you to be my right hand. So, I may say things that really are just between us — or you, me and the team."

She nodded. "Okay. Thanks. I guess I'm not a suspect, then."

"Where were you last night?" he asked her.

She laughed. "Here. Except that I'm not so sure I do have an alibi. I *was* with a friend at a coffee shop until about five, and that I can prove."

"You're not a suspect."

"Oh?"

"Gut instinct. It's never failed me yet," he said.

"Glad to hear it, Agent. Well, good night."

"Good night."

"You're not driving away," she said, eyebrows raised.

"I will when you're inside."

"I'm fine here —"

"It's a Texas thing," he told her, grinning.

"All right. Good night again."

"I'll pick you up at eight."

"To see Alistair?"

"Yes."

"I'll be ready."

He waited until she'd unlocked her door, pulling out his cell phone as he did, then watched her door close.

He sat another minute, gazing thoughtfully at her house. The last half year had been hectic; he'd made an enormous change in his life. And before that . . .

Before that, for a long time, he'd been going through the motions. He still loved film and effects — he always would — and in his new capacity on the team, film was his specialty. Work was the great panacea. It was odd to feel that he already knew Madison Darvil better than half the friends he had back in Texas, although the team had become his family. Of course, one member of the team actually *was* his family. Kelsey O'Brien was his cousin, and maybe it wasn't so unusual that they'd come to the same place at the same time, since they shared their strange talent. But before they'd been brought together to solve the bizarre murders in San Antonio . . .

He'd been going through the motions. Today . . . today had felt real. Something about Madison Darvil had gotten to him. She was smart, and she was beautiful in a completely natural way. But it was more than that.

He hit the cell number for LAPD's lead detective on the case. A weary-sounding Benny Knox answered and gave his grudging promise to meet Sean at the morgue in twenty minutes.

Bogie was watching reruns of *I Love Lucy.*

When she walked in, however, he immediately turned his full attention to her. The way he looked at her, with such concern, was moving. She thought that his ability to focus totally must have been part of what had made him such a great actor — and screen icon.

"You look worn-out," he said.

Madison shrugged. "I showed the FBI guy around the studio. We went down to the tunnel, and I saw all the blood, but that was nothing compared to seeing Mrs. Archer and then Eddie. My heart is breaking for him, Bogie."

"So, you still think the kid didn't do it?"

She nodded, crashing down on the sofa beside him. "This guy I took around today used to work at the studio before he moved back to Texas. How he went from film to the FBI, I don't know. But he believes in Alistair and Eddie, and he must be with some really special unit because they're being given the lead on the investigation. It probably helps that Eddie called the governor to get his way — the first time I've ever seen him throw his weight around. But I understand Eddie's logic. You almost have to understand the business to really grasp that someone could have gotten away with doing this and leaving no trace."

"Isn't there always a trace these days? At least, that's what I see on the forensic shows."

Madison waved a hand. "So they say. You take something and you leave something behind — the law of science. But . . . it does look bad. Of course, I haven't spoken with Alistair yet. And until I do tomorrow, I won't know exactly what he saw and what he thought he saw. But I have to say, I have hope."

"Well, that's good, kid, that's good."

He leaned over and patted her on the knee. She didn't feel his touch, but she felt *something*. Maybe it was movement in the air. Maybe it was some awareness deep inside her. "You're going to do all right, kid. You're going to do all right. Remember, if you need me —"

"Just whistle." She smiled at him and wondered if he knew that he'd been buried with a whistle. She decided not to bring up the subject of his funeral services.

Instead, she got to her feet. "I'm going to bed," she told Bogie. But before she could move, she heard a loud mewl of protest. The sound startled her so much that she jumped, and then realized she'd ignored poor Ichabod. "Correction! I'm going to feed Ichabod, and *then* go to bed!"

The cat followed her into the kitchen, and she stroked his sleek fur as she gave him treats and filled his bowl. "Poor Ichabod! I forgot you. What is this world coming to?" she asked. The cat eyed her soulfully. "Finish up, use the litter box and come cuddle when you're ready," she told him.

Back in the living room, she saw that Bogie was no longer watching the television, which was still on. He stood thoughtfully by the window, staring out into the darkness.

"Good night," she said softly.

He glanced back at her. "Sleep tight, kid."

"Thanks. If you want to continue watching *Lucy,* please keep the volume low, okay?"

He nodded, and gave her his rueful, self-mocking grin. "Want a good old quote? 'Here's looking at you, kid.' And I like what I see. Go on now, and get some sleep." She saw a worried frown creasing his brow as she went to her room.

Bogie had become a true legend, she reflected, and it wasn't *just* the roles he played — the cynical tough guy with a heart of gold and courage to match. He was a brilliant actor, but she thought she was privy to something more. Bogie had been far more fascinating than even his greatest characters. More fascinating than any legend. Yes, he'd been flawed — who wasn't? — but underneath it all, he was deeply moral and unfailingly kind.

She paused at her bedroom door and turned back. "I'm okay, Bogie, honestly. I want to do whatever I can to help Alistair and Eddie."

"So you should. And all is well. I'm looking out for you, kid."

She wasn't sure what he could do for her, but she smiled and said, "Thanks."

Thirty minutes later she'd had a bath and was ready for bed. The lights were out and she was curled comfortably under her sheets. But tired as she was, sleep eluded her.

She found herself thinking about Alistair, and then Sean Cameron. Eddie had chosen her specifically, but it wasn't because she knew special effects better than anyone else.

It was because he'd been with her in the cemetery one day.

She didn't see ghosts every time she was in a cemetery. She'd come to understand that those not ready to move on usually didn't inhabit places where they hadn't been happy; it wasn't that they were *unhappy* at a cemetery — they were just dead when they got there. The ghosts she'd seen and communicated with tended to frequent places they'd loved. For some, it was an old home, for others, maybe a bar or a dance hall. Once she'd even met a young boy, who'd died tragically in an auto accident, at a baseball field.

She didn't always know — unless she reached out to touch and she just didn't touch that many strangers — whether the people she met were alive or dead. Such had been the case with Bogie. She'd been convinced that he was an actor. A damned good look-alike, but surely not the real thing.

But, of course, he was. Like the man she'd talked to in Peace Cemetery, the graveyard that abutted the studio. It was one of the oldest in the city, only a few years behind Evergreen Cemetery, receiving its first burials in 1879. These included the faithful of St. Bartholomew's, which was now just a chapel but had been a small, functioning church. St. Bartholomew's and its parishioners had moved on to a new location in the 1920s and the cemetery had become the property of the county. It was a beautiful place, where late-Victorian funerary art mingled with modern black marble slabs and off-kilter art. The one-time owner of all the land in the area — including the studio and the Black Box Cinema — Lucas Claymore, was buried there, like the rest of his family. It was Lucas she met one day while walking with Eddie to sketch tombstones he liked. She had begun to chat with Lucas, and he'd told her about the property. She hadn't understood that he wasn't real until she saw the way Eddie was staring at her. She'd tried to explain it away, but obviously Eddie hadn't forgotten. A few years later, when one of his old employees died — a master of masks — she had seen him at his funeral. He'd died at the age of ninety-something, and he was pleasantly surprised and gratified by all the people who'd attended. She'd *thought* she'd been unnoticed, assuring the old man that he'd been adored, but Eddie had slipped an arm around her shoulders and whispered, "Tell him goodbye for me."

Maybe she'd believed she could walk into the tunnel and emerge with an instant answer. But life wasn't like that. Apparently, neither was death.

The very first time, it had been her friend Billy. A bee sting on a sunny day had killed him when he was only six. As she'd stood near his grave, her hand in her mother's, she'd seen him across the cemetery. Later, at the reception, he'd come to her and told her he was all right, and to please make sure his mother knew that. He wanted to go along the sunlit path ahead of him; he could hear children playing and the soft voice of a woman who'd watch over him until he saw his own mother again.

But she'd quickly learned that you didn't tell other people when you saw the dead. Her mother had gone white when Madison talked about Billy; she'd pulled Madison aside and told her she mustn't say anything, anything at all. Billy's mother was in enough pain as it was.

Other people, she'd soon figured out, didn't see or talk to the dead. And they didn't believe anyone else did or could, either. To them, the very suggestion was crazy.

Her mother wasn't being cruel; she just didn't believe in ghosts and she empathized with Billy's mother. She couldn't begin to imagine how *she* would've felt if it had been her child who'd died, and she desperately wanted to spare Billy's family any more agony.

Madison listened to the low hum of voices from the TV in the living room and hoped they would lull her to sleep. She started as she felt the weight of Ichabod leaping up on the bed. She pulled him to her and rubbed his ears.

The worst had been during her last year in high school. Josh Bollyn, the sweetest jock in the universe and, at the time, the love of her life. A night of laughter and camaraderie with friends had been destroyed when someone threw something out of a car. A bottle. An empty liquor bottle. Someone who was just careless — a litterbug, maybe a drunk litterbug — had become a murderer because the bottle had hit Josh in the head as they walked along the street. The next thing she knew, he was in the emergency room because of the way the bottle had hit him.

And Josh was dying.

Nothing the doctors could do could change what the angle of the bottle had done, cracking Josh's skull and damaging the brain. She sat there and listened until his parents came, and she had to watch them and listen to the flatline. . . .

And then Josh's words, "Help them, Madison, please, help them. Get my mother out of here, and help her. Just hold her, just stay with her. . . ."

And he'd stood beside her at his own funeral, sad, but saying things to her that he

154

wanted said to others so they could let go. No one had deserved to live more than Josh, and she'd stopped understanding. She had hated herself and withdrawn.

Into work. Dating had to be casual, she'd decided. If she came too close, maybe . . . No, she hadn't caused what had happened to Josh. She knew that. But she couldn't shake the feeling that she was deadly luck for others, and it seemed best to retreat into herself.

And, of course, with Bogie's regular visits, even casual dates became a challenge!

Eventually, she drifted off to sleep, and her sleep was that of the exhausted, the restless — and filled with dreams that really had no beginning or end.

In her dream she found herself at the studio. The L.A. smog had made its way in; low-lying gray mist pervaded the place and swept around all the creatures. Someone was behind her, chasing her, and when she turned around, she saw the evil Egyptian priest from *The Unholy*. She ran, and her only escape was through the door that would lead to the tunnel and the tableau of *Sam Stone and the Curious Case of the Egyptian Museum*.

The door to the tunnel was ajar.

She threw it open.

But when she reached the tunnel, she was slipping and sliding.

In blood.

When she tried to steady herself, another monster stood before her, blocking her escape. But it was actually the same one who'd been chasing her. She stared at what should have been the mannequin of the priest, Amun Mopat — but he wasn't a mannequin. He was alive and waiting for her, brandishing his curved knife.

And he had no face.

You want to see me? You want to see who I am? he asked her. *Come on, keep coming, and rip away my mask. Can't walk? I'll come to you.*

Madison awoke, heart pounding. She was clammy with sweat and had made a knot of the bedclothing.

But she was safe. Safe in her own room. And tomorrow was going to be a long day.

Ichabod let out a worried meow. He was at the foot of the bed, staring at her. She smiled. "Come here, silly cat. I'm okay now."

But she wasn't. The television in the living room wasn't loud enough. She wanted the reassurance of sound, of a benign presence on the television in her room, so she chose a cartoon channel. But she didn't lie back

156

down right away; she walked over to her window and looked out. Chills ran down her spine.

She couldn't *see* anything. Her street, with its rows of small old bungalows, was quiet and dark. A streetlight flickered, and for a moment, the darkness seemed heavier. There was an unrented house across the street, its foliage growing dense. The area around it looked like a dark hole — no, oddly, it was more like some kind of gaping maw. Her imagination was rampant and she saw an image in the shadows created by the flickering streetlights. It was a face, a black-masked face, with malevolent eyes.

Step outside, little girl, it seemed to say.

And she could feel the eyes, the evil in the eyes, and something that wanted her silenced.

She hurried out to the living room. Bogie wasn't there. "Bogie!" she said, whispering his name.

He didn't answer. She walked to the windows in the living room and gently drew back the curtain. She saw the empty house and overgrown lot from a different angle. They still seemed to create a face. And the feeling that the face had eyes that were staring at her was almost overwhelming.

Then she sensed a reassuring presence.

■ ■ ■ ■

The L.A. County morgue was a vast place.

Sean wasn't familiar with it and despite his own credentials, he was glad he was there with a detective who knew the drill.

Benny Knox really wasn't a bad guy. It was ridiculously late at night, and only a handful of the customary staff was working. Nonetheless, getting through the formidable reception area might not have been so easy if it hadn't been for Knox, and finding a medical examiner on duty might have been a lot trickier. In a county the size of this one, few of the many bodies that went through the morgue on a daily basis were considered a middle-of-the-night priority.

Some morgue employees managed to remember that every corpse had once been a living human being, breathing, laughing, working and playing, and, most often, loved by someone. Others became so jaded they could sit among dozens of corpses and see them as little more than evidence or specimens on a slab. In the middle of the night, most of the staff was just holding down the shift — and praying there wasn't an onslaught of bodies due to an accident, earthquake or other disaster.

The attendant on duty was obviously a medical student — he had his books open before him — and yawned. Of course, everyone had heard that it was Eddie Archer's son who'd been accused of the murder, but that didn't make the victim's corpse any more exciting than all the others. The young man tracked down medical pathologist Dr. Herve Rodrique, and Rodrique, though puzzled by the hour, nodded, looked through his documentation and told them to wait. He'd have the corpse taken back out to the autopsy room.

During the day, the high-profile murder victim had been a priority. The autopsy had been performed, evidenced by the Y incision clearly visible once the sheet was pulled away from Jenny Henderson's body. Dr. Rodrique hadn't done the autopsy, but he had the chart in front of him — which, he informed them pointedly, looking over the spectacles that sat low on his nose, had already been sent to the police.

"Yes," Knox said, "but Agent Cameron is not a policeman, he's with the FBI. And he wants to see the corpse."

"And there she is," Rodrique said. "Female, twenty years old, five-nine, weight one-fifteen. If we hadn't had a clean identity on her, we would have discovered it. Breast

159

implant surgery about a year ago, and the serial numbers on the implants match the ID we were given. She was in excellent health when she was killed, and no trace of drugs or alcohol was found in her system, although we're still waiting on some tests. Cause of death — well, gentlemen, that's obvious. I don't believe anyone needed a medical degree to see what killed her."

"What kind of knife was used?" Sean asked.

"Let's see . . . Chang writes that it must have had a sharp point — but the edges of the wound are rough, as if the edge of the knife wasn't sharp, and a lot of pressure was put into the kill. Not a serrated edge, but it's as if the flesh was ripped more than slashed."

Sean nodded, and looked down at Jenny Henderson. She'd been a pretty girl. Her eyes were closed and she almost appeared to sleep — except for the red line of the knife wound that had ended her life.

And a corpse was never truly indicative of the real person who had lived and breathed and laughed . . .

Talk to me, please talk to me. Help me, because even if you were using him, I know you cared about Alistair, and I know you don't want him to pay for what someone else did.

160

But the corpse of Jenny Henderson lay still and unmoving. Not that he'd expected her to rise or to speak. . . .

Jenny, please, I'm here to help. There has to be justice, if you're to find peace, if you're to go on.

Then it seemed — or in his mind's eye, at least that her eyes opened. She looked at him, and her face changed. Her features no longer seemed sunken. She gazed at him, and he heard words that were fraught with terror.

I'm so scared. I'm dead, I see it, I know it, and I'm so scared.

That was when Sean always felt at a loss — when the dead expressed their fears. What lay beyond? He didn't know. No one knew, because once you walked from your own death and into the light that beckoned, there was no returning.

Jenny, you were a beautiful young lady, he told her silently. *You don't need to be scared.*

I did use Alistair! she whispered, sounding miserable. *If I let go, I'll end up in hell.*

I can't claim that I know God, Jenny, but hell is reserved for evil. Of that I'm certain. And if you can help us find the truth, we can help you find your way.

He heard her sobbing. Life. A precious gift. It had been stolen from her.

"What's he staring at?" Sean heard Rodrique ask Knox.

"No idea," Knox muttered back. "Who knows what they teach at the FBI Academy these days?"

"It's late," Rodrique said. And in his peripheral vision, Sean could see the man looking at his watch.

"You got a dinner date?" Knox asked him.

Rodrique flushed. "I have mounds of paperwork!" he said indignantly.

Jenny! Sean whispered in his mind. *Help me. Alistair didn't do this to you. Who did?*

She began to cry again.

Who, Jenny?

No, no, not Alistair. Never Alistair.

Then who?

The man.

What man?

The mannequin man. The one in the robe.

It seemed that she turned her head toward him. That her eyes were open and staring beseechingly into his.

The mannequin man, she repeated. *The man with no face.*

Madison screamed. She spun around, ready to swing and fight.

"Hey! It's just me. Lord help us, it's just me, Bogie!"

162

Madison released a shaky sigh. "Oh, Bogie! It's that house across the street. This is crazy, but I'm seeing a face in it, and it's scaring me, and . . . Sorry, I feel like an idiot."

He studied her expression. "It's pretty creepy-looking, all right," he agreed. "And after the day you've had . . ."

"I need sleep," Madison moaned.

He nodded. "I'll come and sit in that chair in your room. Maybe you'll sleep then?"

She nodded. "Thanks."

"I'll find an *I Love Lucy* rerun. And," Bogie added, "I'll watch that house across the street. If anything moves . . . I'll wake you in a flash!"

Vengeance was angry.

Vengeance had waited. For hours.

Tonight . . . yes, tonight.

No, it couldn't be tonight. Cameron hadn't left until she'd walked in and locked the door. And if Vengeance broke into her house, that would be careless, and might give everything away. Alistair was locked up, and there would be nothing clever or devious about a kill tonight; killing tonight would be against the plan.

The plan was everything . . . at least it

had been. It still was, yes, it was. It had to be.

But . . .

The damned girl! There was something about her, something that made Vengeance uneasy. It was as if she had extra eyes. She kept silent, but there were times when . . .

Times when it seemed that she saw what others did not.

Maybe she was just crazy. Yes, that was it. Vengeance had seen her when she appeared to be talking to someone. . . . Someone who was no longer alive.

Like at a funeral . . .

And Vengeance had seen her walking in the cemetery, as if she was visiting old friends. . . .

Vengeance had felt compelled to come tonight. Because of Madison. She shouldn't have been part of this. And Cameron was back. Vengeance didn't like it at all — none of this was part of the plan.

Control, careful organization and control. And yet, angry, frustrated, Vengeance still felt power in watching.

There was nothing to see. Madison Darvil's house had gone dark except for the night-light on the porch and a pale glow within. The television. The damned television ran night and day. But maybe that would be good. Noise to cover up whatever might happen.

Now . . .

No, not now.

Now was the time to watch and wait. Time to devise a clever way to rid the world of Madison Darvil and her enormous blue, all-seeing eyes. Such a waste; such a talent; such a beauty.

But this was Hollywood. Hollywood could steal beauty.

And Hollywood could kill it.

Outside the plan. Too soon, too close — and outside the plan! Vengeance was not a cold-blooded killer!

Vengeance was . . . vengeance.

6

Sean was glad that Eddie was rich. No matter how hard a city, county, state or the federal government tried, it was difficult to fund decent hospitals on public money.

Alistair Archer was free on bail but required to remain under mental health authority and wear an ankle cuff. Thanks to Eddie's hard work and resources, Alistair was at the Churchill/Dunlap Treatment and Therapy Resource Center. It was an exclusive hospital where many a Hollywood mogul had come, whether to overcome drug or alcohol abuse — or await trial in a high-profile criminal case.

L.A. could be a brutal place, Sean knew. The county was home to some of the wealthiest people in the country — film stars, producers, directors and those who made their money behind the scenes. It also included East L.A., gangs, violence and drugs. In the prisons, habitual criminals often ruled the roost, and men and women accused of certain crimes might not survive to come to a fair and equitable trial. People in the county tried. Not only did the richest and most famous of American royalty live here, but the place was steeped in an artistic temperament and an egalitarian ideology. However, sheer weariness could whittle away at those benevolent impulses.

Technically, Alistair was out on bail, despite the stipulation for the ankle cuff and psychiatric care. But Eddie was smart to see to it that Alistair was in a respected — if exclusive — hospital with a wing for those who might be dangerous to themselves or others.

Had he been someone else's son, Alistair might have ended up in a hellhole.

Instead, he was in a facility where the security guards wore designer uniforms and a valet parked every car that arrived. The lobby, where Sean and Madison checked in, was marble and chrome, and even the metal detectors were high-end. Security was tight, and it took them several minutes to be allowed through and then escorted to Alistair's wing and down a long corridor to his room.

Madison had been polite and quiet through most of the drive and Sean sensed that she was anxious. Her eyes were wide as they neared Alistair's room.

"Looks like a spa," she murmured. "With Uzis."

"They're not packing Uzis, but, yes, it's staggeringly expensive, and while you're awaiting trial for some terrible crime, you can have a massage," he said, a bit cynically. "We may all be equal, but it's true that money talks — and very loudly, too. Eddie managed to get Alistair arraigned almost immediately and his attorney offered this solution while they wait for a trial date. He could be at home, but Eddie thought this was better and safer."

"I agree. Until it's proven that Alistair *is* innocent," she told him, bravado in her voice.

"We both agree on that."

A guard unlocked the door for them.

The room was hardly the customary jail cell *or* hospital room. It was a suite. They could see the bed through an open doorway, while the main door opened into a parlor or seating area with a wide-screen TV and game station.

There was a table in the center of the room, and Alistair was seated there with his father; they both appeared calm and were engaged in a game of gin rummy.

Alistair, dressed in jeans and a rock band T-shirt, glanced up as they were ushered in. When he saw them, a look of hope and pleasure flashed across his features and he leaped to his feet. He raced over to them, throwing his arms around Madison first, holding on to her tightly, and then hugging Sean with equal enthusiasm. "I didn't believe it!" he cried, stepping back, studying them both as if he was afraid they were a mirage. "I didn't believe my friends could have faith in me — I mean . . . I know what it looks like. Oh, God, I know what it looks like. And I'm not crazy, I swear to God, I'm not crazy. I didn't lose my mind and kill her. I was nuts about her — I . . . I don't care what they keep trying to say to me, I'm *not* crazy and I didn't do it."

"Oh, Alistair!" Madison said, hugging him again. "It'll be all right. We *will* find out the truth."

He nodded, then shook his head and burst into tears. "It *can't* be all right. She's dead. Jenny is dead. Nothing can ever be okay again."

"Alistair, I didn't mean that," Madison told him, sorrow in her voice. "We do believe you, and we'll learn the truth, and we'll make sure the whole world knows you're innocent."

Sean hoped she wasn't naively giving Alistair promises they couldn't keep. It didn't look good at all. And yet . . . he *did* believe Alistair. Anyone might conclude that the young man didn't even know what he'd done, that he'd had a psychotic break, killed Jenny Henderson, blacked out — with no recollection of anything. That was the *logical* explanation in a locked-room case in which the accused was so passionately and sincerely sure he was innocent.

But Sean reminded himself that he'd actually communicated with the victim. And Jenny Henderson might not have known who'd killed her, but she *had* been certain it wasn't Alistair.

It was still going to be incredibly difficult to prove what a dead eyewitness knew.

And yet, maybe not. It hadn't been a random murder. Had Jenny been targeted? Not likely. As he'd already observed, Eddie and Alistair were the ones who'd been targeted, and if the Krewe could delve into the situation and find a motive, they could trace a path through the maze.

Eddie had stood, as well, and watched Alistair greet Madison and Sean. He spoke up quietly. "Thank you for coming."

Sean nodded. "I can hardly be effective if I don't talk to Alistair."

Eddie smiled at Madison and let out a sigh. "Sit down, please." He collected the playing cards and set them, with the score pad, on a corner of the table. "Everyone, sit down, and then, Alistair, you tell them what happened. And remember, think hard. Tell them every little detail that comes to mind."

Eddie sat as he spoke; Madison took a chair across from him. Sean followed her, and Alistair sat next to his father, facing Sean and Madison.

"Jenny snuck in to see you, right?" Madison said.

"Yes." He stared down at his hands. "I told the police all of this. I told them everything."

"That doesn't matter, Alistair. You need to tell us," Sean said.

Alistair released a long breath. "Everything. Okay. I went to the Black Box Cinema. I waved in the direction of the camera when I arrived, trying to let Colin Bailey know I was there. I went in."

"You were at home before you went to the cinema?" Sean asked.

Alistair nodded. "Home, and then straight to the cinema. I went and got the reels for *Sam Stone and the Curious Case of the Egyptian Museum.* I love that movie. It's not as well-known as some film noir, but I *love* that movie — and I'm thrilled we're doing the special effects for the remake. I was just watching the part where Dianna Breen comes to Sam Stone's office to tell him how she couldn't possibly have killed her husband when Jenny snuck in on me."

"How'd she get in?" Sean asked.

Alistair looked troubled. "She said I left the door open."

"Did you?"

Seconds ticked by as Alistair's frown deepened. "Well, she *said* I did. That surprised me." He glanced at his father. "I realize I'm privileged. I try to be super careful to follow all my dad's rules. But . . . honestly, I just don't know. I *thought* I'd locked it. Maybe I didn't. I don't know."

"Okay, Alistair, that's fine for now. Thanks. So, Jenny came in and startled you. And she wanted to get into the studio," Sean said.

"She . . ." he started to say, but he paused again, turning to his father. "She really wanted one of the bit parts that still had to be cast for *The Unholy*. And she believed that if she could just see some of what was being done — you know how the props and effects can affect the whole *mood* of a movie — she'd have a better chance of being cast. Oh, God, Dad, I'm so, so sorry," Alistair

172

said, and it looked as if he'd burst into tears a second time. The moment was both ironic and poignant. Alistair was truly devastated over Jenny Henderson's death; he was also heartsick and grieving about the fact that he'd betrayed his father's confidence.

He was in a bad way, Sean thought.

Madison reached out, her hand covering Alistair's. "Hey, come on, now. Your dad's worried about you. He's not angry."

Eddie grimaced. "Right now, that's the least of our worries, son. It's not like I've never been twisted around by a woman. You're young. I understand, but don't let it happen again," he added lightly.

Alistair tried to smile.

They all knew there might not be an *again*.

"So, Jenny talked you into taking her through the tunnel to the studio," Sean said.

Alistair nodded. "And at first, it was fine. Oh, my God! I can't tell you how many times I've walked through that tunnel. I can describe every tableau down there with my eyes closed."

"Did anything appear different about any of the tableaux?" Sean asked.

"No, I don't think so," Alistair said.

"Even the *Sam Stone* tableau?"

"I . . . I remember looking at it and thinking how much I love the movie," Alistair

173

said. "And, of course, that was the movie I'd been watching."

"But you watch that movie a lot, don't you?" Madison asked. She smiled. "You've talked to me about it. We discussed the special effects. Digital is fantastic — but only when it's really right and when the script and everything else is just as strong. If you look back at film history, some images seem amazing because the costuming was so good — and because the actors were so good. Like Lon Chaney Jr., who could turn himself into anyone and *anything*. The effects that were created for the *Sam Stone* movie were excellent. Nothing fancy, certainly not by today's standards, and yet genuinely frightening."

Alistair nodded, staring at her, troubled again. "Yes, I do watch the movie a lot. Most people know it's my favorite film noir. Does that . . . does the movie I was watching matter?"

"Anything can matter, Alistair," Sean told him. "In this case? Yes, I think so. Now, you went through the tunnel, and the tableaux were just as they always were. Then . . ."

"Well, then we were at the door to the studio. And I saw that it was ajar."

"So the door to the studio was open," Sean repeated.

A slight look of annoyance crossed Alistair's face. "I've told that to everyone. Over and over. Yes, the door to the studio was open. Slightly ajar. And it should've been locked. So I walked up to it and that's when I heard Jenny scream."

His voice quavered on the last few words.

Sean leaned forward. "Alistair, tell me *exactly* what you saw then. Try to remember every detail."

Alistair's hands were trembling. He tried to still them where they lay on the table, then gave up the effort. He swallowed hard. "He — he was there. He'd stepped down from the tableau. He had Jenny. And . . . I saw. I saw him slit her throat. I tried to stop him. I cried out. I wanted to think it was make-believe — I mean, we're all about make-believe, right? I wanted it to be make-believe, my dad pulling a stunt on me to teach me a lesson. Or some jerk from the studio playing a game. But . . . but . . . it was real. Oh, God, it was real, and blood sprayed everywhere and I could see Jenny's eyes. Oh, Lord, I could see her eyes. . . ."

"Alistair, it's —" Madison held his hands hard, clutched in her own. Her eyes were locked on Alistair in searing empathy and sorrow; she'd been about to say, *It's all right, Alistair.*

But it wasn't.

"Alistair, we're here with you. We'll find the truth," she vowed softly.

"Son . . ." Eddie said miserably.

"Alistair." Sean kept his voice hard and flat. "Go on. I need everything. Every last detail. You saw him slit Jenny's throat. You saw her eyes — what about *his* eyes? What about the killer in the robes?"

Alistair seemed to stare past him. For a moment, Sean feared that he'd lost him, that Alistair had slipped into some blank realm in his mind.

Alistair finally spoke. "His eyes? He had no eyes. He had no face. It was — the whole area where the face should have been . . . it was just black. He had no face at all. He had no eyes . . . no eyes . . . How . . . Yes, I'm remembering this right! He had no eyes!"

He paused, concentrating. He lowered his head, and then peered up at Sean again.

"He had no face, and he had no eyes. But he was *looking at me.* I knew it. I knew he was looking at me. And . . ."

"And?" Sean asked.

He shook his head. "I — I knew he was laughing. There was no sound. He was laughing, and he was *evil.* Triumphant. Staring at me with nothing, no eyes . . . just evil."

"Madison?"

Madison started. She hadn't been listening. She couldn't forget Alistair's face as he'd spoken about the murderer.

She turned toward Sean Cameron, who was driving. California roads were insane, and if you were smart, you were defensive. But Sean knew that; he'd lived here. Once upon a time, he'd been employed in the very same place where she was now employed. He had done the same things she did.

He was an expert California driver — a specialty in itself — and was able to glance over at her as he said her name in a questioning tone.

"I'm sorry, what did you say?"

"I said, food, lunch. I'm suggesting we go to lunch before our next stop."

"Which is?"

"The morgue," he told her.

"The morgue?" she asked, hoping she didn't sound like the coward she was.

"Yeah, let's eat first. Where do you want to go?"

"Ah, anywhere. Anyplace along the way, I guess."

He nodded; he seemed to like the fact that she was up for *whatever.* And he seemed to know that while he was an FBI agent and probably accustomed to morgues, she was not. Yes, definitely, food before the morgue. She wasn't sure she'd be able to eat afterward. . . .

They wound up stopping at a Buca di Beppo. Homestyle Italian food. It was en route and a national chain that was pretty damned good — a plus, since neither of them cared much about what they were eating; they just needed to eat.

The menu was set up for sharing. They opted for a salad and lasagna. When their friendly waiter was gone, Madison said, "I'm . . . I'm grateful that you're here. I know you worked for Eddie, and I know you're FBI. I don't understand all the dynamics, but it doesn't matter. You're here and you believe in Alistair." She hesitated. "And I believe in Alistair. I work in special effects, so I'm aware of what's possible, but . . . I'm also aware that mannequins don't come to life."

"No," he agreed, "mannequins don't come to life. Unless they're rigged to do so. Or digitized in a movie. So, we know a mannequin didn't kill Jenny Henderson."

"The alternative is almost as bizarre. There were security cameras. From what you've told me, no one came in, and no one went out. You haven't seen the footage yet, have you?" He shook his head. "I'm sure the police have, though. And if anyone *had* gone in or out, the police — as in Detective Knox — would have told you, and that person would be questioned."

He was thoughtful, spearing a leaf of lettuce. "Yes. As standoffish and pedantic as Knox appears to be, I think he's a good cop. And I think he'd pull me in on anything he considered out of the ordinary."

"So, nothing on the tapes. We have an empty studio and an empty cinema. Except for our security guard, Colin Bailey. And while we can't rule Bailey out, he's a totally unlikely suspect — not to mention that the police interviewed him immediately and looked into his background. I love Colin. He's such a reassuring presence. And he's been loyal to Eddie for twenty years and so fierce when it comes to the studio. So that leaves Jenny Henderson and Alistair — and the mannequins," Madison said, feeling bleak.

"Just because a studio is in lockdown doesn't mean it *was* locked down," Sean reminded her.

"But . . . you've seen the security system. You've worked at the studio. And we both know, we *all* know, that if you want to keep your job, you really don't mess around, sneaking people in during lockdown," Madison said. "But, of course, you don't commit murder if you want to keep your job, either. Not if you're . . . normal. But the killer isn't really normal, is he?"

"I've never figured out 'normal,' to tell you the truth," Sean said. "Whoever is doing this is organized. He — or she — has a plan and is thinking it through. And he knows something we don't, because I don't believe in a locked-room mystery. There's a crack in the door somewhere, and we have to find it. Right now, the studio contains secrets that the killer knows, and we don't. Back when I worked for Archer —"

"Why did you leave?" Madison asked, and then regretted it. His face changed; he'd become guarded.

"Texas is home," he said simply. "I was needed at home." He changed the subject. "To return to the concept of normal — the average employee wouldn't know enough about the studio to carry this off."

"You think someone was in the studio. That this person was hiding out somehow, somewhere, someway, and knew that Alistair would be there, and that he'd come through the tunnel," Madison said.

"Yes."

Madison frowned. "First, you have to get in — without the security cameras picking it up. Then you have to hide. Then you have to find the right costume to become the mannequin. And, after committing the murder, you'd have to get rid of the bloody garments you were wearing and get out of the tunnel and the studio without anyone seeing you and without leaving any kind of trace." She lifted her hands. "That's where I'm lost. Suppose the killer did somehow hide overnight and wait and wait — how did he escape without being on the security cameras?"

"Because a locked room with any kind of access or egress is never really a locked room," Sean said.

Madison shook her head. "If Knox is the detective you seem to think he is, and if he respects the FBI, he'll make sure you know what he knows."

"Forensic materials aren't analyzed instantly," Sean said. He shrugged. "And sometimes it's not the forensic evidence that matters most — it's the logic."

"As in, it had to be an inside job?"

"Absolutely. You have to know about Colin Bailey and the other guards — and all about their schedules. You have to know about the locks and the keys and the security system — actually, it's not much of a security system. Eddie is a trusting guy."

"He's not so technologically inclined," Madison agreed. "We're always explaining some feature on his cell phone to him."

"And you know that about Eddie because you work for him, and because he likes you and respects your work. You're close," Sean said.

"Honestly, I wasn't sure I *was* all that respected and liked until I received the call yesterday morning," Madison said. "Don't get me wrong. Eddie is a great boss. He loves his artisans. I just didn't realize I'd been singled out."

"But Alistair is crazy about you, too," Sean pointed out.

"I felt like a very naive kid when I started with Eddie. And now, Alistair *is* a naive kid. He's a lot like Eddie — he has a big heart. I owe them both. And I like Alistair. He's never been — well, for lack of a better term — a spoiled jerk. He blends right in. The only time I ever heard Alistair say anything that made him sound like a rich kid was when he said I didn't need to hurry, that the plane would leave when I told it to. I had to tell him that in the real world, planes left on schedules, and only private planes left on the *owner's* schedule."

Sean laughed. "Yep, that sounds like Alistair. And you're right. He's never been an affected rich kid. And, through three marriages, he remains Eddie's only child. So, what would that mean to you — as a sleuth?"

"That he's a rich kid . . . and . . ."

Sean pushed his plate aside. "Which means that Alistair stands to inherit his father's fortune and the studio and the cinema. So, first suspect? We know that Alistair's mother died a long time ago."

"First suspect — Eddie's wife," Madison said.

"That's right."

"Oh, please."

"Yes, we decided last night that she doesn't seem bright enough to pull off something like this. But appearances can be deceptive. Or . . . she might have been working with someone else," Sean said. "I know we already dismissed that idea. However, I'm not a hundred percent convinced."

"Trust me — I work about eighty hours a week. The only time I have *ever* seen Helena at that studio is when one of the directors, set designers, or casting agents comes through. I honestly don't think she knows enough about the studio to have done any of this."

"You *think*," he said.

"I thought you agreed with me on that?"

"I agree that she appears to be a walking billboard for hair colorists," he said. "She might also be a far better actress than we imagine."

"Doubtful." Madison shook her head.

"Even so, she's the wife — she's not off the hook," Sean said. "Finished with your meal?"

"Yes. Thanks. I can pay my share —"

"No worries. Your tax dollars at work, Madison. If we'd ordered fine wine, well, then, we'd have to argue about the cost."

He stood, ready to move on. Madison got up, too. Their server saw them and quickly brought the bill, and in a matter of minutes they were on the road.

Headed to the morgue.

The morgue.

Madison had never supposed that in all her life she'd be headed to the morgue. . . .

Back again.

No matter how such a place tried to be aesthetically decent — *pleasing* was beyond the realm of possibility — the smell of chemicals seemed to pervade even the reception areas and offices. No room freshener could alleviate that smell.

Sean was growing accustomed to everything he was going to meet along the way in the career he hadn't actually chosen, but which had found him. In Quantico recently, they'd trained in arms; thankfully, as a Texas kid, he'd grown up surrounded by those who expected a man to know about guns, even if he chose not to use or carry them. He'd excelled at the shooting range. They'd sat in on endless classes in behavioral sciences. They'd learned to profile, and they'd learned that profiles could be wrong, but if nothing else, they certainly helped winnow down the pool of suspects. In many cases that pool could be immense. It was necessary to start somewhere, and the best place to start was with logic.

While they were a "special" unit — chosen for exceptional talents that some might consider curses — they were still expected to follow all bureau procedure and to excel at all expertise needed to work as an agent.

That had included days and days at morgues and body farms across the country.

He would never feel at ease in a morgue. But, even in training, he'd never betrayed his discomfort.

Sometimes, in the busy daytime field of a morgue like this one, Sean felt as if he heard voices, dozens of them, crying out to him.

He didn't acknowledge that, but he watched Madison — and it wasn't out of idle curiosity. He had to know if Eddie Archer was right, and if Madison spoke with the dead. If she saw ghosts . . .

She was ashen from the time they stepped into the building. He didn't need Detective Knox today; he'd made himself known as lead investigator on the case. Today, he'd be able to meet with the medical pathologist who had done the autopsy, Dr. Lee Chang.

"I wish there was more to tell you," Chang said as they walked down the chemical-scented halls to the small room, where he'd ordered the corpse of Jenny Henderson to be brought. They were alone when they came to the small viewing room. Chang had his own charts and rattled off information as he withdrew the sheet, saying, "By my best guesstimate, Jenny Henderson was taken from behind. Her attacker was right-handed, seizing her by the left hand and holding it against his — or her — body and then slicing her throat thus, left to right. The artery was severed. The point was to kill, but not to decapitate."

Madison went a shade grayer, staring silently at the corpse of Jenny Henderson. She inhaled on a shaky breath. He saw that the tears she was determined not to shed were crowding her eyes.

"You knew her," Sean said.

"I can't say I knew her well." Madison's voice was low and pained. "But yes, I did know her."

"I'm sorry," Chang said quietly.

Sean decided he liked Chang. The man was a professional with empathy. He didn't let emotion overrule science, but he didn't forget that his science had to do with human beings.

Madison moved closer to the corpse.

Chang cleared his throat. "She has a brother back in Rhode Island. He'll be here tomorrow, although we haven't released the body as yet." He touched Madison awkwardly on the shoulder with a gloved hand. "You may go closer. You may touch her. She was your friend. None of us knows, but maybe she'll sense that you came and you want to help her, that you care."

Chang stepped back, looking at Sean then.

It's easy for us. You and I, we never knew her in life. This girl is here to help. She needs space to breathe, to touch, to see, Chang seemed to say.

Sean nodded to him. He stepped back with the doctor.

Of course, he was using Madison. Watching to see what would happen, wondering

187

what she might see and hear.

"Oh, Jenny!" she said very softly.

Madison, he thought, hadn't wanted to come here. Jenny had been a casual acquaintance, someone she'd met through Alistair Archer. But she *had* known her, had seen the place where she'd been murdered; she'd heard Alistair's rendition of the events that had stolen the young woman's life.

And now, she was seeing her here, naked and lifeless on the gurney, the essence that had made her vital and beautiful and human long gone.

At first, it looked like the last thing in the world Madison wanted to do was touch the corpse.

Sean waited, feeling like a jerk, but knowing he had to.

And in a moment, Madison came forward. A tear dripped down her cheek and fell on her own hand.

She reached out, and her fingers gently brushed Jenny Henderson's arm.

She closed her eyes.

She trembled suddenly, as if she'd been hit by a bolt of electricity. Chang almost stepped toward her, but Sean raised a hand and stopped him.

They waited. Madison stood by the corpse as the seconds passed by. She seemed

188

frozen, unable to move.

At last, Sean took two steps and stood behind her, placing his hands on her shoulders. He looked down himself and saw Jenny. Once again, in his mind's eye, Jenny's eyes were open. And she was staring at the two of them, staring as though pleading for the help that hadn't come to her in life.

Sean felt as if he was picking up on the end of a conversation.

Jenny was saying, *Um, I don't know. I suppose . . . I really care about Alistair! But yes, there were a number of people who knew that he and I were friends. All right, more than friends. That I liked to tease him and sleep with him because . . . because I care about him and because it wasn't such a bad thing to sleep with him. We weren't destined for life but —* She paused, staring at them again. *But I — and many others — have slept with people for much worse reasons. It wasn't a secret. I was talking about it during . . . lunch at the old café down on Sunset. . . . I was with a girlfriend, Molly Ives, and I told her I was going to try to seduce Alistair that night, because I was desperate for a role in* The Unholy. *My roommate, Kathy McCarthy, knew. I was probably stupid. I should have been more discreet. I should have . . .*

Jenny's silent voice in Sean's head was

suddenly stilled.

Chang was standing next to Madison, holding her arm. "Breathe. Just breathe. I know the smell of the room isn't great, but breathe deeply, and you won't pass out."

Sean was dismayed that he hadn't seen how white she'd become. He cleared his throat.

"Definitely right-handed killer?" he asked.

"Or someone totally ambidextrous," Chang said.

"Thank you. Call me when her brother schedules his appointment to see her. I'll be here," Sean vowed.

Chang nodded, covering Jenny's corpse with the sheet. His action seemed to restore a degree of dignity to her poor abused body.

"Is there anything else, Agent Cameron?" Chang asked.

"No, not right now. Thank you. And I will be back. I know you've recovered what you can, but I don't want the body released yet."

"Then she will not be released," Chang promised him.

Sean nodded. He set his hand at the small of Madison's back and led her out of the room, down the antiseptic hallway and out to the light of day.

In the bright sunshine, she was even more pale.

"How are you?" he asked.

"I'm fine," she said, gazing up at him. "Really."

She had beautiful large eyes. He noted that they were perfect — not too large for her face, but the kind of eyes that seemed to give her vitality as well as beauty, that seemed to radiate emotion and life.

He let out a breath and looked at his watch. His team was coming, but they weren't due for another few hours.

"How about we stop by your house?" he suggested.

"My house? But where will that get us?"

"It will get us to your house," Sean said. "And give me time to think about what I want to do next, what I want to say to my team head and what I want to ask my team to start heading up for me."

"Oh. Okay," she said. She was trying to speak casually, but he suspected she was glad of the opportunity to go home.

She needed to regroup herself. She wasn't admitting it yet, but she'd just carried on a conversation with a corpse.

"Fine," she said. "Well, you're driving, and you know where I live. Let's go!"

So he did.

Her little car, an old Pontiac Vibe, was sitting in the driveway.

"That's mine, too," she said, pointing to the space beside it.

When he pulled in next to her car and parked, Madison quickly got out and he did the same. She walked to her door and fit her key into the lock.

"This is a wonderful old bungalow," he said, standing back to admire it.

"Yes, all the houses in this neighborhood are."

The door opened and he stepped into her house. Instantly, he felt an intriguing sensation of being watched — suspiciously.

Madison isn't the only one residing here, he thought.

"Come in. Make yourself comfortable," she told him.

She didn't seem to be very comfortable herself. Her next words confirmed his feeling.

"I'm going to make a drink. Would you like one? I'm not exactly a full-service bar, but I have Scotch, rum, whiskey . . ."

She disappeared into the kitchen and then popped her head back out, continuing with ". . . a questionable red wine and an Irish beer in bottles."

"Sounds like a pretty good bar to me," he said. "I'll take an Irish beer."

He heard her in the kitchen, despite the

fact that the television was on.

"Have a seat," she called to him.

He did. The second he was seated, a ball of fur leaped up beside him and gazed at him with mammoth cat eyes. "Hey, it's cool, I like cats," he said in a low voice.

"Don't mind Ichabod!" she called.

"I like animals!" he assured her, speaking more loudly.

But as he stroked the cat, he felt an odd presence. He turned and realized he was right.

Madison was not residing in the bungalow by herself — and it wasn't just the cat who was residing with her.

There was a man seated at the far end of the sofa, watching him gravely.

"I Love Lucy," the man said. "Love that show. The physical comedy is exceptional. Ah, Lucille! She had some major talent."

Sean just nodded, incredulous. "Bogie?" he whispered.

She wasn't alone. He hadn't merely dropped her off — he was inside the house with her!

Vengeance was irritated. Sean Cameron. Everyone hero-worshipped the bastard.

Could have been a movie star, excellent leader and team player, brilliant, artistic, talented . . .

193

FBI?

Vengeance was thoughtful; it was said that Cameron had left because a friend was dying. A woman. Although they'd been apart, she'd been the love of his life. So he'd gone home to Texas. Texas. Cowboys and guns and ranches . . .

Then he'd joined the FBI. But he was back.

Panic set in. No, just stick to the plan — with Madison now part of the scenario. It was very film noir. She wasn't the love of Cameron's life, but . . .

It made vengeance all the sweeter.

Let him know. . . .

Let him know that another woman, Madison Darvil, had died.

A woman *he'd* brought in on the case. Or, better still . . . one *Eddie Archer* had brought in.

Yes, she must die.

Vengeance wasn't sure that vengeance could wait.

7

Why hadn't she said NO? One gigantic NO, that would've done it. She could have explained that she didn't bring people to her house, that work was separate from her private life, even when it came to saving Alistair Archer and finding a murderer. They could have gone somewhere else.

Anywhere else! She wasn't against being with him — not at all. Under other circumstances, she would've loved to have had him in her house. Every moment she spent with Sean seemed to draw her closer to him, draw her further into the web of fascination he created for her. She liked being next to him, feeling the warmth he seemed to exude, feeling she wanted to come closer and closer. . . .

They were just working together; she was a studio guide for him, and a guide into the lives of those around Eddie, the people she might know better than he did.

And she really didn't need him here! Not when Bogie was bound to tease her and cause trouble. It was going to be hard to behave normally, to pretend that the ghost of a classic film star wasn't sitting on her sofa or leaning nonchalantly against a wall.

But she'd tried to remain casual. She'd been nonchalant. *Sure, what the hell, let's go to my house.*

Bogie would behave. Bogie knew that a murder had taken place. This wasn't like trying to destroy an evening because she was dating someone he considered a jerk. This was different. Sure, the television was on. Lots of people left their TVs on. No big deal. It was all going to be fine.

Madison dug around in her refrigerator and produced a beer for Agent Cameron. Luckily, she was so close to the studio that she brought her coworkers home for week-end evenings fairly often — and Bogie always behaved then. She was well-supplied with snack food and a decent selections of drinks — alcoholic and non. Beer. Beer was easy. She had a case of Guinness her assistant had brought last Friday. Nice cold Irish beer in bottles. What about her? Hmm. Maybe she'd have something a bit harder. Like Scotch or whiskey. She looked around on the counter. She had both. A whiskey and ginger ale. Yeah.

She poured whiskey into a glass with ice.

She didn't add the ginger ale. She knocked the drink back in a swallow, felt the burn and coughed. That was good. Okay, no problem. She poured herself another shot and added the ginger ale. She shook back her hair and managed to call out calmly, "It's Guinness. You want a glass?"

"Nope."

She picked up her glass and his beer and tried to sail smoothly back into the living room. Agent Cameron was seated on the couch, left side.

Bogie was on the right side.

Bogie offered her his charming half smile. She returned it with a warning frown.

"Here you go." She handed Sean the beer, and took a seat in the large upholstered chair.

"Thanks," he told her.

She nodded. "So when does your crew get in?" she asked.

"The rest of my unit arrives tonight."

Why did casual conversation have to be so damned hard?

Because she'd brought him to her house. After a trip to the morgue.

She was insane. Totally insane.

And it was all worse than she'd imagined.

He was staring at her. Just watching her. As if he knew something she didn't know . . .

She gave him her best effort at an expectant smile, as if she was waiting for him to tell her where they were going from here.

But, at first, he didn't speak.

And she was completely unnerved.

She looked at her glass. She didn't remember having gulped down the second drink.

"Wow," she murmured.

"First trip to a morgue isn't easy," he said.

"No. I mean, people don't usually drop in on the morgue," she said.

"Of course not," he agreed.

"Excuse me," Madison said, standing again and hurrying back to the kitchen. She really had to stop. She didn't normally slurp down three shots in ten minutes. But one more . . .

She made herself another drink. She would *sip* it, she promised herself.

Once again, she sat in the big chair diagonally across from him. Bogie was shaking his head in some kind of warning.

She ignored him, looking at Sean Cameron.

And he looked back at her.

"So, about Texas," she said. She felt as if she was awkwardly trying to speed-date. They weren't at a speed-dating event. They were working on a murder case. She was an artist. She could create wonderful special effects and work on her own designs and the designs of others; she was a fabricator, accustomed to fabric and foam and latex and other materials with which marvelous *things* could be fashioned. She knew nothing about morgues and murders.

"Texas, yes," he said pleasantly.

"Nice state. Big state. Lots of horses, cowboys . . . all that." Oh, God, she sounded like she was doing horrendously at a very *bad* speed-dating event.

"Yes, Texas is a big state," he said. He seemed amused, even *charmed,* by her desperate rambling.

But before she could make some other inane remark, he asked, "What did you get from the morgue? Really. Seriously."

Madison frowned. "I got the same thing you got. Exactly what the medical examiner said. Her killer caught up with her from behind. Held her tight and slit her throat, the stroke going from left to right."

"And?" he persisted.

She forced herself to meet his eyes. "If he had any other facts, I didn't hear him say so," she said primly.

He smiled, then looked at her again. "I want to know what Jenny Henderson said to you. If there was something I didn't hear. She did see you, and she did speak to you. I want to know if I missed anything she said, anything at all. You never know what can help until you weigh the words of the deceased."

Her jaw must have dropped to her feet.

He actually reached over to tap it shut with his hand.

"Madison!" He said her name softly but firmly. "Madison, this isn't the time to be shy about your abilities. We've got to get this all out in the open, now, here — and make use of everything we can throughout this case. We need *whatever* help there is. All the help we can get — from the living . . . and the dead."

She was still staring at him. At least her mouth was no longer gaping. But she couldn't seem to speak.

"Please," he said. "Eddie told me you speak with the dead. And Bogie told me he hangs around here because he loved the time he lived here — and because you're the only one he's come across who sees him and responds to him. He really likes you, too. But he'd haunt those he loved during his lifetime if he could."

Her jaw dropped again. And once more, he gently tapped it shut.

She glanced at Bogie, who was watching her gravely, and then turned back to Sean Cameron with total shock.

"I don't know what you're talking about," she said harshly.

"It's all right, kid," Bogie said. "He sees me."

In torment, Madison looked from her ghost to Sean Cameron. He was studying her with his deep green eyes. Eyes that seemed to accept nothing but the truth. Challenging eyes, defying her to contradict him.

Madison couldn't help herself; she sat rigidly silent. She didn't want to hurt other people with what she saw, nor did she relish being ridiculed. In her entire life, she'd never come across anyone else who admitted to seeing the dead.

"You can't begin to know how lucky you are," Sean said, looking at Bogie with awe. "Sir, you were magic on the screen. Magic. And from everything I've read, you were an all-right guy, as well."

"I had my spats with a few folks." Bogie shrugged in that characteristic Bogie way.

"We all do," Sean said. "Every life includes some dark spots and hard times. But, sir, the totality of your life, on-screen and off . . . it's fantastic." He suddenly turned to Madison. "Really! You can't imagine how lucky you are to be haunted by such a legend!"

"Right, there you go, kid. You're lucky as hell," Bogie told her.

Madison stared at Sean. "You . . . you really see Bogie?" she whispered.

"Clear as day."

"Yup, he *sees* me," Bogie said, pleased.

Madison had no idea what to do or how to react.

Sean leaned toward her. "So, here's the thing. I know you saw our victim, as well. I know you spoke to her, and that she replied."

"You . . . you heard," Madison said weakly.

"Yes."

She was afraid she was going to fall off the chair. In a way, her life, her private life, had remained easy. She'd been able to tell herself that she was imaginative — she was, thank God, which was why she had the job she did — but that she wasn't really so strange. That it wasn't real, it was all in her head.

And now she was sitting here with someone who was *making* it real.

She didn't think she liked this reality. Actually, no, she knew she didn't. Reality was Alistair Archer accused of murder, and

202

Jenny Henderson dead on a table in the morgue.

She realized then that Sean was looking at her with far more than speculation.

He was looking at her with hope.

She managed to speak through numb lips. "She doesn't know."

He sighed, leaning back, his eyes still on her. "Yeah, same thing I got," he said wearily. "Except she was pretty honest with you, gave you more detail. We're going to have to interview her roommate and the friend she was with."

"You were expecting something different?"

"Something more," he said. "Well, I hate to say it, but we're going back to the morgue tomorrow. We *have* to find out who else she saw that day. She says people knew she planned to drop in on Alistair. We have to know who those people are."

"I'm sure this young woman wants to help you." Bogie spoke quietly. "And I'm sure she's scared, and uncertain, and hoping to move on from . . . haunting a morgue. But I know she'll help you all she can. Now, just how crazy the morgue workers are going to think *you* are — well, that I can't say."

Sean turned to Madison and grimaced. "Yeah, he's got a point. They'll think we're crazy if we insist on trip after trip to the morgue." He looked directly at Bogie. "Maybe, when the crew gets in, you could join us. Talk Jenny Henderson into . . . coming home with us."

"What?" Madison didn't mean to squeak out the question — but she already lived with one ghost.

"Away from the morgue, at least. She could haunt the studio or the Black Box Cinema," Sean told her.

"God, no," Bogie said. "She was killed there."

"There has to have been a place she loved," Sean mused. "We just have to figure out where. Then she can leave the morgue and haunt a place that made her happy. Until she's ready to move on."

Madison glanced over at Bogie.

"Hey, I gotta say, I'm not sure why *I'm* still hanging around," Bogie said. "Maybe it's for the reruns. Life can't be rerun, but you can now see those old shows over and over again." He pointed a finger at Madison. "Or maybe it's for you, kid."

Sean leaned toward Madison once more. "Most of the time, despite forensics, when perpetrators are caught, it's because someone had a theory. Forensics can be brilliant tools, but they don't mean much unless you have a direction in which to take them. Sure, you can get DNA, and if you're lucky, you'll find it in the system. But I'm willing to bet this culprit doesn't have any kind of rap sheet. So we need a theory. The official theory now is that Alistair did it. Our theory is that someone else did, someone who has a bone to pick with Jenny, Alistair or most likely Eddie. Could Jenny have provoked that kind of hatred at her age? Probably not, but it *is* possible. Could the killer want Alistair out of the picture? Yes, but he'll go to prison for life, which doesn't really remove him. Does his incarceration and the stigma of murder hurt Eddie Archer? To the bone. So I think the murderer is out to make Eddie's life miserable and perhaps close down the cinema and the studio."

"Why not kill Alistair, too?" Madison asked.

"The living can suffer much more — suffer unto death," Sean said.

She nodded slowly, then shook her head. "I still can't imagine anyone close to Eddie trying to hurt him. Helena needs Eddie. I can't believe she'd hurt him or Alistair, even if she had the wits to do it. You know Archer's partner, Andy Simons. There's no reason I can think of for him to do this. And you know my boss — your old boss — Mike

Greenwood. Mike lives for the studio. He'd be out of a job that he loves if the studio fell apart. Let's see . . . Benita. They're divorced. I'm not sure she's happy about that. I actually thought she did care about him, but who knows? There were some rumors about her and other men. . . . But she's not that familiar with the studio, anyway. And then you've got . . ."

"Then you've got?"

She sighed. "The forty-plus people who are usually at the studio and the twenty-plus who come in on specific projects."

"Madison, we have to look at those who are closest to him. I've explained why I don't believe we're looking beyond that list."

"But everyone close to Eddie loves him!" she protested.

"That's what we see on the surface," Sean said. "We have to get below that."

As he spoke, Madison heard her cell phone ring. She was going to ignore it, but he said, "Answer — it might be the curious."

She frowned, not sure what he meant, but she pulled out her phone. Caller ID informed her that it was her supervisor, creative head of the studios, Mike Greenwood. "My boss," Madison said.

"Answer him."

She nodded. "Hi, Mike," she said, watching Sean as she answered.

"How are you doing?" he asked.

"I'm fine, Mike."

"Eddie told me you were helping Sean Cameron. That just beats all — Sean, a G-man!" Mike said. "Anyway, thanks for that. I wasn't sure if you knew that the studio's closed for another day. I don't know when — or even if — they'll let us reopen the cinema. Anyway, the police have finished with the studio, but they're holding off one more day because the FBI team comes in tonight."

"Everything is so . . . so surreal right now, isn't it?"

"Yeah. And we're really going to have to crank it up when we get back in. Not just to do our part for the American economy, but for Eddie. What he's going through is painful enough. He doesn't need to be worried about his studio, too."

"Mike, I'll crank it up. You know that."

"Hard to believe how the world can change, huh? As in overnight," Mike said. "I was in there on Saturday, covering up, making sure we were ready to plow in come Monday morning. Who the hell knew when I cleared the place out on Saturday that Monday wasn't really coming."

"Well, it came — just differently," Madison said. "We'll get through this," she added.

"You think?" Mike sounded weary, defeated.

She kept her eyes on Sean, wondering if he could hear Mike. His face never gave a thing away.

"Of course. Eddie is the best," she said. How many times had she insisted on that fact, one way or another, in the past two days?

"Yeah, well, we'll have to put on our game face and move forward, right?"

"You got it, Mike."

He informed her that he had a few more calls to make, and rang off.

"Mike," she told Sean lamely. "As you've no doubt guessed. He's a great boss. He runs a tight ship, and everyone respects him — and we always hope he'll come to the work picnics and Christmas parties 'cause he's a lot of fun."

Sean shrugged, a half smile on his lips. "Don't forget I worked for the guy. But either we're all lying to ourselves and Alistair is guilty — which isn't true, we know that from Jenny — or one of these nice, great people is guilty."

Madison was thoughtful. "I'm going with

the new wife. I don't hate her or anything, but she's a user with a capital *U*."

"I still believe it has to do with the remake of *Sam Stone and the Curious Case of the Egyptian Museum*," Sean said. "I don't know what her association with the old movie could have been."

"If it was someone associated with the movie, that person would have to be pretty damned old by now," Bogie pointed out.

Madison nodded. "No one old enough to have been in the movie or to have worked on it is still at the studio, in any capacity."

"But there was that death on the set," Bogie said.

"Pete Krakowski?" Sean glanced at Madison. "I read everything I could about the movie when I was on the plane. But while there were rumors running rampant, it appears to have been an accident — partially caused by the fact that Krakowski clowned around on set. His widow was compensated. Still, we should dig a lot deeper."

"I don't know. Helena's out for herself," Madison said.

"And *you* said she wasn't bright enough," Sean reminded her. He stood and looked at Bogie, who'd been contemplating the two of them. "Plus Eddie is kind of her ticket into the movies. She needs him around."

"But not Alistair."

"We'll start sorting it all out," Sean said. He walked over to Bogie. "Sir, it was a pleasure to meet you. This is the kind of thing that makes it possible to live with my crazy sixth sense or whatever it is. I was, still am and will always be a huge fan."

Bogie was on his feet. Sean towered over him, but Bogie retained the essence that made him such a unique man, even larger in reality than on the screen. "Thank you, son. Thank you. And for whatever it's worth, I'm here."

"Thank you, sir."

"Bogie. You can call me Bogie."

"Bogie," Sean said, smiling. He reached out to shake Bogie's hand; Bogie reached out in turn. Madison had to blink. It *appeared* that they'd actually shaken hands.

Sean looked back at her. "All right, I'm on my way to the police station to meet up with my crew. So our plan for tomorrow, if you're up for it, is to return to the morgue and then the studio."

They were both startled by a deep sigh from Bogie. "I guess I'll go to the morgue with you. Maybe make things a little better for Miss Jenny Henderson."

"Thank you," Sean said solemnly.

"I'm just not sure how well it's going to

go for your team when they put everyone who works at the studio through the wringer again," Madison said. "You're accustomed to this kind of thing. Artists usually aren't. Our blood and gore aren't real. People will get edgy."

"Yes, and if a killer is among them, that's a good thing. The police have talked to people, and now my team will talk to them, too. Comparing their notes with what we find will be important. And anytime there's an inconsistency, we can bring you in. Thing is, Madison, you know the studio and you know the people working there. You'll recognize who's telling the truth and who isn't."

"Just like that?" Madison asked. "I'm an artist, not a cop or an agent!"

Sean was already out the door.

She stared after him, incredulous, and then the door opened again, and he poked his head back in. "Oh, I guess I should say this just to be on the safe side — stay away from the studio unless you're with me, and if you speak with anyone, act innocent."

"I *am* innocent!"

"Innocent of knowing anything."

"I *don't* know anything," she said flatly. "And neither do you."

"That will change," he said. And then he

was gone, warning her to lock the door as he closed it.

The more he worked with Benny Knox, the more Sean felt he wasn't a bad cop or a jerk, he was just a realist. And to Knox — being a realist — there was no doubt that Alistair Archer was the only one who could've killed Jenny Henderson.

He wasn't sure of the detective's feelings about him, but at least it wasn't stone-cold hatred, and his resentment seemed to be ebbing now that a real investigation was under way.

Knox met Sean at the police station, introduced him around and then brought him to a large room dedicated to computer forensics. There, a young cop, Officer Angelo Fontini, was working with the security images from the studio and the Black Box Cinema.

"Takes the young ones to know what they're doing with this computer stuff," Knox said. "Hell, so much can be manipulated these days, and I gotta admit, I wouldn't see half of it."

Sean nodded. "I was in film, video and digital special effects before I came into law enforcement. And you're right. It's an area that can definitely be manipulated."

Knox laughed. "Then you and Fontini should get along great. Right, Fontini?"

Fontini looked up; his name might be Italian, but he had blue eyes and curly blond hair, and with his ready grin, his appearance was even more cherubic. "These are pretty much straight security shots. The cameras at the studio are set to catch particular areas. They don't rotate. I've tried to compare the studio film with the Black Box film. And it looks as if they both caught the same stuff. I've been staring at this on and off for hours, and I just don't see how anyone could've been there."

"Let's see the film from the Friday night before the murder up to the time of the murder," Sean said.

"That's forty-eight hours of footage."

"Yeah, I know. We'll speed it up, and I'll call *stop* when I want you to slo-mo."

Fontini hit a key and began showing the footage from the Friday before the murder. Sean watched as people streamed out of the studio on Friday night, the fast-forward making them look like harried, robotic performers. They all chatted as they headed out to their cars; most left between six and six-thirty.

He saw Madison leaving the building close to seven with a tall, lean man who seemed to be in his early twenties. She paused and waved to her immediate supervisor, Mike Greenwood, and Mike waved back.

Greenwood talked to some of the departing employees, then went back into the studio. He appeared from screen to screen as he made his way into the main workroom, stopped to look around, nodded with satisfaction and returned to the guard station. Colin Bailey was on shift, and Greenwood spoke to him before leaving.

Night turned into day. Saturday morning, guard duty changed and Winston Nash came on as Colin Bailey left. A few hours later, Mike Greenwood appeared again, and in time, five other men and one woman entered the building. They all went straight to the main work area, where they completed final construction of the scaffolding he'd seen the other day. The woman made a phone call. A pizza delivery man came to the front entrance, and she hurried out to get the food. The crew ate, then finished hammering and sanding. The workers left. Once again, Mike Greenwood glanced around, checked a power saw to see that it was unplugged and headed out to speak to Nash, who was just changing places again with Bailey. Mike left.

Colin Bailey took out a *Playboy* magazine,

placed his feet on the desk and read — or looked at pictures — for a while, and then seemed to snooze.

Sunday rolled around. Nash arrived; Bailey went home. Eddie Archer came in — there was a clock behind the guard desk, and Sean had Fontini stop the video so he could see the time. Exactly 10:00 a.m.

Eddie went into the studio, walked around and adjusted some of the tarps that were covering works in progress. When he seemed assured that all was well at the studio, he went back to the guard station, said good-bye to Nash and departed. Time passed quickly; Nash and Bailey changed places again.

Sunday evening, Alistair arrived at the Black Box Cinema and let himself in. Then, forty-four minutes later, Jenny Henderson showed up. She approached the door in a crouch, as if she believed she could escape the eye of the camera that way. She went into the Black Box Cinema. Her body hid the door for a minute, and then she disappeared inside.

Sean had Fontini roll the footage over and over again, trying to see what he was missing. Then he got it.

"Interesting," he murmured.

"Did you see something I didn't?" Fontini asked.

"No," Sean said. "But what I *didn't* see tells me a lot."

"What's that?"

"This was perfectly orchestrated. Whoever did it knows all about the security station and the security cameras. Which, once again, suggests that this person is very familiar with the studio."

"Then it could be Alistair Archer," Knox said quietly. He'd returned to stand behind them.

"Nope." Sean shook his head. "No murder weapon anywhere. No bloody trail away from the scene. Come on, Knox! The killer escaped somehow — in a manner we haven't figured out. Don't forget, the studio is missing its robe for the remake of *Sam Stone and the Curious Case of the Egyptian Museum.* That robe has to be *somewhere* — and when it's found, it's going to be covered in blood. Let me see the Friday footage again, toward the end of the day."

Fontini looked over at Knox, and Knox shrugged. They rolled the footage again. This time, Sean concentrated on the dress-maker's mannequin in the costume department. At one point, Mike Greenwood moved it because it was in his way, shoving

216

it behind the curtained area used as a change room when actors came for fittings.

A seamstress passed by and it was shoved farther back. By the end of the day, it was completely behind the curtain.

"One more time?" Sean asked.

"The robe was on the mannequin," Fontini said. "And it's gone now, you say?"

"There's a plain brown monk's robe on the mannequin now."

Fontini started to run the tape again, showing the different rooms. "Stop!" Sean said suddenly.

Fontini did, frowning as he studied the various screens. Then he said, "Got it!"

"Got what?" Knox demanded.

Fontini pointed excitedly to the screens. "There's a gap in the video that covers the entrance. Look — there's the time on the security station camera. It's reading 4:48. And there's the time on the clock in the workroom — 4:50."

"The clocks could have been wrong," Knox argued.

"They could've been. Who would normally notice a two-minute time difference?" Sean said. "And then again, there could be missing footage. And that's where I think we have a theft. The new robe for the new

217

Amun Mopat. The one worn by the murderer."

"It might still show up somewhere in the studio," Knox said.

"Fontini, can we tell if any footage is missing? Could someone have frozen the cameras?" Sean asked.

"It's possible. Anything is possible," Fontini said. "But if something was done, I haven't found it yet. I'll need to go through just about every computer test known to man, and even then . . ." He looked at Sean. "But I'll do it," he promised.

Madison's assistant, Alfie, showed up at her door about forty-five minutes after Sean had left.

"You're home! Thank God," Alfie said in his usual dramatic way.

"Well, if you'd called, you would have known that," Madison told him dryly.

She didn't have to ask him in; Alfie just walked through the door as if there was no question that he was welcome. He threw himself on the couch. Ichabod, who was fond of Alfie, immediately crawled up on his lap.

Alfie was an attractive man, tall and blond and elegant in his movements. Madison watched him with affection. He was really a big kid, one who loved the movies — and loved his job. But, right now, he clearly felt anxious.

"Have you had dinner?" he asked.

"No."

"Do you have any food?" He clasped his hands as though in prayer.

"Sure. I have tuna," she said. He made a face. "I buy a lot of it, Alfie. It comes in cans, and lasts a long time, so it's good when we wind up working nights and I'm not home to cook."

"Tuna sounds great." He followed her into the kitchen, delving into the rack for one of her bottles of questionable red wine as she drew out tuna, mayonnaise, bread, lettuce and tomatoes.

"So?" he said, opening the wine as she prepared the food.

"So?"

"Oh, please! There's a massive rumor mill! You're helping the cops! Or the FBI. The *ghost* FBI."

"I don't know what you're talking about," she insisted. She pushed him aside to get a knife out of the drawer. *Act innocent,* she'd been told.

Alfie rested his elbows on the counter and jiggled his brows. "Studly, macho FBI agent — old employee of the studio — arrives,

219

and you're assigned to be with him!"

"I showed him around the studio."

"Aha!"

"Aha what?" she asked.

"So he *is* studly and macho," Alfie said triumphantly.

"I suppose. It's not something you really notice when you're worried because there's been a murder and a friend is accused of that murder *and* our livelihoods are at stake." *That was a lie.* Sad as it was, she'd noticed everything about Sean Cameron, down to the scent of his aftershave and the single ring he wore, some kind of coat of arms. He also wore a dive watch. His hands were large, his fingers long, his fingernails neatly clipped; his were the hands of someone who was clean in appearance and habits, yet heedless of artificial enhancements. His hair was cleanly cut and simple, too. The way it fell slightly forward was entirely unaffected.

"I don't get it," Alfie said. "I mean, how could anyone but Alistair have done it?"

"I don't know. I'm not an investigator." She took the glass of wine he held before her nose, sipped — it was indeed questionable — and set the glass down. "Alfie, I'm just a friend and an artisan and a fabricator. I showed him around the studio because I was asked to." She cut the sandwiches in halves and bent down to give Ichabod his portion of tuna. "There are chips in the cupboard," she said.

He went for the chips, poured them into a bowl, then put it and their plates on the kitchen table. He pulled out his chair, waiting for her to join him. When she'd done so, he practically pounced on her. "*And* you went to see Alistair!"

"Yes."

"Well?"

"Well, what?"

"Has he confessed?"

"No! Alistair swears he didn't do it — and I believe him."

Alfie leaned back, sipping his wine. "If Alistair didn't do it, then who did?"

"Alfie, we're talking in circles. And I told you, I have no idea. If we knew who did it, the cops wouldn't have to investigate, would they?" Madison demanded. "So, you tell me. How do you know my every movement?"

"Let's see," Alfie said, frowning, "I got the info from Mike Greenwood, who got it from Andy Simons, who apparently saw you with hunk-o-FBI man."

"How'd you find out I saw Alistair?" she asked.

"That one is more convoluted," Alfie said, grinning. "I heard it from Vickie at the coffee shop, who heard it from her boyfriend, Victor — Victor, Victoria, cute, huh? — who goes to the same manicurist as Pierce, who apparently escaped the bondage of the current Mrs. Eddie Alistair long enough to get his nails done this afternoon."

"Well, the fact that I went to see Alistair is no secret," Madison said.

Alfie laughed. "In our world, does *anything* stay secret?"

"Probably not. But it doesn't matter because I don't have any secrets to worry about," Madison said.

Alfie chewed thoughtfully for a few minutes. Then he set his sandwich down. "This is all so horrible," he groaned. "I know you don't *know* anything. But who do you *think* did it?"

"Alfie! I already told you. I haven't got any idea."

"What I'm afraid of is that no one will ever find anything. That Alistair just snapped or something. That he doesn't realize he did it — he's too good a kid — but that he did do it. And then he'll go to jail, Eddie will go crazy — and we'll all be in the unemployment line."

"He didn't do it," Madison said stubbornly. "And it's way too early to worry about losing your job."

"So . . . who could've done it?" Alfie asked.

"You tell me. Who do you think could have done it?"

Alfie frowned. "Ah! The evil Mrs. Eddie Archer. The current one. No, no, never mind. That would mean breaking a nail or messing up her hair. Back to the drawing board. Hmm. Aha! Mike Greenwood. Yeah, that's the ticket. Mike has access. No one knows the studio better. No, no, he likes his job." Alfie looked frustrated. "Colin Bailey! He's the guard, right? He's in charge of security. But why? Maybe . . . somewhere, somehow, years and years ago, Eddie dated a girl Bailey was in love with. Yeah . . . no. No, can't see Bailey and Archer being involved with any of the same women, nor would Bailey risk his cushy job. God knows, he gets to make a mint and snooze and read magazines. Hey! Maybe we *did* create something so real it came to life and killed her. What do you think?"

"I think you need to finish your sandwich and your wine, and go home. I'm exhausted."

"I can't even get you out for some boba green tea?" Alfie asked, clearly disappointed by the dismissal.

"I hate boba," she told him.

"Plain green tea, then?"

"Alfie, I just want to sleep."

He sighed. "Okay, but no holding out. I'm your assistant, for God's sake! Keep me in the loop," he said, rising. "Hey, you want some help cleaning up? Doing the dishes —"

"Alfie, we ate on paper plates."

"Oh. Oh, yeah. Okay, fine — send me out into the cold and the dark, feeling lonely and anxious!"

"Alfie, it isn't in the least cold. Go home. Or go to a club. I've got to sleep!"

She steered him to the door and nudged him out. There, she gave him a quick kiss on the cheek. "I'll keep in touch, I promise, although we're supposed to be back at work the day after tomorrow. Drive carefully . . . and go home!"

"All right, all right!" Grinning, he walked out to her drive where he'd parked his car.

When he was gone, Madison closed and locked the door. She turned to lean against it and realized she hadn't seen Bogie, which was odd, because he loved to talk to her when she had company. He considered it amusing to see if he could push her into answering.

It wasn't that late, but she really was tired. The kitchen received a lick and a promise, as her mother used to call it, she checked Ichabod's food and water bowls and then went to her room and prepared for bed. Tonight, there was no drone of voices from the television in the living room, so she turned on the smaller set in her room, found a ridiculous movie about a massive snowstorm freakishly hitting San Diego and willed herself to nod off.

Just as she was falling asleep, she was awakened by the shrill sound of an alarm.

The noise was horrendous, shattering, shocking — and brought her leaping to her feet, terrified and disoriented.

She rushed into the living room and immediately saw that Bogie was back; he was at the window looking out. The sound was coming from her car. Somehow the alarm had been activated.

She rushed to find her keys, and discovered that they must have fallen out of her purse because they were on the coffee table.

"Bogie?"

He turned to her. "I did it. I managed to press that little key and set off the alarm. There was someone out there, Madison. I saw movement in the shadows across the street. There was someone out there —

225

watching. Watching you. And I . . . I could feel the malice like a wave of hot air, the malice and the . . . evil. Madison, someone doesn't like what you're doing. Someone is out to kill you, too."

8

Sean sat at the desk in his hotel room, studying the handwritten notes Benny Knox had given him. They were photocopies, and sometimes he had to squint to read them. They might be entering a brave new world where younger cops were working more and more with technology, but a lot of law enforcement officers still carried notebooks and wrote down their observations.

He had the crime scene photos spread before him, and from what he could tell, every single notation matched perfectly with what he saw. It could be argued that Alistair had enough knowledge of the studio to figure out someplace to stash the weapon, but Sean didn't believe that was what had happened. And Alistair had been covered in blood. There'd also been trace and cast-off blood along the path he'd taken to summon Bailey.

Colin Bailey had been sitting in security.

He'd been on the property. But Alistair had found him in his little booth, just where he always was. Bailey had not been covered in blood spatter.

He set down the photos and picked up the phone; he'd wanted to talk to Pierce — in privacy — ever since he and Madison had visited the Archer house.

He hoped Eddie wouldn't answer, or Helena. If one of them did, he could just ask how they were doing.

He was glad when Pierce did answer, cordial and proper as ever. "Archer residence."

"Pierce, it's me — Sean Cameron."

"Sean," Pierce said with evident pleasure.

Sean first thanked him for the text messages he'd sent.

"I didn't know if I should or shouldn't, but . . . I mean, their marriage isn't my business, but —"

"This is an investigation. You did the right thing," Sean told him. He asked Pierce how he was, and sympathized with him for a moment. Pierce was a good man, always there for Eddie — no matter who he married.

"I have a few questions for you, Pierce. Private questions."

"Whatever you need."

"Why are they sleeping in separate rooms?

228

Is the marriage on the rocks?"

"No, Eddie is still in love," Pierce said dully. "Mrs. Archer complains that Eddie snores, and that she can't get sleep if he's there. But they do have connecting rooms."

"With doors between them — which, I assume, she closes at night, so she doesn't have to hear his snoring?"

"Yes."

"Anything else wrong with the marriage?" Sean asked.

"You know how much I love Mr. Archer," Pierce began.

"I won't repeat anything, Pierce. But I need to know."

"I don't think Helena ever really loved Eddie. I think that when she went to Benita and Eddie's wedding, she saw that Benita had something she wanted much, much more than what she had herself. I think she waited for the right minute and stepped in. She's been planning on marrying him for a long time. She doesn't love Eddie, couldn't care less about Alistair and, quite frankly, I believe she could be guilty of anything."

"All right, Pierce, I need you to answer this one to the best of your ability. What time did Helena return to the house the night Jenny Henderson was killed?"

"I didn't see the exact time, but I'd say it

was about half an hour after young Alistair left the house for the studio."

Sean had to acknowledge that if she'd come home and stayed home, that definitely removed her from the list of possible candidates.

"Is there any way she could have left after that without you seeing her?"

"Sure. The Archers generally use the grand stairway to the bedrooms, but there are stairs in the back — the family room area — too. I was up in my own room after Alistair left, and I didn't hear her car start," Pierce said.

Sean thanked him, wishing the phone call had allowed him to completely eliminate Helena LaRoux.

She wasn't bright enough to have pulled it off. That was the general consensus. But . . . she could be a better actress than anyone knew. And if Alistair was locked up for life — or, God forbid, worse — Eddie would need her. Then, she'd have even greater power.

And she'd stand to inherit everything, unless Eddie had a will that excluded her.

He called Eddie and felt bad when his old friend and mentor answered, his voice filled with hope since he'd seen that Sean was the caller.

"You have something?" Eddie asked.

"Nothing solid yet," Sean replied. "But — and forgive me, I have to ask certain questions for the purposes of elimination — do you and Helena have a prenup?"

"Yes." Eddie's voice sounded hard.

"What about your will?"

"I have small bequests to various friends and workers. Alistair receives the bulk of my money and investments, and Helena is nicely cared for, as well. My family isn't out to get me, Sean. I'm also leaving Benita nicely set up."

"What happens if Alistair is out of the picture?"

"Out of the picture? How?" Eddie asked, his tone cold. He didn't give Sean a chance to answer. "The killer could have killed Alistair, too. He didn't. Why would I worry about Alistair now? He's safe, isn't he? Alistair is safe?"

"Where he is, yes," Sean said. "Listen, Eddie, I didn't mean to upset you. I'm just trying to make sure I can eliminate certain people, you know?" And, of course, discover what their motives might be.

He bade Eddie good-night. Then he put down the phone and pulled out the crime scene photos again. He'd walked by the tableau of the scene from *Sam Stone and*

231

the Curious Case of the Egyptian Museum dozens of times in the past; he hadn't paid enough attention. He'd been a bigger fan of films like *Laura* and *The Maltese Falcon.*

He picked up the crime scene notes, which detailed everything the reporting officer had seen on the museum floor. There was no mention of the tableaux at all. That wasn't unusual. The responding officer would have waited for a detective to arrive on the scene, once he'd assured himself that there was no help for the victim, and from the amount of blood on the floor, that must have been evident.

Knox had listed studio employees and recent visitors. Records had been checked and interviews conducted by a score of officers, but thus far, that hadn't raised any flags.

Sean was so deeply involved in what he was reading that he started when his cell phone rang. He glanced at the time and realized the Krewe had come in, a fact verified by Logan Raintree's name on his caller ID. "We're here," Logan said.

"Where? Airport, endless highway or hotel?" Sean asked him.

"Endless highway," Logan said. "Endless highway after endless travel. We're heading over to the hotel now. I want to keep your relationship with the local police positive, so we'll use the suite rather than the station. Are we all set?"

"Yes, there's a large dining-slash-work area between two bedrooms, and the other three are just across the hall. So we're all set."

"See you in twenty — or an hour and a half, depending on traffic," Logan told him dryly, and hung up.

Sean eased back in his chair.

He was surprised at the accommodations they'd gotten — and all within a decent budget. Eddie Archer had pulled strings here, too. They were staying in an old mission-turned-boutique hotel that was conveniently located. It was right off the 101, close to the police station and the highway that would bring them directly to the studio door. It was the perfect arrangement for them. The suite included a work area between the two bedrooms, which offered a refrigerator, microwave, wet bar and, most important, a huge table, a sufficient number of outlets and plenty of space. They'd have a designated room at the police station, too, but his group needed privacy at times, and the Hotel Pierre provided them with everything they required.

He was glad the rest of his unit had finally

arrived — Logan Raintree, ex–Texas Ranger, was the head of their team. Kelsey O'Brien was an ex–U.S. marshal — and his cousin. Katya Sokolov, doctor and pathologist, had been an M.E. before joining the team and training at Quantico. Jane Everett, a talented artist, had the uncanny ability to recreate accurate images of the deceased from nothing but a skull or a description. Tyler Montague was another former Texas Ranger. Everyone had his or her specialty in dealing with the unusual, the unknown . . . and the unnatural. As in, he supposed, the supernatural. They'd been carefully selected by Adam Harrison and Jackson Crow. Adam had been involved in mysterious searches and situations so often that the government had asked him to put together his "Krewe of Hunters" teams. Jackson was the only one of them chosen straight from the ranks of the FBI behavioral sciences department, and head of the original team. The six members of their particular unit complemented one another beautifully.

His cell rang again and he answered, expecting to hear Logan again, perhaps telling him that traffic on the 405 had snarled so badly that it would be midnight before they arrived. But it wasn't Logan. He was surprised to hear Madison's voice, soft and somehow sexy even at an anxious pitch.

"Sean, I'm really sorry to disturb you, and this . . . it may be absolutely nothing. . . ."

"Tell me. What is it?"

"Bogie managed to set off my car alarm. He was certain there was someone outside watching me and — Stop it! I *am* telling him what you said!" she whispered, and he knew she was talking to her resident ghost. "Bogie's convinced that *I'm* in danger. I admit to being a bit unnerved, but I really don't mean to bother you. You're involved with the serious law enforcement side of this situation and —"

"Stay where you are. Stay in the house, doors locked. I'm on my way."

"No, no, that's all right. I thought maybe you could just get a police officer to —"

"I'm on my way," he repeated, cutting her off. "Stay inside, everything bolted and locked!"

Sean cursed as he grabbed his jacket and hurried to the elevator, where he pushed the call button far too many times. He was out front, heading to one of the "elite" parking spaces for his loaner car, when he cursed again and returned to the desk, confirming that his fellow Krewe members would be brought to their respective rooms. Then he raced back to the car.

It was late; the roads were still busy, and yet not hopeless, as they could be. He knew he was speeding, but what the hell — so were half the cars on the road. He kept it to a safe level, glancing at his phone — which he'd set on the passenger seat — now and then just to make sure he didn't miss a call.

What had they been thinking? Yes, bring in someone who knew the studio, knew the dynamics and the people. Someone close.

Too close?

Why had it never occurred to him that he could be putting her at risk?

He tried to convince himself that he hadn't blindly led an innocent young woman into danger, that Bogie was being Bogie, a little macho, a little old-fashioned.

He slammed on the brakes, not realizing how fast he'd been driving, when he reached her neighborhood and swung into the space next to her car. He jumped out and hurried to the door. She'd been waiting for him.

The door opened and Madison stood there. He was surprised by the hard thud of his heart and the catch in his throat. Her eyes were wide — perhaps too trusting — and her expression was grave. And still, she seemed as straight as an arrow and disturbed at the thought that she might have interrupted him over something that wasn't important.

They'd barely met, he reminded himself, alarmed by the rise of emotion she elicited.

But that didn't matter. He had stupidly and unwittingly put her in danger.

He was overreacting. But he couldn't take the chance!

"I'm really sorry I made you rush over like this," Madison said. "And I really don't know what good it can do. I didn't even know Bogie was capable of pushing the alarm on my car key."

Bogie was right behind her. "Push an alarm on a key — that I can do. String a fellow up by his toes if he comes in causing problems for the lady? That . . . I'm not so sure." Bogie sounded frustrated.

"You were smart to set off the alarm," Sean said.

"I knew that would wake Madison. She was sleeping so deeply, she didn't feel me trying to shake her."

"The alarm probably scared off whoever it was," Sean told him.

"Being dead," Bogie said woefully, "makes it difficult when you want to be a hero."

"Bogie, what did you see?" Sean asked.

He pointed. Across the street, there were two houses, old bungalows, much like the one Madison lived in.

Between them was an old house almost obscured by the bushes in front. A For Sale sign planted just to the side of the front walk explained its slightly shabby and overgrown appearance.

"You know what it's like when you feel hackles rising along your neck? All right, so I don't really have a neck," Bogie said, "but I still *feel* like I do. I caught a glimpse of movement behind those bushes, and then I saw that whoever was there was wearing something like ninja gear — all black. The kind of black outfit puppeteers use so they're not seen onstage. I knew that this person was watching the house. Madison had fallen asleep, and if the intruder had gotten far enough to break in — well, hell, it could have been too late. I figured if I made the alarm go off, she'd be awake and aware, at least, and maybe I'd scare off the bastard."

"Good work, Bogie. Thank you," Sean said.

Bogie wagged a finger at him. "You see to her safety."

"Of course," Sean said, turning to Madison. "You have a flashlight?"

"Yes." She headed to her mantel, removing the large flashlight there. "What are you going to do?"

"Just take a look. I'll be right back. Lock the door when I go out."

He heard her do so as he left the house and walked from her yard. He crossed the street, quiet and still at that time of night, and came to the abandoned house.

Standing out on the road, he studied the bushes, then carefully moved around behind them.

He found a broken branch on one of the bushes and impressions in the dry earth, but nothing that could help a forensics team. He shone the light on the house, but anyone who'd broken in was long gone now. He considered calling the police, but he was sure that would be a waste of time.

Why would someone come after Madison?

Because she might know, somewhere in the back of her mind, something that could point an accusing finger in the right direction?

Perhaps one of L.A.'s lost and homeless was seeking entry to a place that could offer some shelter. He made a mental note to ask Knox to see that the empty house was checked, just in case. He doubted they'd find anything left behind by such an obviously clever and resourceful killer.

He returned to Madison's and knocked on the door, waiting while she looked through the peephole. Then she let him in.

"Anything?" she asked.

"Nothing useful. We'll have the cops do a search when it's daylight. Can you pack up?"

"Pack up?" she repeated.

"You can't stay here."

"I can't leave Ichabod!"

"You can leave a cat overnight. We have to figure out how to keep you out of danger until this is over." Sean stared at her at a moment; she was staring back at him, frowning and looking extremely stubborn.

"Can't we just call the police, have an officer patrol the area?"

"Madison! Didn't you see the blood in the tunnel — not to mention Jenny Henderson's corpse?" Sean demanded angrily.

"But . . ." She paled. She knew he was right, and she was furious about it.

"This is my home," she murmured. But she wasn't an idiot, and she wasn't going to risk her life.

She'd seen Jenny lying on the cold steel at the morgue.

"It will remain your home," he assured her. "You're not leaving it forever."

"No, no, I'm not. Where am I going?"

"My hotel."

She seemed a little shocked at that.

"I — I'm not sure that's a good idea. I mean, I can't stay with you —"

"I didn't suggest that," Sean snapped. "We have a suite of rooms."

She colored; she went from milk-white to rose-red, and her humiliation at misinterpreting his words seemed to draw her straighter still.

Don't look so embarrassed, he longed to say. *I'd give my eyeteeth to be honest and say, Hey, yeah, what a great opportunity. Come and sleep with me. I really shouldn't feel this way, but can't help thinking the sex would be really, really great.*

He gritted his teeth and tried to ignore that thought.

"This isn't a movie," he said hoarsely. "Come on, Madison! You know you have to get out of here. Do you want to be the idiot girl who's convinced that she's fine — and then runs into the killer in the very next scene?"

"No," she said, with dignity. "No, I don't wish to behave foolishly in any manner. And I'm aware this isn't a movie. It's my *life* that's either being threatened or, at worst, totally disrupted. So, fine. I'll pack. While I do so, would you please make sure the cat's water bowl is filled and he has food? Bogie was wonderful at setting off the alarm, but I don't believe he can do things like that."

"I'll put out food and water for the cat," Sean said. He felt shaky. Dismayed, and furious with himself.

This was his fault.

Hell, no. Eddie Archer was the one who'd thrown her into the fray.

Still, he'd brought her in, inch by inch, and now someone out there was scared of what Ms. Madison Darvil might know . . . or guess.

He found the cat food, which was in a ceramic jar in the shape of a cat's face. He noted other little things about the kitchen that made it specifically Madison's. Like salt and pepper shakers in the form of Frankenstein's monster and his bride. A beautiful kitchen witch dangled above the sink; gleaming copper pots and pans were hung on a rack, along with puppets, some macabre, some enchanting. Creatures everywhere . . .

He gritted his teeth again.

There was a killer out there. It didn't matter who'd involved Madison, whether he'd done it or Eddie had — or even if Bogie was being an alarmist. She wasn't a cop or an agent, as she'd reminded him, and she needed protection.

She was quick; she had a small bag packed

and was standing at the door after he'd refilled Ichabod's food and water bowls and set them down. Ichabod had eschewed both and followed him out. Even the damned cat seemed to be looking at him with accusatory eyes.

Bogie leaned against the wall, arms crossed. "You stay with him, kid. This is ugly. Hollywood can be magic, and it can be ugly as sin. You know that — firsthand now. I'll keep an eye on things here," he told Madison.

Sean hesitated. "We still need you to come to the morgue."

"I promised I would, and I will." Bogie shrugged. "I can probably get there on my own, but why don't you swing by for me when you come to feed the cat again?"

"We'll do that," Sean said.

Madison was grim and silent when they went to his car. He took her bag and put it in the truck, and climbed into the driver's seat.

She turned on the radio and chose a talk station. "Is this okay?"

"No. I'd prefer classic rock."

"Good. We'll listen to this, then."

"Hey! Look, I'm sorry. I didn't do this to you on purpose. I didn't even know you existed," Sean muttered. "You said you'd do anything for Eddie Archer and Alistair. It looks like you're getting to live up to those words."

She didn't reply. She did hit the button on the radio, changing it to an oldies station.

It was still a chilly drive back to the hotel.

Madison didn't say a word as they crossed the lobby, although he saw that she carefully studied her surroundings. The old missionary style was unmistakable, as was the care expended in bringing modern comforts to the historic building.

The hotel was small; it only took a minute for the elevator to carry them to the third floor. Sean headed straight for the suite. Before he could slip the key in, the door swung open. He was greeted by his cousin, Kelsey O'Brien, who gave him a massive hug.

"Hey, we're here — as you can see," Kelsey said, tucking long red hair behind her ears.

"And feel!" he teased her. "Did you learn that power-hug technique with the marshal's office?"

"Sean, where did you go?" Logan asked him, coming up beside Kelsey, a frown knitting his brows. "You knew we were on the way. Did something happen?" He sounded concerned — or was he annoyed?

Logan was his height, and they were both taller than Kelsey, who was still a good five-ten. Logan, however, wasn't about to give him a welcoming hug.

"Yeah, more or less," Sean said. "Can we come in?"

"We?" Logan asked.

"Yes," he said, pulling Madison forward. "This is Madison Darvil. She's doing the job I used to have at the special-effects studio. Eddie Archer thought she'd be the right person to show me around so I'd know what's still the same and what's changed over the years. There's an empty house across from hers, and we have reason to believe someone was watching her from the shrubbery tonight. I couldn't completely check it out. I figured we'd have the cops do it tomorrow. Whoever was there is gone. Madison, this is Kelsey O'Brien, Logan Raintree and, back there — behind Logan, the little blue-eyed blonde — is Katya Sokolov or Kat, as we call her. Dr. Kat, if you will. The guy in the cowboy hat is Tyler Montague, ex-Ranger, and rounding out our team is Jane Everett, over by Tyler."

A chorus of "Hi, Madison," sounded. Madison waved a hand and said hello in greeting. She was trying to act cool and dignified; she looked like a deer caught in the headlights of a massive semi.

"I see you have a suitcase," Logan said.

"That's good. You shouldn't stay at your own place now," Kelsey told her.

"Yes, definitely, if you were threatened in any way, you need to keep close to us, for the time being at least," Logan agreed.

"Thank you," Madison said.

Sean cleared his throat. "I forgot to tell you that as well as being a special-effects wizard and a friend to Eddie and Alistair, she's a great deal like us. She speaks with ghosts. She actually has a close relationship with one in particular, who spends a lot of time with her."

"Oh?" Logan still looked severe. He tended to be mistrustful of others who claimed to be mediums or capable of "reaching the other side." They were all careful with whom they spoke, and careful of what they said. Despite rumors that they were the "ghost busters" of the FBI.

Madison nodded, looking no less mistrustfully at the crowd she'd just met.

She finally answered.

"Yes, sometimes I can speak with the dead. Not always."

"Well, that would be the same of all of us," Kelsey said, smiling. "Sometimes —

most often, really — the dead are gone. And even when they stay, some don't care to talk. But . . . you have a ghost who visits you?"

Sean flinched, not sure if the others would doubt the possibility of Bogie, or if they'd be awed and envious.

It was the latter.

After a few minutes of excited questions, things seemed to settle down. They moved into the central area between the two rooms, and were soon seated around the table.

Bogie had proven to be quite a help in many ways; here, he was an icebreaker.

And questions about him naturally segued into more serious conversation regarding the murder. Madison described the different personalities involved with the studio and Eddie Archer's life, and Sean put forth his theory that it wasn't a random murder, but one that had been carefully thought out — and thought out to hurt Eddie Archer by making Alistair appear guilty.

Logan asked them gravely if they believed there was any possibility that Alistair had committed the murder.

Madison said no — even the victim had told them that. And she seemed gratified when Logan accepted her words without ridicule.

Sean informed them that the clock in the security footage had lost time, while the recording itself had not. "Two minutes. Two minutes are missing from the clock," he said.

"Not a lot of time," Kelsey remarked. "And that isn't when the murder occurred. It's before the murder."

"So what does it mean? Think about it. Say you're underwater, holding your breath. Two minutes can be very long. And if you've plotted something out, two minutes might be all that's needed," Sean said.

"What do you think, Madison? You know the studio. What could you do with two minutes?" Logan asked.

"Well . . . the costume was on the mannequin, and I know that Knox believes we'll find it. The evil priest, Amun Mopat — who could wake the dead and make the mummy rise — came down from the tableau and killed Jenny. According to Alistair. So, if someone had been dressed as the priest and was waiting somewhere in the studio, it's possible that this person — dressed as Amun Mopat — did it. And I suppose you'd look more like Amun Mopat if you stole the robe. And if you could lose two minutes, you might have time to steal the costume you needed. . . . Could the video have been altered? Colin Bailey was out of the security area when he went to the Black Box with Alistair."

"There is no video of what happened in the tunnel," Sean said.

"Why?" Logan asked.

"There's never been a camera down there, I guess because there's a camera that catches anyone going into the Black Box Cinema, and there are several security cameras in the studio," Madison explained. "The museum is more like Eddie's private place. He loves it. And it isn't open much of the time. . . . There are security cameras at the studio because people *do* try to get hold of movie images before the movies are released. Piracy is pretty lucrative. But as for the museum . . . it's just tableaux."

"I think there *was* a security camera down there at one time, but as Madison said, it wasn't an area that anyone worried about," Sean added.

"If there's still an old camera — and if it was used — it probably wouldn't have been active on a Sunday night, anyway. The cinema's closed then. The cameras we do have aren't there because we expect anyone to be murdered. They're there to protect the studio. I assume it's kind of general knowledge that the museum isn't open on

Sundays, because the Black Box Cinema isn't open. And, I admit, you can't discredit the police for their assumptions. To believe that Alistair didn't do it is almost like believing the impossible. As Sean's pointed out to me, you'd really have to be familiar with the studio and the cinema to carry off such a feat. Then, you'd have to know Alistair. And you'd have to know that Jenny was coming — and if you knew that, you'd realize she came to coerce Alistair into showing her the main studio."

"But it *is* general knowledge that Alistair had a crush on Jenny, right?" Jane asked. "And that Jenny was an actress, that she could manipulate Alistair — and that Alistair often went to the Black Box by himself, on Sunday nights?"

Sean looked over at Jane, a slim, very pretty brunette. Of everyone on their team, he'd wondered if Jane would make it. She was an artist, although it was true that she'd worked with human skulls. And, of course, he'd been an artist of sorts himself. Surprisingly, perhaps, they'd all done well on their first assignment in Texas, considering that only three of them had come from a background in law enforcement. Jane had excelled at their courses at Quantico; she was a dead-on shot and would have made an excellent sniper.

"Yes, pretty general," Madison was saying. "I mean, people joked about it at the studio. No one disliked Jenny that I know of," she said. "And I don't think anyone disliked Alistair. He's a sweet kid without a chip on his shoulder at all. The jokes were the usual stuff, like how 'whipped' Alistair was. Some of the guys can be jaded. Jenny was amusing to them, and watching Alistair's reactions to her even more so." She turned to Sean. "And the priest's robe is gone. I *know* it was there, Sean."

Sean nodded, smiling at her. "I watched the security footage. The mannequin gets pushed back, pretty innocently, I suspect — at first. Then, there's the two-minute gap, the time discrepancy — that's when you can no longer see the mannequin in the dressing room area. I have the tech man at the station, Fontini, doing whatever he can to figure it out, and I'm going to talk to Bailey again. He might be the guard, but he's no tech wizard."

"Yes, but he was there, wasn't he?" Logan asked. "Except when he left the security station to go to the Black Box Cinema with Alistair. Have I got that right?"

Sean nodded.

"Okay, then," Logan said decisively. "Tomorrow we'll see the studio, and go to the morgue. Sean, you'll try to find out how the security footage was changed . . . and by whom."

"It's not a difficult trick, not in Hollywood. I'm good, but the kid at the police station is better. Fontini is doing his best, but whoever did it knew what he — or she — was doing."

"There's just one more question I have to ask," Logan said. "You're *sure* — really convinced — that Alistair Archer didn't kill Jenny? I know you 'spoke' with Jenny. Could she have been mistaken?"

"No," Sean said. "There's no discrepancy between her story and Alistair's. Someone came down from that tableau dressed as the priest, Amun Mopat, killed Jenny and managed to disappear without a trace. What we have to figure out is the how, and if we get that far, we can begin to figure out the who."

Madison bit her lip. "Sean's right. Their stories were exactly the same." She hesitated only a moment, surveying those around the table as if she couldn't believe she was with an entire group who might believe her words. "Jenny was certain that Alistair is innocent. She said he was coming back, trying to help her, and that he shouted at the man. She doesn't know who killed her. She does know that Alistair didn't."

"Then that's that," Logan said. He looked exhausted. "It's about four in the morning for us, coming in from Virginia. Right now we need some sleep. We'll get organized in the morning. Sean, take Katya and go to the morgue first thing. I'll head down to the police station and get the team set up there and meet with Knox. And we'll have the cops check out the vacant house across from Madison's. We'll gather at the studio around one. By late afternoon, Sean, the rest of us will go over the police notes, reinterview all the employees and scour the security logs for anyone else who's been in the studio recently. That'll leave you free to question those closest to the Archer family. Agreed?"

Nods went around the table. Kelsey stood. "Come on, Madison, we'll put you across the hall in 302. Tyler is in 301, and Kat and Jane will take 303. This side is 304, 305 and 306. You'll be safe here. I sincerely doubt this person is courageous enough — or foolish enough — to attack you between six FBI agents."

Madison rose uncertainly. "I'm not putting anyone out —"

"We've got the whole floor," Jane said.

Sean glanced at her, grateful for his team members. Jane and Kat had actually had

253

their own rooms, but were quick to accept the new arrangements. They really were a team, a family.

"Well, then, thank you," Madison said.

"I'll take you over," Kat told her, grabbing her bag.

As they left, Sean stood, Logan at his side.

"Eddie Archer is lucky he worked with you," Logan commented.

Sean shook his head, a half smile curving his lips. "Eddie Archer is smart. He looked me up, looked up the team and figured he knew what he needed. He's no fool. He knew, as well, that Madison has our talent. She's a trusted employee, but he told me right away that she spoke with dead people."

"Let's hope that doesn't put her in danger," Logan said thoughtfully.

"It already has," Sean muttered.

"Then we'd better solve this thing damned fast."

Sean nodded, bade Logan and the others good-night and went through the connecting door to his own room. The police reports were where he'd left them. He collected them and stacked them neatly; Logan would need them in the morning.

He lay down to sleep.

Two minutes missing. Two minutes in which to hide a mannequin — and steal a robe.

That was as good as two days if you knew what you were doing.

And then, as he fell asleep, he stopped thinking about the killer.

Because he was thinking about Madison.

He felt as if he'd known her forever. As if she'd been part of his life, part of his consciousness. But it had only been two days. . . .

Vengeance no longer needed to watch. There was something wrong. The girl knew she was in danger.

That damned Sean Cameron. It should have gone so smoothly. The police had seen what was there to be seen, and now —

The phone rang. Luckily, Vengeance was alone.

Seeing the number on the caller ID screen of the phone, Vengeance cursed silently. "What?"

"I'm scared."

"Don't be an idiot!"

"The investigation is getting serious. It was supposed to look like a locked-room mystery. Once Alistair was charged, that was supposed to be the end!"

"And it will continue to look that way."

"No, no, the FBI is all over the place."

"Even if they make discoveries, they'll

never know, they'll never understand, they'll never be able to trace the truth!"

She kept talking; she was panicking. Talk, talk, talk. Vengeance tried to be nicer, to be more reassuring.

"Just keep your story straight!" Vengeance warned.

She calmed down, and Vengeance reminded her again *not* to call.

"If I call you — that's one thing. Don't *you* call me."

Finally, Vengeance was able to hang up.

But Vengeance grew thoughtful.

Vengeance's partner was. . . .

Dangerous.

Vengeance's partner might have to meet with an accident.

"The M.E. is going to think we're ghouls," Madison whispered.

She'd come to the morgue again with Sean and Katya Sokolov, who'd been an M.E. in San Antonio before joining the Krewe.

They'd stopped at Madison's bungalow to feed Ichabod — and bring Bogie with them.

While it seemed natural to Madison that the team's only pathologist would want to view the body and the autopsy report, there was no ostensible reason for a civilian to be there a second time.

"Mortal remains, just mortal remains," Bogie told her. He grinned at Katya. "Now, while you may be the one with the experience in a morgue, you might want to stop staring at me. They'll think you're not right in the head, you know?"

Kat flushed. "Sorry! I'm still so . . . overwhelmed. You can't imagine what a fan I am."

"Thank you." Bogie looked at Madison. "Maybe that's why I hang around. I need the adulation."

"Shh," Sean warned.

"I feel like a ghoul," Madison whispered again.

"Trust me, you're fine. You're with me, and if anyone questions that, I'm asking you questions about the young woman as you knew her in life," Kat said. "Not to worry."

They were met then in reception by an attendant who escorted them back to a private autopsy room. Dr. Lee Chang was waiting there for them, standing silently behind the gurney that held the remains of the woman who had once been Jenny Henderson.

"Dr. Chang, thank you," Sean said. "I'd like you to meet Dr. Katya Sokolov, who is with our team. She'd like to go over your report with you."

"Of course. Dr. Sokolov, pleased to meet you," Chang said, shaking Kat's hand.

He offered her his clipboard. Kat came around the gurney, toward the counter where there was a sink and a huge overhead light.

Madison heard her speaking with Chang as he ushered her closer to the body. Bogie stood on the other side.

She tried not to breathe through her nose. She tried not to hear the trickle of water and smell the chemical scent that couldn't be disguised by any manner of freshener or filter.

Jenny, Madison said silently. She still found it difficult, but she touched the arm of the corpse. It astonished her that a human being could feel so absolutely stiff and cold.

Jenny's eyes opened. They became enormous as she stared not at Madison but at Bogie standing beside her.

Humphrey Bogart! Jenny said in silent awe.

In the — well, not in the flesh, kid. Bogie shook his head. *This is no place for a girl like you, Miss Henderson. There's got to be someplace you can go.*

I don't know how, Jenny said.

Come with us. Just will yourself. Get up, and come with us, Bogie urged.

258

Madison wanted to scream in protest. *No, living with one ghost is enough!*

I can't. I don't . . . I don't . . . I'm cold and I'm scared . . . but I can't.

Thank God, Madison thought for a moment. But that was wrong.

She squeezed Jenny's arm lightly. *You can. You can. Bogie did it, and if he did it, you can, too. Jenny, don't you want to help us catch your killer?*

Jenny nodded solemnly. She glanced from Bogie to Madison to Sean.

You're a cop, right? she asked him. *You came soon after I got here.* She smiled vaguely. *You know I always wanted to be in the movies,* she said. *I guess now . . .*

You're famous, Bogie told her. *And you'll become a legend when this is solved.*

"As you can see," Dr. Chang said, drawing Kat back to the autopsy table, "she was killed with one sure cut. The intention was to kill. I told Agent Cameron earlier that the strike itself was planned. Unopposed, the killer managed what he intended with ease."

Kat nodded. "Despite the fragile position of the artery, it's really not easy to aim so surely and deliver such a deadly strike. There are no hesitation wounds, and poor

Jenny doesn't have a defensive wound on her."

"The whole thing would have taken a matter of seconds," Dr. Chang said.

"Way less than two minutes," Sean commented.

Chang frowned, looking at him. "Yes, of course."

Sean stepped up behind Kat, grabbed her and mimed a knife and the blow.

"I think that was eight seconds," she said.

Sean released her. "And the killer didn't really need the extra time when he was in the tunnel because no camera was running there, and he knew it. I believe he had to be somewhere in the studio or down in the tunnel. Or even in the Black Box Cinema."

"Thank you, Dr. Chang," Kat said, shaking the M.E.'s hand again.

Are you coming? Bogie silently asked Jenny.

I'm naked and chopped to pieces, Jenny said.

No, just rise, and think about yourself in a favorite outfit. The flesh is nothing now, and the soul, the mind, are everything.

"Caleb will take you out," Chang said, indicating the assistant who had led them in.

As he did, Madison walked between Kat

and Sean. She knew that Bogie was behind her.

She felt a little prickle at her nape.

And she knew that Jenny had risen to join them, too.

Jenny was going to help. She was going to come with them, and relive her own murder at the scene of the crime.

9

Logan Raintree was still setting up the command center for the team in the designated room at the police station — and having his own briefing with Knox. When Sean called him, he discovered that the briefing was nearly finished, and that he and the others would still join them at one.

It was just noon, but Sean wanted to get to the studio as quickly as possible. He was convinced that if they could figure out how someone besides Alistair might have gotten in — how the robe had been stolen — they could get on with the rest of the puzzle.

And if they failed, at the very least they'd create reasonable doubt that Alistair was the killer.

But they *couldn't* fail. Because even with reasonable doubt, the press had branded him a killer, and he'd never live a normal life.

As much as Sean needed Madison, he was

afraid that after the previous night, it was no longer wise to involve her. Except that she was already involved and therefore targeted.

The other problem was that he was afraid to leave her anywhere on her own.

But nothing had really happened, he told himself. Bogie might well have been mistaken. He was very protective of his earthly charge.

But in his heart, he didn't believe that Bogie was wrong about the danger to Madison. The killer was devious, with a definite agenda, and wasn't going to let anyone stand in his or her way. Madison wasn't in law enforcement; she'd probably never even handled a gun.

As they drove away from the morgue, he decided he had to try to protect her. "Madison, I know this won't be easy for you, but I'm going to take you to the police station. We'll have you hang around in the team's ops center while we're at the studio and try to get the word out that you have nothing to do with the investigation anymore." He glanced at her in the rearview mirror. She was seated in back, between the ghostly Bogie and Jenny Henderson.

"Don't be ridiculous," she said.

"I'm concerned about your safety."

263

"So am I," Madison said. "But making me stay at the police station while you're at the studio is just . . . worthless. Last night, I felt pretty good — surrounded by six FBI agents. I'm still with FBI agents, so I'm still protected. And thinking you can get the word out that I'm not involved . . . please! Even I know that would be a useless effort."

"She's right, Sean," Kat said. "And she can help us at the studio. I honestly don't think anyone will try anything with all of us around." She turned and smiled back at Madison. "You don't mind hanging with us, do you? You slept okay last night?"

"Yes, I was fine, but I feel guilty, making someone give up a room."

"You didn't, not really," Kat said.

"Yes, I did," Madison said, smiling ruefully.

"My cousin and Logan have been a twosome since we began as a team," Sean explained.

"Kelsey and Logan," Kat put in.

"Kelsey is your cousin?"

"Yes," Sean said simply.

"Do family members usually work together?" she asked.

"No. Our teams are different, Madison. Because *we're* . . . different," Kat told her. "Anyway, you really didn't put anyone out.

Kelsey and Logan were in the king on one side of the suite's work area. Tyler had a room, Sean had his room on the other side of the work area, and it was no big deal for Jane and me to bunk together. We always did when we were in training." She turned to Sean. "But you never know . . . we may want to spend some time at Madison's bungalow. See what we can shake up."

Sean didn't reply. He still didn't like the idea that Madison was being used or could be in danger of any kind.

"We'll see," he murmured.

As he neared the studio and the Black Box Cinema, he saw that patrol cars were still standing guard. He parked his borrowed car just outside the yellow crime scene tape. As he did, he heard soft sobbing, and remembered that the spirit of Jenny Henderson was with them.

Then he heard Bogie reassuring her.

Dear God, the rest of the world would think they were totally insane. *Officers, today we have the victim with us. Painful, yes, but she's going to reenact what happened to her. It's okay. She has a damned decent guy to hold her hand. Bogie, you know him, right? Humphrey Bogart, legend of the silver screen.*

"Agent Cameron!" Duffy said, hailing him.

"Officer Duffy," Sean responded as he stepped out of the car. "We're going into the Black Box Cinema. The rest of the team will be along shortly."

"Yes, sir. We've been expecting you."

"Have you heard from Detective Knox?"

"Yes, sir. He's at the station, sir. I believe he'll be coming here with your people."

The others exited the car, as well.

Duffy frowned, as if perplexed, and suddenly shivered as Bogie and Jenny passed by. He looked sheepishly at Sean. "California," he said. "Los Angeles. You're burning up one minute and freezing the next."

"Right." Sean nodded as he walked on.

They neared the door to the Black Box Cinema.

Jenny stopped suddenly and burst into tears.

"I was murdered here!" she cried. "*Murdered* . . . and you want me to go inside and relive what happened . . . and walk through pools of my own blood?"

Officer Duffy was watching them, Sean knew. They couldn't appear to be a pack of lunatics; dealing with the local police was difficult enough as it was.

"Please, Jenny!" Madison whispered.

"We need you, kid," Bogie said. He had an arm around Jenny's shoulders, strong

266

and supportive.

No good.

Jenny was still sobbing.

Sean could see the strained expressions on the faces of his living companions.

Madison walked up to him, took his arm and whispered, "Oh, God, Sean, should we be doing this to her?"

"Do you want to help the living?" he asked.

"Yes, but . . ."

He wasn't happy about what they were doing himself. He just knew they had to use any method they could to find the truth. Duffy kept staring at them; thankfully, Bogie had managed to move Jenny along.

As they approached the front door to the cinema, Jenny again tried to hang back. Her tears were coming in a geyser, despite Bogie's attempts to calm her down.

Sean waited until they were inside. To the best of his knowledge, the only camera running was the one that scanned anyone trying to enter.

Torn, he tried to touch Jenny, but of course, he couldn't. He could only feel the cold where his hand stirred the air. Lamely he said, "Jenny, I'm so sorry. I am so, so sorry. But you did care about Alistair. Jenny, you said you felt guilty about using him.

Maybe you can redeem yourself by helping us. We really need you to do that. It would be such a good thing for Alistair and Eddie and all of us — and God knows, you must want to catch this bastard."

She wiped her cheeks and tried to square her shoulders. "Do you think I can . . . make up for the bad things I did?" she asked hopefully.

"We stay around for a reason, Jenny," Bogie said. "This may be your reason."

"And I do want that bastard nailed to the wall and skinned alive!" she said.

"I'm not sure we can make *that* happen," Sean told her, trying to smile.

It worked; she smiled back through her tears.

"Everything's okay. We're with you," Madison assured her.

As they walked through the lobby, Jenny sniffed. "I . . . I can almost smell the popcorn," she said.

"There *is* a nice scent of popcorn in the air," Kat agreed.

They passed the cinema, and Sean paused. "Jenny, was the door really open when you arrived?"

Jenny shook her head. "No."

"I didn't see you opening it on the security footage," Sean said.

"I was really careful. I knew there was a camera so I hid my movements with my body," Jenny admitted. "I had a key."

"How did you get the key?"

"I'd taken Alistair's earlier in the week and had a copy made. Can you tell him that?" she asked. "I'm sure he feels horrible. He really loves and admires his dad."

"Of course we will!" Madison said. "What happened to your key?"

"I — I don't know. I slid it back in my pocket, I think."

Sean made a mental note to ask Knox and the medical examiner about the key.

They walked through the office. The poster hiding the door had been moved aside, as it was whenever the museum was open to the public. They started down the stairs to the tunnel, Bogie holding on to Jenny, who clung to him as if she were going to a second execution.

She was, in a way.

They moved past the tableaux. Ahead, Sean could see the chalk marks and the blood still on the floor. He wondered if bringing Jenny here could really help.

"Hey," he said to her. "You said Alistair didn't do it. We believe that. In fact, we *know* it, thanks to you. You don't want to see him go to prison for the rest of his life, do you?

Or . . . worse?"

Jenny looked back at him. "No," she said solemnly. "No. I'm sorry — I'm dead, and I'm still being a coward. What can happen to me in this place now? No, no, you're right. I can fight back. I can help you."

She led the way.

They walked by *The Maltese Falcon, Citizen Kane* and *The Glass Key.* And then *Laura, Casablanca* and more.

Bogie, Sean noted, paused for a moment, a look on his face that was so poignant Sean felt his own heart skip a beat. But the horrible tinny smell of blood and death seemed to have become more intense since he'd entered the tunnel, and he knew that tomorrow, they'd have to bring in the hazmat clean-up crews. It was important that they get it right today, that they get whatever they could.

They reached the last tableau. *Sam Stone and the Curious Case of the Egyptian Museum.*

Jenny stood very still, staring at the chalk on the floor. And the blood.

Then she pointed to the tableau. "It's like it's just a touch off-kilter."

"I thought so, too," Madison said. "But the cops were up there — they probably didn't know how to put it back exactly right."

Jenny nodded distractedly. "We saw the tableau — it's Alistair's favorite film! Then he noticed that the door leading into the studio was already ajar. It should've been closed and locked. When he walked ahead, I heard a noise. I caught a glimpse of gold braid on a sleeve. I tried to turn, but then *he* had me. He came up behind me. I was so stunned and so scared . . . I screamed. Alistair came back — but even as he did, I felt the blade. . . ." She touched her neck. "I don't really remember the pain. I remember the spurt of blood and thinking, Wow, that's so much blood. I'm going to die. And then . . . then I was cold, and the world seemed blank until . . . I knew I was dead. I could feel no pain, and I just wanted to sleep and pretend it wasn't real. There was the morgue — so humiliating. And then . . . then I heard *you* speak to me!" she said, turning to Sean.

"Jenny, this is important," Sean said. "Was there still a priest in the tableau when there was a robed guy with a blackout on his face behind you?"

She frowned. "I — I don't know. I didn't look at the tableau again. I remember falling — or being flung down. And I remember

271

seeing Alistair's face. I think he wanted to fight for me. He would have died for me. He never got the chance."

"Did the killer say anything, Jenny?" Sean asked.

She thought for a minute, then shook her head. "No. Alistair screamed at him, but he didn't say anything at all. The last thing I recall was Alistair shouting and trying to reach me. He started to rush forward . . . and went down in the blood. My blood."

"Is that it?" Bogie asked. His voice was low, rough and raspy. Jenny seemed to be holding her own, but Bogie was torn by the pain of it. "Is it okay if we leave?"

"Yes, you can take her out. Thank you, Bogie," Sean said.

Bogie walked her back toward the Black Box Cinema, one arm around her. They seemed to disappear before they got to the stairs.

"Where did this get us?" Madison demanded. Her eyes were narrowed. Accusing.

"To the world of illusion," Sean told her. He stepped over the velvet cord into the tableau and walked through the scene, studying each character.

Kat and Madison stood there quietly, observing him.

"We need to watch *Sam Stone and the Curious Case of the Egyptian Museum,*" Sean muttered.

"I know you think the movie might have something to do with the murder," Madison said, "but how? And are we talking about the original or the remake?"

"The original. Alistair was watching the movie. The killer knew he'd be watching it, and dressed up as one of the characters — as the *killer* in the movie, to be precise." Sean went from mannequin to mannequin. They were just that. Nothing flesh and blood about them at all.

But the killer had been flesh and blood. No question of that. So how had he gotten in and out?

Sean left the tableau, aware that Kat and Madison were studying him intently. "Okay," he said. "Right now, we don't know how the killer got down here. But he manipulated two minutes from the security video. I think he got in here somehow and that he knew where to hide. Kat, how much blood would he have on him if he caught her from behind? Would he be covered in it?"

"Not necessarily. Not if the blood spurted forward and he pushed her away from him immediately. I'm assuming he'd have gotten *some* on him. From the knife, certainly. And a sleeve probably would have had to have caught some. From what we've reconstructed of the attack, the flow of blood would've been forward."

Madison was still watching him, frowning. She moved from the position where Jenny had been seized toward the door that led to the studio. She shook her head, looking at Sean, a baffled expression on her face.

"Even if it was just a few drops . . . if the killer had gone this way, he'd have tracked blood. I can't believe he escaped through the studio," she said. "Surely, there would've been something here, some clue."

The crime scene unit had gone over the tunnel with fine-tooth combs. But they'd *expected* to find blood there. Spatter, spray . . . drops.

Because Alistair had run back through the tunnel to reach Bailey over at the studio.

Dropping low, Sean began to inspect the area of the tableau again. And it was then that he noticed the slight smear on the skirt of the Dianna Breen mannequin.

"He came back this way," Sean said.

Both of the woman looked at him in surprise. "He came back this way," he repeated, "and then . . ."

The backdrop was black. A black-painted

274

plaster wall. Sean walked over and began to tap it. The sound was hollow.

"There's something behind the tableau," he said.

Standing next to him, Madison tapped, as well. They heard the same hollow sound, and she turned to him with large eyes. "But there's nothing back there. We're actually underground now, Sean. This is just a tunnel."

"We may be underground, and this may be a tunnel," he said. "But there *is* something back there. Keep tapping, press on things — there has to be a release here somewhere. I *know* the killer came back this way."

They spent the next few minutes pushing, prodding, tapping the wall. They were still at it when Sean heard Logan calling out to him. The others had arrived.

"Logan! We're in the tunnel." He stepped down and waited for Logan, Jane, Tyler and Kelsey to join them.

"You've done a great job getting along with Knox," Logan said. "He was receptive to us and actually helpful. We have the notes from all the employee interviews, and he gave us lists of others we might want to question. That's pretty good, considering how unusual it is that the FBI would be called in for one murder in his jurisdiction."

"He was a little annoyed at first. I guess he's resigned, maybe even glad. Whatever happens, he won't be the fall guy."

"So, you've found something?" Kat asked. "This is quite a place. And eerie — the tableaux are really excellent, and being down here is kind of creepy."

"A special-effects studio filled with monsters and surrounded by a cemetery," Tyler commented. "And the work I've seen here is amazing."

Madison smiled at him. "It is an amazing place," she agreed.

"The cemetery was always here," Sean said. "If I remember correctly, the property was all owned by the previous owner — or his father. His father or grandfather, first. They donated the land for the cemetery in the late 1800s. The studio was built in the 1930s, right?"

"Maybe a bit later," Madison said. "The early 1940s."

"Someone had a sense of humor," Kat remarked. "Building a special-effects studio — known for fantastic zombies, mummies and vampires, among other creatures — beside a cemetery."

"Forget the cemetery for now," Sean said. "There's something behind this wall, and I want to know what it is. Or I should say — there *isn't* something. If you listen, you can tell there's no earth behind it."

"You think there's some kind of hidden door here?" Logan asked.

"Yes, but I can't find any mechanism."

The rest of the team joined them, tapping, stamping on the floor, feeling for cracks in the wall's surface.

"We could break it down," Tyler Montague suggested. "We'd need to get some sledge-hammers. . . ."

Sean grinned. Tyler was as muscled as a linebacker. He *could* break it down.

"I think we have to find the trap door or whatever it is," Sean said. "Or come at it from the other side."

"How do we get to the other side?" Madison asked.

"Do you remember I told you that the elevator in the studio could reach the basement?" Sean said. "We have to get Eddie to come over with the key that'll take it down there. The tunnel connects to the studio here. There has to be another tunnel on the opposite side. I'm going to call Eddie and ask him to bring the key."

"And instead of breaking things down while we wait," Logan said, "Madison can show the rest of us the studio."

"Of course." Madison gestured at the door. "We can go that way. I'm sure the forensics teams have gotten everything they can."

"They're just waiting for us to finish in here," Logan said. "Madison, if you would."

Madison glanced at Sean, almost as though she wanted his approval, and when he nodded, she led the others through the connecting door.

Sean found himself alone in the tunnel.

He stood very still for a moment. But he was truly alone. He didn't know where Bogie had taken Jenny, but he was sure she was in good company.

No . . . there was nothing that hinted of a world beyond in the tunnel now. There was nothing at all, except for the sickening smell of blood.

Madison felt as if she was taking a tour group through the studio. Sean's team members were careful and polite, oohing and aahing over the work they saw going on. Logan Raintree was more somber, asking her about lockdown and the current projects, particularly *The Unholy.*

"Anticipation can be the impetus that makes a movie score big at the box office," Madison explained. "So, when we're working on comic characters or some kind of movie monster — especially when there's a nice budget, and it's an important movie for a production studio — we go into lockdown. And you know that we're working on the remake of *Sam Stone and the Curious Case of the Egyptian Museum*." She brought them over to her workstation. "Right now, I'm fabricating all the costumes for Sam Stone, who's being played by Oliver Marshall. He comes here for his fittings. He was due back in this week for his last one. I don't know what the schedule will be now, and I haven't heard from Mike." She paused a moment, then began to explain. "In the movie, Sam is slipped some drugs, and the priest is able to make him believe that jackals and other monsters come to life. He battles that in his mind. We work with foam and latex and all kinds of materials to create them." She lifted one of the tarps covering her work. "He's wearing typical contemporary clothing in most of the movie, but in the hallucination scenes, he has ancient Egyptian weaponry. Of course, a number of scenes are done with his stunt double. In the fight scenes, he's got a helmet on, so you don't see his face most of the time. When the stunt double's working he wears a face shield. In this case, it's easy. The

279

helmet goes over . . ."

Her words trailed off as she raised a piece of black cloth. The material was so sheer it could go over an actor's face and still allow him to see and breathe.

And when an actor wore a headpiece made of that material, he appeared to have no face at all. It worked extremely well for long shots when the stunt double was stepping in for the actor; sometimes, the character was too distant for the facial features to be clearly seen, and sometimes, the face could be digitized in.

She looked at Logan and swallowed.

"This . . . this is what the killer must have used," she said in a hushed voice. "Both Jenny and Alistair said he had no face. If you had a headpiece of this stuff on under a hood, it would look like you were . . . faceless."

Sean went out to meet Eddie Archer when he'd arrived at the studio. He wasn't alone; he was with a woman, and to Sean's surprise, it wasn't Helena LaRoux, his present wife. Eddie had come within minutes of being called, and he was accompanied by Benita Lowe, his ex-wife.

Benita was beautiful, but then Eddie was attracted to women who were showpieces.

She was about five-foot-five, with raven-dark hair, deep brown eyes and exotic features. She was smart, too, and when it seemed that she was getting nothing but supporting roles and leads in B movies, she'd segued into producing and directing, performing only when she was offered a role she really wanted. Sean didn't know what had really split the two of them up; there'd been rumors that she was unfaithful, according to Madison. But then, this was indeed Hollywood, and when there weren't any good rumors to go around, some storyteller would invent one.

"Sean!" Despite her solemnity, Benita said his name with warmth. "It's wonderful to see you. I'm just sorry about the circumstances."

"I'm sorry, too, Benita, but it's good to see you. You're doing well?"

"Yes, very, thank you. I've been wanting to see Eddie, and we got our chance today. We were at lunch. I wanted him to know that he and Alistair have my undying support."

Eddie watched the exchange in silence. "Sean, you have something?" he asked.

Sean nodded. "Eddie, I'd like to take the elevator down to the basement in the studio."

Frowning, Eddie shook his head. "No one's been down there in at least a decade. I'm sure I have the only key. It could be really dangerous down here."

"Where does the basement lead?"

"What do you mean, where does it lead?" Eddie repeated. "It's a basement. Basements don't lead anywhere."

"I think this one does," Sean said.

"Leave it to the master of illusion." Benita gave him a glimmer of a smile.

"I just need the key. Don't worry about any danger. This is what I do now, and my team and I know how to be careful."

"I'll go with you. I may remember something when we're down there," Eddie said.

"The scene hasn't been cleared yet," Sean reminded him.

"The Black Box Cinema and the tunnel museum haven't been cleared yet," Eddie corrected. "The studio — we're opening it for work tomorrow."

Sean looked across the lot, where Duffy and other officers were still on duty. He didn't want to take a chance on someone thinking Eddie Archer might taint evidence.

"I know what you're thinking," Eddie said. "But everyone figures we've got a conflict of interest here to begin with, rather than realizing you're going to understand the cinema and the studio better than any other cop. I'll go with you to the studio and down to the basement. If you find anything after that, I'll keep my distance."

Eddie was grim and determined, and Sean gave in.

"Benita, do you mind waiting?" he asked.

"Well, of course I mind. I'm scared of being anywhere around this place," she said.

"Benita, there are a pack of cops out here. I'd say you were safe. And I'd rather not have to worry about your prints being somewhere," Sean told her.

"How long do they stay on a surface? Because my prints are already all over this place. I used to be married to Eddie, remember? And I came to the studio frequently back then."

"Yeah, but they won't be in the basement, and that's the point. Please wait here," Sean said again.

"Please," Eddie echoed. "Do as Sean asks."

She let out a deep sigh, and then stroked Eddie's cheek. "All right." She turned to Sean. "I expect you to get this whole mess sorted out, okay?" Looking back at Eddie, she said, "I know you'll want to head home or to the hospital when you're done, but I'll hang around for a bit, anyway."

"That's kind of you, Benita," Eddie murmured.

Benita walked toward Eddie's car and slipped into the passenger seat. She had a way of walking that Sean could only describe as *stylized*. So did Helena, but hers was different.

"I told you, Sean. I'm here to provide anything you need — anytime," Eddie said.

"Thanks. You can meet the team in a few minutes. Let's get to the studio and the elevator. I want to go to that basement."

"I'm not sure the elevator will even go there anymore. I can't remember the last time I took it down that far," Eddie muttered. "A decade ago at least. Lord, I don't know if there's any light down there."

"You have the elevator inspected, right?"

"Yes, of course. It's just that we never use the basement. Anything we tried to store down there deteriorated too quickly. The place was too damp, I guess. We didn't really need the space so didn't bother with it."

"Then the elevator should work, and I'll get a flashlight from Bailey. I know he'll have a bunch — he's prepared for the earthquake that'll rip out our electrics," Sean said. He winced at the word *our*. He hadn't worked here in years. He'd always have a soft spot for the studio, though, and would probably always feel a part of it. He'd been an adult — but young, just out of college — when he worked here, so the place was an influential part of his past. The people, too . . .

Colin Bailey was at the security station, as Sean had expected. He snapped to attention when he saw Eddie. Although Eddie was distracted, he seemed aware of Colin's attempts to reassure him and was cordial in return.

Sean procured a large lantern-size flashlight from Bailey and steered Eddie into the office side of the studio and toward the elevator. It was fairly large, a necessity when taking large props or costume pieces from one level to another or to one of the storage areas.

Eddie's fingers seemed to tremble as he fit the key into the lock that would allow the elevator to go down to the basement level. "It's been so long. So long . . ." he whispered as they stepped inside.

The elevator didn't squeak or protest. A moment later, it came to a silent and slightly jarring halt. The door opened.

A black hole seemed to gape before them. A maw. *Stygian* was the word that came to Sean's mind. The basement was pitch-dark and smelled of must, earth, decay.

Sean turned on the flashlight and let it blaze around him. The basement seemed empty, and he couldn't see anything other than the concrete support beams that stood here and there.

Until he saw the arm bone jutting through the side wall, brilliant and opalescent as the light fell upon it.

"So, it's highly probable that the killer stole some of this cloth to hide himself," Logan said. "Do you know how much you had? Is there a way to find out how much is missing?"

Madison shook her head. "No. When it gets low, we just reorder it. It's a staple in many special-effects studios. There could've been dozens of small snatches of it in the remnant bin."

"Where's that?"

"Over there, beside the shelves." She pointed to what looked like massive bookshelves against the wall, surrounded by some of the rat creatures. There weren't any books on the shelves, just endless bolts of fabric — bolts of metallic cloth and glossy knits in brilliant colors, the better to create the world of *The Unholy*. Right now, there was a lot of "blackout" material.

"The large green garbage can against the

wall has remnants in it. We usually have remnants of this stuff because the fabric is delicate and I probably do at least ten masks for a stunt double during filming," Madison explained.

"I assume," Logan said, "that anyone could have helped themselves to a few remnants and not been noticed, correct?"

"Who'd really notice anything around here?" Jane asked, and laughed. "I've worked with dozens of human skulls, sketched hundreds of crime scenes," she said. "But this . . . *this* is creepy."

"I work with dead bodies and I have to agree," Kat said.

"Wait until you see all the mannequins in the hall," Madison warned her.

"I can only imagine," Jane said, staring at their fabricated victims from the Victorian murder movie — Miss Mary, Parson Bridge and Myra Sue.

"Things aren't half as creepy as real people," Tyler stated, and they all nodded. "They're good, but remember — they're not real, they're just *things*."

"Yeah, but it's about the emotions good props create," Jane said with a shrug. "I wouldn't want to be locked up alone in this place."

"It *is* a little creepy when there aren't

many people here, and you're not sure where your coworkers are," Madison told her, smiling. Then her smile faded. "But it never bothered me . . . before."

"Madison, can you give us about half a yard of that fabric?" Logan asked.

"Of course." She went to the bin and pulled out a piece.

As she did, a phone rang, and she heard Logan pick up.

"Right away," he said.

Madison stared at him, as did the others.

"What?" she mouthed.

"We're needed in the basement. Sean and Eddie will meet us at the elevator on this level."

"He needs all of us? What did he find?" Madison asked.

"A bone," Logan said. "A human bone."

10

Despite the heavy-duty lantern, it was difficult to see much in the basement.

But the bone, Sean was certain, was real — and human. He'd soon know for sure; Eddie had taken his key to go back to the first floor and bring the others down to the basement. Kat Sokolov would recognize immediately what they had.

The basic structure of the basement was sound, but there were areas where the concrete that constructed the below-ground walls was worn through. The hard-packed earth beyond might have created pressure on the sides. He'd found the bone stuck in the wall, and what it meant, Sean had no idea.

"It is real, and it is human. A humerus. Hard to say exactly how old," Kat said, studying the bone. "Are there . . . more?"

"No, just that one bone. It came out of the wall," Sean told her.

"Oh, God. Oh, God, what else?" Eddie moaned.

Madison cleared her throat. "Eddie, we're bordering the graveyard here." She looked at Sean. "Is it possible that this arm bone belongs to someone long dead — and with time, it's worked its way through? I don't know that much about funerary processes and certainly not in the 1800s, but weren't pine boxes allowed back then? We've only recently — in human history, that is — learned that disease can be spread, so we started using sealed coffins."

"Yeah, it's possible," Sean said.

"Yes, and it would make sense." Kat seemed relieved.

Sean went to stand by the elevator entrance and surveyed the room. Yes, the basement was larger than the structure above. It stretched beneath the property border, he thought.

"I — I'll need to get someone down here to shore up the walls, make repairs." Eddie sighed. "Oh, Lord, we may have to — to get real structural changes made. I don't think this can be legal. Or up to code. I didn't realize how far the basement juts out. I never spent enough time down here."

"Well, we might have the mystery of the bone solved," Sean said. "But I still think there has to be another tunnel — leading to the Black Box Cinema."

He paused for a minute, getting his bearings, and then walked in the direction of the cinema. He felt a presence right behind him and swung around; it was Madison.

She stopped. There was a smudge of dirt on her nose and he smiled. "You're afraid of the dark?" he asked her.

"I just like to see where I'm going," she said. "And you have the light."

Actually, he saw that the whole group was behind him. He looked back at them all. "This isn't going to work. We need more light," he said.

"I'll go up and see what Colin Bailey can rig up for us," Eddie announced.

"I'll go with you," Jane volunteered.

"I guess I'm not really trusted, am I?" Eddie said. "Everyone's under suspicion, right?"

Jane laughed. "Well, that's true — until we have an answer, we can't really trust *anyone.* But it's not that, Eddie. I just happen to prefer the light."

"An FBI agent who doesn't like the dark," Eddie said, managing a smile.

"Hey! We're human, too. Let's go get some light," Jane encouraged him.

"We have to report the bone to the proper

authorities," Kat said. "Even if it is an old bone. For one thing, there are health issues at stake. Not to mention the dignity of human remains."

"Yes, we will report it. But not yet," Sean told her.

"No, not yet," Kat agreed. "We're supposed to start meeting with the employees in another forty-five minutes, Logan," she reminded him, touching the illuminator on her watch.

"We'll help Sean get some lighting rigged up and then we'll head out," Logan said.

Sean kept feeling along the walls. The place had been built properly, but some of the concrete had been weakened. So far, he hadn't come across anything suspicious. Madison was testing the walls, too — close behind him.

They heard the elevator's soft whisper as it rose again with Eddie and Jane on board. The silence in the darkened basement was eerie as the rest of them continued to walk along the walls, tapping here and there.

"Let's divide and conquer," Sean suggested.

They did so. Sean knew that a few of his team might think he was looking for something that didn't exist. But the rule was that if one of them had a hunch, they all cooperated in seeking the truth behind that person's suspicion or theory.

It wasn't long before the elevator returned to the basement, bearing Eddie and Colin Bailey. Colin had brought not just more flashlights, but cord and nails so they could rig the lights around the basement.

"Agent Everett is acting as security while I'm down here," Bailey told Sean earnestly. "I thought that was all right, seeing as how she's an agent and all."

"That's fine, Colin," Sean said, taking the cord. "Let's see if we can get the angles and corners covered, and position the lights to help us see around the support beams, as well."

They set to work; when they were done with the rigging, Logan spoke to Sean. "Sean, we'll leave you and Madison here, working on whatever you can find. We have appointments to start interviewing employees down at the station, plus the friend Jenny talked to before going to the studio. I could put it off, I suppose, but I don't want to. If each of us takes on a few more people to question, I can have Tyler stay with you two down here. Safety in numbers."

"That sounds fair," Tyler said. "And I agree. It was arranged that we'd do the interviews this afternoon. All those people will be showing up, so we need to go ahead with it."

"But if the three of you stay here, you might discover something. And remember, we're a team. If you find anything, we can all spread out tomorrow. And it's not that we won't share our information with the police, but I'd rather we got first crack."

"Amen," Sean murmured.

"We should take the initiative," Tyler agreed.

"Works for me," Sean said, grinning at his old friend. He'd known both Logan and Tyler Montague before their team was formed. They'd been Rangers in Texas, and he'd been on call with various law enforcement agencies in San Antonio and other areas of Texas, especially when the police were baffled by security footage. Tyler was a good man who always had his back. He glanced at Madison to see if she seemed frightened or ill at ease. She didn't; she looked as if she was anxious to continue their search.

In fact, she said a quick goodbye to the others and returned to examining the walls, running her hands over them, heedless of lichen or mold.

"Hey!" Sean called to Logan as he stepped into the elevator.

"Yeah?"

"Set the elevator to rise and then toss me the key — we'll want to get out of here at some point!"

Logan nodded and did as Sean had asked. When he threw the key, Sean caught it smoothly and pocketed it. He didn't relish the idea of discovering that they were stuck in the basement, calling for help. So far, his phone service had worked down here, but he didn't have much power left.

Again, they heard the soft whir of the elevator as the others left, Colin Bailey going back with them to take over his post so Jane could accompany Logan and Kat to the police station.

Sean wondered how useful it would be to question all the employees, many of whom were relatively recent. The more he delved into the situation, the more he became convinced that the murderer was someone who knew the studio *extremely* well.

Except . . . who knew this building, especially this basement, as well as Eddie Archer?

They began again, working in silence, each on a different side, leaving only the area around the elevator unexamined. As time passed, Sean began to feel that maybe he'd been mistaken. Maybe the basement was just a basement — and the fact that it extended into the cemetery had been kept quiet to avoid problems and complications with property ownership, the cemetery, health codes.

Suddenly Madison let out a whoop of triumph. "There's something here — it's a door!"

He hurried over to her. All the basement walls seemed to be damp and covered in a thin patina of lichen. But, as Madison had done, Sean ran his fingers over that section of wall. And he felt what she'd felt. There was a break, a thin line that indicated the wall wasn't solid concrete.

But the almost imperceptible groove was going in the wrong direction. It was far from the wall that should lead to the cinema, if such a wall, such a doorway, existed.

"It seems wedged," he said. He set his strength against it, and the door started to give.

"Hey, Tyler, come and help!" he called.

Tyler stooped low to put pressure on the bottom while Sean did the same at the top.

"There must be some mechanism holding it in place," Tyler said.

As Madison watched them struggle, she squinted, studying the wall. A moment later, she stepped between them and ran her hands down the opposite side, across from the slit that had shown them there was an opening. She saw what Sean hadn't. There was an actual lever. The discoloration caused by the dampness had hidden it, and made it look like part of the wall.

When she pulled the lever down, the door slid open with only a slight creaking sound. It was a narrow door, with just enough space for one person to slip through.

Sean raised his lantern as Tyler and Madison stood behind him.

For a moment, they were silent.

"Oh," Madison said weakly.

"Well, there *is* another tunnel," Tyler said.

And there was. It led through what appeared to be an underground labyrinth of catacombs. They could see where the walls ahead of them broke and the light diffused, leading to other tunnels. On either side of the tunnel before them there were shelves; some had slabs, the kind found in mausoleums around the world. Some of the slabs were broken, while some had completely fallen away. A few still retained very old plaques, announcing the names of the deceased who lay within the tombs. Some remains were in shabby coffins, old wood that was deteriorating. A few of the deceased were in shrouds, and spiderwebs rather than plaster or stone were their only cover.

"Oh," Madison said again.

"Wow." Tyler looked at Madison. "Those aren't, uh, any kind of special effects, are they?"

Her eyes were huge and bright in the eerie lantern light. "No. No, I don't think so," she told him. "The cemetery was actually the first thing on these grounds, so I believe that . . . I believe these are very old underground vaults."

Sean touched the Glock .22 he wore at almost all times, just for reassurance that it was there. He wasn't expecting trouble from the dead; he was sure someone living had recently traveled through the tunnel. But he didn't intend to be caught down there and surprised by a killer.

"I feel like we've just stepped into a Hammer film — and that we'll find Vincent Price at the end of the walkway, guarding a tomb," Tyler murmured.

Sean grinned. He hadn't expected such a comment from Tyler. He was glad to see that Madison was smiling, too. She might deal in special effects, but it was truly unsettling to be down here, as if they were entombed in the dank, dark, coffinlike interior of the basement, especially now with scores of buried dead stretching before them.

"Vincent Price was cremated," Madison said, "and his ashes were scattered over Point Dume in Southern California." She flushed. "I was a huge fan," she explained. "According to his reputation, he was one of the nicest men, as well as being brilliant on film."

"And he's upstairs — a likeness of him, anyway — in the tableau of a scene from *Laura,*" Sean said absently, taking a step into the tunnel. "If he was here I'm willing to bet he'd give us a hand." He wished then that Bogie was still with them. He might have known more about the cemetery and the original owner of the studio and property.

"Wait!" Madison said. "You're not going in there now, are you?"

He stepped back, looking at her. "Yes."

"We could get help," she said.

"I don't want help right now, Madison," he said slowly. "Until we've got the whole team back, I don't want to tell anyone we've discovered the door. I'd like to check out the place and see what we can find first." He hesitated. "Tyler can take you back up, if you want, and arrange for one of the policemen out there to get you to the station."

She shook her head vehemently. "No . . .

299

Tyler's not taking me anywhere and leaving you down here alone!"

"Only the living can hurt me, Madison. And I'm armed," he said. "FBI agent, remember?"

"Anyone can be in danger — especially alone," Madison argued stubbornly.

"Madison, I'm a really good shot."

"You don't have eyes in the back of your head."

"I have Tyler."

"I don't want to go up. I'm less afraid these days when I'm with you and your team," she said.

"I'm just waiting for direction," Tyler said quietly.

"Madison, you don't have to do this."

Madison kept staring at Sean. She shook her head. "If you're going, so am I. In between the two of you, of course."

Sean breathed a sigh of exasperation. "All right! If I can't get rid of you —"

"You can't get rid of me."

It wasn't proper procedure to involve a civilian to this extent. But, then again, there wasn't anything that smacked of the ordinary or "proper" about their team.

The three of them began the trek down the tunnel, moving slowly. Sean shifted his light, studying the wall, the crypts and the floor, searching for any sign of blood.

He nearly stepped on a femur that had fallen from one of the decayed crypts.

"Some of these must have been illegal burials, even in the late 1800s," Madison whispered, her hand curling around his arm as she came up close behind him. Her voice sounded eerie in the close and fetid air beneath the ground.

"Possibly. And maybe not for a bad reason. Maybe their loved ones didn't have the money for a legitimate burial," Sean said.

"Maybe," Tyler said. He pointed at a simple brass plaque on one of the memorials. "Juan Diaz, born 1891. Beloved. Maybe some of these folks were illegal immigrants, and whoever allowed them to be buried here was doing their families a favor."

"That would make sense," Madison said. "I, um, I know the previous owner." She winced. "He haunts the cemetery sometimes. I think he would've condoned something like this out of kindness."

Sean was only half listening. They'd reached the first fork in the underground labyrinth and his light had picked up something on the floor.

He bent low and touched the stain, then examined it carefully. Tyler and Madison hovered over him. "Blood," he said.

He threw his light to the left. There were more droplets and one larger stain.

"He came this way," he said. "The killer came this way."

"And the tunnel leads back to the northwest," Tyler added.

"Back . . . to the Black Box Cinema?" Madison asked.

Sean nodded. He started to follow the blood trail, walking faster. The tunnels must have contained several hundred burials, and there had to be an exit somewhere that led up to a mausoleum or memorial aboveground, unless it had been destroyed sometime in the past century. But he was pretty sure he knew how the killer had gotten in and out.

He hadn't realized how quickly he was moving until he stopped and Madison crashed hard into his back. At that moment he recognized that he liked the way she clung to him. He liked the softness of her body against his, the sweet scent of her hair and perfume that was a buffer against the scent of death. He wanted to hold her, tell her they were all right, but this wasn't the time — and certainly not the place.

"We're here" was all he said.

"Where?" she asked.

He pointed to the wall before them. It was

302

cleaner than the rest of the walls had been, as if someone had discovered it some time ago and taken pains to figure out how it worked.

"There's got to be another lever to open this wall," Sean said. "And I can guarantee you — it's going to open straight into the tableau of *Sam Stone and the Curious Case of the Egyptian Museum*."

Tyler stepped forward as Sean held up the light. Madison remained between the two of them, but closer to Sean. He had to concentrate on what he was doing. He suddenly wished he'd insisted she go to the police station. He tried to separate his physical reactions and emotions toward Madison from the work at hand. He was skilled at total concentration — usually. And yet it was good to smell her hair and wash away the scent of the bodies surrounding him, if only for a few sweet breaths.

"Got it!" Tyler shouted.

He pulled the lever, and a small section slid back. There was a whisper of metal against metal.

They found themselves staring at the backs of the mannequins — the slightly off-kilter exhibit of Sam Stone, his heroine Dianna Breen and the killer Egyptian priest, Amun Mopat.

"You were right!" Madison said softly.

Sean nodded.

"Um, should we go out this way?" she asked.

He smiled and set his hand on her shoulder. "No, we're closing the door, and we're going back the way we came. I want to keep it quiet for now that we've discovered the killer's mode of entry and exit. We still have to figure out exactly what he did and gather some of the forensic evidence from the tunnels. Tomorrow, we'll bring in the rest of the team — and more light. We know the how. We still need to figure out the *who*."

She released a shaky breath. "But . . . Eddie and Colin Bailey know we've been in the basement."

"And we'll come up frustrated, pretending we made a mistake — that I made a mistake. There's a lot more research we have to do before we make any of our findings known."

"Okay," she said. "But shouldn't we tell Alistair?"

"We will in time," Sean said.

Tyler's deep voice was reassuring. "He'll learn soon enough. We're moving fast on this, Madison."

"It's so sad to think of him sitting there in a mental hospital. He wasn't crazy at all —

isn't crazy at all. Everything happened just as he said," she murmured.

"We've got to close this up and get back now," Sean ordered.

She nodded and stiffened her shoulders. "Let's do it!"

She started back through the tunnel, taking the lead. Tyler grinned at Sean, who shook his head and passed her. "Stay in the middle, Madison. Remember, a killer used these tunnels. Keep an armed man in front of you and one behind you."

"Good plan," she said. Her hand fell on his waist as she positioned herself at his back.

He groaned inwardly when she touched him, gritting his teeth. His thoughts weren't appropriate for this place.

But maybe they were. Maybe human warmth and basic human desires were important. No one was immortal. Living life to its fullest extent was what they were supposed to do while they spent their time on this . . . plane of existence.

She was close behind him all the way, although he didn't move as quickly now. He kept eyeing the crypts and making mental notes to himself.

The robe. The costume robe the killer had used might well be hidden here somewhere.

Tomorrow they'd search; they had enough people and enough time to do it properly.

They walked through the corridors of bones, shrouds, decaying coffins, and vaults where the slabs remained in place. He wondered about Claymore — the elder Claymore. Had the man actually been doing a kindness to illegal immigrants and the destitute, or had he been making a small fortune on the side?

At last they emerged into the basement again. Lights still shone over the walls.

Sean frowned, hoping no one had been there after them.

The studio remained in lockdown. Colin Bailey was standing watch, and there were police cars guarding the area.

And yet, he had to wonder if there wasn't a way to the surface, steps somewhere that led to a vault above-ground in the cemetery. He shouldn't have let Logan and the others leave; someone should have stood guard. But they hadn't known that they'd find what they were looking for. It had been important, as well, that they follow procedure, questioning everyone who might have been involved.

Madison glanced at him as they walked toward the elevator. She laughed suddenly, and her laugh was real, if a bit shaky.

"What?"

"Well, I don't know what *I* look like, but you resemble one of our zombies," she said.

He noticed then that she was covered in spiderwebs and dirt. He smoothed a tangle of webbing from her hair, then inspected Tyler, who was also white and smudged.

"We'd better clean ourselves up a bit," he agreed ruefully.

"Here," she said, reaching over and pulling webs from him. She rubbed away a smudge on his cheek. "A bit of an improvement, anyway," she said, and turned to Tyler.

"We must look like a tribe of monkeys," Tyler said.

"How are we all now?" Sean asked after a moment.

"Well, I guess we look all right for people who've been running around in a basement filled with graves," Tyler muttered.

"Good enough," Madison said.

"And showers are in order. We'll meet the others back at the hotel," Sean decided. "When we're out of here, I'll call Logan and tell him what's going on."

"The studio's supposed to reopen tomorrow," Madison said.

"That's actually a good thing." Sean told her. "We'll get to see the natives in their

307

habitat, and that may give us more to go on."

"But you're convinced it's not a casual employee," Madison reminded him.

"I'm willing to bet the killer will show up tomorrow. He'll want to know what's going on," Sean said.

"For now, let's get out of here," Tyler said. "I'm itchy all over. I'm imagining bugs — spiders, ugh — crawling all over me."

"And that from a Ranger!" Sean couldn't help grinning.

"Hey, I can deal with enemies in human form," Tyler said. "I'm not so big on creepy crawlies. I'd rather wrestle a rattler than a brown recluse or black widow any day."

They stepped into the elevator, and exited on the first floor, passing by the mannequin displays in the small circular areas that separated the offices and the elevator.

For a moment, it seemed to Sean that the years were whisked away as the three of them walked by the young werewolf, a beautiful witch, a chilling vampire and the cop robot who hadn't done so well in his fight. They passed the zombie and it didn't bother him at all. But when they passed the girl from the slasher flick, all he could think about was poor Jenny and how she'd died. The one remaining blue eye in the mannequin-girl's head seemed to stare at him reproachfully.

We will find your killer, Jenny. I swear we will, he vowed silently.

Of course, Jenny wasn't there. He didn't know where Bogie had taken her; he just knew that neither of the ghosts was with them.

Leading the way, he stopped at reception and the guard station. "Hey, Colin," he said. "We're leaving now."

"I'm off pretty soon, too, Sean," Colin Bailey said. "Nash is coming in. He and I are doing twelve-hour shifts, like we do during lockdown. Now it seems especially important that one of us is here to keep guard."

"That's great, Colin. Just hope it doesn't wear you two out."

"Did you find anything down there?" Bailey asked.

"A lot of dirt!" Sean said with a laugh.

"Well, I'm not sure what else you thought you'd find in a basement," Bailey told him. "Bye for now."

Behind him, Madison said good-night and Tyler politely echoed her words. They left the studio for Sean's borrowed car.

Tyler took the wheel while Sean made a call to Logan, and Madison sat silently in the backseat. They reached the hotel, where they hurried through the lobby and up to the third floor.

"Showers. What then?" Madison asked.

"Movie night," Sean said.

"We're going to see a movie?"

"Don't want to be all work and no play," Sean said, but judging by her expression, she wasn't amused. He touched her chin, still smudged despite the repairs they'd attempted. "Like I said this morning, I think we should enjoy a viewing of *Sam Stone and the Curious Case of the Egyptian Museum*."

"Oh. Well, the only place I could imagine seeing that film is at the Black Box," Madison said.

"Precisely." Sean smiled at her. "Your hair looks gray."

"So does yours."

"Any of the three of us would fit right in with those mannequins in the halls," Tyler said. "Sean, I'm going to take a shower, go down to the police station and see if I can interview some of the people who still need to be questioned. Then I'll brief the others and meet you two at the Black Box. Call me when it's been arranged and we'll be there whatever time you say."

"Good plan. I'm going to get on the computer and see if I can come up with any references to the original Claymore and his son, the studio and anything that might've been going on at the time," Sean told him.

They parted and went to their own rooms.

I'm not afraid of cemeteries. I'm not afraid of the dead!

Madison silently chanted the words in her mind as she scrubbed her hair for the third time. Probably useless, because she'd end up back in the strange catacombs beneath the studio again.

No . . .

Tomorrow would be a workday for her, a time to return to the world of *The Unholy* and the specialized costume that would be worn by Oliver Marshall — and his stunt double. Of course, they'd all be feeling awkward, not sure what to say to one another, and there might still be a police presence on-site. No, there *would* be a police presence on-site.

Finally, she rinsed her hair, poured on conditioner, rinsed again and got out of the shower.

Wrapped in one towel, with another wound around her hair, she wandered back to her room. She had the television on and was gratified to see a police spokesman on the news. He was saying that although

Alistair Archer had been arraigned for the murder of Jenny Henderson, new leads were causing police and FBI to delve further into the case.

The spokesman told reporters he couldn't give them any details as that information might jeopardize the case. While still being harangued by dozens of questions, the stern middle-aged man lifted his hand and said, "That is all at this time."

Surrounded by officers, he went back into the station.

Madison was only dimly aware of the reporter as he spoke to the anchor back at his studio, reconstructing the "bizarre" case once again.

She glanced at the bedside clock-radio and saw that it was just after five. She felt as if she'd lived a lifetime that day. They hadn't had lunch, although breakfast delivered to the room had been filling. She was getting hungry, though, and besides being hungry, she was alarmed at the way she felt so *alone.*

But she did feel alone. More alone than ever. Maybe because she usually spent so many hours working. Maybe because she lived with a ghost much of the time. Except it wasn't just *alone* that she was feeling. Because her sudden loneliness had every-

312

thing to do with Sean, with missing him, although she'd left him only forty minutes ago. . . .

She got dressed, determined not to think anymore.

But when she'd donned jeans and a sweater, she was still restless — and alone. Sitting on the foot of her bed, she began to feel as if the hours, the fears and the discoveries, were weighing on her. She couldn't just sit there any longer.

Everything in her life had changed with Alfie's call on Monday morning. She'd liked her life; it was a good one. And she was lucky — incredibly lucky — to have her job. But everything was based on work. Great work, with wonderful coworkers. She was proud of her associations, and outside friends were often envious because she dressed stars like Oliver Marshall and spent hours on movie sets. She'd never recognized until now how much she'd allowed herself to overlook in life. She'd blamed Bogie for the fact that she hardly ever brought a date home, but it wasn't Bogie's fault. Well, maybe it was a little bit. But she hadn't gone out in forever, and the real reason was that she hadn't met anyone she wanted to spend time with, or even one night.

313

She stood; she couldn't stay where she was.

She wasn't sure what she was doing or why, but she left her room, walked across the hall and knocked on Sean's door.

"Just a second!" he called.

A minute later, the door opened a few inches. Sean stood behind it, looking around its edge. "Sorry, I was waylaid by the computer," he told her.

"It's okay," she said, not moving. The scent of his soap seemed to waft into the hallway.

He must have realized she wasn't going away. He frowned slightly, but arched a brow. "I'll be ready soon."

"May I wait with you?" she asked.

He was silent for a few seconds, then opened the door the rest of the way. "I'm sorry — I'm not quite decent."

"You're decent enough for me," she said.

He still hesitated. "Sure, come in. It'll take me a few minutes to throw some clothes on. I'm a little behind — I ended up on the computer. There's soft drinks and probably something harder in the suite's work area."

She walked past him, heading toward the connecting door. It was closed and she turned back to him. He'd been reaching for a neat stack of clothing to bring into the bathroom with him but he paused, his frown deepening as he looked at her.

"Madison, you all right?" he asked.

"I — I don't know," she admitted.

He smiled suddenly, as if he understood. But she knew he didn't.

"It was an interesting day. There's something eerie about those catacombs, even after being in the morgue for an hour."

"It's — it's interesting all around."

"You must feel terrible. And I'm honest-to-God sorry. I never knew we'd have to worry about your safety."

"I'm fine with everything that's happened," she said. "We've already proven how it was done. As you said, we just need to discover who."

He nodded. "The who, and the why." He frowned again. "Is there a reason you're looking at me like that? Are you hungry? We'll eat on the way to the Black Box."

"Yes, dinner will be nice, but . . ."

"But?"

"I was thinking of . . . spending a little time together. Not in the company of ghosts or in a crypt or a graveyard."

He offered her a slow half grin, his head angling to the side in a questioning manner. "I'd almost think you came here to proposition me, Madison," he said softly.

She met his eyes and inhaled, and tried to appear like a woman with a sophisticated sense of reality.

"I did."

11

The moment was ridiculously awkward. It was as if time stood still as he looked back at her — and yet time was ticking away. Madison thought she could actually hear the hands on the room's old-fashioned clock-radio.

But, in an odd way, it wasn't awkward at all.

She swallowed, but she was determined to be honest, and she wasn't backing down, wasn't going to pretend she was just joking.

She wasn't to going to run off in embarrassment, either; if she did, that was how she'd feel forever after in his presence. Her lips curved wistfully. She realized that although she hadn't been sure of her exact intent until she'd said the words, she certainly hadn't expected rejection. It wasn't that she felt any man would instantly agree to have sex with her. It was just that she believed there'd been something between them. Chemistry, if nothing else.

"Uh, you made rather a point about not staying in my room last night," he reminded her.

"I know," she said. "But . . . that was, well . . . I didn't want to be here because I *had* to be here — I mean, in a room with you — because I was afraid. When I'm afraid, I *would* rather be with you, but I . . . I'm not saying this at all well."

She was surprised when he walked over to her at last. She began to feel a trembling inside her when his hands dropped to her arms, and she was intensely aware of his height and physique, his damp bare chest and the towel about his midriff. Whatever it was that she always felt when she was with him seemed amplified, like a drumbeat in her head, or a riveting pulse in her bloodstream.

"Trust me, I have nothing against the idea. I'd be a hell of a liar if I said it hasn't played in my mind more than once," he told her. The sound of his voice seemed to sweep around her, creating a deeper sense of longing with every throaty word, every nuance.

"I guess it's not the time or place," she murmured.

"Actually, it's a fine time and place. Tyler's gone to work with the others, I've called

Eddie and arranged for a showing of the film. We won't meet at the cinema for about two and a half hours."

His green eyes seemed to have a dazzling light as he stared down at her.

"Oh!" she said, about to step back. "I'm sorry — I didn't even think. Is there someone in your life?"

He seemed to wince. "No. There's no one in my life. You?"

She shook her head.

"At least I'm dressed — or undressed — for the occasion," he said dryly.

"I can be, too," she whispered.

"Madison, I'm not really . . . I didn't plan on sleeping with anyone. I'm not prepared. I'm talking about sexual responsibility."

"I am," she told him.

His smile deepened and she added, "No, I mean, really, there's no one in my life. I guess . . . I've been ever hopeful."

He laughed softly. She lowered her head, astonished that the simple sound of a laugh could be so provocative.

He lifted her chin, then pulled her against him, and once more his eyes fell on hers. "You know we live in different worlds," he said.

"Different and the same."

He smiled at that, and there was something amused, something tender and yet still hesitant in the way he looked at her.

"I care about you, Madison."

"Would it be better if you didn't?"

"Yes."

"We can't just take this for what it is — and for whatever time we have?" she asked.

He groaned. "Yes. Yes, we can."

He gazed into her eyes and seemed to struggle, and she wondered if he was worried for her, for himself, or for them both. But his thumb and forefinger were already on her chin and cheek, and he lowered his head slowly. His lips touched hers as lightly as a breath. As if he was giving her every chance to move away . . .

He had no idea how much she wanted to be right where she was. She wished she could hold on to time and savor this closeness forever. His skin was taut and bronzed and smooth. The easy strength in his arms seemed unique, the very feel of his lips was beyond anything she might have imagined.

But his lips grew hungrier, more impassioned, and he drew her closer, his mouth like fire on hers as the kiss deepened. She felt drunk with the luxury of his touch, aware of the hardness of his muscled form, and *very* aware of the rise of his erection against the thin denim of her jeans and the towel that was all he wore. He'd been quite right — he was dressed, or undressed, for the occasion.

His hands moved down her back. She stepped out of her sandals, and together they removed her shirt. His fingers slid beneath her waistband. She imagined that no grace was possible in the act of taking off her jeans, and yet it seemed that they shimmied effortlessly down her body. The towel slipped from him as he picked her up, his eyes on hers once again as they crossed the few feet to the bed. The clothing he'd been planning to wear fell to the floor, landing on top of her hastily discarded T-shirt and jeans.

He leaned over her, stroking her face, but he didn't speak. She had to wonder what was going through his mind. But she didn't speak, either; she was afraid of breaking the enchantment that had seized her.

Then she felt his mouth on hers again, and she ceased to think or analyze and gave herself completely to the sensations that overwhelmed her. His mouth left hers, trailing over her breasts. She felt the pressure of his thighs, the ripple of muscle. He moved down the length of her, kissing her, and where his lips touched, it seemed that fire erupted and spread. She touched him with feather-light strokes at first, and then the hunger inside made her bolder, and she caressed his hair and his bronzed flesh in return. His every movement against her seemed erotic; he was a practiced and natural lover, she thought, a man who knew where to touch and when, and how to tease and elicit and give all at once. She prayed that she could do the same. Again, she ceased to think, she was so caught up in the carnal and earthly sensations that swirled through her, the eroticism of his tongue on her flesh and the movement of his hands. . . .

She cried out softly as he brought her to a fever pitch and then rose above her, sliding into her smoothly and easily, his movements a slow and evocative thrust, then escalating . . . becoming more and more urgent. Her hands and fingers rested on his shoulders. His eyes gazed down into hers and, once again, beyond the physical intimacy they shared in all its heady glory, she felt something deeper. It was as if his eyes could reach where no physical movement could. And yet everything — their breath, the ripple of muscle, the pure eroticism of their intimacy, the pounding of their hearts — seemed so intense that nothing could be deeper.

But it was.

She closed her eyes. They'd taken a step together that neither of them had planned.

Afterward, she lay there for a minute, trying not to breathe, praying they wouldn't speak, that nothing would come to shatter the moment.

Then thoughts crowded her mind again, and nagging fear took hold. For her it had been as if the entire world had glowed and sparkled, but . . .

For him, it might have been sex. Just sex.

Maybe he knew she didn't want words; she wanted to savor the moment. He didn't speak. He held her close, and the seconds seemed to slip away. Outside, the sun fell and shadows darkened the room.

Then he turned to her, and the whole process began again, until once more, they lay side by side, silent in the wonder of aftermath.

Then his phone rang, and the sound seemed louder than music blasting from a disco club. Madison jumped. Sean eased her back down, rolling over to find the jeans he'd discarded before his shower and pulling his phone from the pocket.

"Cameron," he answered.

She heard Logan Raintree's voice, but couldn't really make out the words.

"Yes, fine, all set," Sean said. "We're leaving here, and we'll grab some fast food on the way. . . . Sure, see you in about thirty minutes."

He hit the end button on his phone and looked at Madison. She was afraid he was going to give her some kind of apology, that he'd thank her jokingly, but, hey, they really needed to get going now.

He didn't say anything like that.

"Race you to the shower!" he said, and leaped out of the bed.

Stunned, she watched him for a moment. Then she bounded to her feet and rushed in. "No touching!" he teased. "We'll be late if you do."

He was serious about that. They passed the soap to each other, showered quickly and dressed with equal haste.

They were out the door and in the borrowed Prius before she realized she had yet to say a word.

When she finally did, it was in answer to his question about what she'd like on her burger and did she want onion rings or fries. And that was fine. Since she wasn't sure what to say . . .

That was incredible? Far too clichéd. *Thank you?* Far too sniveling.

Good thing they were going to the movies!

Guilt.

Sean told himself he should've been experiencing a massive sense of guilt — not that he'd done anything for which he should feel *guilty.* Not really. It was just that they shouldn't be involved when there was a chance that she was in danger, when they were in the middle of a case, when —

No. There was no reason to feel guilt, regret or remorse. They were consenting adults with the rights of consenting adults.

He just wished . . .

That they'd met at another time, another place. In a bar, for God's sake. Somewhere other than here and now. Because he couldn't jeopardize her, and he couldn't jeopardize the case.

But did it really make a difference in the practical sense? He'd already determined that she was in danger, and maybe being closer to him was better than not.

Eddie Archer had already begun the film.

Eddie had taken it on himself to have Helena, Mike Greenwood and Andy Simons join them. Maybe that hadn't been such a bad idea; he knew the rest of the team would be observing those closest to Eddie, watching for any indiscretion. Detective Benny Knox had decided to join them, as well.

Sean sat in the darkened theater with the group as they watched *Sam Stone and the Curious Case of the Egyptian Museum.* He tried to remember everything he knew or had heard about the movie.

He'd seen it before — in this very theater. He'd seen it with Eddie and Alistair and a number of the other employees at the studio.

It certainly wasn't the most famous of film noir movies. It had done well in its day, but both of the leads — John De La Torre and Audrey Grant — had died soon after its release, de la Torre in the service and Audrey in a plane crash as she was flying out to entertain the troops. After that, *Sam Stone* had somehow slipped into the pile of the "mostly forgotten." He wondered why. Probably because neither of the two performers had really had a chance to become a big name. There'd been an accidental death on the set as well — a bit player had been electrocuted. These days it seemed that such things would make a movie *more* popular; in the middle of World War II, there was already too much death. Sean remembered the first time he'd seen the movie; he'd thought it was excellent because there were only two suspects in the murder of Dianna Breen's husband — the priest, Amun Mopat, and Dianna herself. But the writing, direction and action scenes were so effective that it wasn't until the very end that you knew the widow was innocent, and you knew because the evil priest killed her just as Sam Stone discovered the truth and killed him. There had been a scene in which the mummy was brought to life. . . . But as Sam Stone fought the thing to save himself, he figured out that it was mechanically run and the priest was a sham. Alistair had loved the movie so much because he'd wanted to direct and produce from the time he'd been a little kid. This movie had exceptional special effects for the day — done at this very studio — and that, too, was part of its appeal.

"Sam!"

They were almost at the final scene. Dianna Breen cried out in horror, and Sam rushed in, pulling the priest off Dianna, nearly insane to save the woman with whom he'd fallen in love. Amun Mopat went flying into another of the museum's displays, a lifelike statue of a warrior carrying a dagger. Mopat was killed, dying dramatically, but when Sam went to help the fallen Dianna, she opened her eyes for a moment, told him she loved him — and died.

The credits rolled. Eddie rose to go back to the projection booth and stop the movie. The lights came on.

Knox stood and looked at Sean.

"So. What did this do? Any good at all?"

Sean stood, too. He wasn't sure why Knox was trying to intimidate him, but he was taller than Knox, so at least he had a physical advantage.

"It did a lot of good," Sean said.

Eddie was coming back from the booth. "What? What did you see in the movie that could possibly help?"

"I don't get it," Mike Greenwood murmured.

"You don't notice it, Mike — or you, Andy — because you haven't been down in the museum since the crime. And you didn't," he said, turning to his team, "because you'd never seen the tableau before and wouldn't know what had changed. Helena, I'm not sure how familiar you are with the tableau —"

Before he could finish his explanation, Madison jumped up with a gasp.

"You know?" he asked her.

Her eyes met his, brilliantly blue.

"Tell them," he said.

"The dagger is gone — the dagger in the

328

hands of the ancient Egyptian warrior. It's gone." She looked at Sean again. "That's why it seemed just a bit off. The mannequins were all turned slightly, not back exactly where they should've been. The sarcophagus was at an angle, the big jackal was too close to the warrior. But the dagger, the dagger that killed the priest in the movie — it's gone!"

"It was a real dagger?" Knox asked.

"Those tableaux have been up for nearly fifty years," Eddie said. "Yes, it was real. Not from a tomb of course, but a replica. The sarcophagus is real, too — made in Egypt by Egyptian craftsmen to the correct proportions and rules of funerary art." He walked over to Madison, taking her by the shoulders. "Madison, you're sure? Is there anything else? I have to get down there myself. I'm probably the only one who'd know if anything else was different."

Before she could respond, Helena stood, coming over to Eddie and speaking in a low voice. "Eddie, the dagger is gone, but . . . how does that help? So now the police know that a prop was stolen from the tableau. All that does is tell us what the murder weapon was — or might have been."

Eddie looked sick for a minute, but turned

to Sean hopefully. "It helps, doesn't it? It helps?"

"Anything we know helps," Sean assured him.

"You're *sure* it's not there — somewhere?" Knox asked.

"Detective, you don't think your team of forensic experts would've missed a *dagger?*" Sean said with more than a hint of sarcasm. "Even if it had been precisely where it was supposed to be, they would have taken it for testing."

Knox seemed embarrassed. "Would the dagger have been sharp enough after all these years to have slashed the young woman's throat?"

"I need to go down there," Eddie muttered again. "I need to go down to the tunnel."

Knox said, "There's no way I'm going to have everyone traipsing around in that tunnel. When we release it, teams have to come in to clean. We can't allow it to become a health hazard. We —"

Logan broke in. "Benny, why don't you and Sean take Eddie down there? With Madison. We've already been, but Eddie Archer might see something else that's amiss." He looked at Eddie. "You definitely didn't go in when you came here the night of the murder?"

Eddie shook his head. "It was a crime scene, cordoned off. I just listened in complete disbelief when Detective Knox briefed me, and then . . . then I was with Alistair."

"I — I can come if you need me, Eddie," Helena said.

He smiled at her. "Thank you, dear, but no."

"We'll wait in the lobby with Helena while you go down," Logan said, indicating the team.

Kelsey stepped forward smoothly. "Mrs. Archer, you're an actress in your own right, aren't you?" she said smoothly. "I'd love to hear about the roles you've played!"

She glanced back at Sean, linked arms with Helena and started walking her toward the lobby.

"Mike, Andy — Madison did a terrific job showing us the studio. Perhaps you two could fill me in on what goes on here, day by day. Andy, you and Eddie have been partners since the beginning, right?" Logan said, leading both men out, followed by the others.

"Let's do it," Knox said grimly.

"Madison?" Sean asked.

She nodded.

"You don't have to come, my dear," Eddie said.

"Eddie, I've been down there," she reminded him.

Sean took her arm as they walked from the cinema to the office and through the door that was usually covered by the poster. They went down the steps and started passing the displays. Knox stopped suddenly in front of the *Casablanca* exhibit. "Is that a real gun in Bogie's hand?" he demanded.

"World War II–issue, yes," Eddie said. "But there are no bullets in it. I swear. Check it out if you don't believe me."

"I don't believe anything around here," Knox muttered. He jumped up into the exhibit to check for himself.

Sean ignored him, and continued down the tunnel, to the scene of the crime. The smell was growing worse. He made a mental note to tell Logan that they needed to bring in the crime scene cleaners the next day. The answers they needed, he now knew, were behind the tableau, not in the tunnel.

With Madison at his side, he stared at the tableau.

"You figured it out the minute I did," he said, and they both looked at the statue of the warrior, standing at an angle, pushed back behind the jackal.

"I can't believe I didn't see it before," she told him.

He shrugged. "Madison, I've walked this tunnel as many times as you have, and I've supposedly been trained to be observant of details, but I missed it, too."

"Alistair wouldn't have missed it," she said.

Sean moved the cord aside and entered the display. He headed straight to the statue of the warrior and turned him around. The way the warrior stood, his shield held high in the other hand, it was easy to see how they'd missed the obvious. They had concentrated on the mannequin of the priest and hadn't focused on the shelves and canopic jars, the sarcophagus, the cobras in their various positions on the floor — slithering and rising in strike mode.

"Gloves!" Knox called to him. He walked over, handing Sean a pair from his pocket.

Sean said, "Thanks," and put on the latex gloves. It wasn't going to matter. The killer had dressed in the black face and a robe — and he'd worn gloves when he killed Jenny Henderson. But it was procedure, and God knew, he'd probably already blown enough procedure that day.

"May I have a pair?" Madison asked. "I can help Sean go through the tableau."

Knox grumbled that the FBI should have carried their own, but he produced a pair of gloves and gave them to her. Eddie stood just beyond the cordoned-off area, outside the chalk marks and the blood. He was ashen as he studied the tableau.

"You see anything else?" Knox asked him.

"No, but I should've come down." Eddie shook his head. "I think I would've known. I'm sure I would've seen that the dagger was gone."

"Hard to say," Knox said kindly before turning back to Sean. "I have no idea what you could possibly find. Our forensic people are good. We've learned to be detailed and make sure the chain of evidence is solid. We've learned the hard way."

Madison had bent down by the mummy that lay on the floor — in pieces. She glanced back at the sarcophagus, frowning.

"What?" Sean asked her.

"All this stuff was made in Egypt — exact copies of items found in real tombs," she said. "They sometimes had secret or hidden compartments. I was trying to see if I could find anything that opened, but . . . it looks like what we see is what there is."

Sean came over and began running his hands gently over the wood, trying to determine if there could be such a compartment. But his efforts failed.

He turned. Eddie was still staring at the tableau; Knox was staring at Eddie. Madison had given her attention to the large canopic jars.

"Empty," she said, picking up the last of them. But then she paused. "Sean, this one — it seems too heavy for its size!"

He took the jar from her and studied it, stuck his gloved hand in it and saw that where he touched wasn't the bottom.

He kept twisting the jar, and he heard a little gasp escape Madison's lips. She was right next to him, almost on top of him. "That's it, Sean! Keep twisting. The design is changing as you twist it. . . . There, look, go a bit further, and you'll see that the two pieces on the design make a sun."

He gave it another twist and heard a click. The false bottom in the jar lifted. Beneath that false bottom, he saw something. He touched it.

Then he pulled the missing dagger out of the canopic jar. It was covered in blood.

"Well," he said. "Looks like we've found the murder weapon."

Madison sat in the suite with the others, listening as, one by one, the team members went through their notes on the people they'd interviewed. They asked her questions and she gave her impressions, but she became well aware that there was a great deal of tedium in what they did. However, repetition was essential to ensure that nothing slipped through the cracks.

They went through the construction crew. Jane, who had interviewed the men and women who'd been working on the scaffolding, told them that every story matched and rang true. Logan had brought back copies of the security footage, and everything they saw verified what had been said. Kat Sokolov had interviewed the seamstresses, the designers and the fabricators, who hadn't been in since Friday. Logan had spoken at length with both Andy Simons and Mike Greenwood and he'd also called in Eddie's ex-wife, Benita Lowe, who wanted to believe that his current wife, Helena LaRoux, had been involved. In fact, Benita had said, if Helena wasn't such an idiot, Benita would be absolutely positive that she was guilty.

"She told me Helena only pretended to care about Alistair," Logan told them. "I believe that, but not really caring about her stepson doesn't make her a murderer."

"Yes, true, she may be just a scheming user," Tyler agreed.

Kelsey had spoken with Winston Nash and Colin Bailey. Bailey had been agitated, convinced that he'd lost all their chances of finding the real killer — because he had left the guard station to rush out when Alistair had come to him, screaming hysterically.

"Everyone's background was thoroughly investigated?" Sean asked.

"No felons in the lot," Logan answered. "The worst we've found on anyone at the studio was a few unpaid parking tickets."

"I'm not thinking so much of criminal activity. I was wondering if anyone associated with either the family or the studio had a relative who worked on the original film."

"No one mentioned anything of the kind to the police or to us," Logan said. "But we can delve deeper. I guess the killer wouldn't announce that his dad had been a grip or a production assistant on the movie."

"What about the dead man, the guy who was killed during filming? Any connections?" Sean asked.

"Not that we've yet discovered."

"Anybody have any theories?" Logan threw out his arms.

"I'm willing to bet it has more to do with the movie, somehow," Sean said.

"The movie was filmed in 1942," Logan reminded him.

"Yes . . . but!" Madison said, glancing around as she interjected, hoping they wouldn't think she was being disruptive and had nothing of importance to say.

They didn't. The six members of the Krewe looked at her, waiting.

"There *was* trouble with the movie. Not with the stars, although they both had truly sad ends. I'm talking about the accident that occurred on the set — the electrical accident that killed a bit player, Pete Krakowski."

"I'm aware of it." Sean looked at her, frowning. "But it *was* an accident, right? He was electrocuted."

Madison surveyed the group, taking a deep breath. "Bogie didn't think it was an accident."

"Bogie — was he connected to the movie?" Logan asked her. "Where is he . . . and our victim, by the way? I would've thought they'd hang out with us."

"The tunnel was too much for Jenny, although she was very brave," Sean said. "I'm sure Bogie is trying to help her find the place she wants to haunt. Maybe he's showing her the ropes. Do you think ghosts sometimes serve as mentors to other ghosts?" he asked, his grin lopsided.

"He's a good guy. That's probably what

he's doing," Madison said. "I'm sure he'll reappear soon, since he seems willing, maybe even intrigued, to help on this. And no, he wasn't involved with the movie. He was working on *Casablanca* at the time. But he knew the electricians and the grips, and he said they didn't make mistakes. That could mean nothing. The movie was filmed well over fifty years ago now. But all the special effects were created at the studio, which was Claymore Illusions back then."

Logan nodded gravely. "We need to look into the past. Because the past can always intrude on the present." He suddenly yawned. "All right. Knox has taken the dagger to be analyzed by the forensics department. Tomorrow, the studio reopens. That won't interfere with our investigation. Jane, I'll ask you to stay at the precinct. Do whatever research you can on the internet concerning the movie. Tyler, Kat, Kelsey — you'll examine the tunnels, see what else you can find down there. We'll have to make sure no one can accidentally wander down to the basement to see what we're doing."

"I guess I'm supposed to be at work tomorrow," Madison said hesitantly.

"That's fine. You go to work. It's going to be important that you do. Keep your eyes open and don't ever go anywhere alone. I'll be out there on the main floor, still talking to people. Even if you need to go to the ladies' room, let me know."

"People are going to ask me questions all day," Madison said. "How do I put them off?"

"Just tell them that all you've done is answer questions about the studio," Sean replied.

"Okay." Madison realized she was nervous about returning to work. She knew she wouldn't have made even a halfway decent actress; her feelings were far too apparent in her face and her voice. But she really *didn't* have anything to tell anyone, so she supposed she'd do all right.

They broke up then, Jane cheerfully calling goodnight as she and Kat headed out, Kelsey yawning and walking to her bedroom. Tyler offered to escort Madison across the hall and she accepted, noting that Sean and Logan were deep in conversation again, their heads bent low as they spoke.

In her own room, she lay down on her bed, exhausted, although adrenaline was racing through her system. These had been the longest days of her life.

And in a way, today had been the best.

But being in the tunnel a couple of hours ago . . . crawling through the mannequins . . .

She inhaled, cringed, sure she could still smell the blood.

Searching through canopic jars . . .

Those had just been props. But it didn't matter; she was convinced she could smell blood on herself and would never be able to sleep. She stripped in a sudden frenzy and hurried into the shower. When she emerged, wrapped in a towel, she heard a soft tapping. For a moment, fear washed over her. But she was in a hotel — on a floor with six FBI agents. She walked to the door, and as she did, hope and anticipation replaced the fear. She looked through the peephole. It was Sean.

When she opened the door, he smiled at her, leaning against the frame for a moment. "I see *you're* dressed for the occasion now," he told her.

She could have asked him if it was really all right for them to be together; he was obviously dedicated to his work and his team, and she'd never want to jeopardize any of that.

But she didn't ask. She stepped back. He walked in. She closed the door.

"A shower," he said. "What a great plan. May I? And, of course, you're welcome to join me. And it's hours and hours before

341

daylight, so feel free to use the soap any way you'd like."

"I'll do that," she promised. Once she'd locked the door behind him, they headed into the shower.

When they finally slept that night, it was deep and wonderful, and yet throughout the night, she knew he was beside her.

12

There was no escaping the fact that the day would begin awkwardly. Sean realized that.

Naturally, everyone at the studio looked at him, Tyler and Kelsey as they walked in. Everyone nodded, not knowing who they were, but obviously assuming they were some kind of law enforcement.

Eddie Archer was a man who tried to be as honest and sincere with his people as possible. Soon after all his full-time employees had arrived, he called a general meeting in the main work area. He raised a hand to ask for silence as people gathered around him, speaking in hushed whispers. Sean and his colleagues stood by themselves, a few feet away.

"You all know what happened here," Eddie said. "Jenny Henderson was killed in the tunnel, and my son, Alistair, was arraigned for her murder. Alistair claims his innocence, and the police and the FBI are

343

investigating. Alistair doesn't want the studio to go down, and he doesn't want any of you having to look for jobs elsewhere, and since the producers of *The Unholy* are retaining their faith in us, we're going back to work. We're going to continue doing what we do best — creating special effects. Anyone who's unhappy about being here is free to leave. But while the investigators continue doing what *they* do best, let's try not to get in their way or disrupt our own lives any more than necessary. So, my friends, ladies and gentlemen, I hope you'll stand by me and Alistair, and that we'll get back to it."

"Eddie!" one of the seamstresses called out. "Will we have police protection through the day? I saw that we still have about four cop cars out there."

"The police are guarding us, yes," Eddie assured her.

"Eddie, how are *you* doing?" another asked.

Eddie smiled. "I get my strength from God, my family and you. Thank you. But if you choose not to be involved, all you have to do is let me know. There isn't a soul working here for whom I wouldn't write a glowing letter or recommendation! And I'll be here," he said. He indicated Tyler, Kelsey and Kat. "These three agents are from the FBI. Please answer their questions and show them around if you're asked. They're here to protect us, and to investigate. Now, I'll be up in my office if you need me."

When he'd finished, Andy Simons took his place. "I could give you a long speech about how much we appreciate your talents and your loyalty. But you all know that. And you know that you're working with one of the most brilliant minds in the business." He gestured at Eddie and grinned. "So . . . work, people, work!" he said, then headed for the hallway.

Mike had been standing behind him, ever supportive. "Okay, people. We've got a few days we have to make up for, if we're going to stick to our schedule."

The employees split up. They'd be whispering among themselves all day, Sean was certain, but they were getting back to work.

"I want to go down to the tunnel," he told Tyler. "I have the key, but I'd like to bring in a few cops to watch the elevator doors. We don't want anyone joining us down there."

"I'll see to it," Tyler promised. "I'll meet you back here in ten." He inclined his head, pointing across the room. "There's a star on the premises," he said.

Sean looked up and saw that the actor, Oliver Marshall, had appeared. People hailed him and he seemed pleased by their friendliness, responding with waves and handshakes as he walked through the work areas to reach Madison's station. She rose as he approached. She'd said they got along well, but Sean studied the man — it was the nature of the game. You had to be suspicious of everyone. And yet he felt his heart beating a little faster. Oliver Marshall seemed to know Madison well . . . and to like her. He greeted her with a kiss on the cheek and a warm hug. She offered him her beautiful smile in return and hugged him back. He could see that she was speaking to him, gesturing at the costume pieces on the table and something she was working on that had to do with foam and rubber and fabric. He realized they were referring to the knee pads Oliver needed for his costume to add a little protection during some of his stunts. Apparently he had a stunt double but was doing the less dangerous scenes himself. Madison was gathering up folds of material to hand him so he could be properly fitted in the costume with the knee pads inserted.

She seemed happy to be working again, seemed to enjoy her job.

"Logan will be up here," Tyler reminded him. "Madison will be safe."

Sean nodded. It was time for them to make their way down to the tunnel, search all the corridors, and when they'd done that, he was going out to the cemetery to look for another entrance.

He kept his eye on Madison as her assistant, Alfie Longdale, a tall, platinum-blond man in his early twenties, approached her and Oliver Marshall. More greetings took place. Then Alfie picked up a measuring tape and some pins and they moved toward the curtained area that was the studio's fitting room.

He watched the seamstresses sit down at their machines and the construction crew collect around a table while the head of the project discussed the plans.

He watched, and it looked like a busy, working studio. The murder simmered just beneath the surface, but as the minutes passed, people seemed to become more and more immersed in their jobs.

Mike Greenwood walked up to him. "Sad thing, huh?"

"Sad, but you and Eddie have the studio up and running as smoothly as could be expected," Sean said.

"We have a good group of workers, and

people believe in Eddie. You treat people right year after year, and in the end . . ." Mike shrugged. "Too bad his choice in women is . . . well, Eddie's such a nice guy. He can be kind of a sucker. Don't quote me on that, please. I've been with him from the beginning, but . . ."

"I don't repeat conversations, Mike," Sean said.

Mike pursed his lips grimly. "Helena acts like she's supporting him all the way, but you ask me, she's nosy. She's trying to keep on top of every move the police make. And you people, of course. She didn't go to that movie last night because she *wanted* to see it."

"Mike, what really happened between Eddie and Benita?" he asked.

Mike shrugged again. "I don't know. He came in one day and asked me if I knew a good divorce attorney. I suggested he might want to attend some counseling first. He hadn't been married that long. But he said, 'No, Mike, counseling won't help. We're amicable, but it's over. I can't live a lie.' "

"And he never said anything else?"

Mike shook his head. "Not a word. I know she still cares about him, and he cares about her."

"What about the rumors that she was

cheating on him?"

"I think they were just that — rumors," Mike said. "But if you were to ask him yourself, he might tell you."

"I'll do that."

Tyler returned with two police officers to guard the elevator.

Then Sean, Kelsey and Kat went back down, armed with flashlights — and their Glocks.

Vengeance was worried. The FBI agents were spending too much time in the basement. Vengeance knew because there were so many people at the studio who innocently gave information away. It was good to be trusted.

Still, even if they found the tunnels, even if . . .

They wouldn't know everything. They *couldn't* know everything.

Still . . .

Vengeance made a call. "It's me, and listen, listen well. Find out exactly what's happening now. We may have to do a little cleanup."

"Not me, no, no, not me!" she replied. "I can't — I'm being watched. I know I'm being watched. I can't — I *won't*. I won't get any more involved. You're being paranoid!"

Yes, Vengeance thought, *because my hands are the bloody ones. . . .*

"You *have* to be involved. I'm going to need help. Tonight. Do you understand me?"

"I may not be able to get out."

"You have to. Do you hear me? You have to."

Vengeance gave her instructions.

"After all," Vengeance reminded her, "the whole thing was really your idea."

"No, no, I was just talking. I never thought —"

"Yes, you did," Vengeance said. "It's what you wanted. Well, tonight, my friend, you're going to get your hands dirty."

"Tough times here, huh?" Oliver Marshall said to Madison.

She nodded grimly. "I'm glad you came in, that you weren't afraid and you didn't stay away," she said.

They were almost alone; she was standing outside the curtain while he changed. She was ready to work on the material and rubber that would go under the shield during his hallucination scene. She needed to be sure it would allow him easy and comfortable movement. Alfie had gone off for some basting thread.

He poked his head outside the curtain. "To be honest?" he said softly. "I'm here with my agent. He thinks it's going to be a popular thing for me to have done. I wish I was brave — like Sam Stone — but I'm not. And, of course, you know how the saying goes: If you repeat that, I'll call you a liar."

Madison grinned. She liked Oliver. He'd already told her he was gay, which she kept a secret as she'd promised. "Oh, one day, with any luck I'll be as big as the guys who can admit anything," he'd said. "I don't lie. I just don't answer. And I do love women and flirt with them all the time. But when you play action heroes and romantic leading men, a certain . . . discretion is best."

"Are we safe here?" he asked her now. "Is there any danger to life or limb?"

She grimaced. "You mean you don't believe what the media say? That Alistair did it?"

Oliver shook his head. "Alistair? Kid's a marshmallow. He'd scald himself in boiling water before he'd hurt anyone, especially that girl. She was kind of annoying, but I'm sure I was annoying to people when I was starting out, too. This is the weirdest business. You can't get an agent or a casting director to remember your name one day, and the next you're in a movie that hits, and you can do no wrong. But . . . are we safe?"

"Oliver, the place is crawling with cops and the FBI. You're safe."

"Yeah, it wasn't some crazy shooter, right? It was all planned out. Man, I can't believe Jenny Henderson could've made an enemy who hated her so much!" he said.

"I don't think she did. I think someone wanted to hurt Eddie — or even Alistair."

Oliver sniffed. He lowered his voice to a whisper. "Well, in my opinion you wouldn't have to look a lot further than the stepmother. I mean, if Alistair's locked up for life, who gets Eddie's fortune?"

"I've thought about that — except they must have a prenup. And Helena's more interested in using Eddie's contacts, anyway. I'd say that most of us who know and love him try to keep our mouths shut about his marriage," Madison said.

Oliver was thoughtful. "Well, if you have an in with the cops, I'd suggest they look at her *really* closely. She was in here with Eddie one day when I was with the producer and director of *Sam Stone.* She was sidling up to everybody, trying to stay in the conversation. I saw her right next to Eddie — just about fondling him in public. I'm almost sure she went into his pockets and came out with something. I don't know what, but I wouldn't trust her any farther than I could throw that yapping dog of hers."

"Oliver, you would never throw a dog," Madison said.

"No, but you get my drift!"

Alfie was hurrying over with the basting needle and thread. Madison leaned back, looking at Oliver, who winked and said, "I think he likes me. And I think he'd like your job." His voice grew even quieter. "Hey, he sucks up to the new Mrs. Eddie Archer whenever she's here. I say watch out for your own assistant."

Kat stopped in the middle of the tunnel and sneezed. "Sean, we shouldn't have to break through anything. If any of the walls were broken through, we'd have seen it. The killer couldn't possibly have had time to cover his tracks."

"Kat, I didn't say try to *break* through, I said *look* through," Sean said. "To the best of your ability. The costume the killer wore is most likely stashed down here somewhere. We've pretty much determined that he — or she — wore gloves, so I sincerely doubt forensics will get anything off the dagger."

Kelsey, who was behind Kat, groaned. "If

I end up wearing any more mold, spider-webs and bone dust, I won't be able to leave the studio until it clears out for the day. I'll be a walking advertisement for the fact that we know more than we're sharing at the moment."

They'd only covered the first tunnel so far; they hadn't even taken the turn that would lead them around to the Black Box Cinema.

He thought it somewhat odd that they hadn't encountered anyone's lost spirit, but then, he knew Jane would have all kinds of interesting information for them about the making of the film *Sam Stone and the Curious Case of the Egyptian Museum,* and that she'd come back with research on the cemetery, as well. They just needed all the pieces of the puzzle; if they could *find* the pieces, they could solve the puzzle. It was a matter of logic. That had been reinforced during their training when they'd met the rest of Jackson Crow's team at Quantico.

"It's here," he insisted. "That costume is here somewhere."

"All right, we'll find it," Kelsey said, setting her hand on his arm. He smiled. She did look like hell, and his cousin was a beautiful woman. She'd come close to dying during their first case, the one that had brought them all together, but even then, she'd understood the risks. She'd been a United States marshal; she'd already signed on the dotted line.

"No one's talking down here, right?" he asked. He was referring to any ghosts who might have remained, but he didn't have to explain. They knew what he meant.

Both women looked at him and shook their heads solemnly.

"I guess it's a good thing they've all gone on. Okay, stick to this path. I'm going to follow the other one for a while, see where it takes me."

He used his heavy flashlight to light the way toward the turnoff that led to the tunnel and museum. He chose not to head back in that direction, though. It seemed unlikely that someone would have retraced his or her steps to hide the robe. However, nothing was impossible. Improbable, but not impossible.

As he moved, she saw that he was going farther beneath the cemetery. The walls here were beginning to cave in; the tunnels were old, and no one had come down in decades to shore them up. Maybe the burials here had been forgotten. Or perhaps there were memorials aboveground, and mourners set their flowers there, having no idea of the labyrinth of dead below. Casting the light around him, he saw decay, broken vaults, fabric and bone in various stages of deterioration.

The crypts were distracting. He tried to look at the floor, seeking any drops of blood. There were none at first, but then on a broken slab of marble that covered half a crypt, he saw a tiny spatter.

He paused, studied it and moved on. And then he turned back. It was a grisly task, but he dug behind the broken slab. His finger curled around fabric that didn't disintegrate at his touch. He tugged on it.

And a robe fell out before him. A robe that was identical to the one on the figure of Amun Mopat in the tableau.

It had to be the mock-up that had been on the mannequin in the studio.

He examined it carefully in the powerful beam of the flashlight. The robe wasn't finished — it was basted together rather than sewn. He felt the material, which was sleek, with the characteristics of a knit, probably synthetic. The robe was a golden brown color, trimmed with gold braid.

And it was dotted with blood.

The killer had come in this direction.

Why?

■ ■ ■ ■

"It's noon. Are you allowed to take a break?" Oliver asked Madison. "Want to go out for lunch?"

"I don't really want to leave the studio today. Thank you, though," Madison told him. She smiled. "You know, there are a million women out there who'd pass out cold at an invitation from you. So I appreciate it."

He gave her a good-old-boy knock on the shoulder. "You're the woman of my dreams, Madison. But you've never flirted with me. How come?"

"Oh, Oliver, you *are* gorgeous. It's not that."

He grinned, leaning across her worktable. "But, hmm, let me see. I'm not your type. You're more into the muscle-bound fighter type. No, no . . . the artist. A nerd? No, I'm not exactly seeing a nerd. Ah, maybe one of the cool, calm, stoic FBI types."

He suddenly started to laugh. "Madison, I was teasing, but . . . ooh, you're going to have to tell me all about your love life."

"You must read enough about *your* life in all the magazines out there!" she chastised him.

"Have lunch with me. Humor me. I'll get something ordered in for us. We can have a cozy costume chat in one of the conference rooms. Come on, what do you say?"

"Okay. But what about Alfie?"

"He can get his own lunch . . . and his own date."

"I can't be rude to my assistant. Alfie's a good kid."

"I'll see that he's kept busy," Oliver said, wiggling his eyebrows.

The young star did have power; in a matter of minutes, Mike had taken Alfie aside, and Oliver was coming back to her with a grin on his face. "Let's go. We're having lunch in the small conference room."

Madison glanced around. She saw that Logan Raintree was keeping watch. He managed to be in a different place every time she looked, either pretending a keen interest in the work going on or engaging a worker in conversation — even pitching in when an extra hand was needed. She was certain that he'd kept an eye on her all morning. What was he going to think about her having lunch with Oliver?

Oliver leaned closer. "Should we ask the FBI guy to join us?" He made a face at her. "Wrong FBI guy, huh?"

"Oliver, would you stop?"

He straightened. "Seriously, just go tell him we're having lunch, and where we're going to be. Tell him we'll keep the door open the whole time. You'll be safe, I swear it. Coward here, remember?"

She laughed. "All right. Let me talk to Logan."

Logan seemed to know she was coming. "I'll be in the conference room having lunch," she told him.

"I heard. Don't worry. I'll be nearby. And there's a cop standing guard at the end of the hallway by the elevator."

"Honestly, I'm not worried. I just didn't want you to be," she said.

He smiled. "Mike told me Oliver really likes you — says working with you is like working with a real human being. Go ahead and enjoy your lunch."

She moved closer to him. "They've been in the basement for a while," she said.

"Everything's fine," he assured her.

She wanted to ask more questions but in the busy studio she couldn't. She rejoined Oliver, and they both spoke to friends among the other workers as they walked to the hallway, beyond reception and the guard station, and over to the conference rooms.

Oliver paused at the first display area near the conference room. He pointed to the one-eyed victim, who seemed to stand there in some kind of strange welcome. "That movie scared the crap out of me when I was a teenager," he told her.

"The werewolf did it for me," she said.

Inside the conference room he paused again, looking at the creation Sean had called Matilda. "Wow. And we're having sushi in here," he said.

As he spoke, Nelly Anderson, the receptionist, came in with a large bag. "You ordered this, Mr. Marshall?" she asked, flushing.

"Yes, I did, thank you so much. It's Nelly, right?"

"Yes, yes!" Nelly said, clearly surprised and happy that he'd remembered her name. Madison liked Nelly, but Nelly didn't seem to notice she was in the room at the moment.

"Hey, that was really fast. Thanks again, Nelly," Oliver said.

"You're welcome." Nelly managed to set the bag down. "If you need anything else —"

"I'll call on you."

Still flushing, Nelly made her way out of the conference room.

"See? Women love you," Madison said.

"I'm a fake in more ways than one, but

don't tell anyone," he said, sitting down beside her.

He looked around the room again, shook his head and dug into the bag. "Two green teas, dragon rolls, California rolls — we *are* in California, after all — and miso soup. That okay?"

"Sounds great," she told him.

He distributed the food, napkins and chopsticks. "You're doing okay, Madison? I mean, really?"

"I'm doing fine. I'm worried about Eddie and Alistair, of course."

He nodded, lifting a piece of sushi between expertly wielded chopsticks. "I have to admit, it shook me up when I heard about it." He hesitated. "If things don't go so well for this place, I'll be really grateful that I chose a stage name for my Actor's Equity card."

"I didn't know your real name *wasn't* Oliver Marshall."

"My name *is* Oliver Marshall. Oliver Marshall Claymore."

She fumbled and dropped the piece of dragon roll she'd just picked up. "Are you related to the Claymores who owned the studio and the land around it?"

He nodded. "Distantly."

"You were born in Ohio! At least, that's

what I've read."

He grinned. "I was born in Ohio. All of that is true. My dad's great-great-uncle was the original owner of the property here. We don't have anything to do with it anymore, and I don't know if the family was still in contact. I do remember stories my grandfather told me about the place. That might be why I wanted to be an actor. Oh! And my name is a secret, okay? I've kept it out of the magazines and trash-azines and I've even managed to keep it off Wikipedia!"

She shook her head. "I don't tell people what others say. You know that."

He nodded. "I do. You're the one totally trustworthy person I've met out here, Madison."

"Well, if someone does find out — although I can't see why it would come up — Eddie owns the studio now and Alistair is the one who's been accused. It doesn't have a thing to do with you. Anyway, it was Claymore Illusions a long time ago," Madison said.

"Yeah, that's true. . . ."

"What kind of stories did you hear?" she asked.

"Oh, funny stories about actors and about the birth of special effects, and how everything's changed over the years. My grandfather used to come to Hollywood on vacations to visit and spend time here. He was an Ohio farm boy, so the studio was really exciting for him. He did become an actor himself. He was fairly successful on Broadway and did lots of tours. My dad, however, became a scientist and decided that since we were from Ohio, he'd put his mind toward creating a better strain of corn." He wagged a chopstick at her. "I'll have you know that farmers consider him a hero."

"I'm impressed," Madison said, meaning it.

He grinned. "Maybe, but my family's boring as hell. Not really. I love my folks and my siblings, and I love getting home for the holidays. Of course, back in good-old-farmboy land, no one knows much about me. I'm just the one who did the family proud in Hollywood." He grew sober. "That's why I feel so bad for the girl who was murdered — Jenny. I know what it's like to be a hopeful. I never thought I'd be this successful." He shook his head. "I still feel like a fake, and I'm afraid it can end anytime."

A loud angry voice suddenly reached them from the reception area. A moment later, Helena LaRoux came clip-clopping along the hallway, her little dog in her arms. Today she was dressed in designer workout clothes. She came to an abrupt halt, in front of the doorway to the conference room.

Winston Nash was hot on her trail. "Mrs. Archer, if you'll just give me a minute, I'll call up and tell Eddie that you're here."

"I don't need anyone to announce me to my husband!" Helena shouted. "Eddie! Eddie!"

"She doesn't know his office is upstairs?" Oliver whispered to Madison.

"Of course — I think they stopped her when she started walking toward the elevator," Madison whispered in return.

"Mrs. Archer!" Winston Nash pleaded. "The studio is in lockdown, *and* we've had a murder, and there are police all over the place. They've asked that any visitors be announced and then escorted in —"

"I'm not *any* visitor! I'm Eddie's wife!"

"Mrs. Archer, if the president came down from Washington, he'd still have to be escorted in. This is lockdown!" Winston Nash insisted.

Winston Nash was Colin Bailey's physical opposite — he was about thirty years old, tall as a beanpole and skinny as could be. His lean face was taut with frustration as he spoke, and maybe a hint of fear. But he'd been given his orders, and he was following them.

Helena LaRoux must have heard either Oliver or Madison rustle a paper or do something that drew her attention. She looked into the room. Her brows shot up, but then she let out a long breath. "There's Madison. And Oliver Marshall. Oliver, you beautiful thing, how lovely to see you. Madison can escort me up to see Eddie. It's not right for me to be kept standing in reception when my husband owns the whole place!"

Madison rose quickly, and Oliver did the same. Oliver was polite and circumspect, walking over to Helena, giving her a kiss on the cheek and a hug, stroking her little dog's ears. "Helena, this must be hard for you. We all know you love Eddie and Alistair," he said.

Madison was astonished that he'd been able to say the words so sincerely — but then, he was an actor, and a very talented one. He'd spoken with just a hint of sarcasm that went right over Helena's head.

"Oh, yes, of course, Oliver, dear. Thank you," Helena said. She had a good two decades on Oliver and she was married, but that didn't keep her from going into flirt mode. She clung to his arm. "Thank you for your kindness. Thank you for being here."

Madison didn't think she'd ever seen a better performance of a heroine cast into tragedy. Her portrait of gracious womanhood belonged on the silver screen.

"Helena, come in and sit with us for a minute," Oliver encouraged her. He was either really being kind or having the time of his life. Madison wasn't sure which.

Nash stood by the doorway and peered in as Oliver led Helena to a chair. He looked at Madison in desperation. "Mr. Archer is with one of the policemen — or one of the FBI people. I got a call that he wasn't to be disturbed. By anyone."

"I'm not *anyone!*" Helena snapped. "I'm his wife!"

"Of course you are, darling," Oliver said. "But give this a few minutes. Talk to me. What've you been doing lately? You know, I saw you onstage once. I think it was the Red Box downtown. You were wonderful!"

"You thought I was wonderful?" Helena asked.

"Absolutely," Oliver gushed.

"Oh, thank you. It's true what they say — film does love you, Oliver," Helena said.

This mutual admiration meeting would be going on for a while. Madison wondered if she should excuse herself and go back to work, but as she started to rise, Oliver kicked her under the table and frowned at her. She sat down again. It was turning into a long lunch.

Sean got most of the bone dust and tunnel muck and grime off before coming to Eddie's office.

As he entered, Eddie stopped drawing on his sketch board and looked up. Maybe he hadn't gotten off enough spiderwebs and bone dust, Sean thought, because Eddie stared at him as if he were seeing a ghost.

"Sean . . ."

"Eddie, we need to talk." He sat down in the chair across from Eddie's desk. "Now."

Eddie raised his hands. "I'm ready to talk."

"You're aware, in a situation like this, that we scrutinize those closest to the victim. When a husband or wife is killed, the spouse is immediately in the running. In this instance, we're pretty sure you were the target. Alistair is the patsy, another victim, in fact, and you're the target."

Eddie gazed at him blankly. "Jenny Henderson is dead, and Alistair is going to trial accused of her murder."

"How does someone hurt *you,* Eddie? Through Alistair, right?"

"What do you want to know?"

"First, why did you and Benita divorce? She still seems to care about you. And you obviously care about her."

Eddie was silent for a minute. He seemed acutely uncomfortable. Then he sighed. "I don't generally discuss this, and neither does Benita, mainly because it's nobody's business. She prefers . . . someone else."

"So she was cheating on you."

"She didn't see it as cheating."

"I don't understand."

"It was a woman. She likes men but prefers women," Eddie said. "Look, I know Hollywood is wide open and all that, but some people feel they'll risk their chances of being seen as sexy or getting certain roles. I think Benita figured she could be loyal to me without being monogamous — either that, or I'd be turned on by the fact that she had sex with women. I don't give a damn about anybody's choices, but it didn't work for me on a personal level. Man or woman, to me it was cheating. Our divorce wasn't ugly, and I still love her as a dear friend. I don't explain it, as I said, because my personal life is nobody's business. And I have no intention of saying things she doesn't want said."

Sean nodded. He believed Eddie. It just

wasn't the answer he'd expected.

"What else?"

"I need to know about the elevator key," Sean said.

"What about it?" Eddie looked confused. "You have it, don't you?"

"Who, besides you, has a key to that elevator?"

Eddie shook his head. "No one. I went to the basement once when I bought the place, with a building inspector. The support beams were all good. The building was solid. I knew I wouldn't use the basement for storage or work. California might be damned dry, but that basement is dank. I don't go there. No one does."

Sean leaned on his desk. "Eddie, someone got hold of your key, copied your key and has been using your key. The basement connects to a labyrinth of tunnels — crypts, like the catacombs. That's how the killer got in and out. I found the bloody robe the killer wore down there, and forensics will be testing it. You need to think long and hard. Because if you're the only one who has a key to get down to that basement, either you're guilty yourself, or someone close to you — maybe someone you've slept with at one time or another — is the murderer."

13

Madison was eager for the workday to come to an end. While Logan had remained nearby throughout the day, she hadn't seen Sean since he'd left her room early. She had a feeling that he'd found something in the tunnels. Something that would directly affect the case.

Finally, people began to leave. She was glad to see that it hadn't taken long for everyone to get back into the spirit of a normal workday. If nothing had been discovered that could allow the state to dismiss the case against Alistair, it would still be weeks — perhaps months — before his trial began. In the meantime, work was necessary, and work was good. It kept everyone sane.

She stayed behind, pretending to finish stitching in the pads for Oliver's costume, as others said good-night and trailed out. She knew that Logan Raintree was near the door that led out of the work area — almost like a farewell committee of one.

But by six-thirty, everyone had left the building except for Mike Greenwood, Andy Simons, Eddie, the cops and agents and Colin Bailey, who'd replaced Winston Nash. Even Helena had gone; she'd gotten her moment with Eddie, shown that she supported him and the studio, and taken her hand-pup home.

Madison felt sorry for the little dog. Helena treated him more like an accessory than a pet.

She realized the agents didn't like to speak about their investigations with anyone else present, and she decided she wasn't going to report what she'd learned about Oliver Marshall until they were alone again — wherever and whenever that might be.

Eddie sighed as they stood in the reception area together. It seemed crowded since everyone who remained was there.

"What now?" Eddie asked.

"Go home," Sean said. "Or go see Alistair. Get some rest."

Eddie gave a weary nod.

Mike set a hand on his shoulder. "It was a good day, Eddie. Not a single employee refused to come in. They started off nervous and chatty, and ended up tired and ready to move forward. Oliver and his agent were in, and the fitting went as per usual. We're going to get through this."

Andy clasped Eddie in a hug for a minute and patted him on the back. "Partners," he said. "And as Mike says, we're going to get through this fine."

At last, they all walked out together, except for Bailey. Everyone said good-night and headed to their separate cars.

"Sean, what did you find?" Madison asked anxiously once she was in the passenger seat of the borrowed Prius. Logan and the rest of the crew were in the SUV they'd rented at the airport, but Madison was sure they'd be connecting soon. "Are we going back to the hotel?"

He looked at her, arching a brow as he put the key in the ignition. "I was planning to go straight to your house to take care of Ichabod."

"Oh!" she gasped, stricken. "Ichabod!"

He smiled. "It's okay. I'm betting we'll see Bogie there — with Jenny Henderson. He wants to make her comfortable. Make sense to you?"

"Absolutely. So, we're going to my house. That's great. But what did you find?"

He glanced over at her. "We found a robe. A robe that's an exact copy of the one worn by the Egyptian priest."

"In the tunnel?"

He nodded. "It was stuffed in a broken crypt. It's with the forensic experts at the police station now. There'll be officers on duty in the basement all night, just to make sure no one messes with the tunnel. Officers will also be posted at the entrance to the Black Box and the studio itself."

"Does that mean they'll let Alistair go?"

"I doubt it'll happen that fast. Alistair's lawyer has to petition the state and get the state's attorney to drop the charges. Before he does that, we need more proof. I think we've proven that someone else *might* have done it, but finding the robe doesn't exonerate him with one hundred percent certainty."

"So what now?"

"We feed Ichabod, get Bogie and Jenny and meet back at the suite."

They did, in that order. As Sean had assumed, Bogie had taken Jenny to Madison's place, where Jenny was learning the fine art of watching *I Love Lucy* reruns. But when Sean explained what had been happening, Bogie was happy to come along to help.

"I wasn't there — and my memory isn't much better dead than it was when I was alive — but I'll do my best," Bogie said, when the six agents, Madison and the spirits sat around the suite's table. "What do you want to know?"

"You believe the accidental death that occurred on that set in 1942 wasn't an accident, that it was murder," Sean began.

"Yeah, but I don't have any evidence," Bogie said. "It just didn't seem right to me when I heard about it. I wasn't there, remember — I'm just telling you what I thought and felt at the time. The head electrician was a man named Richard Wilson, and the key grips were two fellows who worked on lots of films. Donnie Riley and Kevin Baker. I was stunned that anyone could've been electrocuted on their watch. There was an investigation, of course, but it turned out there was a freak power surge — or that's what the police and the insurance company came back with."

"Sounds reasonable," Kelsey said.

"Do you really think what's going on now could have something to do with that movie?" Bogie asked, frowning.

"Hey, strange things, really strange things, seem to be popping up," Madison put in. She looked around the table. "I found out today that Oliver Marshall is really Oliver Marshall *Claymore*. He told me this in confidence. He dropped the Claymore when

374

he went for his Actor's Equity card."

Silence followed her announcement.

"We should have known that," Sean said sheepishly. "Except, of course, we haven't investigated Oliver yet. He's not an employee and there was no reason to suspect he might know anything about the cemetery, the grounds or the studio. The police didn't question him and we hadn't gotten to it yet, although we would have eventually."

"The Claymore who first came out here was a great-great-uncle, from what I understand. Oliver's father is a scientist," Madison said. "His *great-grandfather's* brother was the Hollywood Claymore."

"Let's follow up on that," Logan said. "We'll question Oliver tomorrow. Madison, is he due back in the studio?"

"No, but I can make something up about wanting to check the padding for his costume," she said. "I did promise him I'd keep this quiet," she added in a worried voice.

"We'll respect that. No one else needs to know — unless he turns out to be guilty."

"I can't believe Oliver could be a vicious killer," Madison said. "And even if his name is Claymore, why would he be interested in hurting Eddie? It doesn't make sense. We're working on his costume for what's anticipated to be a number-one box-office hit!"

"The human mind can be a very scary place," Sean told her.

"And," Logan said, "he does have a connection to the studio, and it was the studio back then — Claymore Illusions — that did the effects for *Sam Stone and the Curious Case of the Egyptian Museum.*"

"That still doesn't make him a murderer," she said.

"You volunteered the information," Sean reminded her. "Information that may allow us to eliminate him. Let's find out if any of the other principals surrounding the studio have any associations with the original movie or any of the actors in it."

"I don't know what you'll learn," Bogie said. "I just know I wasn't the only one back then who was skeptical about what they *said* caused that accident on the set. If it was an accident . . ."

"What happened after Krakowski died?" Sean asked.

"They were filming at the old Waterton Studios farther east on Sunset. I think the accident brought the officials in and that led to the structure being condemned. Waterton Studios was used way back in the days of the silents. Right after Krakowski's death, the studios were closed down for a few days while the investigation went on, and then the filming continued," Bogie said. "When it was completed, Waterton was torn down — there's a shopping mall there now. And Krakowski's widow was paid off — some pretty big bucks for the time, I understand."

Logan motioned to Jane. "Find out more about anyone associated with Waterton Studios tomorrow, please. Anything at the police station?"

As Jane began to speak, Sean got up and hurried into his room, returning a moment later with his laptop. He keyed in a few words while Jane described the eliminations she'd been able to make, which included most of the people working at Archer's studio. The majority of them had airtight alibis that she'd been able to check out.

"What about alibis for our key players?" Logan asked.

"Although it was Sunday, Eddie Archer had meetings during the day. Mike Greenwood was at his club in the late afternoon. He was seen there by the bartender and various friends. After that, he claims he went home. He lives in a condo, and the security footage shows him arriving at 7:30 p.m. and doesn't show him going back out. Andy Simons attended a charity event that started at about eight. He was a keynote speaker."

"Anyone see him after the keynote?" Sean questioned.

"I just know that he was there at eight and that his speech lasted about twenty minutes," Jane said. "I spoke to a few people who were at his table. He did eat his dinner, but then friends stopped by and pulled him away and the socializing began."

"Guess who else has a history that relates to this whole thing?" Sean asked.

"Who?"

"None other than the ex–Mrs. Archer, Benita Lowe."

"What's her connection?" Logan stood and walked over to the bulletin board they'd covered with pictures and information, thoughts and theories.

Sean looked up from his computer. "Benita Lowe was actually born in Mexico — the police gave us that much, and I'm pretty sure I knew it already. It was her mother's country of birth. Benita's parents were Austin Lowe, an American casting agent, and Maria Juarez, a seamstress. And Maria was the daughter of Juan Juarez of Mexico City — and Janet Krakowski, daughter of Pete Krakowski, killed in the making of *Sam Stone and the Curious Case of the Egyptian Museum*."

Logan had been writing as Sean spoke. "I

say it's time we had her brought in. I'll call Knox. We'll meet them at the station."

Sean nodded. "Los Angeles may be a city of millions, but there's been nepotism in this industry since the beginning. We may come across more people with connections to the movie."

"We've got a woman with a potential motive and no real alibi," Logan said. "We'll talk to her. Sean, you, Kelsey and I will go. Tyler, get some sleep. If this turns into an all-nighter, you'll be with Kat and Jane at the studio tomorrow. And Madison . . ." he said thoughtfully.

"Madison comes with us. I don't want her alone."

"I think he's saying women aren't tough enough," Jane told Kat.

Sean shook his head. "I am worried, and I have perfect faith in every member of this team. But I'll feel better if Madison is with us. Besides, her take on what Benita has to say could be useful." He looked directly at Madison. Is that okay with you?"

She nodded but then she remembered what else she'd wanted to tell them. "Benita's got the blood connection," she said, "but I was just thinking about something else Oliver said. He was talking about a day Helena came in. Apparently she had her hands all over Eddie — as in, maybe dipping into his pockets."

"Dipping into his pockets — to steal a key? Have a copy made and then replace it?" Sean asked.

"That's how it sounds to me."

"Let's start with Benita," Logan said. "I hadn't expected to get anywhere until tomorrow, so we'll be ahead of the game." He paused. "Call Eddie's house. See if you can talk to his houseman and find out if Helena is there. Make sure she's not out and about and that we'll be able to speak with her tomorrow. If she is there, just lie. Say you're calling to ask how she and Eddie are doing. We won't tell her we need to speak with her again. I don't want to spook her."

Sean made the call, waiting as Pierce went to check on Mr. and Mrs. Archer. Then he hung up. "Pierce said that both Archers retired soon after Eddie got home. They had a quiet dinner and went to bed."

"Let's go talk to Benita," Logan said.

Benita Lowe was at the police station when they arrived; she'd come in just minutes after Knox had called her.

Sean spoke with the detective before going in to question her. He'd been assigned the task, since the interview would seem the friendliest and least threatening if he were to do it.

When he sat across from her at the table, she raised her brows and a smile slowly curved her lips.

"Am I a suspect now?" she asked him.

"Not really or no more so than anyone else at the moment," he said, settling into his chair. "It's just that some interesting information has come up — regarding you."

She leaned toward him. With her catlike grace, Benita could be extremely sensual and charming when she wanted, and her amusement seemed real.

"What, exactly?" she asked him. "The fact that I'm bisexual, or that my great-grandfather was Pete Krakowski? I'm sure you've discovered that by now."

"I'm embarrassed to say we just discovered it tonight. I'm surprised more people don't know," Sean told her.

She shrugged elegantly. "Why would that be? I couldn't see how it would benefit me to advertise that I'm distantly related to some minor actor who ran around all over the place, drank like a fish and wound up dead on a set, electrocuted. Frankly, it's something I'd just as soon *not* have out there, you know? And I doubt anyone cares.

I'm assuming other people can hear this conversation, so . . ." She paused, waving to whoever might be standing behind the two-way mirror that separated them from the police observers. "Hey, you guys! That's not for the news — not until I'm really rich and famous, all right?"

"These conversations aren't for public consumption, Benita," Sean assured her.

She smiled. "You know what, Sean? I really do care about Eddie. And, believe it or not, I honestly thought we'd make a go of our marriage. Granted, there are certain little idiosyncrasies about me . . . if you choose to see it that way. Personally, I consider myself a freethinker and a free-wheeler, and the world is my oyster. Leave it to Eddie! The majority of men would give their eyeteeth to be in a threesome. Not Eddie. I love him, Sean. I really love him. And I care about Alistair, which is more than I can say for Helena."

"But you and Helena are friends."

"We *were* friends, once," Benita said. "Now she's afraid of me, threatened by me. Look, I swear to you — I wouldn't hurt Eddie, and I wouldn't hurt Alistair, and I never even met Jenny Henderson. Come on, Sean. You know me."

"I know pretty much everyone involved

with the studio," he told her. "And I'm not accusing you of anything. I'm asking you to help me."

"People don't always mean to, but they talk." She leaned close to him again, as if they were conspirators. "I understand you've been prowling around in the basement at the studio. Can you imagine *me* in the basement, Sean? Seriously?"

"It's what we least imagine that often proves to be true."

She shook her head vehemently. "Me — in dirty, dusty places filled with spiderwebs? Not in this lifetime."

"Maybe that's not characteristic of what you'd do, Benita, but revenge could be a factor here," Sean said. "Revenge for Pete Krakowski's death. And maybe there's more than one person involved in this — one person to do the deed and another to work on cleanup or alibis or —"

"Well, that's a great theory, Sean," she broke in. "Except what I heard from my grandmother is that Pete Krakowski was a drunk who gave nothing to his family and cheated on his wife from here to eternity — when he wasn't knocking the crap out of her. The best thing he ever did was die on that set and leave his wife a nice settlement. And . . ." She drew the pad and pencil that lay on the table toward her. "I'm giving you two names. Two. They're both my alibi." She looked into his eyes. "We were together all night. You're welcome to verify my alibis for Sunday night — just do it discreetly, huh? Some people prefer to keep their private lives private."

Sean wasn't sure if he was relieved by the conversation and Benita's easy assurance that she had an alibi, or disappointed. Relieved, he decided. He liked her, with all her brash — and perhaps honest — ways.

Gut instinct. He believed her. But . . . she *was* an actress.

"Thank you for coming in, Benita, and thank you for providing these names. We'll be discreet, I promise."

She rose to leave. When she walked out, she saw Madison waiting with Logan and Kelsey.

She smiled, and glanced back at Sean. "I guess you two have a lot in common," she said, "what with the special effects and all." She paused, saying good-night to Knox, Kelsey and Logan. "If you need me, you know where to find me."

When she'd left, Knox turned to Sean, perplexed. "Sure as hell sounded as if she was telling the truth. So, you want the current wife brought in tomorrow?"

"Yes. We'll just tell her it's important we speak with her, and that we're hoping she can fill in some details we need about other people. With luck, that'll get her in here without calling her lawyer and making things difficult," Sean said.

"Tomorrow." Knox yawned. "I'm used to putting in some serious time, but we do have other shifts. You people are dedicated, not to mention workaholics."

"Only on a case like this," Logan said. "Yeah, we're the first shift, the second and the third."

As Logan drove them back to the hotel, Madison asked Sean, who sat in the back with her, "Do you really think that two people were involved?"

"Maybe. I don't understand why time was erased on the security footage, unless it was done just to throw us off."

"I think we might have one psycho ready to kill — and one with another agenda," Logan said. "Or is one simply using the other? I don't know. Or perhaps they both stand to gain from the killing."

Sean met Logan's eyes in the rearview mirror.

"I can't imagine one person close to Eddie being guilty, much less two," Madison was saying. "But suppose you're right. You mean that one person did the actual killing and someone else made it possible? Maybe someone just hired a killer."

Sean shook his head. "I don't think so. It was too carefully orchestrated. The tunnel, the robe, the catacombs, the basement — as we've said all along, it had to be someone with real knowledge of the studio. And even hiring someone . . . That someone had to know how to get around the place *and* have a good alibi." He sighed. "Those two missing minutes are still driving me crazy. I'm convinced the killer always planned to use the tunnels, and I'm beginning to believe the security footage was erased to send us in the wrong direction."

They stopped for takeout along the way; when they returned they met briefly in the center room to divide up the food. Bogie was still with Jenny Henderson, both reclining on the suite's sofa across from the TV. Jenny seemed . . . almost alive.

"Bogie's been telling me the most fantastic Hollywood tales!" she told them.

"That's great, Jenny," Madison said, smiling.

"And we've been thinking, of course. Trying to come up with anything else that might help," Jenny said.

The television was on. They were watching a rerun of *The Danny Thomas Show.*

"Yeah, yeah, and watching television," Bogie said.

Sean grinned. "That's okay."

"Did you get anything?"

"I think we need to look at the domestic situation further," Sean replied.

Bogie nodded. "Yes, closely. Very closely."

Madison walked across the hall with Logan waiting at the door, watching her enter her own room. Sean looked at him. "She's safe," he said in a low voice.

"You're going over there?"

"Yeah."

"Good night, then. We'll get organized to question Helena in the morning. I'll send Tyler and the others to the studio with Madison, and you and I can question Mr. Archer's charming wife."

Sean agreed and crossed over to Madison's room, tapping at her door. She let him in quickly, but it didn't seem to matter to her whether others noted his arrival or not. He handed her his meal, then shed his jacket, gun and holster, and placed the Glock on the side of the bed.

She set their food up on the desk, and despite the late hour, he was surprised to discover how hungry he was. They ate in comparative silence, asking common meal questions like, "Is there another packet of ketchup?" and "Hand me one of those foil things of butter, will you?"

When they'd finished, Madison threw away the trash. He watched her and found himself thinking that she was extraordinary, and not just because she spoke with ghosts. She moved fluidly and everything about her was natural. With Madison, there was absolutely no pretense in a world where pretense was everything; it was even what she did for a living. He'd thought her beautifully, sensually shaped when they'd met, and now he knew that his every lustful thought had been right, that her skin was like satin, her hair like silk. And when she looked at a man with those blue eyes wide and exhaled on a satisfied sigh, she was as erotic as he could have dreamed.

He stood, coming up behind her, slipping his arms around her. She turned easily into his embrace, and for a moment, he cupped her chin and met her eyes, searching them to understand how her shade of blue could be more beautiful than any other.

"What?" she whispered.

"Nothing. I'm exhausted . . . and deliriously happy to be with you. But I'm the kind of exhausted that makes me think I need a distraction — some activity — if I'm ever going to sleep."

"I'll show you activity!" she said, laughing. Her fingers brushed his chest as she undid the buttons on his shirt. Just her touch seemed to ignite something in him. He shrugged out of the shirt as her fingers moved to his belt buckle. . . .

Later, when they lay spent and sated in each other's arms, she spoke to him softly. "So . . . who was she? I don't mean to open any wounds, but . . . when you left here, you went back to Texas. . . ."

He was quiet for a while as he studied her. Then he smiled. "She was the love of my life at one time, and my best friend at another," he said. "We did the mad, passionate on-and-off thing for years when we were in high school, and whenever we were home from college. But . . ."

"But?"

"We went in different directions. I wanted Hollywood. She wanted politics. We fought like wildcats after college, and then split up. I moved to California and she was a mover in Texas, giving fantastic speeches, fierce and loyal to all her causes. I watched her career from afar, and we kept up, mainly through Facebook and email."

He hesitated again, thinking about Melissa. He remembered how the illness had taken her bit by bit, and yet never stolen her passion, her heart, her soul or her courage.

By then he'd realized they were friends. The best of friends. But when she died, it seemed that he'd lost the love of his life. Their histories had been interwoven.

Love could change. Love between them had become something different. No longer sexual. Something different, yes, maybe even something more.

He looked at Madison and touched her face with a bittersweet smile. "We were far apart in distance and in the everyday course of our lives. I was still fairly new out here, working constantly, having that occasional wild night out or superficial fling. And then . . . then I heard about the cancer. Melissa didn't have family. Her dad had departed — left the family, more or less disappeared — when she was two, and her mom died when she was twenty-two. We'd been together during that hard time, and it might have helped cement what we had, I don't know."

"She must have had many friends and been adored."

"She did and she was, but no one knew her like I did. And as she was failing, she didn't want to be around others. It was pride, I guess. She didn't want a lot of people to see her as she was — thin as a rail, balding, drawn. And pretense in front of people who aren't really close can be exhausting. I thought about Melissa and our situation endlessly after she died. Maybe we were never meant to be. And maybe we both believed that we'd get ambition out of the way and then we'd be together when we were ready. It didn't matter. When I knew how sick she was, I had to go to her, and she accepted me. I talked to her doctor. . . . He was a good guy. He never let her completely lose hope — but didn't give her false hope, either. He told me they'd try everything they could while she had breath in her body, but the prognosis wasn't positive. Melissa was an intelligent woman, and she could see that she wasn't getting any better. There were good days when I first got back. Really good days. But what I learned was that ambition didn't mean a thing.

"When she died, I was already gaining a reputation for special effects, especially computer-generated effects, in Texas. I got established in San Antonio, and there was a lot of work going on there. I stayed, thinking I might go back to Hollywood one day, but my heart wasn't in it. I worked with the Texas Rangers and the state and local police on a few cases, and it seemed that I'd found my niche."

He paused, and Madison nudged him to continue.

"A while back," he resumed, "a man named Adam Harrison — who'd been called in by both private citizens and the government in strange and *unusual* cases for years — was approached by the FBI to put together a special unit. He formed the first Krewe of Hunters. Then he found out there was so much going on, some of it genuinely unusual, and some of it people playing at the unusual, that they figured they needed to create another team. No one really knows how Adam Harrison gets his information about people, but he has a knack for putting teams together. Five of us are from Texas and were working there. My cousin Kelsey grew up in Florida, but she'd visited Texas a lot. No one has to join the team, of course. We're all allowed to make our own choices. It's been good for me. It let me really step back, see where I've been and where I want to be."

"You were approached because someone knew you could talk to the dead?" Madison asked him.

"Yes."

"Were . . . were you able to talk to Melissa

after she died?"

He nodded. "Once. At her grave site. She touched my face, kissed my lips — and told me to live my life. But at that point . . . well, I couldn't. She told me she was going on, that it was only right. We had known how to say goodbye in life. Now we needed to do it after her death." He remembered his emotions during that awful time when the cancer had become so unbearable he prayed Melissa would die, so the pain would end.

"She was a wonderful human being," Madison whispered.

He nodded, and hugged her tighter. He didn't have to say anything else. He didn't have to tell her she was wonderful, too.

He felt her gentle touch, and then the way she curled against him. He cradled her chin. "And you?" he asked, meeting her eyes.

"I used to feel like a truly odd loner for a really long time — and yet, I was never really unhappy, just scared and convinced I was crazy, and that I needed to keep my secret. When I was young . . ."

"Yes?"

"There was Josh."

"The love of your life?"

"My young life. He died before we graduated. A ridiculous accident," she said, and told him what had happened to the young man so full of promise. "Even at his funeral, all he wanted me to do was make sure everyone found a way to accept his death. And then after he died . . . I've dated casually. But Bogie followed me home when I was still in college, so my casual dating hasn't been going that great. Maybe I've been afraid of getting close to people. My first experience with ghosts was Billy. I was so young that when I tried to tell people he was going to a better place, my mother was appalled. She doesn't understand."

"Poor baby!" he said, and he smiled. "There are those of us who do understand. You know that now, don't you?"

"I know," she murmured.

They curled together in a comfortable silence.

And then they were both able to sleep.

Vengeance was waiting. Vengeance didn't like to wait. But the night was dark, and a low fog was hanging over the ground, eerie and mysterious. Rather nice, Vengeance thought.

She arrived, angry, as she tiptoed through the grass. "This is totally going to ruin my shoes. And getting here was a nightmare!"

"You're late."

394

"You're damned lucky I'm here!"

"You're damned lucky I just don't tell them you did it."

"*What?* I'd accuse you. *You're* the one who did it."

"You made it possible!" Vengeance reminded her.

She looked away. "I'm not going into the tunnels. I already went into those damned tunnels for you, and I'm not doing it again."

"You don't have to go into the tunnels. Not now."

"Well, you said I have to help clean up. What the hell did you want me to do, then?" she asked irritably.

"Die!" Vengeance said quietly. "Just die."

Her eyes widened.

When she opened her mouth to scream, it was too late.

14

When Madison woke up the next morning, Sean was no longer beside her. She found a note on the pillow telling her that he'd had an idea and she should join Logan Raintree and the others in the suite.

A glance at the bedside clock showed her that he must have risen extremely early, since it was just past six. But then, she was learning particulars about his personality. If he had an idea, he wasn't going to fall back asleep; he was going to explore it.

In the suite, she discovered that coffee was made and there were bagels, fruit and pitchers of juice and water on the table.

"Help yourself," Logan told her, "and then you and I will head over to the studio with Tyler and Kelsey. I'll meet up with Sean there, and he and I will go to the police station. We've decided that we'll bring in Helena LaRoux at ten. Kat and Jane have already gone back to the station."

"Thank you," Madison said. "Do you know where Sean is now?"

"He's at the studio, following a hunch." Logan was standing at the board, writing, drawing lines. Madison studied it. On one side, the name Pete Krakowski was written, and on the other, Eddie Archer. Names were listed beneath, along with the connections between any of those names. Separately, to the far right, he'd listed theories, thoughts, hunches, questions.

Possibly more than one killer.

Benita has a family tie to Krakowski.

Oliver has a family tie to Claymore Illusions.

Madison fixed a plate of food and sat down, watching Logan as he continued to write.

Two killers. Both with knowledge of the studio, one with greater access.

Killing not random.

Motives: Oliver Marshall — related to original studio owner, Claymore.

Helena LaRoux, current wife — stands to gain if Alistair convicted? How? There was a prenup, and she is taken care of in the will. So is Benita.

Alistair — to inherit studios.

Mike Greenwood — knows the studio better than most.

Andy Simons — Eddie's partner.

Colin Bailey — on duty at the time of the murder.

Winston Nash — knows the studio, knows how to work the security footage.

"You really think it's down to one of these people?" Madison asked.

Logan sat down across from her. "Can you suggest anyone else? Anyone we should interview again? We'll bring in Oliver Marshall, discreetly, of course. But other than Oliver?"

She hesitated, surprised by what she was going to say. "I don't know if this is important or not. My assistant, Alfie, has been acting a bit strange. He always acts a bit strange, but I mean more than usual. He's a wonderful assistant and very talented. But he was the first to call me about the murder, and he's almost eager to see what's going on."

Logan rose and added the name of Madison's assistant to the list. Tyler entered the suite, pouring himself a coffee and greeting the two of them.

"Where are our resident ghosts?" he asked.

"Bogie has taken it upon himself to shelter Jenny. He's trying to teach her what ghosts can and can't do. I think he's gone off to show her more of 'old Hollywood,' " Logan said. "We should get going. I'll collect

Kelsey. She's been on the computer looking for any more connections to the studio or the movie." He studied Madison, and she sensed that he was perplexed, suspecting that she knew — somewhere inside — a piece of information that might help them.

"Honestly," she said. "I can't think of anything else."

"You will," he told her. "I'm not sure what it is or when we'll get to it, but I have a gut hunch that you do know something." He smiled. "Now let's get out there."

There simply weren't enough hours in the day, Sean thought ruefully, staring across the expanse of Peace Cemetery. It was aptly named; it seemed to stretch on forever, and beautiful oaks had grown up over the years to shade the winding trails, benches, grave-stones and monuments. The funerary art ranged from the contemporary back to the flowery detail of the late-Victorian era. Fences separated the cemetery from the studio and the Black Box Cinema, but Sean wasn't concerned with the fences; he was still certain there had to be an entry to the underground catacombs. He just had to figure out where that entry might be.

It was a daunting task.

Benny Knox, impressed by the hours the

Krewe seemed to keep, had done his part, bringing the original plan for the cemetery and the roster that noted the burials.

"It's like any other old cemetery, or so says the current manager — who was not pleased to be called at 7:00 a.m.," Knox had said. "Graves have shifted over the years, and before there was greater security, vandals broke stones. Some are almost pulverized by tree roots. Things happen — and the dead are forgotten." Knox sighed. "I was informed that the original Claymore owned the land but donated some of it to the church. At first this place was a grave-yard before it became a public cemetery. Yeah, apparently graveyards are attached to churches, and *cemeteries* don't have to be. In the flux of that turnover, a lot of records went missing. But there are vaults all over — as you can see — and lots of people were buried in pine boxes . . . sometimes on top of one another. There was a rumor that the poor could be buried here when they didn't have money for fancy coffins or grave sites."

"So . . . Claymore worked with the church, to help the poor?" Sean had asked. *That would explain the catacombs attached to the studio and the Black Box.*

"There are over fifty thousand known burials and entombments in the cemetery.

400

Just going through the records is like working your way through a giant maze," Knox had told him.

Now Sean studied the paperwork and tried to get his bearings. So, it seemed Claymore, father of Lucas, *had* been involved, apparently for the most generous of reasons. But Sean had gone to the vault, expecting he'd have to wait for one of the cemetery workers before he could enter the small family mausoleum. That hadn't been true; the vault was open, like a larger, multifamily mausoleum might be. Beautiful iron gates led to a little sanctuary with a bench. There was an altar, and a memorial plaque stated that the earthly remains of Lucas Claymore rested beneath the altar in the middle of various other Claymores, including, of course, his father, who'd been such a benefactor to the church.

Sean was looking over the cemetery when his cell phone rang. He answered it to hear Eddie Archer, sounding frantic.

At first Sean couldn't understand a word he was saying.

"She's not here. She's not here," Eddie finally managed. "The police called. They wanted Helena to come in and talk to them, to help establish timelines, talk about my friends — enemies. Actually, they said you and Logan wanted to talk to her."

"That's true, Eddie."

"But she's not here! I sent Pierce to get her after I spoke to that Knox fellow. She wasn't in her room."

"Eddie, it's morning. She might have gone out somewhere," Sean said. But he felt uncomfortable. Maybe it was the panic in Eddie's voice. Maybe it was just that dreaded gut feeling, the premonition you felt when something really was wrong.

"Did you tell Knox you couldn't find Helena?" Sean asked.

"No, no, not yet. I just said I'd get her up. We need to file a missing-person report," Eddie said.

"It's too soon. We don't know that she's really missing?"

"But Pierce —"

"Let me speak to him, Eddie."

A moment later, Pierce was on the phone. "I've been trying to tell Eddie not to panic — that just because she isn't here this minute doesn't mean she's *missing*."

"Pierce, when did you last see her?"

"She retired about an hour before Eddie yesterday evening," he said.

"Was her bed made this morning — had she slept in it?"

Pierce was silent; Sean could imagine Ed-

402

die staring at him, stricken.

"No."

"Is her car there?"

"Wait a minute."

He set the phone down and came back. "No, it's not in the drive, and it's not in the garage. You think she just went somewhere?"

"Maybe. I take it Eddie tried to call her?"

"Her cell phone goes straight to voice mail."

"All right, we don't want to make Eddie worse," Sean said. "*Yes* and *no* answers will do. Does she ever make her own bed? Couldn't she have straightened up before she left this morning?"

"No," Pierce said.

"Thanks. Tell Eddie that I'll take care of calling Knox, and that we'll get an APB out on her and her car."

"Eddie is extremely agitated, Sean."

"Try to get him to calm down —"

Sean didn't finish his sentence because Eddie had grabbed the phone. "Don't tell me to calm down! I have to do *something*. Helena is not here!"

"Eddie, you saw her last night. And she obviously drove from your house, since her car is gone. She might have gone out for doughnuts."

"She never eats doughnuts."

403

"Then she might have gone out to buy a new kind of diet granola — I don't know. But calm down, please, or you'll end up having a heart attack."

"You can't tell me everything's going to be all right!"

"No, I won't tell you that," Sean said. "I'm just telling you not to panic, and that even if something *is* wrong, the FBI and the police are working on the case. Other than trying to think of anywhere she might have gone, there's nothing you can do. Working yourself into a frenzy isn't going to help anyone."

"All right, all right — I'm calm," Eddie said. He obviously wasn't, but at least he was listening. "Sean, first Alistair — and now Helena. I'm just ill. I don't understand this. Why is someone hurting everyone around me?"

"Eddie, we'll find out," Sean promised him. "We're getting close."

"Helena's dead, isn't she, Sean?"

"You don't know that, Eddie. You don't know that." Sean's voice sounded hollow, even to himself.

He felt a twist in his stomach; Eddie might well be right.

He might be wrong.

No.

Why did he feel that Eddie was right, and Helena was dead? They'd only just discovered that she wasn't in the house.

"I will work with every resource I can summon, Eddie, I promise you. I won't stop until we find her," Sean said.

"Thank you, Sean. Thank you. What do I do now?" Eddie asked hoarsely.

"Go and see Alistair. Be with your son, Eddie. You can support each other."

He hung up, then called Knox and explained. After that, he called Logan, put him on the alert regarding Helena. He'd phone back when he was finished at the cemetery to see if Eddie had gone to see Alistair and if the two were doing all right. With an APB on Helena's car, there wasn't much reason for him to drive blindly around L.A. trying to find her himself.

He returned to his task.

Where the hell is it? Where's the entry? It's got to be here somewhere. The dead in those catacombs didn't get there by themselves.

He cursed and looked across the rows and twisting paths, over winged angels and weeping cherubs.

Neither the original blueprint nor any of the plots and ownership lists had mentioned anything at all about the underground burials.

He started to walk, remembering the cemetery plans, and trying to envision just how far the basement of the studio reached.

"Helena is missing," Logan said. They'd just arrived at the studio. It was still early, barely 8:00 a.m.

Kelsey and Tyler had gone on to check with the guard and the police officers who'd been on duty throughout the night.

"Missing?" Madison echoed.

"Eddie was going to tell her we wanted to speak with her, and she was gone. According to Pierce, she was seen going up to bed last night, but not since. Her bed hasn't been slept in, and her car is gone."

"So do you think she's another victim, or that she's somehow involved and on the run?"

"I think she may blithely drive back home after having gone to the drugstore. Or that she might have skipped town. Or that she might be a victim," Logan said. "I just don't know."

They walked into the studio. "Can you remember *anything?* Anything at all that might have to do with any of this?" he asked urgently.

"I swear, if I could think of anything else, Logan, I'd tell you," Madison said. And then, as she approached the front door to the studio, she paused and turned back to him.

"There *is* something I hadn't thought of," she said slowly.

"What?"

"Lucas Claymore."

"The previous owner of the studio?"

"Yes. And his father owned the land, inherited from *his* father, and founded the studio. I believe the family gave the cemetery to the church for its burial ground, and then, of course, it was outgrown, and a new church was built. But once, when I was going through the cemetery, I met up with the younger Lucas Claymore. He was old, kind, very pleasant. I know that ghosts don't show up on demand, but if we walked through the cemetery, he might appear to one of us. I doubt it'll be as easy as saying, 'Hey, Lucas, did you happen to be around when Jenny Henderson was killed in the tunnel?' But he could tell us *something* that might help — don't you think?"

"I do, indeed," Logan agreed. "In fact, Sean is crawling around somewhere in the cemetery right now. That was his hunch. If he could find the entry to the catacombs in the cemetery, he could follow the killer's path."

"The cemetery gate is on the street," Madison said. "Unless you want to jump the wall?"

"Oh, let's go in properly," Logan said. "I only jump walls when I absolutely have to."

She smiled; she knew that either Colin Bailey or Winston Nash was on duty at the guard stand, and that Kelsey and Tyler had gone to the studio. She wondered if any of them were watching as she and Logan turned away, and started back down to the sidewalk and the cemetery entrance.

The arched iron gate stood at a break in the high stone wall. The letters that spelled out Peace Cemetery were curlicued and ornate, late-Victorian vintage. Actually, the cemetery might have fit an old town in New England better than it did the contemporary bustle of L.A. It was a reminder that while the movie business wasn't old in the history of man, Los Angeles had been around, with hundreds of thousands seeking the American dream, even before the dawn of celluloid fever.

They entered the cemetery. Logan paused for a minute.

"It's huge."

"There's a hell of a big population living — and dying — in these parts," she said wryly.

Logan nodded. "Where do we begin?"

She gestured at a little rise. "That vault there — it's one of the smaller individual vaults. Very pretty, all in marble. The Claymore vault."

"How many times have you seen Lucas Claymore?" Logan asked.

"Just once. I thought he was an elderly gentleman, alive and well and breathing, the first time I saw him," Madison said. "I think that's when Eddie figured I was either crazy . . . or communicated with ghosts. I didn't realize Lucas was dead until I understood that Eddie couldn't see him. Eddie and I were here studying gravestones and monuments. You have to make the not-real look real — if you want movie magic."

"Of course."

"So, let's see if he'll come out today and talk to us."

The kept walking, heading up one of the winding paths that led toward the vault. It was a lovely day, with the sun shining brilliantly. The temperature might go as high as the mid-seventies, since spring was waning and summer was on the way. They passed new burials and memorials interspersed between old stones, other vaults and fenced-in family plots. Fresh flowers had been placed at some of the newer graves.

Other stones were chipped and weather-worn, and the great oaks seemed to dip low, as if weeping sadly for those who had gone on.

They reached the Claymore vault. The iron gate was open.

Logan looked at Madison. "Is this customary?"

She nodded. "There's a little bench and an altar inside. Lucas is under the altar."

"Shouldn't it be locked at night?"

"I don't think they worry about it too much. The walls surrounding the cemetery are high, and the gates are pretty solid. They don't have much trouble out here. In fact, we *never* had trouble out here — until Jenny was killed."

They walked in and Madison sat on the bench. The vault was beautiful, with a circular stained-glass window above the altar, and two more on either side. Each depicted a scene from the New Testament. Above the altar and the coffin beneath, the central window showed Christ with a peaceful look, folding his hands. To one side, the window had Christ surrounded by lambs, and the third window represented the wedding at Cana.

Logan took a seat beside her. "Anything?" he asked softly.

Disappointed, she shook her head. "Did you see him in here the first time you visited?" Logan asked.

"No. I just met him when we were looking for unusual headstones."

"Do you remember where?"

"Beyond the vault, there's another little rise, and something of a potter's field. The burials were for those who died indigent, but the coffins and services were paid for by an actor's fund — those who made it paying for those who didn't. There are a number of really pretty and interesting stones. Some, I suppose, because people were really kind, and some because they didn't want their good deed to go unnoticed."

"Let's take a look," Logan suggested.

They left the Claymore crypt and started along the winding path again. "See," she said to Logan, "isn't that gorgeous? Marian Hatfield had it designed for Shelby McLaughton. They were both silent-film stars." The memorial was carved to picture a feminine-looking angel with a finger to her lips, and beneath it were carved the name of the deceased and the words *In Heaven All Whispers Are Heard Like the Voices of Angels in Song.*

"So Claymore was right here?" Logan asked.

411

She nodded. "We can wait."

They found another bench and sat. Madison began to feel restless; she was sure Logan had to be feeling the same. He'd listened to her, but she suspected they were on a wild-goose chase.

And then, straight and lean, white-haired and a bit fragile, Lucas Claymore appeared. He stood under the shade of an old oak, and he was watching them.

"Logan," she whispered. "He's here."

As he neared the cemetery chapel, Sean heard his phone ring. Caller ID informed him that Benny Knox was calling.

He answered immediately.

"Two of my patrol officers found Helena LaRoux's car," Knox told him.

"Where is it? No sign of Helena?"

"No sign of Helena. The car's on the street behind the northern end of Peace Cemetery. I'd say it's about a half-mile around that back wall to the entrance of the studio. I've called the officers there, but none of them have seen Ms. LaRoux. And the guard about to go off duty — Colin Bailey — swears he hasn't seen her, either."

Sean frowned. "I'm in the cemetery now."

"Do you see anything?"

"A lot of tombstones," he said. "But I'm

412

going to check out the chapel."

Knox was silent for a minute. "What are you doing in the cemetery?" he asked.

"Looking for a pathway to the dead," Sean said.

"I'm heading down there," Knox said. "We need to get on a real search and find that woman. God knows, maybe she met up with a friend, maybe . . ." He groaned. "Why the hell park at the cemetery? There's nothing around it for miles. This just gets worse and worse," he said. "I'll see you soon."

Sean studied the chapel. Once upon a time, it had been consecrated as St. Bartholomew's. But the parishioners had long outgrown the building and the area; St. Bartholomew's was closer to downtown L.A. now and the chapel here was nondenominational. Eddie allowed them to use the building rent-free, as a place for services to be held or for mourners to say their prayers.

Sean had been inside once, years before, accompanying a friend to a funeral service. It was larger than the typical funeral chapel, but then it had begun life as a real church. The main aisle led up to a raised altar, while side aisles converged at the back, where the one-time choir might gather before entering. There were monuments above the walls. The pastor who had first reigned over the old congregation had originally been buried beneath the altar but his remains had been relocated, along with the congregation.

When he entered by the main doors, Sean thought it had been and still was a beautiful place, with just the right poignancy in the decor. The pews were hardwood with dark crimson cushions for kneeling in prayer, and the walls were divided into eight panels, which held Tiffany windows of clear glass with images etched into them — doves, lambs, olive branches and, closest to the altar, looking across at each other, a pair of angels.

Sean walked down the aisle to the altar. He paused for a minute, turning to get a feel for the size and scope of the chapel, and its relationship to the studio and the Black Box Cinema. It was *possible* that tunnels stretched from the chapel to the other buildings.

There was nothing to be seen in the empty church so he went around to the left-side aisle and through a door. He noted that in the rear of the church — where one might enter without being seen by the congregation — was a door.

The staging area for the chapel was in

darkness. There weren't huge cut-glass windows here to let in the sunlight. Two wall lamps were aglow, one on his side and one on the other side. The rear of the chapel was apparently used by the cemetery maintenance workers; several wheelbarrows were lined up against the back wall, a pile of sod waiting to be laid, and shelves holding vases. There were cones that advised Construction Area on the far side of the room. He walked over, trying to see what the construction might be, but nothing gave him a real indication. The place was old and well-maintained, but earthquakes, big and little, had shaken the area over the years, and old foundations always needed to be shored up.

He looked around, waiting for his eyes to get accustomed to the light.

Once they did, he saw a shelf near the pile of sod, and a number of old wooden signs piled up beside it. He dug through them. Several advertised restrooms in one way or another. Ladies, Gentlemen, Men's, Women's. He saw two doors on the right side, one with a large W and the other a large M. He opened both doors to assure himself that the rooms were indeed for the purpose advertised.

Back at the shelf, he dug deeper. At last he found one that read Crypt.

He took a second to look around again; he saw no stairs, and nothing that indicated a crypt.

Frustrated, he returned to the rooms with the large W and the large M.

Nothing, except that when he stood outside, he realized that the depth of the rooms didn't match up with the distance between them.

"This place is full of false walls," he muttered aloud. He studied the wall, tapped on it and shook his head. The crypt stairs had been covered over long ago.

He went into the women's toilet. There was an old dressing table with a mirror behind it. He shoved aside the table and the mirror, uncovering an old pocket door. A large sign read Danger! No Entry.

Sean slid the door open.

A set of dark stairs led downward, into the darkness of the crypt.

Madison stood and smiled at Lucas Claymore. She lifted a hand in greeting, and walked slowly toward him, afraid he would disappear.

"Mr. Claymore!" she greeted him quietly. "Good morning, sir."

Claymore didn't run. He watched her sadly as she approached, then he looked over her shoulder at Logan Raintree. "You work at my studio," he said to Madison. "What used to be my studio, I should say."

"Yes, sir."

"Something terrible has happened," Claymore said.

"Yes, sir." Logan nodded.

For a moment, Claymore became sheer, and almost disappeared in the breeze that moved softly around them.

"We're trying to discover the truth, Mr. Claymore," Madison said.

"I don't have the truth to give you." Claymore sounded sad, even distressed. "People come and people go. There are lights, there are noises, but . . ."

"Mr. Claymore, hundreds of bodies are buried in the catacombs that stretch out from the studio and the cinema," Logan said.

"Yes, of course."

"Of course?"

"That was long ago, so long ago," Claymore said. "But I don't know everything. The property was really my father's, and he died . . . oh, years past. People were flocking here, you know." He sighed. "And then the Depression came. Followed by the war. Most of the burials are very old. Back in the thirties, when there was no social

417

security . . . no assistance for the poor. My father was a good man. When he could no longer help the living, he helped the dead. He wasn't alone in what he did."

"Who helped him?" Madison asked Claymore.

"Why, the Reverend Parker. He was over at St. Bartholomew's. He's been dead for years, too."

Logan turned to Madison. "There's where the tunnels begin," he said. "The church."

"Ah, well, those tunnels have been closed up forever." Lucas Claymore sighed again. "You couldn't have people wandering from a film noir movie into a graveyard now, could you? And Reverend Parker lived a very long life. When he felt it coming to an end, we had the crypt closed off. No one goes down there now. Trust me, I had power in my day. I saw to it that the crypts were kept closed, and that even if the church opened them, there was no access to the studio. Everyone was careful not to let the truth be known. If people had found out, they would have come in. They would've dragged up the dead, who might have ended up in museums, in drawers, like all the specimens they have at the Smithsonian," he said, staring at them as if trying to make sure they understood.

"I think that someone who's very much alive has discovered the secret of the tunnels, Mr. Claymore."

Claymore made a strange sound that, if he'd been living, would have been a disdainful sniff. "That one!" he said, shaking his head.

"That one — who?" Madison asked.

Claymore said, "I saw Eddie Archer with you, young lady. I was glad. He's done the studio proud. But . . . that one he's married to now. She came here. She traipsed around. She lit a cigarette *in my vault* and crushed it out on the floor. She was always waiting for someone here. And she'd be on the phone, yakking away. She was up to something, you mark my words."

"Have you ever seen her in the chapel, Mr. Claymore?" Logan asked.

Claymore shook his head. "I don't stand around here all day, young man. I don't watch people endlessly. Sometimes I come because it's beautiful and peaceful, and I love this land. I can't tell you more than that."

Logan was already tugging at her arm. "Let's go," he said. He pulled his phone from his pocket and started dialing.

"Thank you, Mr. Claymore!" Madison called back.

419

"Thank you, yes, thank you so much!" Logan said. "Damn!" he muttered as they hurried across the cemetery.

"What's wrong?"

"Sean isn't answering," he told her. "He's got to be out of contact. The wretched things worked in the tunnels by the studio, but . . ."

Fear instantly wrapped icy fingers around her heart. "He's here — you said he's here, in the cemetery somewhere. Why haven't we seen him, Logan? Why hasn't he answered?"

"He's probably in the chapel. I know he *was* here. Maybe he thought a chapel that was once a church might have a crypt. And that chapel's a very old building. There might be something blocking cell phone reception. But don't worry — we'll find him. He's a well-trained agent, and he's going to be fine. Now, you, on the other hand, stay close to me."

She didn't intend to do anything foolish. Logan Raintree was tall and long-legged and he kept up with her easily as she ran through the cemetery. When she nearly tripped over a gravestone, he was there to catch her.

"Madison, I'm sure Sean's fine," he said.

"Yes, I am, too."

He smiled, holding her arm. "We'll walk quickly — but we walk, okay?"

She nodded, feeling chastised but knowing he was right.

When they got close to the chapel, she drew ahead again, calling Sean's name as they hurried in. Entering the building, she heard the echo of her voice against the old stone walls. Sean didn't answer.

"Come around here," Logan said, moving past her down the aisle.

She followed him and then entered the sacristy, or staging area, for the church. "Watch it! There are lights, but it's dangerous back here."

"We didn't ask Lucas where to find the crypt!" Madison said.

She walked around and saw a maintenance area. Some of the flooring had been roped off.

"I wonder what happened here, or what they're doing."

Logan joined her. "It doesn't look like they're doing anything yet. Someone who works here might have realized that the flooring is treacherous. They've probably asked for a structural engineer to come in.

Madison walked over to the area that had been roped off. "The ground looks damp. Maybe they had a leak," she said.

"Maybe. I heard it was bizarrely wet last month, lots of rain. But that's good. It'll help keep the fires down this summer." Logan was trying his phone. "Doesn't work in here, either," he muttered.

"Yes, but it doesn't matter. Sean isn't in here!"

"He's here somewhere," Logan said. "Sean!"

He walked toward the bathrooms, but Madison could see that Sean wasn't in the men's room — the door was gaping open.

She crossed the floor, trying to study the roped-off area.

"Madison!"

She turned around. "You found him?" she asked.

"This way."

She took a step and tripped into the roped-off area.

"Madison!" Logan called again.

"I'm all right. I'm —"

She never finished her sentence.

The floor beneath her gave way, and she pitched straight down into a dark abyss.

15

Sean went dead still, hearing the sound of the scream.

He wasn't sure how he recognized a *scream,* but he did.

Madison.

He'd traveled no more than twenty feet into the crypts, straight to the rear of the structure, or so he believed. Here, marble slabs covered every entombment, except for those that had been dug into the ground and were covered with memorials, some in stone and some in brass. He hadn't discovered where the tunnels connected with the studio, but he knew he'd eventually find what he was seeking. There was no other way for a killer to escape without leaving some clue — a drop of blood, *something.*

The scream! It was close, and yet he didn't know where it had come from.

"Madison!" he shouted.

"Sean!" she cried in return.

"Sean!" He heard Logan's shout, too.

"What happened?" he yelled.

"I went through the floor," Madison yelled back.

"I'm trying to get down to her," Logan said.

"Are you all right?" Sean's voice echoed off the cold slabs of marble in the darkness around him.

"I'm . . . up, I'm on my feet. I'm fine, no bones broken . . . but it's dark down here!"

"Keep talking. I'm trying to get to you."

"Okay," Madison said. "I guess I'm going to be a bit late for work. Hey, did you find out anything about our missing Helena? Oh, wait, that would mean you answer and I quit talking. Logan was great this morning and he kept trying to make me remember if there was anything else I knew. I was sure there wasn't, but we were looking for tunnels, and information about the property, and I don't know why it hadn't occurred to me that I knew the ghost of the man who'd owned the studio before Eddie — Lucas Claymore. So we went to his tomb. . . ."

She paused for breath.

"So did I!" Sean called. "Logan, can you see Madison?" he shouted.

"You're so muffled I can barely hear you!" Logan shouted back. "I'm trying to give her some light . . . until you reach her. Then I'll get down there, or you can get Madison back up here."

"Madison, start talking again!" Sean said. So far, he'd been walking in one direction, which seemed to be his only choice. Except that he was moving farther away from Madison's voice, and he needed to get closer. He retraced his steps, using his flashlight to illuminate the grave markers and the floor. Then he froze; there was blood on the ground.

Fresh blood, a trail of it.

"Madison!" He felt a prickle of fear. "Madison, keep talking!"

He followed the blood, and it seemed to lead into a wall of tombs.

"I'm here. Let me see, I'm not sure what to say. Um. It was good to be back at work yesterday. I'm looking forward to going in today. It's — oh, God, Sean, it's really . . . dark down here."

But she kept talking. He realized that following the trail of blood had made her voice seem louder. He'd taken a slight turn to the right, and might be doubling back under the center of the church sacristy.

But there was that wall. . . .

Puzzled, he put his hand on one of the tombs. The blood trail seemed to lead to it, and then beneath it.

He pushed on the marble slab covering the tomb. Nothing.

"Madison!" Logan called. "I'm shining the light down there. Can you see anything?"

"Yes, I can see the floor . . . I'm in the crypt. There are walls of graves down here, and there seem to be more tunnels, like the ones by the studio, except that these are in better shape. Well, I can really only see where your light is shining — Oh!"

Her words broke off in a horrified gasp.

"Madison!" Sean screamed, pushing at the stones. He could hear her clearly, she was so close.

"There — there's something here . . . in a crypt. In a broken crypt."

"Can you see what it is?" he shouted to her.

"Logan!" she called up. "Can you twist the light around?"

Logan must have done so.

Madison let out a long and terrified shriek.

"Madison!" He banged frantically at the slabs on the tombs.

"I'm all right," she said, but her voice was weak.

"What? What is it?" Sean demanded. "Madison . . ."

He'd done something right; the slabs were false. There for show, but perfectly fitted, and probably first engineered when a young pastor and the owner of the property wanted to make sure the down-and-out among L.A.'s dead weren't thrown into nameless pits.

The marble shifted silently, sliding open. He moved his flashlight about frantically.

He saw Madison, white-faced, as she backed away from the wall of crypts.

Sean cast the light in that direction.

"We've found Helena LaRoux," she said, her voice a raspy whisper.

His light fell on the body that dangled from a rope attached to a metal hook on one of the crypts. The hook had been intended to hold flower arrangements and had nearly bent with the woman's weight.

The other end of the rope was attached to the handles on a vault. The blood he'd seen had apparently dripped from the slashes on her wrists. It appeared that Helena had come here, tried to slash her wrists but failed to do so deeply enough and then hanged herself instead.

But there was something really wrong with this picture, no matter how it appeared. . . .

He walked to the body, reaching up to place two fingers against her throat, but he knew before he touched her that Helena was gone, cold as ice in the underground crypt. He moved away from her, not wanting to destroy any evidence.

She looked like a prop, like "Matilda" back in the conference room — victim number one or any of a number of rubber, latex and wax deceased that they'd made over the years at the studio. Except that she was real. She'd been Helena, flesh and blood, but now, she was no more alive than a mannequin in the studio.

"Logan?" he shouted up. "It's Helena. I'm going to get Madison out of here. Can you step outside and call Knox? Tell him he's going to need the M.E."

An hour later, Madison was sitting at the rear of an emergency vehicle, a cup of coffee in her hand, a blanket around her shoulders. She was dirty but not hurt. It was difficult to convince them all that although she'd taken a bad fall, she must have landed right. She hadn't broken anything. She hadn't even cracked anything. She'd probably be sore the next day, but she was fine — just anxious to leave.

She couldn't forget what she'd seen. When Logan's light had first fallen on the crypts, she'd noticed the shadow, more darkness in

428

the darkness. And then the light had focused more directly on what was there in the crypt.

Helena, dangling from the rope, her eyes open, her skin white, just hanging there, the red around her wrists, blood congealing where it had dripped down the marble of the tombs behind her, and onto the marble slab she'd used to jump off in order to take her own life.

Madison wondered if she'd ever forget the sight of her open eyes.

Sean was in deep conversation with Knox and Logan as more and more techs arrived, suited up and looking as if they'd come to contain a biohazard. The manager of the cemetery had joined them with members of his staff, and they seemed to be in shock.

Sean broke away from the group and came over to her.

"Does Eddie know yet?" Madison asked.

"Mike Greenwood is on his way to Eddie's. He's going to give him the news."

"Was she guilty, Sean?" Madison whispered. "Is that why she killed herself? We saw Lucas Claymore. He said she'd been in the cemetery, talking on the phone, waiting — as if she was going to meet someone here."

"Logan told me. And that adds to my feeling — I just don't believe she killed herself.

It doesn't seem like Helena. But her car is parked outside the wall, so she did drive herself here."

"We were sure she wasn't bright enough to carry this off," Madison said.

"I still don't think she was bright enough to carry *any* of this off," Sean remarked. "But the forensic experts will know more than I do. First, I don't see Helena crawling down into a basement tomb to kill herself. She'd do it dramatically — if she was going to do it at all. Secondly, I don't see her slashing her wrists or hanging herself. She would've arranged a grand finale, beautifully decked out, and she would've taken some kind of overdose. I don't believe this at all."

"You think her conspirator killed her?" Madison asked. "And that she was in on Jenny's murder?"

"Oh, she was in on it — that's how she came to be here," Sean replied. "I'm sure she's the one who knew that Alistair would be here watching the movie, and that she's the one who knew Jenny was coming. I think she stole Eddie's elevator key and had a copy made. I don't think she committed the murder."

"You mean, she was in on Jenny's murder, but then her partner . . . decided she was a liability?"

Sean nodded. "Maybe she was getting nervous because she found out we were going to question her down at the station, and she met with her partner to find out what to say. Or maybe her partner was nervous about *her* — that's easy to believe. I don't think she was intended to be a victim at the beginning. Or maybe the killer figured he'd get her, too, when he was ready. I can't help feeling she was involved. Why else do you drive to a cemetery and sneak in? But who knows — we're still missing a piece of the puzzle. When this began, I suspect the intent was just to make Alistair go to prison for the rest of his life. But I think we're close to the truth now."

"You're saying you know who the real killer is — whoever actually carried out the murders?"

"No. I don't know who else is involved. Obviously, with Helena dead, we won't be able to question her at the station and throw her off. But we've found it — the tunnel," Sean said grimly. "I haven't taken it all the way through yet. I will once the tech people are finished down there. I'm sure that tunnel goes to the studio. And I'm sure that's how the killer escaped."

"Why did he leave Helena down there?"

Madison asked.

"I'm assuming it's because he didn't want Helena found right away — in case we didn't believe it was a suicide. But now that Helena *has* been found, Alistair could be released soon." He was thoughtful for a minute. "I also assume the killer didn't think we'd ever find the tunnels. He probably figured we'd go crazy trying to trace the tunnels through the studio, that it wouldn't occur to us to backtrack."

"Can you or Logan speak to the D.A. or the A.D.A. on the case? Alistair should be released now. I don't really understand the legal chain, but all they have to do is drop the charges against him, right?"

"It has to be done before the judge," Sean said. "If they were to release Alistair — or even announce that they were releasing him — it could force the killer's hand."

Logan walked over to join them. "Knox just told me they opened her car. She left a suicide note on the driver's seat."

Sean's eyebrows shot up. "There's a suicide note?" he asked incredulously.

"So I've been told. They'll test it forensically."

"I'm willing to bet it was typed," Sean said.

"Oh, yeah." Logan nodded. "Forensics

432

can try to match it to a printer — and we'll start with the computers at the studio and Eddie's house."

"I need to see that note," Sean insisted. "I need to know exactly what it said."

"I'll have Knox get it."

Sean turned back to Madison, as Logan hurried off. "The police will have to close the studio again, but the work can go on until the last minute. The whole place has to be closed until they really get a grip on what's going on underground."

"How will they do that?"

"They'll bring in a score of engineers. We've just got to find out how the killer's been using the labyrinth, get every bit of evidence from the tunnels before the engineers go down there."

"What's going to happen with the studio?" Madison asked anxiously. She was worried sick about Eddie — first Alistair and now his wife. But the studio meant a livelihood for so many people.

"We'll have to see," Sean told her. "I don't know."

Logan came back, bearing the letter Helena had supposedly written in a clear plastic evidence bag. Sean read it aloud.

" 'I can no longer bear the guilt and the shame. I killed Jenny. I wanted more than you could give. Eddie, forgive me. May my death bring an end to what you are suffering, and may Alistair and God forgive me, too. Helena.' "

"Well?" Logan asked.

"Bull," Sean said. "Helena LaRoux did not write this."

"It *is* dramatic," Logan murmured. "And kind of sad. She asks Eddie, Alistair and God to forgive her — but not Jenny, whom she killed."

"That's because she didn't write the letter."

Knox approached the ambulance. "Agent Cameron, Eddie Archer has heard what's happened. We really don't think he should come here. Mike Greenwood is with him at his house, and Eddie wants you there, too."

"When the medical examiner's taken the body and the forensics team's done, I want to get back in those tunnels. But I'll go over to Eddie's first."

"What should I do?" Madison asked.

Knox looked at her. "You should stay out of the way right now, Ms. Darvil. The teams will be busy for a while."

"Did Eddie want me, too?"

"Just Agent Cameron. You might want to go home and get some rest. Or, if you're up to it after crashing through the floor you could go to the studio," he said, "Mr. Simons has gone in. I still have men posted there. The employees know what happened." He gave her a white-lipped smile. "From what I hear, it's a gossip fest. But the work's going on."

"What do you *want* to do?" Sean asked her.

"Clean up and go to work."

"Okay. I'll get Kelsey to take you back to the hotel."

Eddie wasn't usually much of a drinker.

That day, he was. He didn't need to fight to save Alistair anymore; he couldn't save Helena.

When Pierce let Sean in, he found Eddie sitting on the sofa at the back of his beautiful house. The L.A. sun was shining brightly, casting a benign light on the pool behind the glass and the perfectly manicured lawn that surrounded it. Mike Greenwood was sitting in the chair across from the sofa, trying to lend what support he could.

Pierce, shaking his head sorrowfully at Sean, seemed anxious, worried — and not at all triumphant that Helena had proven to be venomous.

Eddie looked at Sean with dazed, red-rimmed eyes. "It was Helena? You saw her?

There was no mistake? It was really Helena?"

Sean patted his friend's knee and sat next to Eddie. "Yes. I saw her. I'm sorry, Eddie."

"She killed herself?"

Sean hesitated. "Eddie, she was dangling from a rope. It was attached to the hook set into the crypt for flowers. She'd also slashed her wrists, and she left a note."

Eddie nodded. "The police read me the note. I didn't buy it. Did you buy it, Sean?"

"Eddie," Mike interjected.

"Sean, did you believe it?" Eddie demanded.

Sean inhaled on a deep breath. "No," he admitted. "Except . . ."

"What? What the hell are you trying to say?"

"Eddie, it really looks like she drove herself to that cemetery. I think she was meeting someone."

Eddie gulped down his glass of whiskey. "You're trying to say that my wife is a murderer, that she killed a girl — *killed her!* — just to hurt me . . . to hurt Alistair. She's dead, Sean! Helena is dead."

He wasn't sure how to respond. Anything he could come up with sounded lame. "I'm sorry, Eddie. I'm so sorry."

Eddie rose, heading for the Scotch bottle

again. "Be careful what you wish for! That's what they always say. I wished desperately that my son would be freed. I did everything I could to bring in the FBI — to find the truth and prove Alistair innocent. So now, supposedly, Helena wrote a suicide note claiming to have committed the crime. She cut her wrists, and when she didn't do that properly, she hanged herself. That's what the police say. And they think it's all over, that what she wrote is the truth . . . but it can't be. It just can't be."

Sean was silent.

"There's more, isn't there?" Eddie spun on him, whiskey sloshing precariously near the rim of his glass. "You're thinking a lot more than you're saying."

Sean lifted his hands. He wasn't going to lie to Eddie. "I don't believe Helena killed herself. But I *do* believe she was partners with whoever killed her — and Jenny," he said bluntly. "That's no comfort to you, I know."

Eddie let out a long shaky breath.

Sean's phone rang and he answered quickly. Logan was calling from the police station.

"Here's something that might help Eddie," Logan said. "They're releasing Alistair. The D.A. was able to get before the judge

437

and they're dropping the charges. The police will remove Alistair's ankle bracelet and he'll be free to go home."

He hung up. "The charges against Alistair are being dropped. You can bring him home, Eddie."

Eddie stiffened his shoulders, staring out at the yard but obviously not seeing anything. He shook his head slowly. "Alistair is staying where he is. Someone's after my family. I'm not letting them get to Alistair. They destroyed Helena, and they're trying to destroy me and the studio. I'm not going to let them."

Mike stood. "No, Eddie, we won't let them ruin the studio," he vowed.

Eddie took a sip of his whiskey. "So, go back to work, Mike. You, too, Sean. Go get the bastard for me. Don't let the cops put it all on Helena, like they were trying to do with Alistair."

Sean glanced at Mike, and Mike looked back at him unhappily. "Eddie," Sean said. "We're all worried about you."

Eddie lowered his head. "Don't be. Pierce is with me. I'm going to go and stay with Alistair for a while. Don't worry — I'm not driving. Pierce will take me, and we'll stay together. We may be an odd family, but we *are* family. And I'm all right. I've got it under control. Mike, save the studio. Sean, get the bastard. Go — do it, please. We're going to be fine, aren't we, Pierce?"

"Yes, Eddie," Pierce said. "We're going to be fine."

There were still tears in Eddie's eyes. Because Helena was dead or because she had so bitterly betrayed him? Or both?

Sean rose to leave. Mike Greenwood followed suit. "It's all right, really," Pierce said. "I'll take him to be with Alistair."

As Sean and Mike departed together, Mike whispered, "Poor Eddie. Nicest damn guy in the world. And he fell for a manipulative bitch like Helena." He paused, raising his voice as they left the house. "Do you think she really killed Jenny Henderson — and then herself? You can be forced to write a suicide note, but no one forced her out of the house. There's an alarm. Pierce would've protected her, not that he liked her himself, but she was Eddie's wife. Maybe she was going to the store and she was kidnapped — yeah, that's possible!"

"I think she *was* involved. How involved, I don't know."

He stopped at the cars and looked back at Mike. "You're going to manage, keeping the studio open?"

"As long as Andy and Eddie tell me to,

I'll manage. Somehow. And, of course, as long as the police let me. Will they close us down again, do you suppose?"

"They've closed the cemetery for the day, and a couple of cops — as well as my team — will hang around there. This particular investigation could go on for a while, so I don't expect that anyone will ask you to close, not for the next few days, anyhow. If at all."

"Then I'm going back to work," Mike said. "See you later, Sean. Thanks for becoming — whatever it is you've become in the FBI."

Sean watched him go. He remembered working for Mike Greenwood, a steady guy who never raised his voice. He was pretty sure Madison felt the same way. He waved to Mike as Mike revved his car, murmuring, "I always was what I am now, Mike. I always was."

He slid back into the Prius and eased into traffic.

As he drove, a call from Jane advised him that Logan had arranged for a meeting with Oliver Marshall at the police station as soon as Oliver was finished shooting for the day. He expected to be available in about four hours.

Sean mused that Oliver Marshall was

heading into the glare of major stardom. Why would he be involved in a case like this?

But who ever really knew what drove another human being? Who could tell what perceived slights and wrongs motivated acts of vengeance or bitterness? And if Oliver *wasn't* involved, he still might know something they didn't.

How well had Oliver Marshall been acquainted with Helena LaRoux?

He hoped they were going to find out. But for the time being, he planned to get back down to those tunnels.

They were connected to the studio. He wanted to figure out just how and where. It was becoming evident to him that the killer had used the tunnels, certainly to make his escape.

The killer had known the studio backward and forward and had some connection to it. Helena had managed to get the basement key for the killer and she'd probably been the one to reveal that Alistair would be at the Black Box Cinema — and that Jenny would join him. Sean didn't just need to know who was familiar with the studio and the Black Box; now he also needed to know who'd been privy to the information about Peace Cemetery.

People were, naturally enough, tense. But whether anyone had tried to hush up the news about the discovery of Helena's body, Madison had no idea. She did notice that she wasn't included in most of the whispering among her coworkers. As they day wore on, she often caught them staring at her, and then quickly looking away.

She couldn't help being aware of them as she worked on Oliver Marshall's costume with Alfie. He was holding the rubber shield in place on the shirt material while she stitched it in. Simple task, but because of the type of fabric and the need for perfect positioning so that Oliver and his stunt double could rip up his clothing and be clad as an Egyptian warrior, the work required two people.

"Everyone's staring at you," Alfie told her.

"Yep."

"They think you're in the know," Alfie said, "and, of course, you are. Scary. I would've died! You found her — ugh. Weird. Do you have, like, corpse radar or something?"

"Alfie, I fell through bad flooring!"

"How weird! She left a suicide note in her

car, then took herself down to some hidden crypts to kill herself. On the other hand, she never did seem really normal. No, wait, for Hollywood, she *was* normal, trying to play the climb-up-the-ladder game. I just don't get it, though. Can you imagine how she must have done this? Oh, but wait, she'd definitely know Alistair's and Eddie's habits, what they were up to and stuff like that. She'd know how to use the security equipment . . . maybe. I never thought of her as a technical genius. Actually, I never thought of her as a genius at all."

"I guess we'll never know now, will we, Alfie?" she asked, looking up at him.

"So, you think it's going to end? I mean, they're keeping the studio open. First, one corpse, and Alistair is arrested. Then Helena winds up dead! Of course, she was found in the cemetery, so that doesn't affect the studio, but it does affect Eddie. Wow. Who'd a' thunk?"

"To the best of my knowledge, it's been decided that the studio will stay open for the next few days while they explore beneath the church. After that, I'm not sure. At least we're open for now, so let's get this done."

"Yep. And there are still cops in the studio," he said, lowering his voice. "They're guarding the elevator shaft. And Bailey's guarding the building entrance and marching around like a dictator, spying on everyone."

"Well, they're here. Makes you feel safe, right?" Madison asked.

"Madison, come on, give! You're sleeping with the FBI, for God's sake, you gotta know *something* that's going on!"

She glanced up at him, not really startled, but curious about how he'd figured it out.

He just grinned at her, as pleased as the Cheshire cat.

"Alfie, the FBI keeps a lot of things silent," she said. "Personal . . . relationships are irrelevant. I *don't* know what's going on, and you keep easing up on the rubber and the fabric. Hold it tight, will you?"

"Sure." He was quiet for a few minutes. "Can we eat soon? Maybe send out for pizza?"

"Yes, Alfie, we can eat soon."

By the time he returned to the cemetery, the body of Helena LaRoux had been removed and was on its way to the morgue. The crime scene techs were finishing up. No one currently with the studio was still at the site. After Kelsey had driven Madison to the hotel to change and then to work, Logan had sent her over to the hospital to stay with Eddie and Alistair. Logan himself had gone back to the cemetery. Jane remained at the police station, Kat was heading to the morgue and Tyler was at the studio keeping watch.

The cemetery director was beside himself; he'd known about the crypts, but there hadn't been a burial or entombment there for fifty years. They hadn't sealed off access because the supporting structure might need to be repaired or reinforced at some point. Earthquake construction codes had been strengthened since the chapel was built. The managing offices for the cemetery weren't on the grounds but across the street. Police regularly patrolled the cemetery, which was closed to the public at dusk. They'd had a few instances of vandalism but, perhaps thanks to the studio and the Black Box being where they were, they didn't even get a lot of kids breaking in to play pranks, and they'd never had a case of grave-robbing.

Since the young cemetery manager was an emotional wreck, he was allowed to go back to work — or home for a tranquilizer.

Logan and Sean waited, observing the crime scene techs going in and out, doing their last sweeps and bearing bags of dirt, twigs, possible footprints, fibers — minute specks of anything that might lead to the truth.

As they watched, Logan asked, "She didn't speak to you, did she? Helena LaRoux, I mean. Was there any sign of her . . . still being here with us?"

Sean shook his head. "Nothing. Doesn't mean she isn't, but . . ."

"Sometimes they don't stay." Logan shrugged. "Some times they do."

"We'll take a trip to the morgue later," Sean said. "I really want to go into those tunnels, though. I'm anxious."

"Looks like we're getting the opportunity soon," Logan said as the lead investigator emerged.

Armed with his flashlight, Sean moved forward. Knox stood just outside the church. "I'll keep two men on duty out here," he said. He offered Sean a radio. "I don't think any corpses are going to rise up and attack you, but hell, these days . . . This radio should work anywhere in the region of the tunnels, the cemetery, the studio."

Sean accepted it. "Thanks, Detective."

"You want to get in there before they bring in the engineers, right?"

"Yeah," Sean said. "Are you okay with that?"

"Well, you've shaken the tree, that's for

sure," Knox said. "And LaRoux's note proves the kid wasn't guilty — or crazy. I say go for it. But if any of those crypts cave in, it'll be on your head, not mine — no pun intended."

Sean gave Knox a grim smile, and he and Logan entered the church again, hurried to the rear and down to the tunnels.

They took the stairs, pausing to study the false crypts that connected with the area where Helena had been found.

"I'll lead. I'm getting accustomed to the spiderwebs and crypt dust," Sean told Logan.

"Be my guest," Logan said.

"We're assuming that our killer entered the cinema from down here and exited the same way. So we have to find the path that goes toward the Black Box," Sean said thoughtfully.

"There's only one path."

"I don't think so, but let's follow this route for a while. And keep an eye on the walls. I think we'll discover other false fronts — walls of tomb 'shelves' that are really doors to other corridors. This was a major undertaking. What they were doing, or so I understand, was providing services for the poor and for illegal aliens. From what I've heard, the old pastor really cared about people.

I'm sure he gave the family members a lot of solace."

They'd traveled carefully for almost an hour when Sean was startled by a voice on the radio. "It's Knox. Oliver Marshall is on his way to the station. Do you want me to interview him, or are you two coming in?"

"One of us needs to go," Sean said.

"And no one should be alone down here. It's far scarier than any house of horrors ever devised by a master of illusion."

Sean grinned wryly. "That's what the Claymores were — masters of illusion."

"We'll go back. We can spend the entire day tomorrow searching the tunnels," Logan decided. "Or all of tonight, whichever you prefer."

"Knox, Logan and I are coming up," Sean said. "You'll keep men on guard here, right? We don't want anyone else slipping in."

"You got it."

There was nothing on the minds of anyone at the studio other than the discovery of Helena LaRoux's body. Speculation abounded. Some claimed they'd always known that Helena was up to no good. Mostly, however, the speculation revolved around the business itself. Quite a few workers wondered if the business could possibly survive, if the producers and directors who contracted the studio to create the special effects for their projects would continue to do so.

Alfie ordered a pizza, then he and Madison had a late lunch with Mike in the conference room. While she'd never been truly disturbed by any of their props before, Madison found herself studying "Matilda," and feeling ill at ease. It was ridiculous, of course; she'd attended meetings and eaten her lunch in the conference room dozens of times, and all she'd ever felt was tremendous pride in the work the studio did.

Alfie finished his pizza and announced that he was going to the men's room, and he'd meet Madison back at her station.

"How's Eddie doing?" she asked Mike when he'd left.

"I thought he was going to fall to pieces," Mike said. "Then he suddenly pulled himself together. Eddie's going to make it. He was heartbroken when Alistair's mother died, but they were childhood sweethearts — they really had a love match. I think Eddie's married for lust instead of love since she died. He'll get over Helena, especially if he finally accepts that she meant to ruin his life." He leaned over and gave Madison a hug. "We're all going to make it, kid."

Andy Simons came in a few minutes later. He hadn't thought to order lunch and stared at the pizza longingly. "That's all leftovers," Madison said. "Help yourself."

"Thanks." He joined them and wolfed down a piece, then looked at Madison and Mike. "I just talked to Eddie. He's back at the hospital with Alistair. The D.A. has dropped the charges, thanks to the suicide note, but Eddie is staying with Alistair — and they're both staying at the hospital. Eddie sounds like a cat with his tail caught in the door. He's suspicious of everyone. Including me," Andy added wearily. He raised his hands in a despairing gesture. "I'm his partner. We've been together for years."

"His wife is dead, Andy," Madison said. "He's in agony, and he can't accept the fact that Helena wanted to hurt him. He must be suffering humiliation, too, since he didn't have any idea of what she was doing."

Andy shrugged. "Yeah, I guess so. Well, I'm going to take off. I want to get to the hospital to see Eddie and Alistair."

"Give them my love, please," Madison said.

"I'll do that," Andy promised.

He grabbed the remaining two slices of pizza and left. "Back to work," Madison said cheerfully. She glanced at her watch — almost three. "Oliver's suit is just about completed. They can pick it up tomorrow. We already did his stunt double's version, so we're on schedule."

Mike smiled at her. "The monster is ready, too. We're supposed to go out on location soon." He seemed to brighten. "We'll hang on to *The Unholy*. Even if they close us down again, it'll be okay, since we're going to be on location."

Madison nodded as she gathered up the empty pizza carton and napkins and put them in the room's recycling bin.

As she headed back to work, she felt as if icy rivulets were snaking down her spine. She spun around and stared at the creatures in the circular area that separated the conference rooms from the elevator and stairs.

Something wasn't right. She studied the creatures standing there — the werewolf with his golden eyes and dripping fangs, the beautiful evil witch, the victim with her one destroyed eye. . . .

And then she saw movement.

A scream rose in her throat.

16

"Yes, I am related to the Claymores — and therefore the studio and the cemetery," Oliver Marshall said, sitting across from Sean in the interview room at the station. Like Benita, he seemed to realize that others were watching the interview. He waved to the mirror, as if waving to fans. "So, Helena is dead," he murmured, turning serious. "Suicide? Who would've figured?" He looked at Sean, expression quizzical. "Do you really think I could have had anything to do with this?" he asked. "I had an ancestor who owned it all, yeah, but none of it came to my family or me, and I *never* exploit the connection." He seemed earnest, courteous and polite.

"Oliver, we're checking out everything and everyone. In the stories you heard from your family, did anyone talk about the crypts underneath the church?" Sean asked him.

"Sure. I never knew if what I heard was

real or the kind of exaggeration you get when a story is told and retold over and over again."

"What did you hear?"

"Oh, I heard the underground was riddled with tunnels, but I didn't think that could be true! Someone would've found them by now," Oliver said, grinning. "There's often a crypt under an old church, so I figured that part was true. And the original Claymore, the guy who first bought the property, was supposedly a real humanitarian. My dad said he arranged for real religious ceremonies for illegal aliens and poor people who died. Their families, if they had any, couldn't afford funerals or burials, so . . ."

Sean changed his tactic. "Did you ever work with Helena LaRoux?"

Oliver frowned. "Yeah. Well, I never spoke to her on set. We were both in a pilot for a series called *The Legal Way.*" He made a face. "It wasn't picked up by any of the networks. I was playing a character named Harper Mulligan. I was the brash P.I., flying beneath the radar while my partner was a by-the-book guy. Helena was a victim, killed before my character even comes on." He paused suddenly, going pale. "Wow, I'd forgotten about that. It was several years ago. Eddie Archer was married to Benita

Lowe at the time, and I actually remember there was a bit of work done at the studios. Eddie's team created some of the corpses for the show. I remember talking to Benita on set when she showed up with Eddie. I talked with her more than I did Helena."

"Did you know she was related to Pete Krakowski, the bit player who was killed on the set of the original *Sam Stone?*"

"I did." He nodded as he said that. "We talked about our associations with the place and the fact that while they could be discovered if you dug deep enough, we both preferred to keep them quiet. I'm not sure why I did, other than that pride thing of wanting to make it on my own. And, of course, I doubted it would do anything for me. But Benita *really* didn't want anyone knowing about her relationship to Krakowski. She said he might be an ancestor of half the people she knew — he was chronically unfaithful and a deplorable cheat. Pity. She and Helena seemed to be friends back then. But I guess Helena screwed her over, although Benita and Eddie split because of other differences. I never knew exactly what those differences were and they're none of my business. I've never asked. But I know Benita did care about Eddie, and . . ." He lifted his shoulders. "Benita was honestly fond of Alistair, as well. I don't see her being involved."

"Okay, routine question, and you've probably been asked by the cops already," Sean said. "Where were you the night Jenny Henderson was killed?"

Oliver smiled. "In Las Vegas — not having fun. We did some scenes on a set built out in the desert that night. We filmed until the wee hours, and that's something you can verify with dozens of people."

Sean stood and shook Oliver's hand. "Thank you for coming in, and thank you for all the help."

"If I can do anything . . . Archer's studio is great. So is Eddie. I don't want to work with anyone beside Madison — she's fantastic. I'll help if I can. Just call me."

Sean joined Logan and Knox outside the interview room as Oliver left the station.

"Where do we go from here?" Knox asked. "You really don't think Helena pulled the whole thing off, do you?"

"No, I don't," Sean said firmly. "This is the second time we've heard about Benita's feelings regarding Pete Krakowski. The guy was a cheat but what we should do is find out who he was cheating *with*. Trace back some family lines. I still say there has to be a reason somewhere in the past for these murders. And I think we need to uncover it quickly. We were supposed to find Helena's note — but not her body. And if by some chance we did find the body, it was supposed to support the suicide theory, maybe prove that Helena knew about the catacombs. But we're still searching, so it must be obvious that we're not just saying, *Wow, look at that, Helena's guilty.* The killer has to be feeling a little desperate, and that's dangerous."

"Well, the workday is over," Knox said. "The studio will be empty except for our guys, the security guard and I'm assuming you have a man there, too?"

Logan nodded. Sean turned to him. "Logan, can you work with Jane and get on the computer, pull every resource we have, see what we can learn about Pete Krakowski? I need to know who he was having affairs with."

"Krakowski?" Logan said. "You think it's a vengeance killing? According to Benita Lowe, his wife made a bundle. Sounds like he was no loss, and the family was happy to receive the money."

"Sure, his current wife, beaten and ignored and cheated on, might have been happy. But maybe he left someone in the dust. Maybe he had a mistress at the time."

"She'd be dead now or too old to pull this off — Oh, I see! You're thinking Krakowski had an illegitimate child?" Logan asked.

"Yes. And that the illegitimate child had a descendent or descendents who grew up with feelings of hate and anger, believing that if Krakowski hadn't died, their lives might've been different. That if he'd lived, he would have divorced his wife, married the pregnant mistress — if there was one — or . . . whatever," Sean said. "It's a wild card, but Oliver has an airtight alibi . . . and Helena is dead."

"A legitimate child who didn't grow up with any kind of stigma might recognize that Krakowski was a womanizer and an alcoholic," Logan added, "but that he would never have divorced his wife."

"Right. Benita learned that her great-grandfather was a cheat. That's what she was told, at any rate. And as you said, maybe an illegitimate child would teach his or her heirs that *they* would've been legitimate and have everything — if their ancestor hadn't been killed by carelessness on a set. Or murder . . ."

"Do you really think Krakowski was murdered?" Logan asked him.

"It's a case that occurred well over half a century ago," Sean said, "and it was generally accepted as an accident. We may never know — but what matters isn't what really happened, it's what a certain person *believes* might have happened. Hey, even Bogie thought it could've been murder. The killer seems to blame the Claymore studio, which did the special effects on the *Sam Stone* movie, not the Waterton film studio where the accident took place. And he doesn't care that Eddie, who had nothing to do with any of it, now owns Claymore's. At least, that's the only alternative I can see at the moment," Sean said. "It may be a long shot — and it may be the right shot. But there *has* to be a connection. Helena was obviously an accomplice. However, she's dead, and I don't believe she killed herself. There has to be a second suspect, and he — or she — has an agenda. There's a good chance that agenda is connected to Krakowski."

"I'll get on the computer," Logan promised. "I'm pretty good at research, but finding out who a guy was sleeping with . . . hmm."

Sean grinned. "Jane will help you. She's good at reading between the lines. I'm going to the studio now."

"Yeah, you do that. And when you're back at the hotel, maybe you can do some of your computer-whiz stuff and see what you can figure out, too. First, though, why don't you drive Madison home — and maybe find out if Bogie knew anything about Krakowski's sleeping habits," Logan suggested.

"Will do," Sean assured Logan.

He thanked Knox and the other cops and said goodbye, leaving the station. As he did, he called Madison's cell number.

No answer. He tried Tyler's phone next; he did answer.

"Everything all right there?" Sean asked.

"The employees are leaving. The day's ending a bit early but it seemed to go fine," Tyler said.

"Madison?"

"Fine. Don't worry. She won't go anywhere without me. She had lunch with Andy, Mike and her assistant. All is well. Bailey is on the security desk, and the two cops are still in the building."

"Great. I'm on my way."

Madison managed not to scream. The creatures in the circular hallway display weren't moving. Creatures didn't move unless they were radio-controlled or fitted with batteries and run by remote control or manipulated by a puppeteer.

It was Alfie, just standing there.

"Alfie, what the *hell* are you doing?" she

demanded. For the first time, she felt acutely uncomfortable. His curiosity about her relationship with Sean had been almost salacious.

"Waiting for you," he said.

"Why?"

"Half the crew's gone home. I'm . . . I'm not happy out there alone," he said, wide-eyed. "Are we still working?"

"You do what you want, Alfie. I need to finish up that costume. I told Mike it'll be ready for tomorrow."

She didn't know if he followed her or not. As she passed the guard station, she saw that Tyler Montague was there, watching the entrance, as if he was taking a tally of those who were coming and going.

She smiled at him and continued to her station.

As she neared her work area and sewing machine, she realized that Alfie was directly behind her. He shivered.

"What's the matter with you?" she asked.

Madison wasn't worried about being in the studio; Tyler Montague was on duty and there was a cop by the elevator on the first floor and another by the elevator on the second. Poor guys must be bored to tears, except that the cops switched shifts every eight hours.

Eight hours. They still had to be bored to tears.

"I just don't feel right," Alfie said. "Let's go home. I'll walk you to your car. Oh, wait! You're not going home — you're waiting for the studly FBI guy."

"Alfie, I'm going to finish this costume," she said again.

Alfie sighed. "Fine. I'm staying with you."

She began to work on the shirt, and Alfie moved closer, holding the material tightly. He was good at what he did, a great assistant, sensing what she needed before she needed it.

Her cell phone rang. Alfie jumped. She nearly stuck the needle in his finger.

"Alfie!" she said, finding her phone, which she'd placed on the sewing machine. "Yes?" She saw Tyler Montague's name on her caller I.D.

"Madison, it's Tyler."

"Aren't you still in the building?"

"I'm going out. Sean's on his way here. Colin Bailey just got a call from him, saying that something's going on in the cemetery. Bailey asked if he needed any help and apparently he wants me out there. But you're fine. Bailey is on the security desk, and there are two cops in the building. Stay inside, okay?" Tyler's voice was calm and assured.

Madison felt her heart leap, but she made an effort not to let Alfie see that she was in any way concerned.

"I'm fine. Alfie and I are finishing Oliver's costume," she said. "Thanks for checking in."

Madison hung up and looked around the studio, and noticed that Alfie was fidgeting and acting concerned. "We're the last ones here tonight, huh?" she said.

"We shouldn't be working so late. I'm losing it. I think I saw the rat moving," Alfie said.

"The rat did *not* move, Alfie!" His unease was actually making her feel better. She laughed. "Hey, finding you in the middle of those mannequins by the conference room didn't do much for my blood pressure." She gestured over to the wall and smiled. "Once again, the rat didn't move."

"Who was that?" Alfie asked. "On the phone, I mean."

"Tyler," she answered. "He wanted me to know that Sean's on his way back."

"Good," Alfie said. "When he gets here, can we go?"

"Alfie, you can go anytime you want."

"Not without you."

"I'm fine. When Sean gets here, I'll go," she told him, although she suspected that his concern was as much for himself as her.

He confirmed that a moment later, asking, "Madison, do you think the G-man who's still here will walk me to my car?"

She hesitated. She wasn't sure why she hadn't told Alfie that Tyler had gone to the cemetery.

Was she afraid — of Alfie? And yet he seemed genuinely fearful.

"Help me for a few more minutes. Then Sean will be here, and we'll all go."

As she spoke, the studio was suddenly pitched into darkness.

Alfie let out a yelp of terror, and Madison gripped his arm. "It's all right, Alfie. Give it a second. The auxiliary lights will come on."

They did. They bathed the studio in a pale yellow that was deeply shadowed by the distorted shapes of creatures they'd constructed over the years. There were no windows in this interior section of the studio. No glimmer of natural light.

"What the hell happened?" Alfie whispered.

"I don't know." Madison bit her lower lip, fighting fear. In her drawer was a large pair of scissors. She slipped her hand in and curled her fingers around them.

"Alfie, we need to lie low somewhere," she said urgently.

463

"How?"

She thought quickly. Bailey should have been on the desk and there were two cops in the building somewhere. The question was — who *else* might be in here?

"Get into Oliver's Sam Stone costume and hat. Then you can look like a mannequin. Everyone knows we've been working on this all day. *Now!*"

"They can see us! They can see us through the cameras!" Alfie wailed.

"Not if we're on the floor. Drop down and crawl to the dressing area."

"Where will you be?" he demanded.

"Right behind you," she said. "Right behind you!"

Sean had loved living in L.A., but as he drove to the studio, he remembered one thing he'd hated about it.

Traffic.

The rush hour in California seemed to start at 5:00 a.m. and end at . . . 5:00 a.m.

Annoyed by the traffic, he called Tyler again, using his hands-free device.

Tyler answered, sounding equally annoyed.

"I don't know what the hell I'm doing out here, Sean," he said. "There are still a pack of cops by the church. I've gone over there, but they say nothing's changed. They've been watching the grass grow all day."

"What are you talking about?" Sean asked.

"Bailey sent me out here — he said you wanted me at the cemetery."

Fear shuddered through Sean's heart. "I didn't send you anywhere. *I didn't call him.*"

"Ah, hell!" Tyler said. "I should've known! But Bailey said you called — it must've been someone pretending to be you, someone who wanted to make sure I went out. Dammit, I should've phoned you myself to confirm. I'm heading back, Sean. Oh, shit!"

"What?"

"The studio just went dark."

"Screw traffic. I'll be there in five minutes," Sean said.

He hit the gas pedal, moving illegally onto the shoulder. If the cops wanted to come after him, they could chase him to the studio.

Manipulating the wheel, he tried Madison's number.

There was no answer. He flattened his foot on the gas pedal. His phone rang. He answered it, praying that Madison was returning his call, that there'd been a power short, that she was with one of the cops and whoever had called Bailey pretending to be him had been caught.

The call wasn't from Madison. It was Logan.

"You were right, Sean," Logan said. "I found a reference in an old magazine — or Jane did, I should say. Krakowski had an affair that hit the tabloids in the late 1930s. He was seeing a woman named Elissa Sinclair. And you'll never guess who she married or the name of her grandson."

"Tell me!" Sean screamed. "And get the police over to the studio. Now!"

Madison was on the floor, slithering over to the curtained area, when she heard her phone ring.

She'd left it back on the sewing machine.

Cursing her luck — and trying to tell herself that it was just a power failure — she kept slithering across the floor. Someone could be watching them from any of the cameras, so she didn't dare go back for her phone.

Where was Sean?

Alfie was ahead of her. "Keep going!" she told him.

He did. He was ready to do anything she said.

She froze when she heard a voice coming over the speaker system. She didn't recognize it. The sound was distorted, low-pitched and seemed to be male.

"Madison, yes, it's me, and I've been watching you, and you've ruined everything. I haven't got much time, so don't make things any more difficult. Come out . . . come out . . . and your little friend might live."

Alfie kept going. She paused. Was he going to die because of her?

But Alfie looked back, his eyes glittering with fear — and courage. "Come! Come, now!" he urged her.

She caught up with him. They made it behind the curtain, where she found the rest of Oliver's Sam Stone costume. If she could get Alfie dressed and standing completely still, she could distract the killer.

And then what?

Hide, get away. The person who wanted to kill her knew the studio well — but she knew it just as well. And she had an advantage.

She was desperate to save her life.

"Alfie!" A chuckle followed the calling of his name. "Come on, Alfie! Do you want to die for *her* — Eddie's favorite? You know, *you* could be the favorite. It will be all over tonight. It's Madison. She ruins everything. Don't die for her."

Behind the curtain, a terrified Alfie

pinched her, and she wondered at the courage that was making him stay silent, even in the midst of his fear. "You keep quiet! He's not going to get us both!" Alfie whispered. "Sean's on the way. Keep quiet."

"Get dressed," Madison hissed. "Please, Alfie."

"Don't believe a word he says — he's killed twice already. He'll kill me, too. You have to save yourself, Madison," Alfie said. There were tears glistening in his eyes. It was dark behind the curtain, but she could tell that he was nearly crippled by fear.

"Get into this."

"I gotta get the jeans off," he said.

She helped him tug down his jeans while he ripped off his T-shirt. In the meantime, she dug through the costumes left piled on the floor, offcasts from various other projects. She found some kind of material, thought it might be the widow's costume from the Western they'd done the scaffolding for. It was. Her fingers fumbled with the fasteners but she managed to get into it. She felt something silky — a wig. She crammed it on her head as Alfie reached for a hat.

She nodded, gesturing with her chin to indicate that he should slide against the wall and freeze. He looked at her, shook his head and tried to fix her wig. It was a long black one. After a moment, he seemed satisfied.

"Madison, Alfie, come out to play. . . ."

The disembodied voice wasn't coming over the loudspeaker anymore. It was in the room with them.

And it was very close.

Tires squealing, Sean drove into the parking lot, cursing that they'd missed the obvious from the start.

He got out of the car and looked at the studio. The auxiliary lights had come on, making the place appear ghostly and indistinct. He hurried to the door; when he couldn't open it, he threw his shoulder against it without success.

He peered through the window at the entry, trying to figure out why he couldn't budge the door.

And then he knew.

A man lay blocking the way. A man in uniform. One of the cops.

Blood was trailing over the floor and a knife protruded from his back.

He was coming nearer and nearer. In a minute, he'd find the two of them cowering behind the curtain. Madison groped on the floor for the scissors she'd brought with her.

She hardly dared breathe.

She heard the footsteps of their stalker approaching. He was just beyond the curtain. She rose slowly to her feet, ready to pounce, hoping to wrap the curtain around him, at least blind him with it, and then slam the scissors into his back.

Her phone started to ring a second time, and their stalker paused.

He was just standing there, listening. But then she heard him laugh. He was on the move again.

"Madison, Madison . . . come out to play!"

She wrenched at the drapery, ripping it downward and throwing it at him. She slashed with the scissors and he fell back, the drapery falling on top of him. Her scissors caught in the fabric and fell on him, too.

She started to leap forward, ready to attack. But their stalker was almost up. Alfie grabbed her, pulling her back. "No, run! Run now! He's got a knife!"

She ran with Alfie. The man was still down, only his large hand, the knife clearly visible, emerging from the fabric.

"Out the front, out the front!" Alfie shrieked.

They ran along the hallway, headed for

the front door.

Madison saw the dead cop blocking the door. "No!" she cried. "We don't have time to move him."

They tore down the hallway; he'd be there any minute. He was still coming toward them. They could hear his harsh breath, his heavy footsteps. She shoved Alfie into the first conference room.

"Stand there! Just stand!"

"Madison, no! Don't do it!"

But she was already moving, making sure she was heard. She stopped at the second circular display, slid in between a robotic cop and a vampire. She breathed slowly and shallowly, looking behind her.

He came . . . walking slowly. He didn't know where they were. He paused, staring into the first conference room. Madison stood very still. If he saw Alfie . . .

He peered inside, and then came back into the hallway.

"Ah, Madison . . . you're here . . . somewhere!" he said.

She saw him. Saw him in the yellow glow of the auxiliary lights, and he was more frightening that anything the mind could create. He wasn't transformed by makeup; no latex could ever change a man from a calm and friendly demeanor into such a demented monster.

It was so hard to believe.

He paused. "Madison!" he said. "I know you're there!"

He went into the second conference room.

Madison turned and ran. There was only one escape. She ran to the elevator. For a moment, she panicked; she needed the key!

But the key was in the lock. She twisted it, and the elevator brought her down to the tunnel.

Heedless of the dead, she raced through it.

Sean tried to stay calm, running to the car for a tire iron, and then back to the door, swinging as he approached it. The window shattered; he reached in and broke the lock, and shoved with all his might. As he did so, Tyler came pelting down the road. They didn't try to talk — they burst through the doorway, pushing the body of the dead man out of the way.

"Madison!" Sean shouted her name loudly.

There was no answer.

"I'll take the main work area," Tyler said.

"I'm going to the conference rooms."

As he sprinted down the hallway, he suddenly heard a shout. A man in costume came bursting out of one of the conference rooms. Sean reached for his Glock.

"No!" came a screech. "Sean, it's me, Alfie — we dressed up and went in different directions. He — he walked right by me. He kept going . . . he tried the next room. Then he heard the elevator. Madison would've taken the key . . . wouldn't she? He couldn't . . . he couldn't have gotten to her . . . he couldn't have."

"He has his own key!"

"I'll come, I'll come . . . I'll help you —"

"Alfie, go wait by the entrance. Find the other guard. He must be patrolling the perimeter. Go on, find anyone! Tell the cops and everyone else where we've gone — into the tunnel. Get them down there fast!"

Alfie, a comic book hero for real, dashed toward the studio's front door.

Sean tore past him, out of the entry and to the Black Box.

Madison charged through the museum to the rear of the *Sam Stone* exhibit. She nearly tripped over a cobra as she made her way through the mannequins. She was just about to rush down the hallway to the cinema when he burst in behind her, leaping over the jackal and landing a few feet away.

For a moment, she was frozen, staring at him in horror. He carried a knife, but he had a gun, as well.

He smiled at her.

She shook her head. "Bailey, what are you doing? It's over! I don't know what kind of agreement you had with Helena, but you were stupid to kill her and rig it as a suicide."

He frowned, angry, still a few feet in front of her. All she had to do was stay alive, she told herself. Help would be coming. All she had to do was stay alive until it did.

"It wasn't stupid. Helena was an idiot. As long as everything went smoothly, she was fine. But in an interrogation room? She'd have spilled everything, would've lied and said it was all my idea, and she'd have walked — and I would've gone to prison for the rest of my life. No, Madison. I'm sorry you were so instrumental in my downfall. You're a decent kid. But I should have guessed. You know things you're not supposed to know. You . . . well, it's your fault. Yours and that fed's. Who the hell knew Eddie wouldn't believe the cops, that he wouldn't accept what was obvious? Involving you and the damned feds, finding the tunnels —" He broke off, chuckling. "Finding the dead."

"That's right, Bailey. I talk to the dead," she told him.

"Good. You'll have friends to talk to."

"Why did you do this?" she asked him.

"Vengeance," Bailey said. "I am Vengeance! They seem to think the new *Sam Stone* movie, *The Unholy* they named it, is going to be such a brilliant piece of work! They don't care — just like they didn't care back then! — that a man died. Murdered. I heard the rumors. Pete Krakowski was murdered. No one sought justice. So, when you can't get justice, you've got to get something else. Vengeance — and I am Vengeance. You still don't understand? I was pretty sure your G-man was getting close to the truth. Pete Krakowski. Yeah, he was killed on the set. I knew the truth, you see. The wiring was faulty because of the effects they were using — they'd wired the mummy, and it came to life. But they screwed it up — the wiring was loose, and the power shot through Krakowski. I call that murder!" Bailey's eyes never left her. "He was in love with my grandmother. They should've been married, and if they had been, she would've seen that his death was avenged. This place should've been *mine*. The widow got all the money — and my grandmother got nothing but directions to the soup kitchen. People whispered about it being murder, and that it was Claymore's fault. They didn't let Pete live to divorce his wretched, whining wife and marry the woman who loved him, who would have avenged him. She would've taken the studio for all it was worth. And it should've been mine, and I shouldn't have been sitting at a guard desk all these years — yes, sir, no, sir, can I help you, sir — no, I shouldn't have been. Alistair needed to go to jail, because Eddie needed to know what it was to lose everything."

"Bailey, that is the most messed-up thinking I've ever heard!" Madison said. "Alistair is just an honestly nice young man. Jenny didn't do anything to anyone. And Eddie was loyal to you." She stared at him, knowing that she shouldn't be making him angry. "Eddie isn't a Claymore —"

"Not a Claymore, no. But you know who would've been next? When Alistair was on his way to jail? Oliver Marshall, that bastard. I would have gotten to him. And Eddie's whore of an ex-wife. Benita Lowe — the bitch who badmouths her own blood."

Madison suddenly realized that he'd planned more, so much more. . . .

"I don't understand how you did all this. You were on duty. But you — not Helena

476

— killed Jenny. Helena met you in the tunnel, right? You weren't on camera because you're the one who was trusted to watch the cameras. There was a time discrepancy on the video. Two minutes were missing from the clock in the workroom because you had to stop the camera to steal the Egyptian priest's cape. Helena had gotten you the key to the basement and she was keeping you informed of Alistair's schedule. She listened to gossip, and she knew that Jenny was coming to see him. Then she met you at the site to hide the robe. She escaped through the tunnels — into the cemetery. Meanwhile, you'd taken care of the murder weapon, hiding it in the canopic jar." Madison took a deep breath. "You know the system so well, you could freeze all the tapes at exactly the same time — so perfectly that not even a forensic expert could tell what you'd done — and back them up so no one ever knew you'd left your position. You did that in the video room behind the desk, then ran around to the front — and there you were, Alistair's sympathetic savior when he regained consciousness and came looking for you."

"It was still a locked-room mystery, Madison. It should have stayed that way," Bailey said.

She was startled when she heard another voice, one she hadn't expected.

"Keep him talking, kid. We're here. We'll help you when we can — when we figure out *how* we can."

"Thanks, Bogie," she whispered. He was there; her resident ghost had made it here to help her. Jenny Henderson, as nervous-looking as a toy poodle, was standing slightly behind him. They were in the *Casablanca* exhibit.

"What?" Bailey said.

She'd unnerved him, and she hadn't even done it intentionally. Maybe he was feeling the cold some people felt when a spirit was around . . . or the creeping sensation of another presence that seemed to raise the hair on a person's neck.

Bailey turned. It wasn't enough for her to make an escape, but he turned.

He stared back at her. "What are you up to?"

"Bogie is here. You know — Humphrey Bogart. I told you I talk to the dead. And Jenny's here. Jenny Henderson. The girl you killed."

"That's not true! It's time for you to die. The cops will be here soon. I may go down, but you're going down with me."

He took a step toward her. She jumped

478

back into the exhibit, standing behind the mannequin of Sam Stone. When Bailey tried to reach her, she thrust the mannequin toward him. He tripped backward, but righted himself. She looked at the sarcophagus, ready to shove that in his direction next.

But before she could do so, the mannequin of Humphrey Bogart came flying out of the *Casablanca* exhibit. It didn't go far, but it hit the ground, surprising Bailey. He drew his gun and shot at it. She counted the shots. She didn't know anything about guns. How many bullets did he have?

"What the hell? Who's there?" he demanded, searching the exhibit.

Another mannequin came flying toward him — Ingrid Bergman as Ilsa Lund.

Bailey started shooting again.

And then he turned the gun on Madison. She screamed and leaped behind the sarcophagus, her heart thundering.

A bullet . . . a clean kill . . . better than a knife across her throat?

But then she heard a shout from the living. Sean had arrived.

"Bailey! Drop the weapon now!"

He was racing in from the Black Box, Glock in hand, aimed at Bailey.

Bailey whirled around, gun raised.

"Drop it!" Sean yelled.

Bailey didn't.

Sean fired.

Bailey fell back, a spill of blood spreading on his shirt.

She wasn't a coward. . . . But her knees were so weak.

She was barely standing by the time Sean stepped over Bailey and the fallen mannequins, pushed aside the sarcophagus and drew her into his arms.

That was when her knees failed completely. He swept her up and carried her from the tableau, and as she fell against his chest, she was exhausted and safe and . . . in love.

It was just like a movie.

EPILOGUE

Madison awoke feeling a sense of luxury and comfort that was wonderful.

The sheets were an incredible blend of silk and cotton, cool to the touch, sensuous against her skin. The drapes at the large lanai windows were moving with the slight breeze, and the sound of the waves and the ocean were just beyond them.

Best of all, of course, was the man beside her. Sean, naked and strong, his arms creating a haven, a sanctuary. It felt so right. In the long run, of course, she couldn't live in a Hawaiian paradise; Ichabod was at home. Alistair was taking care of him, and when she returned, she was also taking Helena's little designer lapdog — mutt, as Sean called him — and she loved having her pets.

But for now . . .

She opened her eyes, trying to see if he'd awakened. He had. He was watching her with amusement, lips curved in a smile.

481

"Good morning," he said.

"Yes, it is." She sighed luxuriously and smiled up at the ceiling fan.

Eddie Archer really was a great friend.

With the studio closed while the tunnels were cleaned out and sealed and the dead within them reinterred in peace, her work was on hold. Next week, she'd be heading out to the desert on the outskirts of Las Vegas, and Sean would follow the members of his team to Chicago. Something strange was going on in Lake Michigan; people Sean had worked with in Texas had begun a documentary on shipwrecks in the Great Lakes, and in the midst of their work, a diver had mysteriously died.

She bit her lip, worried about him, and then realized it was what he did, and if she wanted them to fashion a life together, she'd have to accept that, just as he understood her love for her own work.

His mind was apparently moving in the same direction. "You really think you'll be able to take a three-day weekend after the action sequences are filmed on location?"

She nodded. "But you're taking a few days first to meet me in Vegas."

His eyes were brilliant as he looked at her and smoothed back a lock of her hair. "I learned once upon a time that we all need a focus in life, but that focus has no meaning if we can't remember that life is really about people, the people who are most important to us. People we might come across only once in a lifetime. Twice if we're lucky. And when you get a second chance, you don't blow it."

"I would go anywhere for you," she told him.

"You're with me now." He smiled and kissed her, and the fan continued to whir and the breeze to wash over them. His kiss deepened and he moved against her, his body as sleek as the sheets, and the kiss naturally segued into much, much more. . . .

Later, they went to lie on the beach. They'd already spent long hours with the team and with each other, retracing every moment of the case, trying to understand how a person's mind could seize on injuries of the past, even the distant past, and become crazed by them. "Hatred is so often taught," Sean had said. "Be it against an individual or a group." And she thought he was wise in that assessment. They'd talked about the fact that when they were ready, when they had a family, they would take the greatest care to see that their children learned tolerance instead of hatred. That had been an especially nice conversation, because they were still shy with each other. They didn't bandy the word *love* about easily, so when he'd first whispered, "I love you," she knew it was real, and that it was for a lifetime.

Their Hawaiian conclave was exclusive, a really wonderful present from Eddie, and they should have been alone, completely alone, so naturally Madison was surprised when she felt the air and the sand stir. Someone was approaching them.

She glanced up. Bogie was coming along the beach; he looked as if he was ready to film the sequel to *The African Queen*.

Jenny walked beside him, close, but as a daughter would be close.

"Hey!" Sean said, standing and dusting sand from his swim trunks. "I thought you hated to travel. This is a very long way. You're welcome here, of course," he added huskily. Madison knew that Sean believed Bogie had saved her life, far more than he had himself. And he was grateful.

"We're ready to go," Bogie said.

"Go?" Sean asked him, puzzled.

Jenny smiled, slipping an arm through Bogie's. "I think Bogie's right. We stay for a reason, a purpose. No matter how long it may take for that reason to come along, or what that reason may be. We're almost sure we've fulfilled our purpose. So we came out to be with you until the sun sets, and then . . . well, there's nothing like a Hawaiian sunset. We decided that might be the time to see if . . . if there's another light."

For a moment, Madison thought Bogie would argue. But he didn't. They were spirits, visible to no one but them. Then again, they were alone on a beach, so what was real and what wasn't didn't seem important.

Sean spread another blanket, and Bogie and Jenny joined them on the sand, and they spent the day talking about good things, Bogie laughing about incidents on set, Jenny enthralled by his tales of the past. Sean and Madison listened eagerly, as well; they'd never hear these stories again.

Then the sun began to fall in the west. The sunset was striking and beautiful, shot through with what seemed like a hundred shades of gold and red and mauve.

A light seemed to burst brilliantly as the rest of the sky faded.

Bogie turned back to Madison. "Here's looking at you, kid."

Tears sprang to her eyes as Bogie reached for Jenny's hand, and they walked toward the light. Then they walked through it and were gone.

Sean pulled Madison close and touched her cheek gently. "And now," he said softly, "to life."

"To our lives," she agreed.

They walked through the sand and the softening breeze of the night back to their cottage, and the time they could seize together before the journey that lay ahead.

Before the journey and during it. Now and forever.

ABOUT THE AUTHOR

New York Times bestselling author **Heather Graham** has written more than one hundred fifty novels and novellas, has been published in nearly twenty-five languages, and has over seventy-five million copies in print. An avid scuba diver, ballroom dancer, and mother of five, she still enjoys her south Florida home, but loves to travel as well. Reading, however, is the pastime she still loves best, and is a member of many writing groups. For more information, check out her Web site, theoriginalheathergraham .com.